The Light
Possessed

Other Books by Alan Cheuse

Candace and Other Stories

The Bohemians

The Grandmothers' Club

Fall Out of Heaven

The Tennessee Waltz and Other Stories

The Sound of Writing
(edited, with Caroline Marshall)

Listening to Ourselves
(edited, with Caroline Marshall)

Talking Horse: Bernard Malamud on Life and Work
(edited, with Nicholas Delbanco)

The Light Possessed

A NOVEL BY

ALAN CHEUSE

New Foreword by Rick Bass

New Afterword by the Author

SOUTHERN METHODIST
UNIVERSITY PRESS
Dallas

Copyright © 1990 by Alan Cheuse
Foreword © 1998 by Rick Bass
Afterword © 1998 by Alan Cheuse
First Southern Methodist University Press edition, 1998
All rights reserved

Originally published in 1990 by Gibbs Smith, Publisher

Requests for permission to reproduce material from this work should be sent to:
Rights and Permissions
Southern Methodist University Press
SMU Box 750415
Dallas, Texas 75275-0415

Cover art: Georgia O'Keeffe, American, 1887–1986, *Cow's Skull with Calico Roses*, oil on canvas, 1932, 91.2 x 61 cm, Gift of Georgia O'Keeffe, 1947.712, photograph © 1997, The Art Institute of Chicago. All rights reserved.

Cover design by Tom Dawson Graphic Design

LIBRARY OF CONGRESS CATALOGING-IN-PUBLICATION DATA
Cheuse, Alan.
      The light possessed / a novel by Alan Cheuse ; new foreword by
Rick Bass ; new afterword by the author. — 1st Southern Methodist
University Press ed.
            p.   cm.
      ISBN 0-87074-430-5 (pbk. : acid-free paper)
      I. Title.
PS3553.H436L5   1998
813'.54—dc21   98-12774

Printed in the United States of America on acid-free paper

10 9 8 7 6 5 4 3 2 1

For James and Denise Thomas

ACKNOWLEDGMENTS

The author thanks Graywolf Press and William Stafford for permission to quote the lines from "At Archbishop Lamy's Church in Santa Fe." Some lines on pp. 209–210 have been adapted from an essay by Marjorie Pryse.

Thanks to John Slack for his geologist's eye. "Charleston" appeared in the Autumn 1990 issue of *Gulf Stream Magazine*. "The Rose and the Skull" appeared in *Story* (Autumn 1990) in slightly different form.

Grateful acknowledgment is made for permission to use lyrics from the song "Hit the Road, Jack" © 1961 Tangerine Music Corp. © renewed 1989 and assigned to Tangerine Music Corp.

FOREWORD

What are the rules for this sort of thing – what Alan Cheuse has done? Two things should be said immediately: that he has written a wonderful novel, and that the main character in the novel, the artist Ava Boldin, reminds one tremendously of the artist Georgia O'Keeffe: so much so that the novel, first published in 1990, seems to push new boundaries for how intimately a novel or any work of fiction can follow history and fact – bending fact, tempering it, only slightly here and there, in just the right places, after which bending, the artist then hands us a work of art. The piece, the work, seems all the more organic – still living, almost – because such care has been taken with materials already in existence. The raw materials of fact have been used, rather than simply the raw materials of the artist's vision of the truth. The title of the novel is not inappropriate for what the author has done; it is as if Cheuse has sent light through the lives, the fact-of-the-lives of O'Keeffe and her associates, and that the facts of their lives have reflected or refracted that light. Surely, some large part of it is Cheuse's own light, Cheuse's own eyes landing upon and passing through these raw materials, to create this novel.

One of the things I love most about this book is how unflinchingly it approaches those facts. Cheuse, rather than fretting about it, seems to have embraced a situation other novelists might have viewed as a dilemma – how close does one dare to approach the facts, and still consider one's self a novelist?

It seems as if his full embrace of facts, rather than pussyfooting around and attempting to weed them out of his story, comes from an inspired confidence as well as a profound love for the subject: the characters from history, who died, and their twin characters who have blossomed in his mind, and now in ours.

Cheuse's book is voracious and brazen, even gluttonous with the facts; it summons the rich past and hands it to us in the future. So strong and secure is the voice, or voices, of this novel, that from the very beginning one is unaware of Cheuse. One hears and views the story rather than the author.

It seems paradoxical that an author should become less visible in addressing the challenge of inhabiting fact in a novel. Facts are everywhere in this book, like termite-chewings riddling the structure of fiction, traditionally a wonderful house of lies, but now hampered by the structural inflexibility of fact.

Understand, however, that it is Ava Boldin whom we love in this book, not Georgia O'Keeffe; and that it is Ava's brother Robert, her friend Harriet, Ava's husband Stig, the photographer, and Ava's lost-at-birth twin, Eve, whom we love. I do not believe it is any disrespect to the lives of the dead that they have become shadows, and that the art, the novel, has come closer to life. So gracefully told is the story that it seems as if the two, those-lives and this-art, are in some slow swell of rhythm, like those waves far out at sea that never crest but which carry so much power – trough and ridge, trough and ridge – and that O'Keeffe and her friends and lovers have been gone a while, and now it is time for Ava and hers to ride the earth for a time.

What is the story, in *The Light Possessed*? A simple one: the making of an artist, as shaped by her friends and family and the landscape around her, yet powered, fueled, by her own candle-fires within; and then, against deepening odds, the fierce care and nurturing of that artist: the struggle to retain, to possess that artistic identity, and to improve upon her craft, all the way through to the vanishing of her physical life – leaving behind "only" the art, as a residue of that fierce life, fierce grace. It's a story that's little different, really, from any heroic journey. Obstacles, hardships, are laid down as challenges to the creative spirit and its energies, but Ava's fire pushes her over, through, or around these obstacles, often converting them – creating them – into opportunity. The fact that Ava was a girl, and then a woman, in the early 1900s, is sufficient in itself to provide a steady headwind of travails – a headwind which helps, of course, to sharpen and hone who she is, and who she becomes.

And as Ava develops towards greatness, Cheuse makes live masterfully the unspoken, uncomplaining but aching loneliness attendant to this journey. It is a loneliness – neither good nor bad, but simply a loneliness – that is sometimes present, or at least always in the background, even in the midst of the joy of work. As Ava experiences it, it seems almost to be a joy from the addiction of creation – and the loneliness of addiction, and of creating; for in creating, the artist turns his or her back on the world, even if only for a while, in order to enter that other one.

This is one of the many deep cores where Ava's strength is stored – her commitment. Early on, her credo is established clearly, when the girl coerces her brother into letting her draw him nude: "Nothing is [wrong], if I need it to draw."

What is the source of Ava's fire, her soul? Neither novel nor history book can pin that down; some momentary intersection, perhaps, of cauldrons within the earth, stars above, and wind sweeping through the sky, and all the other things we do not know from the other world, conspiring to focus in the time and place of Ava's body, Ava's life: but of the other factors that influence her – the knowable factors – Cheuse paints them beautifully. Ava's growth seems partly sculpted, and partly metamorphosed – heat and pressure applied with intensity, but in just the right amounts – from the very beginning.

A mad mother who vanished into the other world early, a father who fell into alcoholism; an upbringing by an alien housekeeper who set down rules and boundaries at every possible juncture – what option was there for Ava, then, but to seek to break those boundaries? And like a river that begins cutting down through softer sediments, the pattern of her life became set.

At the same time that the hardships were occurring, there were also mentors in her life, appearing almost magically: benefactors, fairy godmothers, and always, Ava's brother Robert supporting her, helping to hold her aloft so that her fires could continue to carry her along. Cheuse crafts these scenes wonderfully, so that the sense we get from these mentors passing Ava through the stages of her life is like that of a forest protecting one of its trees from storms – a tree which will eventually grow to be a giant in that forest – or of a herd protecting one of its young – an individual who will someday grow up to be the herd's matriarch.

Cheuse explores other themes of the artist's identity, the artist's chemistry, in the relationship between Ava and her brother Robert:

the sibling nature of the artist in the "other" world – and the masculinity and femininity of art. It's not that art is one or the other, Cheuse seems to be saying, nor is it that art is neither, but that it contains both, and that both genders are elements in Ava's life and work. Her relationships reflect this duality, as does her art.

Like relatively few other novels, and despite its historical component, *The Light Possessed* is a novel grounded more in place than in time; and I would call it very much an American novel, from the buffalo skull so revered by Ava and Robert as children, which presided over the elemental past, to the landscapes of wind and light and stone to which they are attracted, and which they soon come to require, as they require food and water and shelter. Scarcely a page can be found without the appearance of some raw essential element of nature – a thing not yet touched or bent or sculpted by man – owl, blue jay, rock, clay, clouds, water, light.

From these elements in which Ava Boldin surrounds herself, we gradually gain the understanding that it is the landscape, and her friends and lovers, who are sculpting her, as is the unchanging nature of the light in her southwestern home – but it is that one element, time, which does *not* sculpt her; or at least not on any scale that we, the readers, or the characters around her in the novel, can perceive. In this regard her life and her work gain the qualities of bedrock – a geological kind of endurance, and power – a metamorphosis.

Such structural and narrative complexities – constructed always along clean lines – abound. The novel is told democratically, by many voices – Amy, the young artist and mother; Michael, the bastard son of Ava's husband and their housekeeper; Ava herself, and Ava's never-born sister, Eve, and Robert, and many more – but always presiding over all the narratives is the quiet power of Ava's work, and the example of Ava's life, which is committed to that work.

The book's major theme is nothing less than the theme of all life: birth from death, growth from decay – and the artist's desire to continue creating, shifting, changing, weaving, throughout a life's journey. The blossom erupting from the skull; the grandmother made young again by the caring-for of her grandchildren; the mother dying in childbirth; an old life in the East being rebuilt in the West, in a new landscape; life-from-death, stability and art from disorder . . .

FOREWORD

One is surprised, in examining this book, upon completing it, that the heft of it, the physical density of it, is like that of any other book. There was for me in rereading this novel the strange sensation as I thumbed through pages I had previously bookmarked with dried leaves that it was not just their crumbles that should sift from the pages, but that so too should showers of desert sand; that I should find dried flowers and snakeskins pressed between its pages. The book seems more like a life, or at least the organic residue of a life, than it does a book, or "art" – which is, I suppose, the finest thing toward which art can aspire.

Rick Bass
January 1998

The Light
Possessed

The heart of another is a dark forest.
You can never know it.

WILLA CATHER
The Professor's House

Here in late winter light
remembering a clear, still life in the sun,
I touch a door with my shadow . . .

WILLIAM STAFFORD
"At Archbishop Lamy's Church in Santa Fe"

Shot gold, maroon and violet, dazzling silver, emerald, fawn,
The earth's whole amplitude and Nature's multiform power
    consign'd for once to colors;
The light, the general air possess'd by them – colors till now
    unknown,
No limit, confine – not the Western sky alone – the high
    meridian – North, South, all,
Pure luminous color fighting the silent shadows to the last.

WALT WHITMAN
"A Prairie Sunset"

RIVER

Robert

The world didn't begin with my sister, although I have sometimes thought that it could hardly go on without her. The earliest I know of the rest of our family, or so it was passed down to us in a tortuous way, comes in the story of a small farmer from Kent named Wander who sold his plot in the old land and took his wife and two small children to the New World, there to buy cattle and raise them on one of the Georgia Sea Islands. But on the voyage over his wife fell sick and died, and so when he arrived here, this widower needed someone to attend to his two babes.

On the other side of the island from his farm lay a small village of dark-skinned people, a mixture of Africans and Cherokee many of them, it was said, a beautiful blend, to hear the story told to you, so that the tall dark-haired girl he hired to help him with the rearing of the children had skin the color of mahogany, and eyes a miraculous blue that seemed to mirror the ocean that she so often gazed upon. Melissa Tree was her name, and she was an artist of sorts, the first and only in our family before the present generation, who collected seashells and painted with inks on the smooth inner side of bark.

None of these artifacts survive, of course, except in the story. And I don't even know how many of the facts about Melissa Tree are actual, or embroidered upon to create a tale for a lonely child of the plains. This makes me slightly uneasy. Scientists like myself don't enjoy wondering if things are made up. But even as I try to recall these matters, sitting in bed with my pad on the little lapboard, staring at the buffalo-calf skull on the table alongside me, a mighty-fine Midwest blizzard blowing past the window of this Chicago old folks' home where my aged heart and I have found some comfort,

1

they seem to me substantial, or as substantial as anything can be on this seemingly solid earth that is ready at any moment to buck and shift and crumble to dust, and on the other hand takes millions of years to create such things as oil and uranium, powerful products of time. The eons, an instant—I've loved my profession for what it has shown me about the links between long periods and short.

But in thinking of time, and the past, I can almost hear that skull murmuring to me—it has seen so much itself—to go on and say what I know while I still have the chance. Starting with what I heard.

The story has it that Melissa and Wander grew as close as sea and sand, and that she produced a light-complected child of her own as a result, and then another, and that she and the children were rowing to the mainland one afternoon in late summer when the sky suddenly turned from milky blue to dark purple bordering on green-black, and that a waterspout whirled up from the horizon and flipped them over as easily as a child might turn over a card.

"Help! Help, Mama!" the older children screamed.

"Follow me!" their mother is supposed to have called to them as she scooped up the youngest in her arms. "Walk!"

And they found solid stuff beneath their feet and walked to the shore, their mother waiting for them to catch up with her, and then prodding them from behind, on this hidden sandbar.

Such was the feat that my own mother described to me as Mother Melissa's Miracle on a warm Sunday afternoon on the edge of the Sand Hills when we were supposed to leave for church and she took my hand and said that we were going for a walk instead. I was four years old, an obedient child, though I had been wondering lately about the size of my mother's belly. It had grown and grown, and my railroad-man father, chief engineer for the region, had told me only that I was going to have a wonderful surprise one day soon, to be delivered by angels.

Father had a flat voice that sometimes sounded as though he were chewing pebbles. Mother's voice flowed slowly and thickly like caramel or honey. Father was upstairs still dressing. Mother led me out the door and I did not protest. But after a few hundred yards of walking over the prairie behind our house, I complained, because

2

this was not the way to church, and that was when she caught me up in the story, to keep me going on our trek. We passed the tall cottonwoods that marked the border of our property. Who knew what was beyond, except that because of the train whistles I understood that the roadbed for my father's rail company lay in that direction.

"You're a good boy, Robert," my mother said, squeezing my hand as we walked.

"Can we rest?" I said.

"Save your strength, because we have a ways to go."

"Where are we going, Mama? Not to church? Will we have a picnic?"

"Do you want to go to church?"

I shook my head, and she laughed. "Listen to me and you won't ever have to go again."

There was something in her voice, but I didn't question it, only followed along a dusty narrow path lined with scrub trees. She was, after all, my mother, and I had been trained to obey her.

"My feet are tired," I said, as the path sloped down through the underbrush.

"Take your shoes off if you like," she said, allowing me to stop and do so.

"Is Father coming?" I said.

"He'll catch up," she said.

"Where is the food?" I removed my shoes and now carried them one in each hand.

"What food?"

"For the picnic," I said.

"That will come later," she said, taking my shoes from me and tossing them over her shoulder into the brush.

"My shoes!" I said.

"You don't need those anymore," she said, herding me along ahead of her. "We're almost there."

"Where?" I said.

"Here," she said, pointing toward the river, which at this time of year still flowed with some force. "I want you to know something. When I was a girl . . . " And she proceeded, as she led me to the river's edge, to tell me of the miracle of Melissa Tree.

3

"You can't do that," I said, meaning that she could not walk on water.

"But I can try," she said. "I'm going to show you."

"The water is cold," I said.

"No, it's not," she said. "Give me your hand."

I looked at her, but kept my hands at my sides. "My clothes," I said.

"Such a good boy. Well, you don't have to come if you don't want to. But I'm going to do it," she said, and before my amazed stare, pulled her dress over her head. I couldn't take my eyes off her stomach, something I had never seen before without it draped by clothes. Goose bumps played up and over her belly and her arms.

"Mama," I said, and began to cry.

"We can do it, little Robert," she said. "It's in our blood. Here." Once again she offered me her hand.

I shook my head.

"Very well," she said. "I'll go alone. Or not alone." She patted her distended stomach. I was staring at it, its bulk, the odd wild tuft of hair that grew out from between her legs, when she laughed, and I looked up, saw a hawk circling nearly directly above us. "Are you sure, Robert?" she said. "I have to hurry now." Tears burst from my eyes and I stood, fists clenched, as she came toward me.

I backed away up the path. "No, Mama."

"No, what? You don't know, you don't know. Let me take you back with me to Georgia. Come now."

An animal called out along the river; at least that was what I thought it was at first.

"All right . . ." I said, feeling lost and awful and lonely and wanting her to love me. I couldn't look at her much longer without thinking that I would burst—or float away—some terrible thing.

"Come now," she said, reaching up to take my hand. "You don't have to undress. There's no time."

She led me to the river's edge. The current was strong, but I paid more attention to her pendulous breasts, to the light on her belly, the way her skin seemed to glow under the sun. And that hair, the animal hair, was how I saw it.

4

That was how close we came before my father burst upon us from the trail, knocking me aside as he leaped toward my mother, capturing her roughly in his arms.

"No," she said in a wail. "I want to go; I want to go and you can't stop me."

I rushed at him, and beat at his thighs with my fists. "Let her go! Let her go!"

He removed a hand from her in order to bat me away, sending me tumbling into the dust.

"Mama, Mama," I was crying over and over again as I watched him attempt to dress her even as she kept on struggling.

"Louise," he said. "Louise, you stop this. Hold still. Hold still."

She made a horrible noise, like something you might hear at night from a distance while trying to fall asleep and feel it necessary to call out for your mother or father, and she slipped from his grasp, leaving him holding her dress while she stood panting and moaning, her arms hanging limply at her sides. Her eyes, oh, her eyes were wild!

"I won't," she said, raising her fist above her belly. "I won't!" A few horrid thuds sounded in my ears before my father had her in his arms again, this time wrestling her to the ground.

"Robert," he called to me. He was short of breath and sounded hoarse, like an animal himself. "Go back to the house."

That was when I discovered my own shortness of breath. "I d-d-d-d . . . "

"Go," he said.

"Let me go," she said.

"Get," he said.

"I c-c-c-can't . . . "

"Go."

"My s-shoes," I said.

"Go," he said.

"No," she said. "I want to take him with me."

My father raised his hand. A flat ugly thud echoed across the clearing. I looked around to see blood seeping from the corner of my mother's mouth.

We returned to the house, though I don't remember the walk. Father took me in his arms and put me to bed, and I know that I heard the doctor's voice drifting up the stairwell, a sour dry speech that was punctuated now and then with small birdlike chirpings from my mother. I listened a while without hearing any words.

"James!"

My mother's shout awakened me early the next morning. The house filled with her anguished moans, the sharp barked orders of the doctor, the odor of salve and steam. Who knows what intimations she had had of it, except that as her attempt at the river showed, my mother was fearful of many things, particularly this birth. As it turned out, she had a right to be.

"A girl," the doctor came out of the room to announce around six that evening.

Then there was a second girl, born a few minutes later—born dead.

My mother died around midnight.

And our real lives, Ava's and mine, had just begun.

DOOR

Some of us took longer than others to get here, and to find our vocations as well. Myself, I was only a few years past twenty when I started in this westerly direction in Michael's little maroon pickup with new tires that we bought with money that Cissy, his mother, gave us as a farewell present.

Though I suppose I had taken my first step much further back than that, perhaps on a day in Virginia when I was walking and dreaming, as little girls do, along the banks of the Rappahannock where my parents had always kept a summer house, and something about the way the sun caught on the rushing current drew me to a halt, and I stared for a long while at the dancing patterns of light. I came out the next morning armed with one of my father's yellow drafting pads and a grease pencil, trying to sketch the flow. Oh, how unmercifully my brothers teased me when they discovered what I was doing!

I kept on drawing—oh, Ava! my Ava! I did!—all through grade school and the upper levels, too. I took a giant step toward where I now live and work, with you, when I applied to Bennington as an art major—and was accepted. There I learned, among other seemingly useless things, that though I was only five foot five and rather slender, I could drink with dirty old men and weld pieces of steel into sculpture. I remember the look my father gave me when he came up for the student show where my first creation appeared.

"Is it going to be architecture then, Amy?" He had a pitiful look of hope in his eye. None of my brothers gave a damn for what he did.

"Gee, I don't know, Daddy," I said, frightening myself with the sudden understanding of how much I wanted to please him. "Could

7

be." I pushed some of my hair from my eyes and struck a pose that I had seen other girls put on when talking about their work. "And then again, who knows?"

"Well, I like this," he said, going up to the piece and giving it a good rap with his knuckles.

"Daddy!" I cried out in alarm at his brazen act of philistinism.

"Steel," he said, and I think he would have said it whether I was standing there or not, "we're both lovers of steel and structure."

This was not exactly true. I liked to work with steel. As I said, it gave me confidence to put a torch to those big sheets of metal, splashing sparks about with the alacrity of a welder on a bridge high above the New York docks. But I didn't *love* steel. I didn't, couldn't love anything. Until Michael came along, and we began moving west.

On those tires supplied by Cissy, his mother, who is bound to this story's beginning with ties of steel. And love. Though I didn't know any of that at the time.

"And so off you go," she said with a wave of her red-knuckled hand as we went out the door of her little brick house on Washington Avenue in Albany. We had swung by on our way out of Vermont to show her the tires and to thank her once again.

"We'll bring you back some red dust or whatever it is they have out there, Mom," Michael said. "She's never been west of Buffalo," he turned to me and explained.

"Rochester," she said by way of correction. "Though I used to hear a lot of stories about the place. And it's all red dust, and skies the color of turquoise stone and air so clear you cannot even see it. That's what I've heard."

"You've heard so much about it," Michael said. "Maybe you ought to come with us, Mom, after all this time."

"Oh, me?" she said. "Oh, no. It's not for me. I'm just a girl from Washington County who fell into some interesting luck." She leaned toward her son who stood next to me on the little stoop and kissed him on the cheek. "You, Michael, you go. And your Amy, who will be the new Mrs. Gillen."

I blushed and reached for her hand, feeling much more horrible about lying to her than I did to my own parents about our situation. But Michael didn't want to get married just yet – he said –

8

and I didn't want to push him too hard, I had my reasons. And a little *surprise* as well.

"I'm going to keep my own name," I said. "It's been mine for so long . . ."

"Don't apologize for it," Cissy said. "We're not so particular with names in this household, are we, Michael? After all, the boy's got my name, not his father's."

"Okay, Mom, that's good-bye then for now," Michael said and tugged me from his mother and led me to the curb.

"Bye!" I called after her.

"Good-bye, my darlings," she called out.

"You shouldn't have been so short with her just then," I said.

Michael gave me a look I'd never seen before and started up the engine with a vengeance. He threw the truck into reverse and we lurched backward, nearly banging into the car behind us.

"I know that you don't want to get married. But at least be careful," I said. "You're driving for three of us now and I want you to be more careful."

His mother was waving furiously at us from the curb as we drove off, rubber burning in the already-thick Albany air.

"Three of us?" he said, holding the wheel as though it were a weapon.

It was then that I explained what I had been planning to tell him after we had been on the road a while, finding perhaps some lovely romantic place for it, wherever that place out there might be.

"You're joking," he said. "You're trying to fool around with my brain."

"No, Michael," I said in a voice that sounded to me quite strange, as though it belonged to someone I had just met. "I'm going to bear you a little Cross."

"The road! the road!" Stanley Hyman shouted this to us in Lang. and Lit. class one morning. "All life is a road!" And then he smacked his hands together in rhythm and began shouting out that Ray Charles tune:

> Hit the road, Jack! And don't you come back
> No more, no more, no more, no more!

Hit the road, Jack!
And don't you come back
No more!

The Myth Man, my Michael called him, and practically sat at his feet like a disciple, sometimes even showing up in class and demonstrating by his comments that he had read everything on the reading list with more care than most of the students on the roster. If it was unusual for a working-class boy from New York State to drop in on classes and engage us girls in long discussions about Lord Raglan's *The Hero*, Stanley's favorite book, and Freud and Fraser and Marx, if it was unusual we didn't know it; even when he prefaced the things he said with, "Well, hey, I'm the bastard son of a Manhattan photographer and a housemaid from Cossayuna, but the way I see it . . . ," if this was unusual we didn't know it. This was Bennington and anything could happen.

As you already may have figured out, some of it happened to me. Michael, of course. He was painting a lot, but also working outside on some small metal pieces. One night I saw him as I came out of the painting studio—he was wearing goggles, the sparks were flying, and I thought to myself, this is some man! this is some man! So I guess I have to admit that I'm a coward, or maybe just a realist, because I never told him about me and Stanley, not that it was more than a tiny little fling. Michael would have died, or worse, he would have brought it up to me a lot—I remember hearing my mother's whining voice all through my childhood about a thing that my father had gotten involved in, and it might have been one night or ten years, didn't matter, because my mother never let it drop—Stanley stumbling in drunk to my room, trying to take off his pants. I worshiped him; he was so smart and sweet and tough all at once. I helped him off with his trousers and let him do it. I knew about half-a-dozen other girls who had the same experience, and it was exactly the way they described it when they talked about it, a little incestuous, a little bit like a visit from the family doctor.

"Jesus and Moses!" he shouted when he came. "Oh my God, Jesus, and Moses!"

So when, as we were driving through Illinois on our way to New Mexico to see Michael's Aunt Ava who had moved out there

10

to paint before Michael was born, he suddenly broke out into a war whoop, honked the horn, and shouted, "Hey, I got it, if it's a boy we'll name him Stanley!" I nearly went into convulsions. Though I managed to recover quickly enough to say that I didn't think that we ought to saddle any kid with the burden of that funny name.

"He's not funny to me," Michael said. "He's a great man. Him and Paul Feely. They're my fathers, you know. They really are. The fathers I never had."

We were whizzing through cornfields near the Iowa border, and I couldn't really pretend that something fabulous lay outside the truck windows, fabulous enough for me to turn around and stare at it, but I wanted to hide the deep red blush that I could feel as heat on my cheeks at the thought of having made love to Michael's adoptive father.

I stopped blushing after a while, but the cornfields ran on. And then the grainfields of Nebraska, receding to the horizon, broken by little farm towns, bordered by straight roads and by railroad lines, along one of which Michael's Aunt Ava, as he called her, had grown up. However we didn't know that then; we didn't know much more about her than the few things his mother had said. We even had the idea that Ava and Albert Stigmar had divorced when Michael was conceived, not that it mattered much. Not to him. He loved that, being the bastard son. Not many men would. But Michael was special, a thing which had both its good side and its bad, and I had the worrisome feeling—only women know what it's like—that the baby might bring out as much of the negative side of him as the positive.

First of all, no matter what we had told his mother or my parents about our intentions, we still weren't married, which had been all right for me before I got pregnant, but riding along the interstate with the weight of the new child in my belly, or imagining the little reed that he was at that stage as a weight, I wondered if we ought to break this chain of birth out of wedlock that Michael sometimes reveled in and stop in one of these small towns, find a justice of the peace, and, as they say out this way, get hitched.

"Beautiful," Michael said, and I was pleased with his reaction. When he suggested that we wait until we got to New Mexico, because

11

we'd have to take blood tests and all that, as he reminded me, I was more than satisfied.

But around the time we turned southward and crossed the border of Colorado, he was already of another mind. "Amy," he said, taking my hand and squeezing it hard, "I know this is going to sound crazy. It's just—we don't have to rush into this marriage thing, you know, just because you're having our baby. I mean, I spent all my life so far being a bastard and it hasn't been bad at all. Hey, and you know how—Stanley pointed this out to me—in Shakespeare the bad guys, the bastards, get a lot of the good poetry. The gods stand up for bastards!"

"Oh, Michael," I said, feeling a sigh rise within me, "you are such a stitch!" I leaned over and lay my head on his right knee, feeling the power of his leg as he worked the gas pedal. In a moment he was pulling over onto the shoulder of the highway, and in the next we scrambled out of the cab and onto the truck bed and into his bedroll that still reeked with the oils and resins of the studio back in Vermont. You could hear the cars roar past on the highway.

Nice girl from northern Virginia, college educated, pregnant now, making love in the back of a truck parked off the interstate in northeastern Colorado. And then again as she crossed the border into New Mexico. What do these notes say about how happy I was? I was hot with joy, happier than I had ever been! I was having his baby, our baby, and we were nearing our destination, his legacy, our destiny. No matter what has happened since, wonderful as well as pain filled and miserable, I will never feel as calm in my intensity as I did throughout that trip.

Michael, however, seemed to be reacting the opposite way—the closer we got to our destination, the more agitated he became.

"Christ," he said as he lay back just after having finished with me, "Do you realize . . . ?"

"Realize what?"

"My God," he said, and then closed his eyes and made an odd sound with his tongue.

"Michael, what is it?" I was fast losing the good feeling that I had, becoming the victim of his inscrutable mood swing.

"We're nearly there," he said.

"I know." I reached over and touched a hand to his cheek.

"Maybe we should go back."

"Why? I don't understand."

"What if . . . what if she's just some crazy old lady?" He took a deep breath, and I could almost hear his lungs filling up as much with fear as with air. "What if . . . she doesn't want to see us? If my mother was making this all—"

"Michael!"

"Or what if she's mean as hell? What about that? And we've spent all this money coming this way to get turned right around?"

"Not for nothing," I said, sliding up alongside him so that my mouth was even with his ear. "We've had some fun. And it's beautiful out here. Maybe . . . we'll even stay."

That sat him up, looking kind of sweet and silly, as he gazed out over the rocky landscape. "I can't stay out here," he said. "I've got my work. I can't stay *anywhere*. I'm going to be a father . . . "

"Oh, Michael, don't worry," I said in my first official act as a mother while cradling him in my arms.

His mood lightened, though, the closer we got to Santa Fe. Whose wouldn't, given the mountains around us?

"That sky!" he kept saying in a voice filled with real wonder. "Look at that sky! And there! Look! The mountains, the colors!" All the way to Santa Fe, and beyond.

And that beyond! I have to admit that it got to me as well, despite the fact that the baby growing inside me was just about everything to me at that time. Having grown up in the demure and manicured landscape of Virginia—and gotten something resembling an education in the tempered mountains of Vermont—my notion of height and distance left much to be desired, though I might have lived something like a full life without ever having known this. Space out here resembled the ragged edge of a painting, with all the lines and colors bleeding off into some infinity, the presence of which we in the East could easily hide from, but which nevertheless was always present, always lurking about the wings. When we stopped in a village a few miles off of the main highway, Michael ate a Mexican lunch he repeatedly declared was the hottest meal he'd ever had. I couldn't do that to my baby, and so I nibbled on bland tortillas and drank a little milk. The view from the patio was a feast in itself.

13

The mesas leading away toward the eastern horizon seemed like some kind of topiary made of stone. But the best view for me, of which we saw more and more as we got closer to our destination, through Taos, then Espanola, was the ancient seabed that lay to the west, toward the mountains. Here and there we could see dust devils spinning up out of the dry desert floor. Now and then we passed a car or truck driven by a brown-faced man with long dark hair, many signs were in Spanish, my breathing was slightly altered by the climb toward the sky, there was a sign here for a reservation, a turn there, and then we were passing through a crossroads — a gas station, a small weathered adobe general store — and on toward the mountains again, climbing slightly. Suddenly — the sign bearing the name we had seen on the map — the road dipped into a little bend at a dry riverbed with a few cottonwood trees and clusters of cactus; there was a turn to the southwest at the next bend in the road, and within minutes we were rolling up a small ravine toward the old ranch house and outbuildings.

I could have sworn my baby gave a little kick for joy, but it was much too early in the pregnancy to feel any movement.

Out of the cab, stretch toward the sky, blink at the odd sun, a strangely white, nearly translucent brightness, gasp at the altitude, Michael kisses me on my dry cracked lips, limbs creak from sitting for so many days, walk up to the house, up onto the stoop, knock at the striated black wooden door, knock again; no answer. We walk around to the side of the house, peer in through a large new window that takes southern light, see its counterpart across the room to the north, a desk, a few books, rocks, on the wall a large steer skull, dried flowers within it, walk along the adobe corral wall behind the house. Stillness, except for the sound of our feet in the dust. And my breathing. Another black door, this one slightly ajar. We enter the corral. Large wooden barn to the rear. The door open at the north end. Odd odors on the air, a slight resin tang, dusty odor of native light, no sound, smell of oily wind, wind shifts, no sweet streak of scent, wind subsides, a dog barks in the distance, or is it a dog? could it be a coyote? Now the barn, where inside a shadow hovers like a large pool of dark water, the very air turned to liquid, there a table covered with tubes of paint, small orange rocks,

14

bones, feathers, dried flowers, a bird's nest. "Look at this," Michael says, holding up a large dried fish. I look in his eyes, what do I see? Then we turn at a sound outside the barn, look to the adobe wall across from the open doorway, and we blink, and see a slight, weathered figure in jeans and tattered white shirt; old man, no, slight old *woman*, stick in hand, no, long thin *brush*, standing perfectly still, as a lizard might, as though she herself might have been painted on the wall, listening intently, not to the dog or wolf or coyote, not to the noise of the wind like the soles of feet brushing across the soft stone, not to my cry of surprise, not to Michael's whispered breathing, but I could almost swear it, or so it seemed at that moment, as if she were listening to the sound of the tiny gurglings of my child within.

She turned then and looked at us — at me, to be specific — and again in that instant, those eyes made me see that it was true.

PRAIRIE

Eve

Up on the widow's walk atop the house of a Saturday afternoon, late, the old woman with hair the color of tarnished silver flicks her eyes back and forth across the horizon. It has been hours since the girl was seen and Mrs. Boldin is beginning to worry. Aside from the time Ava is in school, her grandmother always keeps her within sight, or at least within earshot, a habit that goes right back to the baby's earliest moments, after the old woman received the wire from her son and within a day had packed, closed up her house in New Brunswick, and boarded the train for the West.

She has stood here many times before, overlooking this vast sea of grass, many times with her tiny granddaughter in arms, marveling at the rows of rolling hills that run all the way to the broad and sometimes frightening expanse of sky. Eastern skies never seemed larger than the earth on which you stood. They never reminded you of the long stretch of eternal oblivion toward which you were probably headed. Probably? Definitely! She had never been much for religion. When her mother had left her father, she had left her belief behind as well, and though mother and daughter attended church, it was more out of custom than devotion. Out here on the prairie she had begun to think of such questions as where was she going and where would she end. Somehow she thought that had she remained in her house in New Jersey, such matters would not have arisen as large.

Yes, she had to admit to herself, it was this sky, this huge and looming sky—the broad sea of sandy hills seemed a mere reflection of it, the grass a wide stretch of beach, the sky the ocean. And out there, near where the row of cottonwoods marked the Boldin property line, she had last seen her granddaughter, now eight years old and as full of vigor and contention as anything Mrs. Boldin had ever known. As she had just been a while ago, when against her grandmother's expressed wish she had gone dashing out of the house on some mysterious errand for her brother.

Robert was so different from his younger sister, so much like his father, studying his science and his mathematics, collecting his rocks.

Ava was like no one she had ever seen, with her fearsome eyes and her quick, lithe body, looking more like an antelope than a human child, when she had rushed away from the porch, her long red hair trailing behind her.

"Ava, where are you going?" she had called after her.

"I have a mission!" the girl had shouted back over her shoulder.

"Mission?"

Robert came bounding down the stairs. "Let her go, Gram," he said. "She's promised me something. It's important."

Mrs. Boldin turned to her other charge. Now that her son James was away in Omaha almost as often as he was home, she had more responsibility than ever for these two poor motherless children. "And just what has she promised you?"

Robert made a puckering of his lips and for a moment seemed to be about to reveal what he knew. But then he lowered his head and said, "Secret mission."

"A *secret* mission? I'm your Grandmam, Robert, surely you can tell me."

He shook his head. "She made me promise."

"But where is she going? Not near the river, I hope."

"She's not alone," Robert said.

Mrs. Boldin could feel her heart surge up into her chest, as though it were some kind of small animal about the size of her fist. She took a deep breath or two, felt her words catch dry in her throat, and then tried again. "What do you mean that she's not alone? Who went with her? I didn't see anyone with her."

Yet even before Robert said it, she knew what he would say.

"She went with Eve."

"I thought she had given up with that story," Mrs. Boldin said, trying to calm herself.

17

"I don't know," Robert said from the stairwell. "That's just what she told me."

"And you didn't tell her to stop playing that silly game? I thought that your father told her . . . "

"I'm not my sister, Gram. He told her, not me."

"You should know better. Robert, I want you to come with me now. We're going to find her."

"She's not lost, Gram," the boy said.

"She shouldn't be out there alone."

"I told you, she's not . . . "

"Robert!"

"Yes, ma'am."

"No more stories."

"Yes, ma'am."

"Come along then."

"Oh, Gram, you can stay here. I'll go fetch her."

"Thank you, dear boy."

"Yes, ma'am," he said, and yanked a coat from the clothes tree near the front door and went out while Mrs. Boldin slowly climbed the stairs, making her way to the widow's walk where she would keep her little vigil.

A good boy, she thought. The spitting image of his father. While the girl had her mother's coloring, such as the old woman remembered it. She wondered what else she might have inherited on her mother's side, recalling the stories her son had told her—not in any great detail but enough for it to stand—of her strange behavior just before she gave birth to their second child.

And then the birth and sudden death of the other child, and the mother's sudden demise, leaving Ava the only one of the three to survive the agonizing labor.

It was no wonder that she had made up her story about the company she kept with the figure she called Eve, after her late twin sister. She had been so small when she had first begun to talk of it, she hadn't thought that there was anything out of the ordinary about it; she hadn't even tried to keep it a secret.

James was so often away. Mrs. Boldin was the one who had to listen to all of the tales.

Of how Eve had come to little Ava in the night and told her that she was going to have a visitor. "And it was you, Grandmam," Ava had said.

"You were just a week or so old when I arrived," Mrs. Boldin said. "So I think that you were too young to have heard this."

"Oh, no, Gram," Ava said. "I remember. She told me you were coming. She told me about the train, and your suitcases, and the hat you would wear."

"Was I wearing a hat? I suppose I was."

"See," said Ava, a big smile on her usually dour face. This child didn't smile enough, and so Mrs. Boldin was content for a while to let these stories pass, if they amused her motherless granddaughter and helped to pass the time in good cheer.

These stories: the girl said that her sister Eve spoke with her, sometimes at night before sleep, sometimes while out walking in the grass behind the house, sometimes while playing indoors.

"What does she say to you?" Mrs. Boldin had asked.

Ava gave her that look of hers and said, "Gram, it's just for me."

"But you can tell your Grandmam, can't you?"

"Eve says it's just for me."

She grew tired of asking Ava to confide in her, and the one time she tried to discuss it with her son, he dismissed the conversation out of hand. He was much more with his drink and his cigars than before Louise had passed away.

There were nights when she herself wished that she had an imaginary playmate with whom she might converse—or at least the ghost of her late husband, a great talker in life. Ava's ability to conjure such things apparently didn't come from this side of the family.

Mrs. Boldin kept after the girl, and eventually coaxed her into revealing a few details.

Eve was her own age, her twin, in fact.

What did she look like?

She didn't look like anything. She had no shape, only a sort of feeling that she gave you that she was there when she was speaking to you.

But what was the feeling?

Ava didn't know. Colors maybe. Sometimes a little flash of light, like a star peeping out from behind thin clouds.

Well, and what did her voice sound like?

It didn't sound, Ava explained. It was more like color and light.

At church that Sunday after the conversation about Eve, Mrs. Boldin leaned over and whispered a question in Ava's ear: "Is it like this? The feeling that God is near?"

Ava shook her head no.

After that, her grandmother gave up trying to understand it. There was too much else she had to do: clean the house, and make the meals, and keep the children on the straight and narrow with their schoolwork, and be sure that they had clean clothes of the proper size — Ava now eight, Robert twelve, and still growing like a prairie fire! — and generally keep the peace in a household where the father, her son James, the engineer, of whom she had always been quite proud, was more often gone than present.

It had to do with the death of Louise, of course. Though he denied it.

"I'm redesigning the signal system for the plains, Mother," he told her one night after a few glasses of the stuff that usually got him talking. She despised the drink, but loved to hear him talk. His voice seemed almost a replica of her husband's, whose arguments in court she had loved to witness in times that now seemed so long ago she recalled them almost as if they were part of a long-departed dream. "And so," he said, "it means that I'm required to visit these sites and see that the system is working properly. This is modern life, Mother, and our trains carry the life-stuff all across this part of the country. Think of me as a surgeon on call, making his rounds."

Which she tried to do after that, though she knew that whatever he argued, he was finally just running away from the house where Louise had died.

She knew that he was a good engineer, her son, but she didn't like the fact that he was drinking so much and neglecting his children and generally behaving like a coward. The only good that came of all this was that she got to spend so much time with the children. But the bad part of taking care of the children was that it tired her more and more each year. She was a grandmother, not a mother, and grandmothers were not made to work as hard with their grandchildren as they had raising their own children. Or, in her case, child. James was her only child, and now and then she wondered what it would have been like to raise more than one, and this made her quite weary, particularly at times such as this when she was dying on her feet, staring off over the grasslands trying to make out the figure of her granddaughter somewhere off near the row of cottonwoods.

But those trees marked the border of the river and Ava would not dare to go there. The river was forbidden territory for either child, even though the river was mostly a dry bed with a thin stream lying nearly placid in the center between the low banks, except in springtime and early summer. It was autumn now, nearing winter. Even as she stood here, dreaming, a great slant of clouds had assumed the horizon to the west—like a large crowd of turtlebacks making stepping stones to the far northwestern corner of the sky.

And if the girl looked up from wherever she was walking, on her secret mission charged by her older brother, what would she see?

Islands?

Islands, says Eve in a voice the color of certainty.

And what are we walking on then? the girl Ava asks.

The sky, Eve replies.

Everything's upside down?

The best way, says Eve.

In the picture books, everything's straight.

And everything's boring. We miss our Papa, for example, but if he were here, could we play like this? Absolutely not.

I don't like it when he drinks, Ava says, stooping and idly pulling at a twisted root. It doesn't give. Another tug. Still it stays.

Come along, her sister says. *We've got to find the you-know-what.*

If we can.

I thought I saw one a few days ago.

We need it for Robert.

We'll go to the river, we'll find something there.

Ava stops again, looks back at the house, the roof just visible behind the row of low rolling sand hills.

We're not allowed at the river alone.

21

Oh, sister, sister. And how will we find something special then? I ask you that.

You're right, Ava says almost at once. But we just can't tell Grandmam. Or Robert, either. We just have to say we went out somewhere.

That's where we are: out, somewhere . . .

I have to water the bushes.

Do it, Eve says. *I'll keep watch for Indians.*

Ava makes a most unladylike pose in the scrub grass, her eyes lidded over, her mind turning inward, her body performing all by itself while her sister keeps watch.

She then scampers down past the tall cottonwoods to the bank of the river. Grandmother, from her vantage point on the widow's walk, can only imagine the mischief and even danger she can suffer here, of which attack by Indians (who haven't lived in the vicinity for a number of years) is mild. Death by drowning is her fear for Ava and for Robert, the children slipping down the sodden bank into the muddy water and sinking under the weight of clothing, suffocating amidst the soggy branches and old vines, their bodies to be found later far downstream. Not that this would be such a horrible death, she imagines. Only that it would come so soon for the child, the children.

A woman like herself, on the other hand, could go that way, the soft enfolding water pulling her under as if with fingers of flesh, and closing her eyes to the blurry light, opening her mouth to the long drink; a cough or two, and then sleep would come to embrace her. But this is a fear she reserves for another season. And for Ava, she will not suffer such awful luck.

Not Ava, no. She has a long life ahead of her, something that only a grandmother can imagine for her in its entirety, since she herself has come such a long way to be standing here at this moment conjuring up the girl's future: her own childhood near the Jersey shore, winters there, winter after winter; meeting her husband, their life together; raising James, his schooling, his leaving home; the girl he married, Louise, meeting her family, the wedding day; and that was so long ago it seemed another life, some story she had heard, and there she had been in New Brunswick, living out her last days in a teacup, walking in a tiny circle from house to market to house, barricading herself against the awful winters—not knowing if the weather was growing worse, or if she had merely grown old, or could it be both?—when the telegraph message had arrived:

AVA BORN JUNE 20 LOUISE DEAD COME SOONEST

The shock of the news had started up a new life in her, as though her heart, which dull days and the pressure of old age had slowed down, was then struck by lightning to inspire it to new pulsations.

But what was that child doing out there?

"Ava!" she called. "A-va-a-a-a! Dar-ling!"

The wind caught her cry and ripped it to shreds.

AVA BORN LOUISE DEAD COME SOONEST

Oh, the way the wind whipped her thoughts and memories about! Then came a cry and she turned around. Where had the sound come from? She scanned the horizon, squinted and raged at the incapacity of her eyesight, trying to focus on the line of cotton-woods but failing. And then, as if some invisible hand had tapped her on the shoulder, she looked up and saw it, a young, white-wing-tipped eagle soaring overhead. But was that the creature that had cried out? Could she know?

"Gram! Grandmam!" Young Robert was calling to her from the yard below.

AVA BORN DEAD COME SOONEST

"She's here, Gram!" the boy called up to her. "Come see what she's brought me!"

These children, she thought as she started down the steps, they'll be the death of me yet—they brought me back to life and now they get me so riled up, they take the life right out of me; watching and watching for her, and all the while she had already come back, that girl so sly, too old for her years; she needs some seasoning, and that's a mother's job, not a grandmother's; the mother gives the clues and the grandmother need only give her affection and stand like an arrow in the earth or a beacon lamp upon the horizon to show the way through the years, to show that you can move through time like a ship through water and reach a destination that lies even beyond the horizon you can see from where you now stand in childhood, in youth, in the early days of marriage; almost like a pillar of fire the grandmother stands, nearby and yet far away, far in the past and far in the future, and though her body does falter

23

and her mind, too, if she can only persist long enough for the children to thrive, she will have done her duty to family and the Lord and the light.

And who did this poor girl have without her? She had nothing: she had no mother, she had only James, and who was he to raise her? A man who ran from her, who ran from the death of Louise, and this made-up creature she talked to when she felt the urge . . .

AVA DEAD SOONEST

. . . the thoughts that ran through her head as she descended the stairs, walking unsteadily, holding the banister to be sure of her balance, for if she fell there would be no one for these children.

And here she was at the bottom of the stairs, the girl with her hair wildly frothed by the wind, those eyes burning, in her outstretched hands the animal bone, hideous in its nakedness, whitewashed by the water and the wind and dried by the sun. A cow's skull, it looked like, splintered, raw.

But the child, Ava. Alive!

DOOR

"Or something like that," Ava said, blinking hard at me after she had finished the story. "That is the past, isn't it? Something like the way we remember it? But I can show you . . . " She started to get up from her chair but I stood first.

"Let me," I said.

"I'll get it," she said, rising slowly. "I don't require another servant yet. I've already got Socorro, and she's the one who needs all the help now that her mother's dead." Ava sighed deeply and stared past me as if at someone who had just come into the room. But Socorro had gone home for the day—she had moved out of the spare bedroom now that Michael and I had arrived, and returned to her daughters in the village—and I felt a bit guilty about that, but Michael told me not to worry, so I'd been trying to avoid it—and Michael was out in the barn studio, cleaning up and putting things in order after another day of helping Ava set up for work. I thought for a moment that it was he who might have just come in. But I followed her stare, and it was no one I could see.

"I'll show you the photographs," she said, picking her way across the room as I had seen her walk across the corral, steady, unyielding to the fragility of her bones. I was too young when my grandmothers had died to remember much about them clearly. Ava was the first really old person that I had spent any time with at all, and the way she walked, it was not so much that she was carrying the weight of all her years—nearly eighty of them by the time we arrived—but that she was walking face forward into a strong wind blowing—this is ironic, I guess—out of the past.

"Is it in here?" I caught up with her and reached with her toward the box on the shelf below a stack of books.

25

"I said *I'll* fetch it, Amy." To soften the effect of her voice, she smiled at me, and in that glance I saw something of the mischievous girl she had been speaking about for the last few nights.

Michael's mother had, in fact, been in touch with her on our behalf, not just sending along Michael's early drawings but also asking Ava if it would be possible for us to stay here a while.

I shook my head vigorously when Ava told us that our first night around the dinner table.

"It's almost as if she knew . . . " Michael looked at me and then at Ava. Socorro hovered in the doorway, a beautiful brown-faced woman with several gold-capped teeth in the front of her mouth.

"Knew?" Ava spoke up. She might be old and having trouble with her eyes, but she had all of her wits about her. ("This is a woman you can't *bullshit*," I said to Michael later that night in bed. "Oh, and you think that I tend to *bullshit* people?" "I didn't mean that at all," I said. But he was miffed and turned away, and—another story, I guess, for later. He's changing, I'm changing, the little thing inside me is growing . . .)

"That we were restless," Michael said. "That we were, like, ready to put the East behind us . . . "

"I understand that," Ava said tartly. In that dry direct voice I'm still not used to, just a touch flattened out, the western sound. But I was hearing a lot of it, in the stories she had begun to tell me almost as soon as we arrived.

"Do you want someone to write all this down?" I asked after the first—well, I have to say it, since that was what it was like—after the first session we had about her past. (Michael, meanwhile, out in the barn studio was apprenticing himself to her in the present—and he was both utterly humble about it to her, and filled with it all, the glory of it, when he spoke to me.)

"I don't know about the writing part," she said. "All I know is that I want to be saying it."

"Yes, ma'am," I said, feeling the full force of what she was telling me. Though I may have gone to Bennington, where everybody looked to the future, usually at the expense of the present, not to mention the past, I was still a Virginian, a state in which when someone tells you about what has gone before, you listen well.

And so she began to show me documents to go along with the stories: letters, diaries.

And this photograph that she took out from an old cigar box. "Even the box," she said.

"What?"

"Even this *box* could tell stories," she said. "It was Stig's, one of his old cigar boxes . . . " Another sigh, no, well, perhaps only a deep, deep breath. Reaching inside. "Here. That's it."

Picture of an old man sitting up in bed.

"I'm sorry," I said, shaking my head. "I don't know who this is. Uh, Stig? you called him?"

"No," she cut me off. "This is not Stig. This is Robert. My brother, Robert. And let me tell you, two men could not have been more dissimilar. Except in certain respects. This is *Robert*. Dear Robert." She made another sound in her mouth as if to spit. "But that's not the point. I wanted to show you *this*." And she pressed the photograph quite close to her face, and then whipped it over to me. I stared at it a moment longer, trying to see whatever it was she wanted me to see in the face of the old man with the great wisps of white hair sticking up around his ears and balding head.

"Do you see, girl?"

I sighed myself a little then, feeling so stupid. "He's . . . "

"Not him! Not him!"

And *then* I saw it on the table next to him. "Ohh . . . " I let out the sound as a sigh louder than before.

The skull!

"The same skull . . . "

"Yes! All these years!" Ava shook her head, snatching the photograph from me and whirling about as though indeed someone else had just come into the room. "He saved it! All these years, who knows what else he saved. My darling brother! Oh, my, oh, my. Geologist he was all his life. Never threw a single rock away if he could help it. And there it is right there on his night table. Oh, I'll bet those nurses wondered sometimes what the hell he had up *his* sleeve!"

And I took the photograph back from her and I studied it, looking from the skull to the man and back to the skull again.

The baby in my belly, Michael in the barn, this grand old stick-thin woman painting, talking—it was going to be quite a visit, I told myself. Quite a visit.

TOWN

Robert

From that same riverbed where my mother had once tried to lead me to sleep forever, my sister fetched the skull of a buffalo calf worn smooth by time, and it may have been that gift that showed me the direction for the rest of my life. I had collected rocks before this, but her gift inspired me to consider what it was about objects I found in the earth that fascinated me so. All these years later, staring this same skull in the face, I understand that it was the skull that first spoke to me of time and its dual nature of both constancy and change, time, like gravity, pressing down on us, transforming us from one stage to the next by the pressure of its presence.

Four years passed, for instance, between the afternoon that Ava handed me that skull and our move to town. I had begun my study of geology and Ava had taken up drawing, and yet it all seemed to take place in an instant, which came about when Gram, who was standing at the stove preparing supper for Ava, Papa, and me, suddenly turned to us at the table, said, "I do believe I hear the waters rising," and then fell like a stone to the floor.

It was just like a book ending for us, a story coming to a close. At the small cemetery behind the church on the outskirts of town, Papa, a little in his cups, I realize now, took us in his arms and vowed that he would take care of us now that only the three of us were left. But within a few days of Grandmam's demise he moved us into a large white house near the railroad depot — much closer to school, he pointed out to us, than our prairie house — and a few days after that, he came through the door out of a cold rain just before suppertime in the company of a birdlike woman in bonnet and shawl who, when she removed her head covering, revealed hair the color of corn silk and just as fine. She wore spectacles, and these were all steamed up from her breath and the heat of our new house.

"Children," said our father, "this is Mrs. Halme, who will be taking care of the house."

"And you," she added in a voice with that odd lilt of the Scandinavian marooned on an island town in the ocean of prairie.

"And us?" I asked.

Ava, I noticed, turned her face away.

"She will be moving in," Papa said, "and she will be looking after you."

It went like that, and it would have gotten worse had not at that moment our visitor removed her spectacles to dab at her tearfuleyes with a handkerchief, and we saw that without the strong lenses lenses to correct her vision she was utterly and most comically cross-eyed.

However, my sister and I didn't laugh. We sneaked a quick look at Mrs. Halme and then at each other, and—it was almost as if we could read minds—decided then and there without speech that this was a woman as pathetic as we felt, having been left without a mother, and now without a grandmother and without our prairie home. I don't know what kind of a listless, dispirited life we might have led in town if it hadn't been for our entertaining Mrs. Halme. She was an awful cook, cried at the drop of a pin, and never knew just how silly she appeared when she took off her spectacles to drop her tears.

"You are fooling me," she would say in a rising wail on occasions when I would do some mean-spirited thing to her, such as hide her rolling pin just as she was about to smooth out the pie dough. "When your father comes back from Omaha, I am going to tell him everything you done." *Ever-tink you dunn* was more how it sounded in that immigrant lilt. Her name was Finnish—it was her husband's—but she herself was Swedish, a farm girl of strict upbringing who, whether singing at church or trying to conduct our household with what she took to be the dignity appropriate for the family of a widowed manager for the rails of the Great Plains, just never understood her possibilities for comedy. In times of sorrow—and there were more to come—she kept us on the edge of ludicrous laughter, and in ordinary hours she was never far from showing us by her example that everything we did on this earth — eating, work-ing, speaking, or just the simple act of looking out a window or picking something up from the floor — had the potential for the pre-posterous.

But for all of her inadvertent silliness, she possessed the innate sense — it had to be innate since there was nothing about her out-ward manner that suggested it — to recognize in me the desire to be left alone with my growing love of science, and in Ava the begin-nings of her vocation for art. After having cleaned Ava's room the first time — the attic room at the top of the big new house in town which I had seen immediately was the perfect room for me but, talk about innate understanding, had given over to Ava because of the quality of the light — Mrs. Halme declared, "This chickadee needs lessons!"

"She does not!" I said, assuming that the housekeeper meant that Ava's sketches were not very good. And I had seen for myself over the past few years just how well she captured objects and trees, stones from my collection, or just the ordinary things of the house.

"I do!" Ava said, understanding exactly what Mrs. Halme meant while I was the one left behind in this.

When Papa returned from his latest trip — he had been to Laramie this time — the housekeeper was ready for him. "Mees-ter Ball-deen," she said, "there is a voman I think you should meet."

It was at the dinner table, of all places, that she said it, and despite my now mature sixteen years, there was something about this announcement that made me jump.

"Woman?" I said, looking directly at my sister, but Ava gave me no sign at all that she felt the same embarrassment as me.

"Robert," said our father, his speech slightly slurred from drink, "you're talking out of turn. Let Mrs. Halme speak."

And speak she did, which is how we found out about Dora Rix, the sister of a woman Mrs. Halme had worked for in town sev-eral years back. Dora had attended the Chicago Art Institute for a drawing class one summer after she had lost her husband and then had moved back to the plains.

"She has the learning, Ava has the talent . . . "

31

"Talent?" I spoke up, not to disagree but to enunciate the word that had eluded me in my attempts to understand what my little sister was doing.

"Robert!" Papa put in. "For the last time!"

"Sorry, sir," I said.

"Continue, please, Mrs. Halme."

Continue she did, quickly arranging a meeting among the interested parties, and thereby changing the direction of our lives.

"The secret about art," I heard this thin, long-fingered, dark-haired person say to my father one evening after he had had Mrs. Halme invite her to supper in appreciation of her devotion to Ava, "I used to believe, is that anyone can learn to draw . . . "

"Not me," said Papa.

"Well, I was going to finish," the art teacher said, looking somewhat dismayed. "But your daughter is so good at it that she has made me think twice before ever saying such a thing again. I don't even know what I meant by that. Ava is . . . she draws . . . like an angel."

"Excuse me, please," Ava said and looked at our father.

"Do you make a living at this?" Papa asked, nodding his assent at Ava's request to leave the room.

"I beg your pardon, Mr. Boldin?"

Papa reached for his glass, the one that always seemed filled with brownish liquor no matter how many times he raised it to his lips. "Do you support yourself from your drawing?"

"From my lessons? Well, no, I . . . "

"So if she wants to draw, she'll have to find a husband."

"Again, I must beg your pardon?"

"If she is as good as you say she is, she will want to do it all the time, and so she will have to find a way to support herself, some other way. So she will need a husband sympathetic to her desires, isn't that correct, Mrs. Rix?"

"Dora," the woman said. "Please call me Dora."

"Dora," Papa said.

"As a matter of fact, Mr. Boldin, I am managing quite well by myself and still keeping up with my drawing and painting."

"It depends on what you call 'quite well'," my father said.

32

Their voices dropped into the realm of near whispers. Feeling like the odd man out—odd boy, I suppose I should call myself, odd *boy* out—I left the room in search of Ava, but she must have climbed up to the attic, because she was nowhere in sight in the lower floors of the house.

" . . . difficult," Dora was saying as I returned.

"I know," my father was saying.

I watched carefully as he walked her to the door. "I'm going to walk Mrs. Rix home," he called to me over his shoulder.

"What?" Ava seemed quite agitated when I told her about it.

"That's right," I said. "That's what it looks like to me."

That next evening she took a walk herself to the edge of town, where the streetlamps stopped, and the prairie began.

Is this what we want? I imagined her asking her sister, who was still always with her.

You like her, Eve would say.

It's true. It's just . . .

Our real mother's gone. No bringing her back.

I know.

And Dora is a good teacher. She's helping you. You won't need me much longer.

Yes, I like her, but Papa hasn't stopped his drinking.

She's a good teacher, not a miracle worker.

But he likes her, and so he might stop.

He might.

You don't believe that will happen.

I want it to, but I don't believe it will. I always try to see the difference between what I want and what I think can happen.

I'm the opposite. Dora calls it the dream side of me. She says every artist has to have this . . .

Don't you know I know that? You know I was there when she said it.

Oh, don't be angry with me. Please don't be angry.

Look!

A shooting star!

So late in the season, too.

That's right. Robert said the big meteor showers come in late August.

Look there!
Another, yes! And now there!
There!
Oh, I wish I could draw that!
What?
The fading star, the streak of motion turning into . . . I don't know a word. I'll try to draw it.
And so you will.
I caught up with her at the edge of an open field. "Fourth of July sky," I said.
"You should be a poet, Robby," she said.
"I'm going to be a geologist," I said.
"Oh, rocks!" she said.
"What's wrong with rocks?"
"I was just joking. I love to draw rocks. I love rocks, too."

Rocks. I should say something about them, how I collected stones of varying textures and hues from the prairie and laid them in piles on my dresser.
"Dirt, dirt, dirt!" Mrs. Halme hated my hobby, sometimes pretending that it never existed at all and throwing out stones that had taken me hours to find and even more time to polish. We had terrible fights about it, and only after the wedding, when Dora moved in with us, did our housekeeper, now second in command, stop harassing me for my love of rocks.
It took me a little time to come to terms with my new step-mother. It took Ava less, for she had been won over after her first lesson and never felt that sinking motion of dreadful fear that we would be betraying our mother by allowing ourselves to enjoy life with Dora. But then she had never known Mother, only that she had passed her, coming into the world as Mother was going out, as it were. Talk to me about schist and marble and metamorphic process and I can respond with alacrity. It's the human pressures that I have always found difficult to understand. Ava and I could converse about stars and rocks, but we never found a way to talk about Mother. This was a flaw, and my sister paid for it in later years.
My sister. Picture her, as I often saw her, up in her room, dreaming. She told me once that she loved that room more than any

other place she had ever inhabited. Nestled under the slope of the roof beams on the southwestern side of the house, it collected early afternoon heat and stayed bright late into the day. If she had taken the room originally assigned to her, now my room on the second floor, with one window looking east, and that window shaded by the long tin gutter, she would have had nowhere near the amount of light, however changing, that flowed into the upper room, the room in which, I like to think, began some of the changes in her work that led ultimately to the Ava Boldin known today.

I know that I had something to do with the forming of her. Despite all the affection I felt for her, beneath the surface lay a resentment I could not suppress—Mother had died and Ava had survived, and I know that I went out of my way to be good to her, as with the room, to avoid facing up to the fact that there were times when I truly wished that she were dead. In times such as that, my rocks were good to me. I could touch them and feel myself caught in the massive drama of upheaving earth and ocean that made them the way they were. I could lose my Nebraska, household, family, older-brother self on the vast stage of volcanic eons that I conjured up in my mind. Some boys my age dreamed of flying. I heard their stories at school. And some imagined sailing the seas of the world as captains, admirals even, if their souls could stretch that much. Others pictured for themselves heroism in war, and indeed in just a few years there would be a war for them to go to. For me geological time loomed large, and I needed no windows on the plains to pic-ture the hemispheric sea that had once surged there. Those boiling tides swelled and roared in my mind, building and falling to the measure of an ancient moon that shone down on a planet not yet fully formed.

What a theater my small room was! And presiding over it was the calf skull found for me by my little sister. I'd touch that pitted, blanched bone for luck, and sink down onto my bed, already sail-ing back into a past so distant that even the first ancestors of the old buffalo herds that had once roamed beyond our former prop-erty on the river were nothing more than a slender possibility in the nervous system of creatures more alien than anything I could, at that stage in my studies, even picture. And I roamed about like some eye with wings above all the furor, seeing the youth of the planet, and wondering now and then what it might be like if I could stay forever in this foyer of the ancient geologic ages, never to be born in the future, and thus never to know the mournful miseries of life without our mother.

However Dora was settling into the household, which is to say winning my affection, encouraging Mrs. Halme to make my favorite desserts, ordering from exotic catalogs gemstones from faraway places and giving them to me for holidays and birthdays, and generally helping to create the illusion that with Mother and Grandmam gone and our father on the road almost as much now as ever, we still had a family worth belonging to. Some weeks I could go along with this, some weeks I couldn't. But I was enough of a scientific-minded boy that I could face up to the facts: that Mother and Grandmam were dead, and the smart thing to do, if I didn't find sulking and feeling sorry for myself very interesting for too long, was to appreciate what this actually rather wonderful woman was doing for us.

"Robert," she'd say, if she caught me unawares, coming in the door from school or coming down from my room for supper, "how's the world treating you?"

A simple thing like that. I suppose that some boy might have allowed this to get under his skin. I took her greeting as a sign of affection, which it truly was, and began to return her generally sunny ways with pleasantness of my own. One night at the table she asked if I might show her my rock collection.

"Say yes," Ava said.

"Yes," I said, "sure." I had to admit to myself that Dora had won me over.

I was working with my rocks on another evening when Ava knocked at the door. "I'm busy," I called to her.

She knocked again.

"Busy."

"I would like to speak to you," she said—this way of talking from a twelve-year-old!

"I need your help," she said after I allowed her to enter and sit down.

"I'm busy," I said.

"I know, but this is important." She had that expression on her face, which only later did I understand as the conviction of Ava *and* Eve come together for a serious moment.

"I have homework," I said.

"You've already done your homework. You always do it right after school."

I nodded, admitting that she had caught me in a lie. "Well?" I said.

"I need you," she said.

"All right." I closed my eyes and thus blinked away the Jurassic reverie I had been caught up in. "You want me to lift something, little girl? What is it?"

"No, Robby, something else."

I raised a hand in question. "What?"

"And please don't call me a little girl."

"You are a little girl."

"I'm twelve. Dora calls me a young woman."

"*Dora*," I said.

"Don't say her name that way. You like her."

"I suppose," I said.

"You do."

"All right. But what's the favor?"

Her smile broke out, a cute, cunning smile. "Something."

"What is it? Tell me. I have things to do."

"It will take a little time."

That was when she explained that she wanted me to take off my clothes.

"What?"

My amazement, embarrassment, consternation, outrage—all were present. I leaped up from my bed and was making to throw her from my room when, as if by magic, tears spurted from her eyes and she began to howl.

"That's . . . wicked!" I used that word because I had no other.

"No, it's not. I need to see you . . . "

I stopped short of taking her by the arm and twisting hard. Standing before her, I was not that much taller—that's what a big girl she was, not little at all.

37

"I knew I never should have given you that room. It's made you think you're a princess or such. And that I'm your slave, one of your subjects. Do you want to put me in manacles, too?"

"Please, Robby," she said. "Look." That was when I realized that she had been carrying a drawing with her all this while. "Look at this."

She held up the stiff sheet of paper to show me—a study of a bird feather, a chunk of malachite, a library copy of *Little Women* with the spine turned so that you could see both the title and the embossed design on the front of the cover, and a slice of apple on which I saw, in the marvelous drenching light that she had somehow captured, several beaded spots of moisture so real that you could almost have touched the tip of your tongue to them and tasted the juice.

"So?" I said, so impressed that I did not want to give her a single hint of the awe in which I held her talent.

"I can't do any more of this for a while."

"Take time off then."

"I can't do that, either. I want to draw the body."

"My body, huh?"

"I can't ask Papa, can I?"

That remark was so preposterous that I burst into a great convulsion of astonished laughter, during which I spit out so much saliva that Ava pulled the drawing closer to her in order to protect it from my spray.

"Ask Dora," I said, and felt a shiver of titillation as broad as the mixture of fear and amazement at her remark about our father.

"I need to draw a man. I can draw a woman by looking in the mirror, silly. You have different bones. They look different."

"If you know how my bones look, why do you need me to pose for you?"

"Not pose. Sit. Just sit. Posing is old-fashioned. I just want you to sit and look natural."

"Without any clothes?"

"You do it every day, don't you?"

"I do?"

"In your bath."

"How do you know about me in my bath? Are you spying on me?" I reached for her arm, but she drew back.

"I've never *seen* you in your bath. I just know that you take one. Just the way I do."

"You probably only take one once a week," I said.

"Don't be smart. So will you let me?"

"Let you exactly what?"

"Draw you."

"In my bath?"

"Well, I didn't think of that, but that would be good enough. I could at least get your upper torso."

"My upper torso? Does Dora teach you to talk like that?"

"Robby, it's no different from your rock talk."

"That's science."

"So is drawing. That's just what I do. Science. That's why I need to see your body."

"My upper torso."

"If that's all you'll show me."

"And you'll be lucky to see that much."

As it turned out, I didn't know how lucky she thought she was.

There was a concert in town by a visiting Chicago chamber group the next Saturday evening. Dora, always a lover of the arts, took a reluctant Papa who—I know since I smelled his breath as he went out the door—must have thrown down a few precautionary drinks before departing the house.

"What will you do?" he said to me on the threshold.

"Sir?" His question threw me off balance, fearing, as I did, that he had some power that allowed him to read my mind.

"This evening. Will you chase hawks or sand the boat for our expedition?"

"What expedition, Papa?"

But he was already out the door. Ava waited while I heated the water for the tub. I tried to figure what it was my father had been saying as I carried the buckets, but nothing came clear.

"Tell me when you're ready," Ava said and left me standing at the side of the tub.

"Are we really going to go through with this?" I called after her.

Ava stuck her head back in the bathroom door. "I *need* you, Robby," she said. "I can't advance if I don't do this. Dora gave me a book about the human body, but looking at diagrams of muscles is a lot different from seeing them for real."

"In the flesh is how you say it, I think." I blushed at my own remark, and turned my back on her. The door closed. How did I get myself into situations like this? I asked myself. I had a few good friends in town. If they ever found out about this, I'd be a laughing-stock, is how I thought of it. Nevertheless, after a few minutes I began to undress, and, despite the fact that I imagined the water to be ten times hotter than it actually was, after a few more moments of indecision, I climbed into the tub and lowered myself into the tepid little pool.

"Ready?" I heard Ava call.

"No!" I replied, still agitated. It was supposed to be the other way around with the sexes, I knew, from the stories some of my friends had told me. But this was life with Ava Boldin, and nothing much in it was like life with anyone else.

"Ready now?"

"One minute," I said; then, "okay," sinking back down into the water.

Ava came into the room and immediately sat down on a chair and began sketching.

"I don't see what the big deal is," I said.

"You made it into one," she said. "Don't turn your head. Just keep looking forward."

"I could have taken off my shirt and sat at the window," I said.

"It's not the same," she said. "When you're all . . . "

"What?" I stirred the water with my toes, my arms stretched along the side of the tub.

"Robby, you're not doing it."

"Doing what? I'm sitting here, just the way you asked. Look, Ava, this is . . . "

"You have your underpants on."

I could feel my whole body clench up like a fist. "How do you know?"

"I can tell. And it's not fair."

"How can you tell?"

40

She got up from her seat and leaned down. "Just as I thought."

"Get out," I said.

"You promised," she said.

"Get out, you spy, and I'll do it," I said.

"You're a liar," she said.

"Get out and come back in a minute," I said. "I'll call you back."

"All right," she said. "But don't lie to me."

"My own sister," I said. "Would I lie?"

Ava left the room and I stood up again, splashing water indiscriminately over the floor. I stripped off my wet pants—they felt like dead skin—and tossed them aside. Back I sank into the tub, muttering to myself as I did.

"Okay," I called.

Out of the corner of my eye I saw Ava come back in. "You look and I'll kill you," I said.

"I'm looking at your head and neck and shoulders and arms," she said.

"I'll bet," I said.

"It's true," she said. Something in her voice, a certain tension, convinced me that she was up to something, that she was probably working with her quick pencil. But I didn't try to look.

"The water's getting cold," I said after a while.

"Does that mean you're going to get out?"

I nodded.

"Wait, don't move your head. Another minute."

"It's too cold," I said.

"Just a minute."

"I'm ready, Ava."

"All right, Robby."

"Well?"

"What?"

"Aren't you going to leave?"

She stood up, holding her pad and pencil, saying nothing. "I want to see you," she said finally.

"You can't." The water was cold, but I stayed beneath it.

"Stand up," she said.

"No. Get out."

"I need to see you," she said.

41

"Go look at yourself in the mirror," I said.

"I do that. I want to see you."

The cold water, it felt now like a hand clutching me in the groin. "Go," I said.

"Please," she said.

"You're my sister," I said.

"That's why it's all right," she said.

"No, it's not," I said.

"I won't go near you," she said.

It was quite cold now, and I wanted to stand. "No," I said. "Now get out. If you don't, when I get out I'm going to get you."

"Please," she said. "It's for my drawing."

"For your drawing?" I asked.

"I need to see things," she said.

"You don't need to see me," I said.

"Yes, I do."

"No, you don't."

"I do."

"You don't. Now leave so I can get out."

"I'll just stand here. I'll be drawing."

"Drawing me?"

"Yes."

"My . . . "

"You don't have to say."

"Ava, you get out. Or I'll tell Pa."

"Tell him what?"

"What you asked me."

"You will not."

"I will."

"Look," she said. "We can trade." She set down her pad on the chair and unbuttoned her shirt.

"What are you doing?"

"Showing you," she said. "You show me and I'll show you."

"What?" I said, but I didn't say stop.

"There," she said, slipping out of her shirt. She had on an undershirt and pulled that next over her head. Her chest was flat, except for her nipples, which were like bulbs bulging under the earth just on the verge of spring. "Now will you stand?"

I sat there silently a moment, feeling myself in my senses in a way I never had before, wanting to stand but not standing, about to stand but not wanting to. "This is wrong," I said, as if in someone else's voice. I tried quickly to figure whose it was, and decided that it wasn't our father's and it wasn't our dead mother's; it was Mrs. Halme's, her singsong little way of speaking.

"Nothing is, if I need it to draw," Ava said.

"What?"

"I know what's right." She glanced down at her chest. "This isn't enough, is it?" she asked.

"Enough?"

"All right." She began to unfasten her skirt.

"Ava," I said quietly, unable to think of any other sound to make.

She stripped to her white lace underpants. I had not seen her this way since she was a child. She was long there and thin, and as I was wondering, she made a small noise in her throat, and leaned down and stepped out of her pants. "You're still sitting," she said.

So I was, for I was so transfixed by the sight of her, the tiniest pale red patch of hair she wore between her legs. I had seen my mother like this down by the riverbank—and I grew excited at the same time I thought of her death. Ava sat back down now, drawing pad and pencil on her lap, her legs crossed. "Ready," she said.

"I guess you are. But I'm not," I said.

"You have to be. Or it's not fair. Robby?"

"Well," I said. I looked down at myself. No matter what else passed between us, it was the fairness of it all that mattered at our age, at that time. And so I stood, glad, actually, to get out of the by-now cold water of the bath.

"Good," Ava said. "You're dripping wet, but let me draw."

I watched her eyes flit back and forth from me to the pad, the pad to me, and saw the pencil move as she eased her wrist through the air. It would be difficult to say how much time passed, though it seemed to me not all that much. My legs grew tired, but surprisingly I didn't mind the cold. Something about this pose—me and my sister caught up in this equation—kept my mind off the chill. One moment I was standing there dripping water, the next I was relatively dry, and found myself thinking once again about embarrassment.

"Don't put your hands in front," she said as I moved to cover myself. "One minute more."

"Ava," I said.

"You're a great brother, Robby," she said. "You know you are."

"I'm a fool," I said.

"No, you're not. You're wonderful."

"Ava," I said, "you're a *crazy* girl."

Her pencil moved swiftly now, as if it had only a little life left to live, a thing alive, apart from her wrist. "Okay, I'm finished. But I want to draw you again," she said, still sitting there.

"Not now," I said, holding the towel around me.

"Of course not. Another time," she said.

I was standing above her, staring at her, staring down into her lap. I could scarcely breathe, and my chest felt as though it were about to explode.

"Can't see," she said, and turned the drawing pad away from me, holding it to her chest.

"I wasn't looking at the drawing."

That was when she stood, holding the drawing pad at her side.

"Let the towel go," she said. "Be fair."

I slowly let the towel slide to the wet floor, after which Ava studied me.

Though *studied* is all we did that night or on any of the other nights when Ava drew me. By anyone's standards, then or now, we were wild, but there was also something in each of us that kept us at a distance no matter how close we came to the other thing.

Where that quality came from is another matter, a question that neither scientists nor artists usually address. It was nothing that I wondered about then, and I can't imagine that Ava gave it much thought, either. We were both so busy with each other. We had so little else when it came to family. If Mrs. Halme and Dora had not come into our house, it's hard to believe that we could have carried on at all, though I suppose we would have somehow. Papa was not much help, and actually his drinking made him more and more a hindrance, not only to us but to himself. At first Dora seemed to have a good effect on him. But after a few months he began to take up his old ways, leaving home a man slightly tipsy and arriving home a drunkard in his cups.

Dora sometimes had to carry him from the door to the stairs. We could often hear him alternately raving and groaning where we lay in our beds.

"Birds of passage!" His words echoed through the house.

"Hush!" We could hear Dora trying to calm him.

"The echoes! The echoes!"

"What echoes, James? Will you please hush! The children!"

"And the roaring!"

"James . . ."

"Infernal roaring!"

Within a year he was gone, roaring and all.

The horrible news came to us from the telegraph office, and then a few hours later in the form of another manager from the yards in Omaha. "Mr. Boldin was checking some switches when a freight backed up over him, I'm afraid . . ."

I was afraid for the lack of weeping and wailing. Ava and Dora and I had been sitting there in a kind of daze ever since the man from the telegraph office first delivered his words. And now this more vivid description, which should have sent us into a frenzy of tears, instead drove us deeper and deeper into silence.

"If there's anything the company can do . . ." The man might have been speaking to a group of statues.

The three of us spent the night in one bed, Dora's and Papa's, Ava and I on either side of this woman who was now the only person resembling a relative we had in the world. We spent the night huddling together. Still silent. Now and then a cough. A catch in the throat. No more.

It wasn't until Mrs. Halme, who had been away for the night, arrived early the next day that the sounds of real mourning echoed through the house. "What is this?" she called out. "What is *this*?"

And commenced all the shrieking and screaming and hair tearing and eye rolling and teeth gnashing and rending of clothing that any family might have required on an occasion such as this.

We buried him in the little cemetery on the outskirts of town, alongside our mother and his, and returned home to sink deeper and deeper into an awful funk of misery.

* * *

"Your stones!" Mrs. Halme would sometimes again berate me after
trying to clean my room, and her voice cut into me more deeply
than before. "When are you going to throw out all that dirt?" She
rolled her eyes up in the back of her head and carried on as though
she had found stolen bank notes instead of my rock collection. "You
are an educated boy. You are going to go to college. You should
choose to become a lawyer; you speak well, you should use your
God-given talents. Throw away that dusty pile of stones and become
something useful!"

My stones!

But she was even worse when it came to Ava's drawings, carrying on what she apparently took to be our father's crusade. "I don't
care if I was the one suggested it, your drawing lessons. It would
make a good pastime was what I thought. A girl should have a skill,
I believe in that, but make it something useful, like my cleaning.
Where will all this picture making get you? A husband wants someone to cook and clean for him and to raise his children. If he wants
decoration, you can learn to embroider, Ava. But you must learn a
practical thing or two or you will never get married."

This conversation took place up in Ava's attic room, she later
told me, with Ava sitting at her worktable that looked out over the
prairie, and our dear old housekeeper, seeming ever so much like a
flustered prairie hen flushed from hiding, rushing back and forth,
picking up and setting down, dusting and folding.

"But what if I don't want to get married?" Ava asked. She might
as well have told Mrs. Halme that Jesus was a meadowlark.

"Sure, sure, Ava," she said. "You can mock me now, but when
you meet your intended, you are going to have to show him that
you know more than how to draw an apple on a plate."

"Mrs. Halme," Ava said to her, echoing something that I had
once heard Dora say, "this is the twentieth century, and girls are
no longer just chattel to be traded back and forth between families
for power and land."

Our housekeeper couldn't believe her ears. "What?" she said in
a kind of low wail. "What kind of talk is this from a girl your age?
Who teaches you such things? Oh, but sure I know." At this she
came right up to where Ava sat and leaned over and said in a near

46

whisper, "The calendar says the twentieth century or whatever. But in here," and she balled a fist and tapped it against her chest, "in here, we still live in the forest."

I'm not sure that Ava fully understood what the Swedish woman was saying, or else she gave a reply well beyond her years. "I like the forest, Mrs. Halme," she said. "I've seen pictures. There are a lot of wonderful things to draw there."

"And Indians," the housekeeper came back at her. "Indians what would eat you up! And don't go tell me that you would like *that!*"

Ava made a little smile and nodded to her. "Then I could draw the inside of an Indian."

But Mrs. Halme, who was so wonderfully amusing to us even in our gloomiest hours after Papa's death, did not take Ava's joke lightly. She kept after her to acquire some domestic skills, and Ava, because at this age she could hardly go on working all her waking hours, sometimes acquiesced.

For example, I came home from school late one afternoon to find them both hunched over the stove, watching, as it turned out, for some reaction to occur in a dish.

And then there was the year of the embroidering. Mounds and mounds of it all around the house.

"You do such a wonderful pattern," Mrs. Halme said to my sister.

"But it's a pattern and I don't like that," Ava said. "I don't like to make something that's already *there.*"

Still Mrs. Halme kept after her, as if she recognized that this might be the world's last chance to divert young Ava Boldin from the far border of her gift and turn her talent toward the conventional lands where most of the rest of us live all of our lives. It's not that she was a mean or vengeful woman wanting to break Ava's spirit. She was, after all, as she pointed out, the one who had introduced us to Dora in the first place. She believed, I'm sure, with all her heart—tap your fist against your chest and remember the ancient forest—that Ava was, what? sick, perhaps you might put it, from an excess of zeal for her drawing, and needed help to be cured.

Nothing proved this to her so much as when one day while

doing something or other with cleaning up in the attic, she found Ava's sketches from our bathtub encounters.

Oh, the wail that went up through the house; you'd have thought that she'd stumbled on Christ Himself nailed to the Cross. "I knew it, I knew it, I knew it! these children living here without any parents could only come to a bad end! Oh, Jesus, give me the strength to help them; help me, Jesus!"

She wailed on as she wandered back and forth across the attic. From my room I could hear her clearly, stumbling about as if in a stupor, and I wondered if she knew that I had come home already from school—while Ava was still out, as was Dora, who after Papa's death had taken to giving drawing lessons again to make some extra money for the household. I lay there, very still, while our house-keeper raged, and clumped down the stairs in her comical way, a stilt-legged woman in big housekeeper shoes, looking for someone to blame.

"It is a sin against the light!" I heard her rage to Dora as soon as our stepmother came in the door. "That girl is going to burn in hell! And that boy will go with her!"

"Don't be ridiculous," I heard Dora say after Mrs. Halme had sputtered out the story of her discovery. "Now come and show me what you found."

Clump clump clump: housekeeper shoes thumped up the stairs, followed by the lighter step of our Dora.

I was seventeen years old by then and about to leave for the university in Lincoln that autumn, but I was feeling in those moments that I was about eight or nine and that I was heading for bad trouble!

"These!" I heard Mrs. Halme's voice ring through the attic rafters. "And these! This! Oh, may Jesus save us all from burning in the Devil's fire!"

I couldn't hear Dora's response beyond a few muttered words. I did hear Mrs. Halme again, shrieking out her siren warning against the sinful products of my sister's pencil. "Oh, oh, oh, first the mother dies, and then the father from the train, and now this sinfulness! Where will it end? Where will it end?"

"Mrs. Halme," I heard Dora coming back down the stairs, "the girl needs . . . "

48

Scream from the housekeeper. "Encouragement! What are you saying?"

"It's true," Dora said in a calm, careful voice as they passed my door on the way down the hall to the stairs to the first floor. "Drawing figures like that, it was the best . . . "

"Figures!" Mrs. Halme sounded as though she were going to fire herself up into a flame of screeching voice and impassioned flapping of arms—I was watching from behind my half-opened door now as they descended the stairs. "This is no *figures*; this is her brother! the boy! Oh, the boy led her on."

My heart sank. My knees trembled.

"Of course he didn't," Dora said, and I tried to calm myself with that, but I kept on trembling. "*I* led her on."

"You!" Mrs. Halme let out. "You?"

"Oh, calm down, Mrs. Halme," Dora said. "We'll talk to Ava when she comes home from school. As for the rest of it . . . "

Their voices faded from my hearing as they reached the bottom of the stairs.

I dreaded dinner that evening and in anticipation of it, dug myself so deeply into my books that I didn't even hear Ava come in. Her knock at my door set my heart to pounding. "Yes?"

"Me."

I told her to come in even as I found myself short of breath and wishing I were anyplace but here.

She walked in, fresh from some meeting at school where, I could tell by the burning light in her eyes, she had probably stood up and challenged one of her classmates about some subject or other—the song they should sing at the spring pageant or the color of the bunting, who knew?—or perhaps it was just from the wind on the walk home, or perhaps from a combination of her usually brisk pace and the wind while she walked along our little streets, thinking to herself about Rembrandt and Mary Cassatt, Gericault and Holbein and Homer, all of those painters whose work she had heard about from Dora and longed to see—the subject of many a discussion between them while Dora was working with her on her drawings, ah, these famous drawings, some of which within the last few hours had made me feel as sick as our housekeeper believed me to be.

"Hello, Robby," she said. "I have some good news."

"You'd better hear what I heard first," I said.

"What did you hear?" She sat on the edge of the bed and touched a hand to my foot.

My sister, my artist!

I began to tell her my story when she burst out laughing.

"Do you think it's funny?" I asked.

"No, no, yes, yes, yes," she said, giving my foot a good squeeze. "I just talked to Dora on the way in. She wants me to go to the Art Institute in Chicago just as soon as I finish high school!"

"So, she's not mad at us?"

Ava shook her head vigorously. "She loves us, Robby. She loves my work."

"But Mrs. Halme . . . "

"She quit, Robby." Ava snapped her fingers, a most unlady-like gesture, the likes of which I had never seen performed before.

"But who will cook?"

"Dora says that she will. And I'll help her."

"I'll . . . I'll help clean up," I said.

"Oh, you will not," Ava said. "Not you and your rock collection." And with that she went into a wonderful mocking re-creation of Mrs. Halme, beginning with, "You and your stones! Oh, your dirty, dirty stones!"

I laughed so hard I couldn't catch my breath.

"So it's just the three of us, Robby."

I was still short of breath, getting up to walk with her down-stairs to dinner. "The three musketeers," I said.

"Is that from a book you've read?"

"Yes, from a book."

Ava slipped her arm through mine as we went out into the hall. The odors of dinner—meat, bread, coffee—drifted up the stairs. "I can't believe she found those drawings," she said. "I wish I could have been there."

"It wasn't fun," I said.

"You were there?"

"I heard her screaming." And now it was my turn to imitate our old housekeeper—except that just as I launched into it, I heard a familiar voice at the foot of the stairs, and there she was standing in her apron looking her same old silly self.

"Mrs. Halme, . . . " My voice caught in my throat.

"Come down, you naughty children, and let me feed you. I'm staying on, just to make sure that you don't do nothing further to make you both burn in hell."

DOOR

Naming.

The name.

During a week when I was suffering a series of Braxton-Hicks contractions, which Amalia Anaya, the midwife Socorro had found for me in the village, called "dress rehearsal," Michael turned to me in bed and said, "I've got her name."

"Who?" I said.

"The baby."

"You know that it's a girl? I wish I knew."

"*If* it's a girl," he said.

"Then what?"

"Cecelia."

"Cecelia?"

"After my mother."

"Oh, Cissy. I get it. I should have gotten it right away." I took his hand and guided it under the covers to the mound within which our little kid was playing. "Feel this."

"Wow," was all he said.

"Wow?"

"Wow."

But then we artists have never been known for our way of speaking. We don't speak; we *do*, don't we? At least that was what Michael lectured me about when I burst into tears and told him that it was his child inside me growing, and that he could at least find something more inside him to say about it than *wow*.

Oh, I grew weepy, weepy, weepy. And I *hated* myself for it.

"And if it's a boy?" I asked when I finally gained control of myself again.

52

"I don't know. I'm not sure."

"What about after your father?" I said.

He gave me a look.

"Did I say something wrong?"

He shook his head.

"When you're working out in the barn, painting with Ava . . . "

"We're building a kiln," he said. "I'm going to teach her how to pot."

"She's not painting?"

"She's painting. But we talked about potting, and she said she wanted to learn it. Her eyes are getting bad. She's preparing for that."

"Well, you talk a little while you work, yes?"

"Some."

"Does she talk about your father?"

He gave me that look again.

"Well?"

"We talk about what we're doing," he said.

"You could ask her about your father, you know. You don't have to go through life not really knowing anything about him; it's not required."

"I'll ask her sometime."

"I know you. When you're her age."

"I wonder if you really know me, Amy, when you talk to me like this."

"Like *what*?"

"Like . . . oh, look, just shut up, okay?"

I felt his words like a slap in the face. It took him a while to calm me, and he apologized, told me he was thinking about work all the time, about working with Ava out in the barn, about the potting project, and I reminded him that I had a few things on my mind as well, and that I didn't spend all day with chores, going to the village with Socorro and baking bread and getting things for the baby and trips down to Taos for nothing, that I had just as much right to think about the art stuff as he did, and he agreed with me, and tried to calm me with his kisses, and I let myself go with that, and pretty soon he was stripping off my nightgown and trying quite hard to get me wet, and then sliding himself inside me

53

and working—gently, I have to admit it, very gently, to the point where I had to tell him that he could be just a little bit more vigorous—working around my big mound of a belly as though it were some kind of precious piece of art in itself.

It was around this time, with my due date both coming fast upon me but also seeming as though it would never arrive, that Ava went beyond the storytelling and asked me if I would help her out with some old papers. When I saw what it was she was asking me to sort through, I grew quite excited. "Some of these . . . "

"Yes?"

We were sitting at the table in her small studio inside the house, the room that Socorro sometimes slept in when she worked too late to return to the village. Michael and I used a larger bedroom just alongside it. We never heard a sound from the room when Socorro was there, though now and then I wondered if she could hear our little quarrels.

I held up a sheaf of notebooks. "These belonged to Michael's father?"

Ava squinted down at the papers. Up close I could see that her pupils seemed oddly shaped, not the perfect round of most people, although their color was evenly black. Not so the irises of her eyes. These were each, right and left respectively, flecked with blue and green, with an almost-red flanged shape in the left and a dot of vermilion in the right. If they were not the strangest eyes I'd ever heard of, they were certainly the strangest I'd ever seen. Or perhaps they had been normal and this was what had happened to them now that Ava was having trouble with them. In any case, it was difficult not to stare at her, though even when I was sure she noticed that I was staring, she gave no sense that she knew.

"They belonged to my husband, Stigmar, yes," she said. And for the first time in all the months that we had spent with her— well, perhaps Michael had been present in the studio when she showed this emotion, but I had never seen it—she let out a long, long sigh.

"You must be tired," she said, almost as though she were speaking to herself. "You need your rest."

I allowed myself to agree, although I wasn't yet ready for bed. When she noticed that I hadn't moved, she sighed again and gave me one of her infrequent smiles. "Have you decided on a name?"

"Oh, oh, yes, we have. Hasn't Michael told you?"

"We don't speak a lot when we work," Ava said. "But tell me the name." Ava reached out to me, and I could smell the clay on her fingers as she touched my face. She gave off the odor of the earth, as though she were one of those creatures I had read about while studying mythology with Stanley, a creation of the gods made out of mud and blood and hair.

And I told her the name, and she was glad.

CHICAGO

Ava

"I am your fairy godmother," the white-haired woman in black velvet and pearls says to me as she opens the door. A black man in a black uniform stands half a step behind her. The black driver, also in black, stands behind me in the foyer, holding the bags he took from me just as soon as I stepped down from the train.

The lights of the city would have been enough to bewitch me, though I have some knowledge of the world from the reading of novels—Dora pushed on me the work of both Jane Austen and Balzac so I would know, as she puts it, "the two different sides of the same odd world . . . " But even beyond the thousands and thousands of lights outside the train window, and the thousands of people milling about in the streets outside the station as we climbed into the handsome black car, there was the height of the building that we entered and the electrical room that hauled us vertically through the heart of the structure—horseless carriages, elevators, the thronging crowds, skyscrapers: all these things made me believe within minutes that I had not just left the prairie for the city, but that I had left one country for another.

Chicago cannot be another planet entirely. The people appear human enough, though their language seems rough and sharp both at once and grates on my ears, even as I'm amazed by sight after sight that I hastily set down in this notebook, afraid that I shall forget one wonder because of the next that appears. Chicago. September. My arrival in the city. Why do I have to record any of this on paper? How could I ever forget it?

"Darling," says the woman, offering me her hand. "I am so pleased to meet you."

Dora had described Rebecca Finchey as a frontier woman, though that is the last thing that comes to mind as I take in her beautiful white hair wound up atop her head in ribbons of dark velvet to match her dress. At her slender throat there are pearls and on her fingers white gold bands, and in her eyes – diamonds, sparkling diamonds.

"I'm pleased, too," I say, taking her hand, hoping that this awful sense of dumbfounded admiration for her beauty doesn't show too much on my face. She's everything I picture when I imagine my mother's voice in my ear. Perhaps she is indeed my fairy godmother – and I'm certainly ready to be enchanted. That prospect is a lot less daunting than beginning classes tomorrow morning at the Art Institute.

"And how is your Aunt Dora?" she asks as she leads me into the apartment, a place so splendidly appointed with urns and drapes that for a fleeting second I almost believe that *this* is the Art Institute itself.

"My stepmother? She's well, thank you," I say. "But . . . " I want to bite my tongue.

"Yes, my dear?" says Rebecca Finchey as we come upon a table set as if for a holiday feast.

"Are you sure you come from Laramie?" I hear myself inquire.

She does indeed come from Laramie, and how she came from there to here is a story that keeps me interested all through dinner, though the facts of it seem to me less important than the moral lesson it contains: stand up for yourself, since no man will do it for you.

"This is the century in which women must take a stand," says my hostess, raising a glass of wine in my direction.

"Of course," I say, hoisting my own glass. I suppose I would have tried a drink before this evening, but then no one had ever offered me one before.

"To us," says Mrs. Finchey, drinking, and licking wine from her lips.

"To us," I say, thinking upon the father, brothers, and several husbands she has populated her story with in the hour before. Of my own men, of course, there are only my lost father, and Robert, who has gone to Michigan to study science and engineering. As for husbands, the thought has come into my head, but only as an abstraction, and usually only when I happen to be reading a novel.

"It is true," she says, "that they have bestowed upon me my initial investments, but it is I who have turned them into my fortune. The brutes who first gave me the cash would only have squandered it eventually." She reaches out and snatches the bottle from the black servant who is about to replenish her glass. "Here! I can pour my own!"

I allow him to fill my glass again, enjoying this light-headed voluptuous sense of nothingness and everything in a sip.

"Oh, and if it weren't for *them*," Rebecca Finchey says. "If it weren't for *them*, or if *we* were better, what a world it would be! Oh, Evelyn . . . "

I don't correct her but rather take another sip of wine and sit back in my chair, allowing myself a posture unfamiliar but comfortable. "I would miss them," I say.

"Oh, and you would miss them? But of course we would miss them, but it is that we have to *breed* with them that gets me down, darling. There's something a little bit soiling to think that my mother had to have something to do with a man so that she could produce me. All those years on the ranch, you'd think, would make me find it natural rather than humiliating, the bulls mounting the cows." She rises suddenly and lurches toward me.

"We stand alone," she says.

"We do, ma'am," I say.

"Don't 'ma'am' me now, Evelyn. You call me by my name."

"I'm Ava, Rebecca," I say.

"Oh," she says, giving herself a little shake. "I've got to tootle. Come along . . . "

I follow her from the dining room, hoping that by tagging along after her I'll find my room. Halfway through the library she stops, and to my amazement (and some horror, too, I confess) bounces off a wall, stumbles toward a large urn decorated with oriental flowers, raises her skirts, straddles it, and with a contented smile crossing her face gushes into it.

It's a strange way to start off a year, I write to myself before sleep. Which takes me a while, though I am tired from my train trip. We're how many stories above the street? For a prairie girl this is quite discomforting. Dreams steal lightly through my night, though I remember not the dreams, but only that I did dream them. I awaken early to the feeling that someone is in the room, watching me. I carefully open my eyes to find myself surrounded by extraordinary light, light drenching the room from the undraped window through which, the night before, I had looked for a moment to see nothing but blackness. Now when I look, blinking hard against it, I see that the light is a great upward flooding from an immense body of water, a vast and silvery sheet that makes me dizzy to stare at it, and yet I force myself to stare.

Breakfast—at the same table as our strange dinner of the evening before. Rebecca Finchey wears a green silk robe and gives no sign whatsoever of her actions the night before. "Johnson will drive you to the Institute in my car," she says.

"I'd like to take the streetcar."

"Plain old midwestern girl, aren't you?" she says.

"Don't be angry. I don't mean to be rude."

"No, no, no," she says, sending waves of French perfume my way with each word. "I just want to give a young girl the help she deserves."

"How do you know what I deserve?"

"Don't be modest. I've seen your drawings."

I sit up in surprise. "How could you have seen them? I sent them to the Institute."

"I told you, darling, I am your fairy godmother and I have my ways."

"Your ways don't include having them admit me, do they?"

Rebecca Finchey leans forward and squints at me as though she is about to try and wrestle me to the ground. "Don't doubt yourself, darling. Don't doubt yourself. I will only work my magic for you when you run out of resources of your own." For a moment longer she bears down on me with those eyes, and then she leans back in her chair. "I'll have Johnson show you where to meet the streetcar."

The Art Institute looks more like a temple than a museum. I stand on the steps a while looking up at its columns before going around

59

to the back of the building where I am told by a guard the entrance to the school is located.

In the bowels of the museum I find the classrooms. A clerk discovers my name on a list . . . the look she gives me! I am taking Greek and Roman art and literature, aesthetics, and my drawing and painting classes. Nothing out of the ordinary there, the clerk's face says. But there's something else. It takes me an hour to discover what it is. After the literature class I find the studio where the drawing class is to meet. Twenty young men stare at me as I come in the door. The instructor at the front of the room looks up at me and asks, "You are Miss Boldin?"

"Yes."

Suddenly the room is filled with whispering, a strange sound coming from the lips of the young men.

"May I speak to you . . . outside?"

I nod, feeling my heart sink as premonition of whatever bad news he will deliver.

"Miss Boldin," he says when he has led me out into the hallway. "I am your instructor, Geoffrey Banks."

"Yes . . . sir," I say.

"And I have been fretting over your arrival ever since I first heard the news."

"The news?" My hands flutter before me, wild birds that I cannot capture.

"You are enrolled in my life drawing class."

"That is what I requested, Mr. Banks."

"Yes, and the clerk put your name on the list." Now I see it in his eyes, the terrible news. "But you cannot attend."

"I'm here, Mr. Banks."

"I see that you are, Miss Boldin. But you cannot attend. I simply will not have it," and here his voice begins to rise into the upper registers, "or have you, shall I say, in this group."

"And may I ask why not, sir?"

Several of the young men have come to the door, trying to overhear our conversation. When they catch my eye, they draw back into the room.

"I believe you know why not, young lady."

"Mister Banks, I . . . "

"I will arrange for you to have a tutorial rather than the class. You're not being penalized, Miss Boldin, merely given the courtesy you deserve, and require."

"I don't require it personally, Mister Banks."

"Don't get cheeky with me now, young lady. I will be taking the time to give you this tutorial myself and I am personally paying for the model."

"Please don't bother, Mister Banks. I will pay for the model."

"You will pay?"

"Yes, I will."

"Very well."

The whispering starts up louder than before in the room behind us. I notice that Mister Banks's stare, like a fly, has landed on my bosom.

"Fairy godmother!" I call to her as I come through the door of the apartment, "I need you now!"

Before she hears me out, she takes me to dine in a restaurant more like a church than a dining room, with tall columns and quiet music by a string quartet and candlelight, lovely odors of perfume and food.

"Paris in Chicago," Rebecca Finchey says to me, sweeping her large bare arm across the table. The uniformed waiter arrives and she proceeds to order enough food for a week. And drink. I have little appetite myself after my encounter with my drawing teacher, but I do have a desire for a glass of wine. A few sips and I'm reeling about even while sitting still. Large-eyed women move past our table dressed in diamonds and ribbons and gowns, their fingernails long as crayons, accompanied by men with slicked-down hair that fairly glows in the candlelight, wearing capes and carrying walking sticks. One of these men winks at me as he goes by and Rebecca Finchey hisses at him to move along. She stands; I'm afraid she's going to relieve herself into an urn again!

Or am I dreaming?

"And now your fairy godmother would hear your request!"

The same clerk who showed me my list of classes shows me the list of models. "You pick," she says in her flat Chicago voice.

I choose a name: Helen Vislawa. We heard of Helen today in our literary studies. So Helen.

The clerk looks me up and down as though I'm the one who's going to disrobe. I feel more betrayed by this woman than I do outraged at Mister Banks!

I turn on my heel and leave, indebted perhaps to Mrs. Finchey but much less so than I could be in the power of the awful art teacher. I pray that he can help me with my drawing, because I already despise the situation I am in.

Nearly a week has gone by and my education, as I imagined it, has not yet begun; yet clearly in a number of other ways it is already in motion. At the library, for example, where I am looking for the myth of Helen, a young man surprises me at the card catalog. "Excuse me," he says.

I step back, thinking that I'm in his way.

"No, no," he says. "It's you."

"Me? Me what?"

"It's you I've been watching."

"Don't make me laugh," I say.

"I'm quite serious," he says. "My name is Leo. I attend the university."

I don't even think to ask him which one, and he assumes that I know that he's referring to the local university. A smug little fellow, rail thin with a sharply chiseled nose.

"*I* attend the Art Institute," I say.

"You do?"

"Yes, is that strange?"

"I didn't know . . . "

"They do enroll women," I say. "Though they're not polite about it."

"What part of town are you from?"

"I'm not from this town," I tell him.

"You're not? Then where do you live?"

"With my fairy godmother."

Leo invites me for a walk along the lakefront and I accept. I'm not sure that I ought to encourage him, but then I don't have much experience with boys and don't know how to *dis*courage him. So off I go, walking to the lake. I don't have to do much except listen, since he loves to talk: about a bear sighted walking on the ice of the frozen upper lake last winter, about a philosopher he's reading named Nietzsche—he spells the difficult name out for me with a finger in the air—about his plan for building a socialist community near the Canadian border where all would share their worldly goods and all would be sisters and brothers.

"I have a brother," I tell him, and proceed to talk for a while about Robert, stopping halfway through the story of how I found him the buffalo skull because it makes me so sad and homesick to speak of it.

"I have neither brother nor sister," says Leo, striking a pose that he seems to think defiant. It occurs to me then that I must sketch him sometime, he's got such a funny way about him, something almost like an animal, a prairie dog, or a bird.

But then I realize that I don't have my sketchbook with me, and it gives me the shivers, I feel so naked without it. Never again, I tell myself. Always carry it with.

We part, making promises to meet again. Next time I'll have it.

Mrs. Finchey's out to dinner somewhere this evening. I eat alone, retire to my room early, and suffer a sleepless night in my bed high above the lake. I feel quite innocent, but miss the dreams.

And then at school this day, it all begins.

I'm waiting in my little studio, reading Homer in Pope's translation, which all races along a bit too merrily, I think, compared to what the art would make life out to be back then, when a girl my age comes through the door, blonde, heavy boned, it would seem, beneath a coat that makes her seem all the bigger still.

"I am Helen," she says, going immediately to the little platform in the front of the room. "You got a screen?"

"What?"

"You got a screen? Where I can get undressed?"

I shake my head, feeling only a sudden thundering in my breastbone and a fluidness about my knees.

"Oh, aw right," she says, "since they tell me it's only us girls." She modestly turns her back to me and begins to remove her clothes, laying each article—coat, then dress, then slip and wool stockings,

63

and her thick cotton underwear – atop the other in a neat pile at the edge of the platform. She mounts to the stool and only then turns to me, with a simple gesture of compliance. Full-breasted, thin-waisted, long legs classically perfect in their plumpness at the thighs, her only defect is her hoarse and halting voice. After posing her atop the stool, I might never have had to listen to another word she said. But over the course of that hour, and many more hours during the next weeks and months I pray will come, I bid her to speak. There is nothing about her, I think, that I do not want to know.

Helen lives behind the stockyards, in a little place, as she calls it, with her infant son.

I wet my lips and set to work.

She was born here. Her father was not.

Oh, that feeling, the good feeling of moving at the wrist and making the line.

He was born in a place in the Old Country, as she calls it, in a place called the Pripet Marshes, born to a family of peasants who fought to keep their small plot of land to themselves, struggled with great Russian landowners who wrestled territory away from Polish princes, warred with Jews who lived in villages alongside the marsh over who would use the good wells and when, worshipped their icons of Christ and his Blessed Mother, the Black Virgin, black not as in former slave as we might understand it here, but black – it seems to me as I inscribe this – from the blood of her only son's sacrifice, from this part of the world, where the family went from drought to famine to blizzards and then to floods and mud that could swallow you up . . . Her father knew this life as a boy, and ran away from his father's house of slapdash brick and straw and branch, ran west to Warsaw, where he found a job as a butcher's boy, and was lucky he found that. He lived off the bits of meat that his butcher threw away, and this was a boss whose motto was never to waste any part of the beast, and sometimes he even sold bits of meat on the sly. The only milk he ever drank (I blush as I enter this) was what he stole from the tits of cows brought in for slaughter, so never much milk he had.

A pal of his, a leatherman's apprentice, was the first to talk to him about Chicago, a golden city to the west of the great ocean, and years went by and he saved, because he was in a contest with his friend, and one day they both discovered they had enough for passage to America. So they sailed here, late in the history of the country, if you use my own ancestors as a standard, but they sailed here nonetheless—not to the Georgia and Carolina coasts, as did our people, where they mingled with the natives (and what is that story I faintly remember about my ancestress, the miraculous Melissa Tree? That she walked on water! I remember that story, but how? from Robert? from Papa? but why do I hear it in a woman's voice? Is it Eve telling it to me?).

A woman's voice! Which reminds me, I could record this story as Helen told it to me one dark November afternoon as she spent hours posing for me, and I worked harder than ever before with her figure before me . . . the story she began while posing, and continues while we sit knee to knee in my small studio and drink tea.

"Next thing you know . . . " she says.

That voice!

"Next thing you know, they's in the boat again, and they's sailing to Chicago . . . "

They reached Halifax is what happened, and took another ship that carried them up the St. Lawrence River, and heaven forbid, they nearly decided to stay in Canada! But way led on to way, and driven by the stories they had heard about life in Chicago, they finally found their way here. Now from the pictures of him, this lean blond farm-boy-turned-butcher appears as though he had good bones and a way of squinting into the sun that make you think that he might have some purpose that would carry him on his way as soon as the photographer had finished his work. Though he seems an ordinary-looking man. It is her mother who was different. She, too, had been born in Poland, but had come to Chicago with her parents when she was a little girl. She was still nearly a little girl when she met the lively butcher who had just arrived on the boat. She was all of fourteen, and he was a nearly ancient twenty-five.

"She had just got the curse," Helen says in explanation (I have to put this in her actual voice; it's such a way of speaking about these private things!), "and so what did she know about these things: what he says to her, what he shows her, what he wants her to do with him? But you know, I feel sorry for her, but I don't, because if she was smart, she would have stayed away from him, this fast talker the butcher with good cuts of meat he offers her for her family, and a walk along the lake at night, and she's gone after that, in his arms—she told me all this—but if she was so smart, I would not be here talking with you, would I?" (Now she says something in Polish, and I have to ask her to put it in English.) "What?" she says. "Oh, that, yeah, 'there is a garden, there is a snake.'

"Ava, I got to go. I got a baby at home and the little creature has a cold, and I have left him with the neighbors. So I may? Thank you. But if sometime you would like to come this week, I would make you a little supper. And we could talk. You. Me. I will cook you my special supper. I will cook you a special delicious Polish meal . . . Ah, can I see the drawing? A'h, you make me so beautiful. But what about this, darling? Hah! Smell the garlic? Can you draw me with the garlic on my breath? Can you show how this tit, here, droops ever so slightly to the left? See, you know it does. You can see it; you watch. Why don't you do something with how you can draw and make a picture of things like they really are? And why are you always talking about those Greeks, Greeks, Greeks? I have told you about the Polacks, and you have drawn me, and you have come closer to me than anyone, Ava. Come here, see, the door is shut, no, no . . .

"See? See how it droops? And look—little bubbles of milk—I must go now. See? Ah, little daughter, friend of mine. I know, I know, your own little mother was someone you never knew . . . "

This is my life, day in, day out, seeing Helen, drawing her. I come to despise weekends because I cannot work with my Helen. Rebecca Finchey, who at first seemed so glamorous to me, now has paled in comparison. Little Leo, whom I first wanted to sketch, has come around to visit several times but I am not much interested in what he has to offer, whether as a model (though I haven't asked him) or a friend. Well, perhaps he might serve as both sometime. But not now. It is Helen I want, Helen I live. I correspond with my stepmother and my brother, but it is the blonde-haired Polish girl who seems closest to me now.

This is what I discover about art and love: you must be ready to die for them. The weather, as it often does in Chicago, or so I learn, conspires with me in my quest. It begins to get quite cold after Thanksgiving, with now and then a golden day in which the lake seems to take on the qualities of polished stone rather than freezing water. Christmas Day is bright and glorious. But nothing like the morning into which I awaken just after New Year's, with light that pierces upward from a frozen sea and convinces me that I must not stay too long in this city for fear of going blind.

I mention this to Mrs. Finchey at the breakfast table, where we usually exchange the few words that pass between us during the day.

"Take what you can from Chicago, and then leave," she says. "Behave like Chicago's a man. That's the only way you'll get ahead in this world, darling."

It would all be very amusing, if it weren't for Helen. Helen— whose future I try to probe with pretended idle conversation while I work. "Do you ever think of leaving here?" I ask.

She makes her eyes cross and gives a little laugh. "Excuse me— but where would I go? To Warsaw, hey?"

It's snowing at the end of the day as I head up Michigan Avenue for my streetcar, thoughts of Helen swirling around in my head with the ferocity of these wind-driven snowflakes. At the end of each session she goes home to her "little creature," and I finish my classes and return to the palace of my fairy godmother. A tale of two cities. Today, just as I'm about to board the car, Leo comes rushing up to me out of the crowd. "I saw you," he says, all out of breath.

"I guess you did." Other passengers climb aboard, but I stand back. "Want to walk?"

We stop at a little teashop near the waterworks. He asks about school and I can't help but study his mouth while he speaks, the odd way he has of pursing his lips just before letting the words out. Nietzsche, building socialism: these same things are still on his mind. Did I have in mind sketching him? All my thoughts lie with Helen— where can she be at this hour? In her little apartment? I try to imagine it, cooking supper for her infant and herself. He'd like to get to know me better, he says, but I'm too distracted to be a good friend. He wants to meet again. Who knows? Perhaps, I say. And I might sketch him, who can tell? I'm quite confused.

Rebecca Finchey and I meet in the lobby of the building, she on her way out — in velvet cape and pearls, as though to say damn the weather! — and I on my way in.

"Champagne and laughter!" she declares, whirling suddenly in front of me. It's as though she's my age, and I am hers. "I'm off to the opera. The cook will fix you a meal."

"I'm not very hungry."

"Girl," she says. "What is it? Tell your . . . "

"Fairy godmother," I finish. "I wish I could tell you."

"But you have to know first?"

She makes me smile, blush, almost. "That's it."

"Well, maybe what I should do is skip the opera, and we'll just spend the evening talking about this whatever it is."

"Please, no, Rebecca, you go to the opera. I'll be fine. I have a lot of reading to do this evening."

"Is it that boy?"

"Boy?"

"The one who just called."

"Who just called?"

"I left a message for you by your plate. Leo, he said, was his name."

"Leo," I say. "He's quick. I just saw him . . . on the street."

"Should we have a talk about these Chicago boys?"

"Go to your opera," I say.

I take a meal by myself in the kitchen and over the course of the evening, when I should be working out various assignments, I stage my own little spectacle in my mind, and it is very curious to me the roles which I assign to myself and Helen — and little Leo, who, I'm afraid, is not going to like what he has to sing or hear.

All through the night visions of Helen course through my mind, and I pose her in every way possible for me to learn all there is to know of her, of her body, and where the body meets with the spirit, if that is what I should call it, the essence of her Helen-ness. I sleep, I wake, I sleep. And in one of the intervals when I do doze off, I am awakened by a tapping at my window. Impossible! I leap out of bed and throw back the curtain to see nothing but snow driven in a fierce wind in the faint light of a full moon behind racing storm clouds. I sleep, and wake again. It's early morning now, and outside my window – crazy blowing snow.

It seems to be snowing *upward*, out of the ground, up from the lakefront, up from the frozen surface of the lake itself, so that this snow might reach the moon!

I fall back onto my bed and pull the covers over me, pretending that I am being buried in snow, the thick covers falling on me like snow, and I am a seed that will stay buried all winter . . . the bulb of a beautiful spring flower . . . a fox cub . . . an eaglet still forming in its egg, warmed beneath the hot-blooded body of its mother . . .

But then I sit up suddenly, wrenched up almost as if by a hidden hand. Helen, I think. What if Helen . . . ?

What if she, poor dear, undaunted by the storm has set out for the studio? Quickly I dress and go to find my boots.

"Where are you going?" Mrs. Finchey calls to me from her bedroom. She has heard me clumping about in the hall.

I'm into the elevator before she can raise herself up from her bed and stop me.

"Going for a stroll? It's a blizzard out there," the elevator man says.

I remain silent, pulling my mittens tighter onto my fingers.

"Come down to have a look at our beautiful weather?" the doorman across the lobby says as he leaps from his chair.

"Yes," I say. But no more.

He tentatively pulls open the barrier to the wall of solid white flakes, and I step out and around the corner where the wind whips into me and sends me reeling backward, as though a hand has pushed me in the chest.

"Taxi?" The doorman comes rushing up to me. "You'll be needing a taxi!"

"Very well," I say, feeling the snow on my tongue. The wind shifts and shoves me back toward the corner.

"I thought you was just taking a peek at the snow, Miss," the doorman says. "I'll get you that cab, but there's been only a few . . . "

Minutes go by, and I'm shivering from my wait inside the doorway.

Helen, I'm thinking, picturing her setting out for a streetcar, for the el, finding none, but, devoted to her work, knowing in her

heart I'll be there, sacrificing her health for my art, trudging forward into the blizzard.

"It seems, Miss, as though there ain't no taxis . . . "

"I'll walk then," I say, and head straight into the heaving snow.

"Miss?" the doorman calls to my back. I cross the empty street—
empty except for shifting drifts of piling snow—and when I turn, I
can barely see him in the door. When I look up, the higher stories
of the building fade into the thick sheet of snow that seems to be
falling from a point in infinity, and when I look down, I stumble,
confused by the whiteness above and around me and now below. A
corner of a building comes up on my right, and I feel my way along
the wall and start what I know to be southeast along Michigan
Avenue.

No one is in sight, nothing except the snow that shifts and
undulates in some dance whose pattern adjusts to the wind. I can
see no further than my hand sometimes, and then the moving wall
will part and I can see all the way across the street, and once all the
way to the amazing empty white void that must be the space above
the lake itself, and then the curtain closes on me and I'm back leaning against a building before I push on again.

"Miss?" Another doorman calls to me from his little haven
beneath the lintel of a neighboring apartment building.

I pay no attention, move forward one foot at a time.

A vehicle rolls slowly past at the next corner. "Taxi!" I call to
the driver.

The car keeps moving slowly away from me.

"Taxi!" I run after it, slip off the curb and fall face forward into
the street. I'm not sure how long I stay there, though I notice that
snow has piled up on my hands. My gloves are gone; why I don't
know. I raise myself to my feet and stuff my hands beneath my cape
and keep moving.

For an instant, I see the shape of another traveler, as if from a
vast distance across the plains, though it is only the width of Michigan Avenue that separates us. Is it a man or woman? I peer through
the rippling snow, and wonder if it is Helen herself. But she lives in
some other distant part of the city and would not be walking this
way, would she? Or has she lost her path? Has she come to look for
me? Ridiculous, ridiculous, I chide myself, and turn my head down

toward the icy pavement and trudge forward. She must have taken the elevated to our destination. In a mile or so, I should catch sight of it at the Loop. I'll keep on walking, I tell myself, rubbing my hands beneath the cape, feeling how numb they are, but then how can one feel numbness, since numbness is the opposite of feeling?

My eyes sting, and my feet are heavy. I trudge forward, looking up only at a strange sound, stranger still since the walk has been so silent, the usually raucous street so silent. "Whoa!" a voice calls, and I look to my right to see a dark beast moving at a fast pace towing a wagon behind it. The snow's so thick I can read only part of the sign . . .

—BERG'S DAI—

. . . as horse and wagon disappear into the whiteness that has become so dense that it might as well be the dark of night, for all that I can see. Still I try to follow beast and cart. A few feet and I find myself in what must be an alley. I fear that if I keep going forward, I'll be stranded here, and turn to head back to the street. I feel around with my hands for the building, find it, make my way forward, turn with it when it turns.

Was I carrying a briefcase with pad and pencils when I set out? If so, it's gone, all gone. Eyes tearing, I walk forward into the open space before me, holding out my naked hands for fear that I'll walk into a wall without them. Another horse whinnies in the distance, but I can see nothing. I might as well be alone on the prairie in this storm, tracking a lost beast.

"Hello?" I call.

Or was it a cow? Have I walked all the way to the stockyards? Impossible, I know. Hands burn with cold. Toes sting.

Or was it a buffalo?

"Hello?"

Or some prehistoric beast of the prairie, the mammoth my brother described to me?

He's dead! It suddenly comes to me. Robert's dead! They're all dead! Frozen! And I'm alone in this storm; I'm lost, and we're all dead.

Then suddenly there is glass under my fingers. Shop window cold to my numbing touch. Inside I imagine another world: calm, silent, beautiful in its pristine unsnowed-upon condition. A white bridal gown and veil, white shoes, white gloves.

I shake my head, feeling the hood of my cape fall off, my hair fall loose, snow in my eyes, in my ears. The wind grabs me as if it had fingers, and spins me around by the cape until I find myself without a boot.

I take a breath, and realize that I have been breathing snow, inhaling this weather, ingesting it, feeling its icy being creep into my chest. Where am I going? Where have I been? Nothing answers me, and then I remember *Helen*, and I keep on moving into the hands and mouth of the storm.

"Two buildings over," Mrs. Finchey says when I look up into her worried face.

"What?" I feel around in the bed. I'm piled over with covers, though I begin to shiver and rattle in my bones like an old railway car on a nearly ruined roadbed.

"You asked where they found you. I told you, two buildings over."

"Found me?" Horse, I remember vaguely. Bridal-shop display. The snow. Snow. I cough hard, and my chest feels as though a carpenter were taking it apart, rib by rib.

"How could you have done it?" Mrs. Finchey touches a cold, cold hand to my forehead, and I flinch, and draw back deeper into the covers. "The doctor will be back this afternoon, but I want you to rest – those were his orders – until then."

"Rest?"

"The doctor commands it," she says. "You little fool, you. Wandering off in the storm that way. I didn't know, when you went out . . . well, I never would have let you. Like a calf on the range, you were. You might have died . . . " She pats the covers around me. "Why on earth *did* you go out? Was it that boy?"

I can honestly say to her that it was not that boy, but beyond that I can tell her nothing, nothing that I can admit to myself. My coughing takes over, a Krakatoa erupting in my lungs and chest so that I believe I am going to fly apart, bones and flesh and all.

"Calm down," says Rebecca Finchey. "Tell your fairy godmother. Tell her, or she may put a spell on you!"

But there's no spell like the one I'm already under.

Two weeks go by before the doctor will declare that I am ready to return to the Institute. "But do not exert yourself, Miss," he says. "The coughing may return when you least expect it. I don't expect that you are the sort of woman who keeps late hours. Just pay attention to what I have told you."

Off I rush the next morning in a taxi to the museum; my hair, though tied in red and blue ribbons, still flying behind me, my heart beating wildly, as though I were a mare that I was riding past the frozen drifts on Michigan Avenue in a great passion to reach my destination.

"No, I haven't seen her," says the hard-eyed clerk in charge of keeping track of our models. "What was her name again?"

"Vislawa," I repeat. "Helen Vislawa."

"Polack," she says, as if thinking aloud in her vile way. "They all live out by the stockyards."

"Which way is that?" I ask.

"You don't want to go there," the woman says.

"But if I did?"

"Follow your nose," she says.

"Oh, please, be civil," I say.

"Don't get on your high horse, Miss," she says.

But I ride it out into the corridor, wondering how I will ever find Helen.

"Good morning," says a man from behind me. But it's no man after all, only little Leo, an odd smile on his face.

"What are you doing here?" I ask.

"Mrs. Finchey wouldn't show me in to see you. But when I saw you go out this morning, I thought I'd catch you here."

"You saw me go out? Why are you following me?"

"Don't you appreciate a fellow who's devoted to you?" His eyes brighten with anticipation.

"I'm sorry, Leo, but I can't speak to you." I'm studying the crowd in the corridors, men, mostly, but here and there a model, none of them Helen, alas.

"I thought that I might take you out for tea," he says.

And now here comes Mister Banks, the last person I want to see.

"Will you, Leo? Can we go right now?" I turn away, but Mister Banks will not be denied. "Good morning," he says. "Miss Boldin. May I speak with you?"

"Good morning. Yes, sir. My friend, Leo . . . Leo, this is Mister Banks, my drawing teacher. I'm sorry, I must go."

We leave the dejected Leo behind, heading for Mister Banks's studio.

"I've been ill, Mister Banks. That's why . . . "

"That's why, what?" he replies as we step inside the studio.

"Why I haven't been working."

"It's not the amount of work, it's the quality, Miss Boldin. And if I were you, I would keep on with it."

I'm shocked at his sympathy, this man who barred me from his class. "I don't know what to say, Mister Banks."

"Your drawings are saying it, Miss Boldin. The true artist speaks through his work." He stares at me a moment, making the inevitable trail with his eyes across my breasts and then back to my face. "Or *her* work, as the case may be. And in your case you have a fine hand and a good eye." He clears his throat, as if he's been preparing this little speech all the time I've been away. "I know that one day we will see your work in the newspapers. The rest of my students will be starving in attics in France trying to paint, and you will be a great success." He gives his mustache a little tug. "You should try hats, you know. There's a lot of money to be made in hats. More and more Americans, as they learn their manners, will be wearing hats."

"Hats," I say.

"Hats. You wear one. Every young lady wears one. And as more and more American men desire to look like gentlemen, they will be buying them also. That's the key. Hat stores. Competition for the heads of millions. And if you can draw hats to show off their good qualities, these stores will reward you. They'll need to put pictures of their hats in the newspapers. Do you follow me?"

"I think I do, Mister Banks. Thank you."

"And by the way that Polish girl who models for you has been looking for you."

"She has? When?"

"About ten minutes ago. I sent her to your studio."

"Thank you, Mister Banks."

I rush back through the labyrinthine corridors to my little studio, my heart beating heavily, my mouth dry as cotton, and I nearly pull the door off the hinge as I enter (I never knew I was this powerful!). The studio is empty, and my heart sinks. I feel like such a goose, looking around for evidence of her having been here, muttering at Mister Banks under my breath for having toyed with my emotions in such a way.

"Hello," comes the voice at the door behind me, and it shocks me to realize how much I am shaken by it. "You been sick, I hear."

"I'm better now," I say.

"You don't look so hot."

"Maybe not, but I'm recovered."

"Me, too."

"Were you sick?"

"I wasn't working. That's like being sick for me."

"Let's get to work then," I say.

"Good," she says, and undresses. For a moment or two I feel quite faint, and then get the better of myself. She sits on the stool. I nod. She unfolds her arms and drops them naturally to her sides, so that her breasts show forth in perfect proportion to her neck and shoulders. Even when she sits with her legs crossed, her belly does not puff up, though neither when she stands does it appear all sunken. Her abdominal muscles are surely as perfect as the flesh that covers them, despite childbirth, despite the long days of carrying the infant about outside the womb.

"Uncross your legs, please," I say, taking up my stand at my drawing easel.

"Like this?" Helen casually straightens her legs and keeps them close together. "Or," she says, before I can reply, "like this?" And with the most lewd look upon her face that I have ever imagined an angel might pretend to, she spreads her legs open as wide as she must have in giving birth, and with her fingers spreads apart her nether lips as well, showing off to me the light pink cleave, where the hooded bud still remains to my eye nearly perfect in form despite the trouble of labor. "See my clump?" she says.

75

"I'm drawing you," I say.

"You drawing my clump?"

"All of you," I say. "I'm drawing all of you."

She says something Polish. "That's how we say it in Polish." She says the word again. "It's just a word," she says. "It has nothing to do with the real thing."

"Does my drawing?"

"I ain't seen it yet." She is still sitting there in the same position, as though it were the most natural thing in the world.

"Drawing is closer to the real thing," I say. "Closer than words."

"Ava?" she asks.

"Yes?"

"Does you ever look at yourself in the mirror?"

"You mean, down there?"

"That's what I mean."

I shake my head. The talk for some reason doesn't distract me. My hand flies fast over the paper, as though it has a life of its own. "Have you ever posed this way for any of the men?"

She shakes her head.

I say, "Don't move, please."

"I wasn't moving down there," she says.

"Please," I say.

"Please what? Please don't move or please answer?"

"Both."

"Well . . . that teacher of yours, he asked me to pose while you was sick."

Cramps seize my stomach. I feel so betrayed! But by whom? which? "How did he ask you to pose?"

"How? He asked me politely."

"No, I mean how did he pose you?"

"Oh!" Helen smiles serenely. "With the creature."

"Babe in arms?"

"He was on the tit."

"Madonna with child," I say.

"The Black Virgin," she says with a laugh.

"Oh, blasphemy," I say.

"What's that?"

"You as the Black Virgin."

76

"Why, and she can't be a mother? She *was* a mother. Ava, you got a lot to learn. You got book learning but there is other things." At which she takes her hands and folds them again across her chest and draws her thighs together as well. "I want to go home now," she says.

"We have at least another half hour," I say.

"Now," she says.

"What about . . . ?"

"You want to pay me for only half an hour, do that."

"No," I say in a quiet voice. "No."

Helen dresses quickly, and I move with her toward the door. "No, no," she says. "I know the way."

"I thought that I would walk you upstairs."

"I *says*, I know the way."

She leaves me standing in the doorway of the little studio.

Dear Dora,

You know that I have been ill and now you know that I am well again, and that I am back at my drawing class. I managed to keep reading the tutorial lists for my other courses even while I stayed in bed. Such dreams I had, too, inspired by the Greek poets and the stories out of the history books I have read! I could have nearly lost a month, yes, that much of a chunk out of my year, but I think I salvaged a great deal of it. And I now know how to survive a winter in Chicago. By staying indoors!

Even now when I go out to the museum or to shop with Mrs. Finchey (who is, by the way, everything you said she would be, and more, including playing the role of my fairy godmother, as she puts it), I bundle up as though winter has not ended. I don't think it has. You see, I fell prey to the notion that just because I was living in a city it would not be as cold as a winter on the prairie. A foolish notion!

I am trying to break myself of the habit of drawing things perfectly. I am slowly discovering that the real beauty of what I see is in the slight imperfections. I have enclosed a small drawing of a model I have been working with. Her name is Helen Vislawa, and she has become a good friend. She has a small child, and this has gotten me interested in children in a way that I never thought about before. Usually Helen leaves her child at home with a friend when she comes to sit for me, but every now and then she brings the little creature, as she calls it—a delightful little child named John, after her brother, who died in a fall from a roof about a year before the baby was born. Her parents are both dead. I won't go into the details, except to say that this woman, who is just about my own age, has endured much more than most people we will ever have the chance to meet. Her experiences have, among other things, taught me something about city life as compared to where we grew up. The city is a frontier of its own, that is for sure.

I hope that this drawing shows the progress I believe that I am making. One of the instructors will put others in a show this year. Although I am kept separate from the men in the class, I think I am learning from the instruction I do get. You were the first one to declare that I had a sure hand for drawing. In fact, I have heard through the Institute of a teaching position in a girl's school in South Carolina which I am thinking of applying for. What do you think of that idea? It would mean that after classes end here I would be coming back to Nebraska for only a short while. Dear Dora, would you mind if I left you alone for yet another year? If I am going to support myself for the rest of my life, I am going to need a way of earning money. And teaching girls younger than myself how to draw might not be such a bad way to earn it. You taught me. Perhaps I could teach others? Let me know what you think.

Lovingly,

Ava

I don't like Mister Banks. But he says something I think about: The work comes so easily the tree "draws itself," the bowl of fruit "draws itself."

Helen draws herself.

Almost.

From the first moment she walks into the studio, something passes between her body and my eyes, and when she slips out of her robe, the power leaps to my wrist.

"From your wrist?" she says when I try to explain. "Don't you sound funny."

I blush when Helen speaks. We have grown up in such different ways. But when I say this to her, she says, "Oh, sure, we grow up differently, but we're both girls, Ava."

Helen relaxes her pose and her body turns fluid, silk or water in motion. Thirty or forty minutes pass. I look up and she catches my eye. "I want to see the picture now."

I bid her to come forward and look. "This is a mistake," she says upon first glance.

"What do you mean?" I ask.

"No one is this beautiful," she says.

I laugh, laugh, laugh; I am so nervous over this! "I draw out the light in you," I say.

"The what?"

"The light. The light you have inside."

"Ha!" she says in her own way, not at all nervous, though. "I got a stomachache and my feet hurt. There's a little tickling under my left tit, and my eye is winking without me having anything to do with it. So who turned on my light? I never heard of it; I don't know what about it."

The next session she arrives with a small package in hand. "I got to give you this," she says.

"For what?" I reply.

"For making me look so beautiful in the picture," she says.

I blush, and unwrap the small package. Ribbons! A packet of beautiful ribbons, my favorite colors, red and blue!

I wander through the halls of the museum above the Institute thinking
   perhaps I'll draw hats,
   ladies' hats,
   men's hats,
   on every street heads, on every head a hat.
I study this large Hudson River painting: the fading trees, the sun in retreat,
   old-fashioned light,
   European light on an American river.
I must be learning! I can tell European light from American!
But where are the paintings with American light as I know it?
I walk up and down these halls and cannot find them.
It must be . . . that . . . I haven't painted them yet!

And then I learn that while I was dreaming about painting with light – or painting light itself! – my brother lay in a hospital, clutching his chest and wondering where his next breath was coming from. Or so he describes it to me over tea a few months later when he turns up in Chicago for a job interview. As he tells me about it, I couldn't feel any worse – or so I believe – if it were happening to me.

"But you're all right now?"

I want to wait on him; I want to make him comfortable. But he's already moved past this ordeal and is thinking only of his impending interview.

"And what is the job, Robert?" I say.

"Rocks, Sis," he replies.

"Rocks?"

"My first love. Rocks."

"I've applied for a teaching job in Charleston," I tell him.

"So Dora informed me. That will be dandy if it comes through. If both of them do. My rocks, your art. You will be teaching art, won't you?"

"Yes," I say, caught up suddenly in fleeting pictures of Helen passing through my mind.

Robert begins to talk about a girl he's met – Margaret, her name is – quite old-fashioned. "My real heart problem," he says with a smile.

Helen, sitting on the stool, her pale white throat. I have a heart problem of my own.

"I like it," Helen says after our next session. "Your pictures are really getting good." Nice of her to say this. It's a special afternoon – she has invited me to her house. All the compliments I get from the other students, and now and then from instructors, mean nothing compared to how Helen's invitation makes me feel.

"So will we go now?"

"Yeah," she says. "Come on."

I watch her carefully as she dresses. With her clothes on, she seems mysterious to me – and immediately I would like her to undress again.

But we have to hurry.

80

"Like this?" she asks, putting on a snappy, little, broad-brimmed hat. "Sort of makes me look like a man, you think?"

I can feel a little redness spreading across my cheeks. "Do you want to look like a man?"

Bright light flashes in her lovely blue eyes. She holds out her hands as if in supplication. "What do I know?"

"I was only joking. You never could."

"Thanks."

We leave the museum and head for the Loop. I notice all the hats on the street. Yes, there is a business to be made out of it, drawing these hats for advertisements. What's-his-name might be right. Maybe my future lies in hats.

Tenements fly past us on the el, or rather we speed past them. The city, all aglow this evening in early spring. But though I have been watching Helen for months now, I still find myself unable to take my eyes off her for more than a few seconds.

When we reach the back of the yards, I find that I cannot breathe very well. But Helen seems to pay no attention to the smell. It's so ferocious it makes me wonder why it doesn't stick to the clothes of the people who live in the neighborhood. "Helen?" I say.

"What is it?"

"Oh, never mind."

We go shopping for our meal, to the butcher shop first where Helen buys sausage, and then to the vegetable market where she buys potatoes, and then to the saloon.

The noise in this place weighs on my head and shoulders.

And all the men follow her as she walks ahead of me to the bar. "Hey, Helen!" a number of men cry. "Helen!" Some voices call out in Polish. Big beefy men, their arms seem stuffed with rocks and their eyes almost bleed from raw redness. Smoke billows up around us. The world stinks of beer and garlic. Helen borrows a large bucket from behind the bar and gets it filled full of foamy brew.

"I didn't know you could buy beer like that!" I say.

"Sure you can," she says. "We just did, didn't we?"

And we carry our purchases to her apartment where a neighbor has been taking care of little John all day.

I volunteer to go to the kitchen to start the dinner while she nurses the baby but she shouts at me to stop. "You're my guest," she says. "You're going to have to wait till I'm finished here. You don't know bricks about cooking."

I wait, gratefully, picking up the little geegaws that lie about the tables and shelves: a card in Polish that might be the announcement for a special mass—it's got a drawing of the Black Virgin on it. And how do I know the Black Virgin when I see her? I simply have to raise my eyes to the wall to see her there in all her quiet solemnity. Crockery animals in miniature, a wolf, a bear, a horse, a deer, line the shelves along one wall. On another hangs a sepia photograph of a man in a dark suit—the face is blurred, as if each time someone has held it up to the light, her thumb has come down right through the glass onto the man's face. Helen puts the baby down and leaves the room. Soon powerful odors, of sizzling meat and boiling cabbage, drift in from the little kitchen.

"Hey!" Helen calls to me.

I peek into the alcove where she is cooking.

"Hey," she says, "wait till you taste this, what I am making."

The smell grows stronger by the minute—the house is a small cave of a place—and then John begins to wail from his little cradle near the far wall. In the middle of all this whirls Helen, so beautiful that she might have been born in another age—in Greece—and thrust by accident down into this mess. Is that what I am to learn from all this? She rushes past me, throwing me a smile, and picks up the baby from his bed, and rocks him a bit.

"Can you take him for a little?" she asks, thrusting the child toward me.

"Sure," I say. "Sure, sure, sure," I say to the noisy child, walking the room in a tight circle, the only kind the cramped space allows me. "Little John," I say. "Little John . . . "

"Her," he says. "Blue. Glow. Glow."

He's a small weight in my hand, he's a dampness, he's a gurgling mouth, he's a stink, and a bother, and he's got his mother's eyes.

"Thanks," she says, coming back in a few moments and taking him from me and putting him back in the cradle. "So, you hungry?"

She pulls a small table out from the wall and points out a chair for me. She brings a plate filled with good, hot, greasy, garlicky sausage, potatoes, cabbage. It burns my mouth but it is delicious and I eat with relish, washing the hot down with gulps of the beer, still cold even after all this while.

"After that beer, I suppose now you got to go?" she says when we've finished our meal. "Down the hall, top of the stairs."

Another glass of beer, and I am out in the hall, looking for it. The first door I try doesn't open. Behind the next I hear voices, so I don't try to open that one. The third opens inward, and I'm inside the stink of a closet. I step back out.

"That's it," Helen says over my shoulder.

"You followed me," I say.

"I didn't want you getting lost."

"Well, I'm all right now."

"Sure you are. Okay."

She goes back down the hall, and I have no choice but to step into the dark, awful-smelling closet, find the light string, and close the door. The stink, the beer, the food, the baby, voices, my stomach, past fevers—I'm drawn into the vortex of smells, sounds, falling forward, my head stopped by the wall.

Odd sounds—Helen in Polish, I finally figure it—come to me when I return, lying on the small bed off the kitchen.

"You all right?"

"I don't know. I felt dizzy. I couldn't breathe . . . "

"Well, that was good, because who wants to breathe in *there*? It stinks, don't it?"

I nearly pass out again when she mentions it.

"Hold it," Helen says, taking me by the shoulder. "Stay awake, yeah?" She pats me gently. "I give you some water. Yeah?"

I nod, letting my head fall back on the musty-smelling linen as she leaves me in order to fetch the drink. "Was I . . . out long?"

Helen comes back with a cup of water. "Yeah," she says, "about, I don't know, two, three days!" And she gives a horrible cackle; oh, that sound coming from those perfectly sculpted lips!

"No, it's not . . . "

"Oh!" she says in a kind of shout. "I got you! You truly thought . . . !"

The baby makes a wail. WA-I-L-L! "Wait," she says, "I got to see to my other child."

I shake my head, wondering how I have done this to myself, strayed this far. But it's Helen—Helen so beautiful is why I have done this. And I lie there quietly, breathing softly, waiting.

And she says to me when she comes in, her breast bare after nursing, her eyes glowing with mischief, "Which do you think is better? A picture of me? Or me like this up close?"

"Both," I reply, reaching out my arms for her.

"Both? How can both be better?" she says, dancing back from the bed.

"Both," I say. "That's the truth."

"The truth?" she says, buttoning her blouse as she sits down next to me on the bed. "What's the truth?"

"Darling," says Rebecca Finchey in the doorway of my room, "there is only so much magic I can work for you. If I'd known you were staying out all night, I would have sent Johnson with the car for you this morning. Why, you must have come in at dawn! I won't ask you where you were. Too many old mouths working in my own head always asking me questions like that. But I was worried, darling. But I had faith in you; I did, indeed." I haven't moved, lying here on my pallet while she clucks at me. "No, I wasn't worried. I wondered, but I didn't worry. I said to myself—this is what I said—I said, 'Becca, this is a western girl; she just got stuck somewhere for the night but she is not in trouble. She is definitely not in trouble.'" She touches a finger to her perfectly combed hair and shakes her head slowly, slowly. "And I was right, as it turns out, wasn't I? But I must have been crazy to think I would be. This is Chicago, honey, so why should I have thought that you weren't lying dead in an alley somewhere? Tell me that."

But I keep silent. There is no way that I can explain or want to explain. I scarcely understand myself. I do understand how tired I am though, and how much I want to sleep.

"But you can tell *me*, darling," Mrs. Finchey says. "Where have you been? Or better, don't tell me. Do I want to know? This is the twentieth century, darling. But you still have to be careful. Was it that little Leo? I never would have guessed that boy had a night's worth in him. He's still a child, and I don't know that he'll ever grow up. Don't give him your good time, honey. It's a real man you need, to go with what you're worth. I've seen your drawings, so don't be shy. If your fairy godmother doesn't know your gift, then who does? But let me just give you some advice. You had better be careful in your life if you're going to protect your gift for art."

"My gift?" I say from the bed. "I'd give my gift for an hour of sleep right now."

"No, you wouldn't," says Rebecca Finchey.

"No, I wouldn't."

My gift: I can do nature sharply, though I still don't feel as though I can get to the heart of things. But I am good with surfaces, very good!

And yet.

Staring out at the lake. The great lake has shown me. There is a light within it that makes the surface glow, that comes up from beneath the water. You can never see it directly if you look at it, but it is there. Everything, from trees to stones to the human body itself, glows from a light within. How do I know this? Because I can feel the burning inside of me, I can feel the heat of my internal fire! And I believe that what I do is a matter of focusing—of linking the two points of light, the one from without and the one that flows out from within the subject. Where the two points meet, that is where my work appears, which, if I am any good, becomes a third source of light!

Helen. Helen is light.

Helen's body is a body of light. And yet it is not without substance. And my own body, when I am with her, I feel in such a way that I know if I could view it from the outside in any fashion other than as I have already done, if I could pose the two of us before a mirror, I might see my own skin of light!

At the Institute. A delegation of faculty passes through the studios to review student work. Mister Banks shows my drawings to his colleagues. They stare and stare but say nothing, one of them making noises with his tongue, another touching a fingertip to his chin and then his nose.

"Beautiful girl," says the man who is making the clucking noises.
"Polish," says Mister Banks.

I can feel the fiery blush rising to my skin, but I hold my tongue.
Let the work speak!

"She's had quite a year," one of the men says. How do you
know what Helen has had or hasn't had? I want to shout at him.
But then I realize that they're talking now about me.

"Thank you, Miss Boldin," says Mister Banks, and leads the
delegation from the room.

Dear Robert,

*Thank you for your letter, which I read with great pleasure. I have
had good news about the position for next year myself. And my drawings
are going to be in a schoolwide show, with me the only woman in it. Not
that I am so good as to be better than the rest of the women. There are, as
you know, no other women taking classes. But one of the instructors who
taught me this year came to my studio and looked over my work and just
this morning told me that he wished to include it. Your news about work
is good, too. Does Dora know of it yet? I will write to her about my own
good fortune but I won't mention yours on the grounds that she should
hear it directly from the oracle's mouth. I am planning to come home for
a visit when school ends here and hope to see you when I do. How is your
heart? Please send me all the details.*

Your loving sister,

Ava

Spring—and I'm missing the prairie so unbearably I never could
have predicted it. I'm thinking that I would love to show my Helen
the home country, the fields that lead down to the river, and walk
along the weaving bank where the spring rains have washed the
stones clean after a winter buried in the frozen mud, and listen to
the song of the meadowlark, and dip her child in the cold water
just for a second, and then bundle him back up and walk out into
the hills until the wind picks up, and the sky begins to tint toward
darker blue, and you know that within an hour or so, you will be

able to look up in that western space and see the first glinting of the evening star.

What if she were to come with me to Charleston, she and little creature John? Is it madness to think that she might come with me? It would be a cleaner life, out of this city with its mud-spattered spring, its dirty snowdrifts, its air of urine and beer and smoke, and the raucous cries of peddlers and news hawks, and the grind of metal on metal of the elevated. Helen and I could explore the new territory together, and in that state we could find some nanny to look after John while Helen went to school and I gave my classes, and at night we could talk while we prepared the meal, and I could help her with her lessons, and John would sleep, and we would all have a very nice time.

"What's that?" she says when I bring it up in a lightly joking way. "Hey, you just don't know. You want to know? If you really want to, I could show you."

"Show me what, Helen?"

She had been late for our session, something very unusual for her. "The creature is sick," she had said as soon as she came through the studio door. And that was when I made my remarks about living in a place where the winters wouldn't be so hard on the child and her.

"Well, who is taking care of him?" I motion for her to take her place on the raised platform near the wall. "Milly?" That is her neighbor.

"Naw, somebody else," she says, disrobing with the ease of a practiced model.

"Who?"

"Somebody," she says. There is something in her voice.

"Does that mean you're calling off our dinner tonight?"

"Don't know," she says.

"You can't tell me? I have to let Mrs. Finchey know. She got very upset the last time . . ."

"So who ain't upset?" She settles onto the chair, lowering her head a bit so that her long golden hair falls forward over her breasts.

"You're worried about little John. I'm sorry."

87

"Yeah, yeah," she says, and raises her head a little, looking at me with a stare I have never seen before, not in her, not in any person I have ever met. It is sometimes more animal than human, but also upon occasion like what an angel's glance might reveal. "What do you know?" she asks. "What do you know?"

"I'm trying to understand," I say.

"Keep on trying," she says. "Maybe in a million years. You and your Mrs. Money."

"Mrs. Finchey?"

"That's who."

"Helen, are you worried about money? Do you need some?"

"Oh, naw," she says, "I'm going to sell my diamonds, so don't worry about nothing."

"You need money for the baby?"

"That's right. How did you know?"

"You just told me he was sick."

"I did, that's right. I did."

"I can help you. For medicine, is it?"

"For everything," she says. "But I don't want you helping. You don't have much except what Mrs. Money gives you."

"If I ask her, she'll help."

"You, but not me."

"I don't have to tell her what it's for."

"No!" she says, and sits straight up in her chair. The sight of her like that, upright and angry, sends a hot wave of passion and fear and other things I cannot explain right down into my womb! "Helen," I say. "Don't be angry with me. Please, don't."

"Aw, how could I be?" she asks, relaxing her pose a little. "Hey, so's we going to do some work today, or what are we going to do?"

"I have the job in Charleston," I say to Mister Banks when I see him advancing toward me along the corridor at school the next morning.

"I know," he says. "I recommended you, Miss Boldin. I told them that you'll be a credit to the teaching profession, and I'm sure I'm correct. Can we step into your studio for a moment?"

He begins to speak to me about the forthcoming show, something that I haven't allowed myself to become awfully excited about.

The preparation itself was quite enough effort. It takes me a moment or two to understand what he's saying, that the committee has decided it would be *indecorous* – that's his word, but I know that he means *unseemly* – if my paintings of Helen were included..

"A few weeks ago you told me you wanted them," I say, unable to suppress the childlike pitch of my voice.

"We've simply decided against them, for fear of upsetting the decorum of the show," he says, his fingers moving nervously across his shirt pocket, touching a pencil stuck there jauntily in haste, then up to his weedy little Vandyke beard.

"I'm out of the show," I say, and, just as suddenly as I was nearly wailing, am now unable to raise my voice above a whisper.

"Not at all," he says, staring past me at the empty platform. "We all recognize your talent and would like you to be represented. But . . . by some other aspect of your work this year."

"I haven't done a hat," I say.

He blinks at me, uncomprehending. "I beg your pardon?"

"I don't have anything else. Just Helen."

"Surely you did some earlier studies, some still lifes, objects."

"I told you, Mister Banks, no hats."

"What about . . . ?" he casts his eyes around the studio, acting out my own desperation.

"Mister Banks," I break in, "how can you have a show without any nudes? You can't . . . "

"Miss Boldin. As you will see when you view the show, there will be nudes. To be frank, it is the nudes by you, a woman, that we cannot . . . "

"Cannot what, Mister Banks?"

"Cannot," he says. "Cannot . . . Miss Boldin, we have made our decision. The rest is up to you. If you have some other work . . ."

"I told you that I don't."

"Do you want to be in the show?"

"Yes, I do. More than anything."

"Then do something today. Tonight."

"How can I?"

"It need not be a painting. A drawing. A sketch. We'll allow you that."

"Very well," I say. "I'll give you something."

"So you have other work after all?"

"No. As you suggest, I'll try something today."

He leaves me standing there in the studio staring at the walls. Students pass by the door, talking and laughing. Some time goes by. I walk over to the desk and pick up a charcoal stick, then set it down. At the mirror I stare at myself, blouse buttoned, then unbuttoned, then buttoned; hair up, then down, then up again. Then down. I move the desk over to the mirror and set up a large sheet of paper. I'm working hard on the drawing when the door opens and Helen comes in. "Hey," she says, "what are you doing?"

"Drawing," I say.

"This is what they call a self-portrait, huh?"

"Yes," I say, not turning for fear of losing my concentration.

"Tired of doing me, are you?" Helen asks from across the room.

"No," I say, "I just have to do this right now."

"Some kind of assignment, huh? Well, hey, since you don't need me today, I'll just go home."

"Do you have money for the train?"

"Sure. You give me money last week. I got some left over. How you think I got here right now? I even saved some so I can come over to that show you're putting on this week."

"It's off," I say, still without turning. But I can watch her in the mirror and I do.

"I seen the signs outside," she says.

"My part's off," I say.

"Naw," she says.

"It's true."

"Naw, you changed your mind. You just don't want me to come."

"That's not it at all, Helen." I set down my charcoal and turn to face her, not the image in the mirror, but she is already going out the door. My heart leaps, but I can't follow her right away. I must finish this drawing.

Hours go by before I leave the building and hail a taxi. I no sooner give the gray-haired driver the address, when he turns around and says to me through thick lips pasted onto a face red with drink or arrogance or both, "Now, why is a nice girl like *you* wanting to go to that part of town?"

"I live there," I say in anger.

"Sure you do," he says. "You don't even live in the city. Where you from? St. Louis, or something?"

"None of your business," I say, feeling tough enough after eight months in this place to fight back against one of its monsters.

"You got some Polack boyfriend, huh?"

"Please let me out." I thought I was fighting back, but I decide to give up and find another taxi.

"Naw, I'll take you there," he says. "A nice girl like you, wanting to visit with the Polacks and the . . . "

"Do you mind?" I ask, trying to conjure up my fairy godmother's most imperious voice.

"Naw," he says, "I told you I don't mind. I'll take you there." And he pulls away from the curb, leaving me no choice but to scream for the police or go along for the ride.

My mind is racing as we travel deep into the other part of town. None of the landmarks I noticed in the winter seem familiar to me now, nothing except the smells. The streets are filled with people, a city within a city, whose life goes on like this with all its noise and joys and fears and trials and labors every minute of every day while I live high above the lakeshore, or work in my studio in the bowels of the museum. Just my good luck—as we pull up before her building, Helen emerges from within, child on her shoulder.

"Hey," she asks once I pay the cabby and meet her at the stoop, "what are you doing here? You looked like you had work to do."

"I've done it," I say. "Helen, I'm sorry. It's so complicated. I didn't mean for you to think . . . "

"Yeah, yeah. Hey, you want to walk with me, you got to keep up." Her arms pump back and forth as she strides forward, and her long golden hair streams behind her, almost as if she is moving through water. Her sweater flows behind her, too, and her white blouse has opened two buttons down, so that as I keep up alongside her, I can see the fullness of the top of her breasts heaving with her as she breathes.

"Helen, you're not angry with me, are you?"

"Angry? So who's angry? I got stuff to do myself."

"I'll explain it all to you."

"You don't have to explain nothing to me, Ava." She gives the baby a little jiggle. "Hey, you, say hi to your Aunt Ava." We cross the street and then turn into an alley that opens into a vacant lot. There's a smell here worse than anything I've breathed yet, a clotted soup of animal and who knows what else, as though things have died here for a long time, and the very air fears it will become weighted down with more and more deaths by the minute. I follow her across the lot, where the odor becomes so thick it seems as though my own body has begun to decay. Helen bends down and snatches up a shard of animal skull from the weed-rife ground. "This one got away, huh?" she asks.

And she hands me the piece of bone.

"Thank you," I say, and not knowing what else to do—I don't want to toss it away, not a gift from Helen, however horrifying it is—I slip it into the pocket of my coat. "Can you at least tell me where we're going?"

"Where do you think? Ain't you got a nose?"

A flood of cold rushes through my chest, so awful is the way she's speaking to me, as if we have never felt close, never worked together, everything else. I keep my hand on the filthy bone shard in my pocket.

"Here," she says, and leads me through a small door in the fence at the other side of the lot. We're walking toward a huge open-sided, barnlike building, with row upon row of stalls, from which has been coming—and I only just understand it now, the sound hitting me like a great gust of wind all of a sudden, even though it has been slapping at me all the while—the noise of a thousand animals in torment. Big men in stained white coats and small white caps wave their arms; some hold long-handled hammers, others swing knives; they are shouting, but I can't hear them. I see only their open mouths.

"Helen, . . . " I reach for her arm, feeling my knees buckling beneath me.

"Here," she says, taking me around and leading me to the side of the infernal scene, to a little outbuilding where the big men gather around and drink beer from large white cups.

"Helen! What are you doing here?" A young man, big, with a thick, bent nose and powerful arms, comes out of the crowd to meet her. His coat is stippled with dark blood and the remnants of dung and hair.

"What *are* we doing here?" I say to Helen, still holding her arm.

"Peter," she says to the big fellow, "this is Ava. Ava, this is Peter."

He looks me over, as though I'm just another cow for him to slaughter. "Who's this?" he says.

"My teacher," she says. "The artist."

"Your teacher?" I ask.

"You know," Helen says to me with a smile, "you are in the school, and such."

A huge roar rolls across the lot. I have nearly forgotten how noisy it already is, until this great wave of shrieking passes by us. "I got to work," Peter says, looking back over his shoulder at his comrades.

"Well, so?" Helen says.

"So what?" her friend says.

"You know what," she says.

"You come all the way here to stare at me?" he says.

"You just tell me and then I'll go," she says.

"Tell you?"

"You know," she says.

"All right, all right," he says. And then mutters something in Polish.

Helen's face lights up in a way I've never seen. She leans forward and raises herself up on tiptoe and kisses her giant friend on the lips.

More Polish words spill from his mouth, as he steps back, gives a little wave, sneaks a look at me, but says nothing, wandering back to the group of men in stained coats.

"So that's good," Helen says, leading back the way we've come.

"Tell me," I say.

"Well . . . " she says.

Back to the alley, into the alley.

"What?"

"That Peter . . . "

"Yes?"

"He is going to marry me."

"Really?"

"Oh, yes. He is the father."

"John's father?"

Helen takes me by the arm and keeps me moving through the alley. "No, not the father of that one," she says. "He is the father of the one that's coming."

"Which one?"

"The new one."

"The new one?"

"That's right. I got a new one coming." She laughs at me, and I turn my head away as we step out onto the street, a street that seems quite clean after the filth and bloody rummage of the lot and the slaughter barn. "You think I don't live when you ain't drawing me?"

I take to my bed, an ancient remedy I've read about in novels.

"My dear," says Rebecca Finchey, hovering over me in her spring best like some great white moth, "I'm off to the country for the weekend. Will you be all right here by yourself?"

I nod, rather unconvincingly, I suppose, because Rebecca leans down and whispers in my ear, "It's not that boy again, is it?"

"No, not that boy." I reach for her hand and give it a squeeze.

"My powers fail me here, I'm afraid," she says. "I can bring you to the borders of love but I cannot make it go either well or poorly."

"What?" I can feel my face crinkling in consternation.

"My powers as your fairy godmother." She returns the squeeze of the hand. "I've reached my limits. You're on your own."

"As if I didn't know that."

"But not *that* boy?"

I shake my head. I take a breath, part my lips, but no words come.

However that boy is a stalwart friend, I must admit. He turns up a few days later at the show, a stodgily dressed exception among the crowd of young aesthetes with cigars and long flowing hair, one of whom even wears a wreath of flowers. "Ava," Leo says, "I love your self-portrait."

"And I hate it, so we're even."

"Don't be so disparaging. I want to buy it."

94

"I want to give it to you," I say, spying the traitorous Mister Banks and turning my eyes away.

"It will help me to remember you always, not that I could forget you even without it." Leo pulls a thin cigar from his pocket and lights it.

"And I'll be glad to get it out of my sight."

"But why? It's so very good."

"Because it's me," I tell him. "And I can't bear to look at me right now." I want to smoke myself, but I dare not try, not just now.

"One day you'll be famous and you'll regret having given it away."

"Leo, one day I'll be famous," I say, feeling my heart rise up in my chest like a full moon over the prairie, "and I'll regret nothing."

DOOR

Living out this way, I have come to regard water as quite precious, which to most people where I grew up in Virginia would seem like a rather extravagant statement. But I have taken to washing my hair only once a week, and to bathing quickly, without the luxurious soaking that we easterners take so much for granted. And so there I was, undressing so that I could wash myself as sparingly as possible—when my own water broke, splashing down my leg like a flash flood along one of the usually dry little arroyos that spread out from Ava's compound.

Socorro heard me cry out and came running. She telephoned Amalia, the midwife, and then went out to the barn to tell Michael, who was at the potting wheel with Ava. I lay down on our bed and must have dozed off. The next thing I knew, Socorro was standing over me, explaining something about how to breathe.

"Where's Michael?" I asked.

I was a few centimeters dilated before he arrived. "Where were you?" I asked, unable to keep the disappointment, and the little pain, out of my voice. Before he could answer, a contraction took hold of me and I tried to work with it, as I had seen dancers move in performance at school. My breaths came rhythmically. I snorted. I chuffed and howled.

"Baby," Michael whispered in my ear, "I made something for you."

"Go away, you bastard!" someone called out in my voice. And I tried to shut him out so that I could rest before the next contraction. It seemed like hours went by before we spoke again. I could hear whispers, and I recognized Ava's terse low vowels.

"We made this for you," Michael said.

I blinked my eyes open to see him holding before me a large brown bowl with figures all around, blurred by my vision.

"Her first production," he said. "We just fired it the other day."

"What?" I knew he was trying to distract me, but it didn't help much.

"Sorry, I know it hurts," he said.

"You do?" I replied. I clenched, unclenched my fists, and went off again on another ride.

The next time I opened my eyes, there was Ava leaning over me, a leathery, almost-otherworldly look on her face, seeming neither female nor male but something other—what you grow into when you reach a certain age.

"One thing I've never done," she said.

"So she made this," Michael said from over her shoulder. He held it out again for me to see.

The bowl.

"For the afterbirth," Ava said.

"Which we then offer up under the stars," Michael said.

"Good Catholic boy like you?" I asked, hearing the strain in my voice along with a certain sense of satisfaction. I had been working; he had been standing there watching, holding his precious bowl.

"He's changing," Ava said. "His father was a lapsed Jew, a pagan, of sorts."

I wanted to speak but was called away again for a while. When I focused on him again, he was smiling. "So what do you think?" he said.

"About what?"

"About the name 'Albert'?"

"Robert," I said.

"Who's that?" he asked. "Who the hell is that?"

"My brother," Ava said behind him.

Someone made a sound just then: a grunt, a howl, a growling howl of a wail that seemed to come up through the ground beneath the floor and through the floor and up through the bed and into my throat—and out into the air like a mating cry, an alarm, an

97

announcement that the very plates of the earth were starting to come apart.

"It begins," I heard Amalia the midwife say.

"I thought it had already . . . " Michael's voice.

Then Ava's, cutting him off. "It's always beginning. Always."

CHARLESTON

Harriet

Had I had hair like corn silk, Ava Boldin and I might never have become friends—and oh, how different my life would have been then! But because of who I was, Harriet Cardozo, and because of how I appeared: busty, wide hipped, dark wires for hair, and with the habit, I've been told, of smiling almost constantly, no matter how dire the situation—*and* because of where I lived, which was Charleston—of course, this woman and I fell in together and over the years have remained as close as sisters, and more.

Thank God for making me who I am is all I can say. Unlike most of the other teachers at the Taverner School, my interest in art—music, then, with poetry a distant island—set me apart from the crowd, those amateurs at mathematics and natural science who seemed always to be barely a lesson ahead of their brighter students. From the moment I saw Ava, I knew that we were kin of one kind or another. She was such an attractive girl, her dark reddish hair all done up in bright ribbons, so delicate in appearance (such an illusion that was!), and much taller than I. There was a mixture in the way she looked, of the exotic and the familiar, that made her stand out so much that—yes, I will admit it—she actually quite swept me away!

"Your figure," I heard myself say soon after we made our introductions to each other on that first day of school, "however do you keep it?"

"Chicago did it for me," Ava said with a laugh. "It's a city of such urgency—they say it's because it's always trying to catch up with New York, though I wouldn't know about that since I've never been to New York."

"You haven't? I've just come back from living there for two years and I'm telling you you must go!"

"Well, I must then. Chicago made me run about so, I ate like a hog on the way to slaughter, to use a Chicago image, but I never gained a pound."

"But you were in art school," I said, "so how was it that you had to rush?"

Ava gave me that smile again, the mouth turned up ever so slightly at the corners, the full lower lip, almost a child's pout, with her eyes declaring there was something more than childishness to the look. "I rushed," she said. "Let us just say that I rushed."

Time in Charleston doesn't rush much at all, yet it seemed as though it were only about ten minutes from the moment that the headmaster introduced her to the rest of the faculty at school before she and I were talking as though we'd been friends a long time, walking out on the common before the main building, since Mr. Curry had asked me to explain some of the regulations to our newcomer.

"I'm looking forward to teaching," she said, fiddling with long fingers at the buttons of her cloud-white blouse.

"It passes the time and makes a contribution," I said, seeing Mrs. Trenholm coming toward us across the grass.

"That's a good way to look at things," Ava said as the secretary approached us, smiling. Her mother and Mr. Curry's mother were second cousins, and she watched over the school as though it were her family, without ever letting us feel at home. "Good morning, Miss Cardozo," she said to me while looking Ava over. "And this is Miss Boldin, our new art teacher?"

"Good morning, Mrs. Trenholm. Yes, it is. Ava . . . "

"Is this your first time in Charleston?"

"Yes, ma'am."

"And what do you think of our fair city?"

Ava paused, looked to the sky. "I enjoy the light, ma'am," she said.

"The light?" Mrs. Trenholm looked surprised, as though, yes, for the first time, she, too, were noticing that we had light here. "Now, Miss Boldin," she started in, "there is something that I'm sure you'd like to see. Every art teacher before you over the years has enjoyed looking at it, and I would like to show it to you as well. It is a painting that my mother and I have at home, a scene with birds and flowers, really quite beautiful, and we would very much appreciate your paying a visit to see it."

Ava appeared momentarily puzzled, but then recovered, smiled, and said, "I'd love to, Mrs. Trenholm."

"On Sunday, then?"

Mrs. Trenholm seemed rather forthcoming about the invitation, about as forthcoming as a hunter about to spring a net on a bird.

Ava looked to me for advice. I nodded my approval, as if she needed that.

"And Miss Cardozo, would you be so kind as to show her the way? And come for tea yourself?"

And so it came to pass that Louise Trenholm invited her first Jew to the house on the Battery where she had been born, and her mother before her.

A few years earlier, before my accident of a marriage and short life in New York, I would have been thrilled to visit the Trenholm house. With its several columns in front and the sleeping porch running along the west side, it made the very picture of the prettiest building, a design sturdy enough to withstand fierce autumn weather yet almost demure, and nearly part of the landscape, like our palmettos and shifting dunes.

But as life would have it, now that I was finally invited for a visit, I wasn't going to look at the house; I was going to watch Ava Boldin look at the house.

The day before our visit we sat on the rough, scarred pinewood benches under the cool roof of the old market—sat opposite each other—and Ava sketched me. Odd how when you're posing, you can't truly see what's before you, the objects, in this case the slatted walls of the building and the old bricks, fading into a series of lines and curves, sun and shadow. I found myself sinking into one of those reveries such as usually only overtook me when I sat at the keyboard, and a certain expression must have passed across my face, because the next thing I knew, Ava was quietly laughing.

"Do I seem that comical to you, Ava?"

"You look so pleased with life," she said, "that I couldn't help but laugh. Don't pleasant sights sometimes inspire you to laughter?" Her fingers flew as she spoke with me. Flew! I felt as though she were a pianist, and that I was watching an inspired performance of some of the romantic music that I loved.

I stood up, wanting to embrace her—I had that feeling about her from the start, the desire to hold her—but she motioned for me to sit back. "Wait, wait! Here!"

And she held up the drawing for me to view—and never have I seen my head and hair depicted with such clarity and classical lines, lines that showed to me the history of my people and affections back almost to the Portuguese merchant who first signed the name Perera (my family name) on a manifest hundreds of years ago. I had been pounding at the piano since I was a child and had settled at the level of music teacher to uninspired children. Ava, from what she told me, had been drawing seriously—I mean, with a teacher—since she was a young girl herself, yet she seemed to possess a talent such as I could never imagine in myself, not with music at least, however much I loved it. "Ava," I said, "you are such a good sketch artist! You make me see myself alive on the page!"

"Take it," my new friend said, with a cunning smile, "and do with it what you will. Because I have just decided that it is the last sketch that I am going to make for a long time."

"But, Ava, you're so good at it. You can't quit it now."

"I'm not quitting," she said. "Not hardly. But I want to do other things now, more difficult things."

Her face seemed to turn darker right there before my eyes, and whether it was the shift of sun and shade in the market space or some deepening and congealing of the blood in her cheeks, I couldn't say. But it was not a blush the likes of which reddened my own face from time to time. Mine grew out of embarrassment, the kind that often overcomes a young woman when she understands of a sudden in company that she has shown herself to be innocent of the rules of life, or the opposite: that she knows more than she should let on. No, Ava's darkening visage seemed to grow from another impulse, a kind of visionary glance that allowed her to look upon you and yet beyond—so hard to explain in straightforward prose. As if she understood everything she would do in the future but suffered from the impatience of not having yet met up with it. Oh, all my life people had told me I was a strange one and set apart. But nothing in me compared to Ava.

"You are my first real friend here," she said, catching me off guard in my wandering of mind. And she offered me her hand, as though she were a man, and I were, too, and we had just been introduced. "I already know I'll never forget you."

I was so overcome with the emotion of the moment that I didn't think to wonder why she spoke of me as though she were already leaving me behind.

Coming back to Charleston after my time in New York City, I used to dream a great deal, and it's not a surprise that many of my dreams were filled with water. Water, water everywhere! Hurricanes and waterspouts assailed me in my sleep. Once I dreamed that I was taken up on the back of a giant turtle that carried me far across the waves to an island where pickaninnies danced and played. "Possum!" these children sang to me upon my arrival on the sandy beach. "Possum ate a milkweed!"

Whatever that meant, I never could figure out, for though I knew of possums, it was milkweeds that I had never seen. Negroes aplenty passed through my life, of course, but milkweed? Where had I read of it? Had I seen pictures? It was one of the small mysteries I would never solve.

I don't even know why I am telling this now, except that a storm was said to be approaching, and that night I dreamed of the largest waterspout I had ever seen, and I don't know how you understand these things, but somehow the dream marked that time for me as the time when I was making this friend for life.

Fits and starts—I played the piano this way. Why should I be surprised that my recollections take the same zigzag course, with strong tides—always water!—and breaking waves, like the music that I love— Debussy, Rachmaninoff, and later Satie—I loved to sit at the piano and play his music that I brought back with me from a trip to Paris years after. It would have done well to play it in Charleston in those years when Ava and I worked together. That languid, almost-limpid line, marching forward but seeming always to stay the same, at least in mood – that was our city back then.

Other cities call out to me – old Lisbon, where my ancestors made their business and their families – and certain port towns on the Ivory Coast of Africa. Africa! I can never run my comb through my own wiry hair without wondering about David Levi, my fabled great-great-and-so-forth grandfather who, supposedly, after being shipwrecked off the coast of the dark continent, stayed some years there and founded the family trade, importing to Lisbon along with the ivory and the precious stones a wife the color of cocoa with milk. Ava and I had that much in common from the start: a woman in our blood whose skin was dark complected. For she told me the story of her great-great etc., Melissa Tree, whose walk on water took place – and I have no doubt about it, not these days, and certainly not in those days when I first heard of it – not very far south along the same coast where we stood on the second afternoon that we were friends, barefooted, walking in the easy surf, telling stories to each other.

Ava spoke to me about a love that she had just ended in Chicago, and I could see by the way her eyes burned when she mentioned it that it was not a subject that I ought to pursue. And she spoke of her older brother, fragile from heart disease, who had to take very good care of himself. He was a geologist and worked with stones and the very pediments on which our planet balanced. And of her family, her mother who had died giving birth to her! and her father, who after that took to drink, and of her late grandmother, and of the only living parent she had, her stepmother, who had given her her first lessons in art.

"Though I knew from the earliest moments that I had something about the way I saw that made me different," she said as we walked along, now and then bumping shoulders and hips, kicking at the froth on the sand, "I didn't know what to *do* with that power until Dora – that's my stepmother – showed me the way."

"Where is she now?" I asked.

"Back in Nebraska. I wanted her to visit me in Chicago, but she wouldn't travel. When I went back home to see her before coming out here for this job, I understood. She suddenly finds it difficult to walk, and even holding a crayon takes some concentration. She trembles and quakes. Oh, Harriet, I refuse ever to get so old that I can't draw a line!"

Music was my passion then, though I do remember an encounter with paintings that turned out to change everything for Ava and me. After a pampered childhood and a moody adolescence (filled with music, mostly of my own making), I married Benjamin Cardozo and moved to New York City where my new husband would manage the office of the import-export company owned by his father. This story of my marriage I may write another time. It is not the point here, except that after a few months we both grew tired of each other alone together at home in our apartment and began to range restlessly about the great city looking for amusement. I associate that time with a taste—steel, stone, glass—that seemed to flavor the very rain that fell on us one night in autumn as we stepped out to hail a taxi on an uptown street. I was terribly homesick, though much of this feeling, I understood only much later, grew out of my disgust at myself for marrying someone my family had selected for me and not someone I had chosen myself. That bitter rain only increased my misery. A mixture of business and pleasure was how my dark young Benjamin later described the nature of the evening. He might have been speaking about our marriage.

"We recently helped this photographer bring some paintings in from France," he explained to me. "You should see the junk. You *will* see it. The colors all run together, the figures are blurred. How he's going to sell it, I don't know, except maybe to the nearsighted crowd." Benjamin had a sly wit, but this only made him seem more the caricature of the boy I had married than the boy himself. The taxi splashed through the streets, and I doused my thoughts in the rain and thought of the harbor at home, the ships on the rivers, lights bobbing on dark nights when air and sea seemed one because of the way the rain fell, straight, hard, down, piercing the surface of the ocean with such ferocity that you could for a moment imagine the rainstorm as shafts of water shooting up out of the sea, rather than falling from the clouds onto the waves.

"Are you all right, pigeon?" he asked, taking me in his arms. He was not all a waste, this boy-man I had married, but then even an idiot might have noticed that I had slumped to my left on the seat, my head against the cold window of the taxi.

"No," I said, no longer able to pretend, "no, I am not all right, and I don't like this, and I want to go home."

"We'll only be a few minutes," he said. "I've got to take a look at the gallery; the owner invited me and I couldn't turn him down."

"Not *that* home," I said, thinking of the apartment, my New York prison. "I want to go to Charleston; I'm cold and it's wet here, too cold and wet, and I want to go to my real home."

"Poor pigeon," he said, and it was as if nothing had passed between us since our wedding night.

"I *do* want to go home," I said as our taxi pulled up to a storefront on Fifth Avenue and we stepped out into the rain.

"Upstairs," Benjamin said.

I trailed behind him on the broad staircase like a child forced to come along with her parents on a deadening social visit.

AN AMERICAN PLACE, read the sign on the upper door. We entered, and I discovered paintings that were music.

I didn't last much longer in New York. Within a few days of that trip to the gallery to see the paintings from France imported by a photographer named Albert Stigmar, I packed a bag and took the train home. No one in my family paid me much notice. I was a married woman, no matter how young in years I might be, and that was what mattered to them. Though I lived at home, I had a lot more freedom to move about the town than I had ever had as a girl. No boys tried to court me, though a married few, boys Benjamin had grown up with, made such remarks to me, when I encountered them in town or at synagogue, that I was led to see for the first time—considering that in New York I had learned about the sadness of adult life and not any of the rest—that the world was quite unlike the way I had imagined it to be when I was growing up.

Music became my life, the playing and the teaching of it, something quite similar to the role that drawing began to play in Ava's life after her father died.

"You got a good head start on me," I said as we talked about these matters on that Sunday that we walked toward the Battery to pay our visit to the Trenholm house. "I'm jealous," I said. "You have a brother as well. I'm terribly jealous of that. If I had had a brother, I might never have gotten married. At least I would have been prepared for life with Benjamin."

Ava squinted at me and then stared up at the sky. All week it had been a hazy but distinct blue. Now it was clouding over with the kind of unfurled scrolls on which you could read: storm coming, storm on its way, have a care.

"I don't know that I was ever prepared for anything," she said. "I haven't married yet, and I don't know that growing up with Robert has helped me decide that. I don't think that I ever will marry."

"I wouldn't say that if I were you, Ava. Any day now someone might come along and change your mind."

"I want only to make a profession so that I can support myself and my desires," Ava said, dividing her glance between me and those gathering clouds. "Are we going to have a storm?"

"Indeed, it looks as though we are," I said. "I've never felt the wind this hot and fierce before. If you look out that way . . . you can't see the flags flying atop Fort Sumter from here without a spyglass, but I know that in this wind they must be flying taut, pointing straight at us."

"Fort Sumter?" she said. "That was from the war?"

"The war between the states."

"Oh, yes. We studied that in school. But I never paid much attention. I don't think I'm . . . made to think of such things. Robert, my brother, does. He and his rocks and his layers of ages . . . " She turned her face to me as she said this, and it was as if the large ball of the sun had slipped out from behind the blowing haze. Her eyes, there was something about her eyes. She touched me on the shoulder, and I had to glance away. "I miss him. I don't want him to die. They all die on me, Harriet. Don't you go and do that either, now that we've become friends."

"No," I said, daring myself to look her full in the eye again, "I won't do that. I promise I won't."

Ava was wearing a plain blue cotton dress with a little lace collar, the kind of smock she must have worn for art classes in Chicago. I had on a flowered dress that was tight enough to show my figure—though in retrospect I have to ask myself, to whom? to whom?—while still loose fitting enough for me to breathe. The wind blew even stronger and by the time we approached the Trenholm house, our summer clothes seemed somehow too flimsy for the gathering weather.

Behind the gate laden with bougainvillea, jacaranda and jasmine, the house appeared whiter than white in the portentous atmosphere just before the storm – dark, brilliant flowers in the foreground and the deepening purple-gray of the sky above gave the wood such contrast as I had never seen before – and I know it wasn't just me, because I noticed that Ava was staring. "Isn't it strange?" I said as we opened the gate and walked up to the house.

"Sometimes it is," she said. "All of it like this."

Before I could question her as to what she meant, a servant opened the door for us and bid us enter. "Hello," Ava said, and we followed him into the entryway. As many flowers lined the hall as grew in the gardens, it seemed, and when we met Louise Trenholm at the entrance to the sitting room, we found her with her arms full of flowers.

"The cutting before the storm," she said, looking up at us from where she stood contemplating her colorful burden. "If the wind comes up later on, as well it might, given the signs, every last blossom will get torn away, and I just couldn't stand the thought of it, so I went out and did it myself. Please take some."

"I like that," Ava said, taking a handful of flower tops from the load in the woman's arms and then handing one to me.

"Thank you," I said.

Mrs. Trenholm handed over her burden to a thin, dark-skinned maid, who had entered the room as if by a signal neither Ava nor I could hear, and bid us be seated. She then proceeded to talk for many minutes about the school, to which she contributed too much of her time, and then about the weather – she had heard from the port authorities that a storm might be boiling up to the south of us, over that portion of the ocean where the worst storms got born – and then about family members living and dead, some of whose names were as familiar to me as the names of our streets and islands, and some of whom rang unknown on my ear.

"And you, dear," she said to Ava after a while, "tell me about your people," as if my friend had come to our city from the steppes of Russia rather than someplace just west of Chicago. And Ava spoke a little about her dead and living family, and I watched her as she spoke, and then I studied Mrs. Trenholm as she listened, and I understood that Ava's life did seem exotic and foreign and strange to those of us who had grown up along this southerly coast, and lived with our mothers in houses surrounded by high walls of flowers and palmettos – and family history that went back to the first European settlers who beached their boats in weather calmer than we saw rising this afternoon.

At first I thought I would feel thrilled to enter this house – but as she talked on and on, and then led us before her awful painting, I grew angrier and angrier. By the time we finished our conversation, I was ready for anything nature might throw at us, furious at the way the woman had ignored me and courted Ava in the hope that the new art teacher at Taverner might say that her family painting was a masterpiece. Ava said nothing of the kind; in fact, said very little about the painting at all. But I could hear Mrs. Trenholm already telling her friends that this gifted art teacher had told her she owned something approaching a masterpiece. It clearly didn't matter what the painting was – just a drab collection of birds and flowers on a blue background – but what was said of it, that counted more! And this lesson stayed with me, and later stood me in good stead in my business, in years to come.

But the storm! the storm! Puny mortals! Not even old families like the Trenholms could stand in the face of such a turbulence as this, a hurricane that within a day of our departure from that house came down on us like a fist! Trees sailed past rooftops like sticks flung by petulant children. An entire stable of animals far from town floated down the river. So too, alas, went the library at the school – thousands of dollars worth of books sailing out to sea alongside the struggling horses. Buggies sank in the harbor. Sailboats, pushed by the winds of the angry storm, churned across East Bay Street and headed full tilt toward the center of town, later to settle, their sails torn to shreds, against the battered walls of bank buildings and gardens.

On this portentous day Ava and I watched this marvelous destruction through the dormer windows on the top floor of my parents' house. Everyone else in the family had departed inland for Columbia, and the two of us, who they mistakenly thought had preceded them on the road inland, were left alone in our reckless-ness to bear witness to the storm that wailed on around us for hours and hours into the dark of night, and then through a dawn that we never noticed amidst the black whirlwind of hurricane. We should have been terrified out of our minds but as only we could do, we showed just the opposite face, utterly fearless in the face of fero-cious nature: two of a kind, despite our many different traits, in the stupidity of the brave.

"Now I know why I came *here* to work," Ava said to me at one point over the roar of the wind. "I love this! I want to live here forever!"

"We don't have storms like this but once every few decades," I said.

Ava clutched my hand and gave it a hard squeeze. "I'll live here and wait for the next one. This is how I want to paint! I want my work to show all this! It's how I feel when I draw! This excitement, this *fear* . . . "

"Ava!"

She let me go and stood up. "Come on!" And raced down the stairs. I followed, fearing I knew not what.

"Don't," I called to her when she reached the front door. "It's too dangerous. We should go . . . "

But she was out the door, and I followed to see her, hair stream-ing behind like a sail as though she were a vessel and moved upon the waters.

A hundred-year-old tree came crashing down nearby, as if to punctuate the passage from this music I would never play.

When the winds finally subsided, the town lay under a foot of water, some African children were missing, a two-masted schooner was found atop the steeple of a Baptist church several miles inland along the Ashley River, and—see how it all comes together here!—Ava had completed the first of a remarkable new series of drawings, the so-called Storm Sketches, her first nonrealistic work.

I took one look at the paper she unfurled in front of me that morning and understood why I had done penance in New York. I knew the gallery where she had to show this work, and I asked if I could keep the drawing, and rolled it up and sent it with a

110

letter to my dear Benjamin and told him where he must take it and show it, saying that there were dozens more. When the answer came that the photographer and gallery owner Albert Stigmar wanted to see them *all*, and would be interested in meeting the artist, I told Ava.

DOOR

And then one night he came to me smelling of clay and oils and cigarettes, and it was just like the old days, the way he could thrill me with only a gesture or a word, sometimes only a sound, half a word, and then he touched me, and I felt cheated at first because I came so suddenly undone, after all the labor, all the weeks since the baby, the hurting and caring and nursing, and Michael off in the barn as though things were just business as usual, and who knows but maybe they were, maybe they are, and I'm a fool.

"I love you, Amy," he said.

Put a bowl of butter under the noonday sun. It would take longer to melt than I did at his word. But as I was reaching up so that I could slip off my nightgown, he said to me, "No, wait, I want you to come and see something."

I wasn't sure what he was talking about. But in a moment or two he explained that he wanted me to come out to the barn with him. I got up and got dressed, checked on Robby, and then followed Michael out the black door and across the corral to the barn. He unlocked the door and I stepped inside. It had been a long while since I had been in there. The potting wheels, the large canvases stretched midway across the barn, the small finished paintings stacked against the walls, and where was the kiln? I said to myself, outside somewhere?

"What is it that you wanted me to see?" I said, taking Michael by the hand. "Something you're working on?"

"No," he said, "just this. All of this. This is what I've been working on. I'm organizing things," he said, "for the first time in my life. Do you know, if we play our cards right, just how much all this is worth?"

112

"Michael," I said, shaking my head. "Is this really you talking like this? How much is it worth? None of it's ours. You're supposed to have your own work. I don't think you ought to forget that for a minute."

"Listen, listen, listen," he said, trying to keep hold of my hand as I struggled to free myself from him. "You're organizing her old papers, right?"

"I've started to work on them, yes," I said.

"And I'm helping her get back to painting. We got new glasses for her . . . and I'm helping her with the preparation."

"We're helpers, Michael. You used the word. That's what we are."

He shook his head vigorously and though I tried to break away, he kept his hold on me. "Uh-uh," he said. "That's not who we are. Do you know who we are?"

"Tell me, please," I said, wanting to end this and go back to our room.

"We're her children," he said. "That's who we are."

"Aw, Michael," I said. It took me hours to calm him.

WEST

Ava

That cold afternoon in late winter when Ava set her collar against the wind and walked out onto the plain behind her house in the direction of the quickening sunset, she had never carried so much with her in her mind and in her chest—the heart part of it. Her student, Billy. Her brother's marriage. So much in her thoughts when all she wanted to do was savor the new and exhilarating light. Three years in Charleston had not prepared her for the marvelous transition from western day to western night. Back there the best light came at sunrise, from the east over the ocean, and it was difficult to set up and work for more than a short while before it became commonplace, either blinding in its immediacy or muddied by an atmosphere thick with moisture.

But here! here was all luminosity and shimmer, a palette that showed raw reds and yellows and blacks with the audacity of a student who has just discovered the rainbow!

She wasn't accustomed to the cold now anymore than she had been when winter had first set in, supposing either that her body had forgotten about growing up in Nebraska or had been transformed somehow by living in the warm lap of Charleston, where only now and then a day or two in December or January reminded the inhabitants that in other places in the world heat was not the usual issue. Cold! She balled her fists against it and kept on walking, hoping that somehow with this next step or the step after that, she might leave behind for good the turmoil that had driven her out the door.

And on top of all this, she still couldn't forget that a young girl had died so that she might walk beneath this beautiful sky turning toward evening. Ava didn't know the poor thing's name, but she

114

had been a teacher. Ava's former instructor, Mr. Banks—traitor, now friend!—had written to her in Charleston about the opening. Influenza had hit hard again in the West, and one of those taken—may her soul rest in peace—had been the art instructor at this little west Texas town's local college. The school, though bereft, had had to fill the vacancy and had put the staff at the Art Institute on alert. Thus Banks's letter. A serious opportunity for advancement, he had written. And no hats!

But first, New York! her first time—so unlike Chicago, no matter what comparisons they made for themselves out there! She and Harriet took the train, a quiet, nearly serene journey north, and then suddenly she was let loose in this capital of everything—horsecars, horse carts, automobiles, trucks, bicycles, fire engines, whistles, screams, shouts, hallooos!, sneezes, belches, whimpers, whispers, tearing of wood, grating of steel on steel wheel. At night she could not see the stars, scarcely a moon, on this rock of steel surrounded by waters, the flowing sights and sounds and odors, the air thick with the fears and sighs and pleasures of multitudes.

And through it all the piercing sight of buildings pointed toward heaven!

No fairy godmother to assist her. But she had Harriet, who led her to their hotel for young women where they washed off the dust from the trip and prepared their faces to be powdered with the soot of New York. Ava managed to add a few passages to her notebook and make a few sparse lines for a sketch. Then out onto the street again.

Fifth Avenue: upper swank on the street, women the likes of which she had seen only in the rotogravure. Here they were, alive and moving their lips in quiet speech, speaking perhaps of the odd way that she dressed. Ava wanted to flee before she had even arrived.

Only those tall spires, spiking the sky—they took her by the eyes and led her about.

"Here she is!" said a black-and-white-bearded man in spectacles as she came up the stairs and entered the gallery full of people. There on the wall . . .

"How did you know it was me?" she asked, staring for a moment at the hand he offered in greeting and then giving it a vigorous western shake. Her eyes flew back to him, this man old enough to be her father.

The bearded man—it was Stigmar, the owner, photographer—pursed his full lips and smiled. "The anxiety," he said. "It shows on your face, even in a room full of Manhattanites." She didn't know what he meant by that. He asked her if she had more of those hurricane drawings. She said that she might. It was odd. He was so much older than she, yet something held her attention besides mere curiosity.

An hour of loud talk and wine, shuffling from subject to subject, meeting—not true but it felt this way—everyone in the room, then back now and then to Albert Stigmar, king of this court. Something about his mouth, those lips curled now around a cigar, and a dancing light in his eyes behind those spectacles.

And then it was over, and the pair of them rode the train back to Charleston, Ava trying to calm herself, calm herself, calm herself, and sleep, thinking of those towers, those eyes, seeing the spires reflected in those spectacles—finally, sleep.

Soon after their return to Charleston, she and Harriet had a tearful farewell, a farewell much more painful than Ava had imagined, walking along the beach under a half-moon that passed in and out of low, moist clouds. Wet sand sucked at their shoes.

Will I miss this place? Ava asked herself. "I'll miss this place," she said.

"No, you won't," Harriet said. "You won't miss our stuffy old Mrs. Trenholm and the heat and the way we sit out here on the water, so set apart from the rest of things."

"I will miss that," Ava said, concentrating on moving along in the sucking sand.

"Will you miss hurricanes?"

I've done those, Ava thought to herself, but this was her friend and so she said, "I'll miss it all."

"So why . . . ?"

"I knew you'd ask again." Harriet had asked when Ava had first told her about the Texas job and had listened dutifully, but Ava could see in her eyes that she hadn't accepted her explanation. "Tell the truth," Harriet said, producing the wine bottle from her bag.

Ava took the bottle from her and as she had seen working men do along the railroad tracks years ago at home, she put it to her lips and sucked. "Ah!" Wine dribbled down her chin and spilled onto her dress. "Ruined!"

"Mine, too!" Harriet poured the dark liquid down the front of her own dress.

"Oh!" Ava let out a cry as though she had been surprised by someone at her shoulder, but it was only the moon coming out from behind those low clouds.

"Come," Harriet said, "we'd better do our wash." She led Ava by the hand to the low-lapping surf.

"How do we do our wash?" Ava said.

"This way." Harriet walked her into the water.

"It's cold!" Ava spoke up in spite of herself—the wine, the cold tickling at her ankles. "And deep!"

She stared out across the moon-tinted horizon. When the water reached her hips, she stopped and pulled her friend to a halt along with her. "Where is that wine?"

"Gone," said Harriet. "But there's more where that came from."

Ava dipped a hand through the water. Waves splashed against her breasts. She edged forward a little, until she could taste the next wave. It was smooth underfoot, one long ledge all the way out to the place directly beneath the moon, it seemed. She strained her eyes in that direction, hoping for a glimpse of a woman walking on water. But not a sign of her. Now the undertow pulled a little harder, and she could feel the sand slipping out from under her. "I'm laundered," she said. "Let's go back."

"Don't want to swim?"

"Not in this dress."

"Take it off." Harriet made to pull her own dress over her head, but the water made it too heavy, and it was a struggle. "Help me," she called.

"Are you all right?"

"Help me with this dress," Harriet said.

But just then something brushed sharply past Ava's leg, and she screamed, and Harriet screamed, and whatever it was, by the time they beat their way back to shore, their wet dresses as heavy as

117

armor, was gone. However, Ava was convinced, a woman could walk on water.

Who knows but that a marvelous sunrise might have made her regret her decision to put Charleston behind her? But the sky was overcast the next morning, and a cold wind played in off the ocean. In her damp dress she returned to her room for her suitcases. There was a letter waiting for her, which she did not open until she had boarded the train and the train had begun to move.

Texas, he had written, *what's Texas compared to a future in New York? Up here we don't even know where Texas is, but you know where we are. Ever since we met I have had the odd sense that I can help you with your work. I cannot say the same about your life. You say that you are taking a position at a college in Texas. But if a stranger—though I do not, after having seen your drawings, feel as though I am a complete stranger to you—may give you some advice, it is this: take your job as seriously as your art, and your art will come to no good end.* As the train rolled forward she tried to picture the man: slightly built, wearing wire-rimmed spectacles, a mostly white beard, that odd light in his eyes. *You know,* said the inscription. *Stig,* he had signed.

Did she know? She felt as though she knew nothing at all, that her mind was the prisoner of her body, and her body was a captive of the train, rolling her toward the horizon at a noisy, high rate of speed. Normally at a time like this she might read or draw. But for hours and hours she sat in her compartment perfectly still, as though time and the future were some poison against which only immobility could serve as an antidote. Like a rock in a rushing streambed, her stillness might allow the future to roar around her and leave her fixed forever where she was now. Why had she chosen to leave Charleston and her simple job and her good friend? She had a number of reasons and none of them seemed to make much sense right now; none of them, at least, seemed to have the force to help her to stay calm as she felt the power of the train that carried her west toward she knew not what. Her hands trembled, and Ava could feel a coldness growing around her heart, like ice forming on the edges of a stream in deep water.

Now and then she would recognize that other passengers rode this train, that a small woman wearing a large white hat sat next to her for a while and then left the car, but most of the time she sat as still as she could, looking neither to the right nor the left, drained of power, fearing that she might stop breathing. Papa, she called out in her mind, like some prisoner in a gothic novel entombed in some dungeon far below the base of a mountain; Dora, she called— Mama! Robert, she thought to herself, Robert, Robert, Robert! Could a woman truly walk on water? Hours later she found that she could steal a glance at the land outside the window only to discover that it was growing dark, and that she had little chance to try and figure out her location, except that they were traveling in the direction of the fading light.

She was still moving in that direction the night she set her collar against the wind and, carrying her heavy burden, walked off behind her little house on the edge of town, where the grounds of the state college left off and the dry and dusty plain began.

Who is he? who is he? she asked herself as she stepped smartly forward, her face jutting into the steady breeze that blew from the west. Something about him pushed her into thinking about Billy Aitkins in ways no other boy had. That she found quite unaccountable. There was that look about his eyes and the way he carried himself. Ava didn't even like to think about it; it made her feel so helpless and irresponsible. She held tight to her work and her life, and it didn't please her to find Billy Aitkins's face rising before her as she walked toward the horizon.

The light was disappearing fast now, and the vast sky served as a kind of screen onto which she projected all of these events that had passed before her arrival, and some of those events that had taken place since then, particularly in the classroom where that boy had first appeared.

"Yes, *ma'am*," he had said the moment she had read his name from the roll, and she had looked up and seen those eyes. It was a shock.

First the old bearded stick of a man in New York, and now this *boy*? At least she had been able to flee from Stigmar on that first meeting. But now here was *William Aitkins* on her roster, and her job could last a long time. At first she buried the meeting in the rest of the day of classes and paperwork.

119

It was quiet in the room at the end of the afternoon, when she was packing things away in her briefcase and quite ready to return to her little house at the edge of town for a meal and a rest. Her plan while teaching was to wake early and be ready to catch the first light, which here on the plains seemed to enlarge upon itself rather than dissipate as it did on the East Coast. Even an hour or two of work before meeting her classes would do a lot to help her balance these two parts of her life: what she had to do for her pocketbook, and what she had to do for her heart. *Take your job as seriously as your art, and your art will come to no good end.* She had to admit that Stigmar's letter still lingered with her.

"Damn him!" she said because of it, and looked up to see *William Aitkins* standing in front of her desk. She started, and then snatched up the briefcase and began searching through it, trying to hide her embarrassment at her surprise.

"Ma'am," he said, again in that quiet but insinuating way. And that was how she came to see the barranca for the first time.

"You got to take a look at it," Billy had said. He hadn't had to do much convincing, not when she wanted to escape the small room with him in it. He was boasting about the town—after all, he had grown up here, or near the town, anyway, on a ranch—even as he began to tell her how much he wanted to get away, to go east, or maybe to California to school—he didn't know where, but he just wanted to get away.

She was staring as much as listening, trying to avoid those eyes by studying his big bushy head of dark hair, the musculature of his arms and shoulders. He babbled on about the barranca.

"What?" she said, and it was almost as if she were reading poorly from a script.

"Oh, that's a sublime spot," he said, using language most un-Texan—what a strange boy, she said to herself, and who has he been reading? "Come on, I'll show you."

So they had stopped at her little house on the way—it was, in fact, directly on the way, lying as it did on the western edge of town—and she dumped her briefcase and picked up a coat and off they went, walking in this same direction she was walking now.

She admired the way he moved—what was he? nineteen? twenty?—and thought about how she might ask him to pose for her without him thinking . . . well, as yet there was no way. But later on?

Meanwhile he was asking a lot of questions and she was answering when she could—where was she from, and what had she done before this, and how had she heard of little old Canyon State College, and what kind of drawing did she do? All these interrogatories merely prefaced his own disquisition on his life, on the ranch just outside town, and the kind of art he loved to make—drawings of horses, mainly. It was clear to her that he had been storing up these things to say for a long time, something she understood. If it hadn't been for Dora, she herself might still be waiting for someone to say such things to. And so she helped to calm herself as they walked by turning herself into the willing listener, the kind of person a good teacher must often be.

Once they left the town they slowed down a bit, picking their way across the scrub plain as Ava imagined a horse might, or a mule. After a few minutes they found themselves surrounded by tall cactus and, here and there, another variety of desert plant that spread out across the ground like roots that seemed unable to find a home. A cry went up at their approach. "Owl," said Billy. "Sounds almost human, don't it?"

Ava, studying her surroundings, kicked herself for not taking along her sketchbook.

"Now where is . . . ?" Billy brought her up short by the sleeve. She looked down and saw that they had reached the edge of a crevasse that dropped precipitously down toward a small stream already bathed in shadows. It was with a little shiver that Ava stared into this place of descending curves and configurations, large striations and overlappings of levels of sandstone and clay.

Moving along the lip of the barranca, she noticed a gentle grade, a natural path resembling slightly worn steps, and by this means they made their initial descent into the ravine. A shadow passed overhead just as she climbed down to where the rim stood higher than her shoulders, and Ava turned but saw nothing—perhaps it was a bird passing across the fading sun—and continued the downward passage. After a few more steps Ava found herself standing on a small ledge, a place she could not have made out by merely looking down from the rim, where the face of the cliff had been carved

121

with sticks by wanton boys, whose names—*Tex, Stony, Mike*—mingled with crudely lettered inscriptions of forbidden words.

"Sorry, ma'am," Billy said when he noticed she was staring. She ignored his embarrassment.

The remains of a fire lay at her feet, and a small black cooking pot sat amidst the rubble of an old camp. Ava smiled at the evidence of the boys' play, wishing she had been with them at that supper, or that she could be sometime. She was sure these wild and woolly boys of west Texas had more fun than most girls in most places.

A few feet further down, on another, smaller ledge, she found the remains of some nameless small beast, a dog, perhaps, that someone had thrown into the ravine and left to rot, whose bones lay bare and roughly worn by who-knew-how-many seasons of sun and rain and snow and wind. Nothing stirred near its blanched white surface, as smooth and inviting as piano keys.

Many times thereafter Ava returned to this place, alone, armed on these occasions with her sketchbook and pencils. Her teaching schedule made it difficult, if not impossible, for her to come here anytime but late in the day—except for weekends. And she avoided coming on the weekends since she did not want to encounter any of the schoolboys who had carved their names in the soft stone walls of the ravine. After a full day in the classroom it was solitude she craved, the kind of solitude that could be filled only with work of her own choosing. So it was a trade between quiet and the necessary time alone, and the best light that she might have available.

Nevertheless she made the most of this, and had done so on the evening when things began to change. She had just made her eighth or ninth version of the dog's body, and was packing up to leave, when she turned at some noise on the rim above her. She looked up and saw nothing but the fading, nearly purple, bruise of sky. When the noise came again, she did not look up. A stone and a handful of loose dirt rained past her; she strained and caught a glimpse of a shoe disappearing over the rim. "Who is it?" she called up into the fading light.

"Nobody but us Injuns," came Billy's voice down the crevasse.

"You followed me," Ava said when she had climbed up out of the ravine.

A shy smile spread across the boy's face, and it was all Ava could do not to blush. "You come out here a lot," he said. "I'm just watching out for you."

"Thank you, but I can take care of myself."

Billy kicked at the dust at his feet. "Well, say some Gila tried to attack you."

"What's that?"

"A lizard. Could bite you and leave you for dead."

"Don't try to scare me," Ava said. But for the moment she was scared. "I appreciate your thinking of me. But I can do just fine by myself."

The wind was blowing, as usual, and it made her shiver. The season had angled into winter, the sun descending a few degrees further south every time she thought to study it. On this particular afternoon a few clouds had drifted up from Mexico, showing bumpy undersides like knuckles above the mountains to the west.

"You're a good teacher," Billy said. "But there are things I could help you with."

His meaning was clear, and Ava considered it, wondering what to do, what she would do. It was just then, because of his remark, that she turned her head away. That was when she saw it, the bright and slightly gauzy emblem of the evening. She raised her sketchbook, but for a while she just stared at the light. It wasn't the way the old Greeks believed; it wasn't as though some god had poked a hole in the backdrop of oncoming night and showed a candle through it. It was as though a fire had broken out above the horizon in a sky made of paper, and it was consuming the very stuff of darkness, locally, just in that place.

She was staring, poised to sketch it, when Billy took her by the shoulders and kissed her awkwardly on the mouth.

The next day she received a letter from Harriet, a note that contained, as Harriet's letters always did, news about Charleston and the weather—hurricane season had passed in a rather benign fashion this year—and more than a few paragraphs about her life and mood at this moment. It seemed that she had begun a love affair with a visiting actor from New York City, and that, though the town was large enough for her to keep this liaison covert—or so she

123

hoped, at least for reasons of family reputation and her standing at the school—there were things going on which anyone with an eye for such matters might notice. For example, Harriet had put on weight. Some women caught up in love, she wrote, grow thin. For me, she told her friend, it is just the opposite.

When Ava found herself skipping supper that evening, she made a little note in her mind to Harriet, saying to her that it was clear which side of the river she stood on when it came to such matters. And then she caught herself, her heart racing along. Can this be happening to me? she asked in her mental letter to Harriet. Here was a boy some four or five years her junior, and here she was, a woman who believed that she knew what she wanted out of life— her work, the solitude to make her work—a woman who had known love only once before, and then not conventional storybook love, the kind the boy seemed to believe in, given the circumstances of that first kiss, a woman who . . . what? . . . was a little worried.

I don't want to be condescending, she told Harriet in this letter. I have to be honest. He is awkward and, I do believe, in many ways more innocent than I am, but I have to admit his kiss thrilled me. But I don't know *him*. What if *he* is different from his kiss? And he is a *boy*!

She was standing at her worktable in the corner of the little dining room of her house, pressing herself against the edge of the table as she sometimes did in the minutes before beginning to work. The work trance was how she put it when trying to describe to herself the peculiar state in which she found herself making her drawings these days. And now here she was in that condition, thinking not about work but about this boy!

Nothing had prepared her for this. She issued a low cry in her mind that she hoped might reach all the way to Charleston: oh, Harriet, would that you were with me!

A knock at the door! It was as though a fist squeezed down on her heart.

This was absurd, ridiculous! Had it been this way when Helen had come into the room? She tried to remember; at the same time she tried to forget.

"Miss Boldin?"

Ava opened the door to a woman in town clothes, who introduced herself as the mother of one of her first-year students, a priss
who wanted to learn to draw so that she might impress her husband-
to-be (whom she had not yet met).

"How did you ever find where I lived?" Ava said to her, asking
her with a gesture to step inside.

"Everyone knows where everyone lives in Canyon," the woman
said, proceeding to deliver to Ava a cake she had just made, and a
speech about her daughter's abilities and how much Ava had helped
her to find them in such a short while.

After the woman left Ava stepped just outside the door and
watched her grow smaller and smaller on the road back toward the
center of town. It was evening, but late enough so that the sky was
crowded with stars. Ava stared a while, and when a cool wind came
up, caught hold of herself and went back inside.

"I'd given up on you," she said to Billy when he arrived about
an hour later.

"I met some friends in town," he said. His voice trembled a little, and his breath smelled of beer.

You don't have to be afraid with me, Ava wanted to tell him.
Because nothing is going to happen.

But he came up to her, this time forthrightly, took her in his
arms—it was almost as if he had been practicing with a dressmaker's
dummy and who could say that he hadn't?—and kissed her again,
and her resolve immediately disappeared.

With the coming of cold weather Ava's regular trips to the barranca ended, though once or twice, even with the threat of a
northwester in the offing, she bundled herself up in sweaters and
headed out to the cut and spent her time alone with her eye and
wrist and hand, no thoughts in mind but the way the line flowed
onto the paper, sorry only that after a while fingers became too
cold and stiff to hold a charcoal crayon. A series of drawings of a
feather grew out of these expeditions: the large, singular artifact of
an absent bird. She drew a fern leaf many times as well, the leaf
pressed deeply into the wall of the ravine. And that dog's body,
washed clean now by a big rainstorm and shoved a few feet further
down the ledge. There was a snakeskin, too. She drew that. And a

125

wooden axe handle she had found midway down into the pit, and the remains of another animal whose bones she did not recognize.

Thus went her days: up early and over to school, teaching her classes until late afternoon, and then home, possibly to steal time out at the ravine or draw at home in the small bedroom, a corner of which she had turned into a little studio. Nights became more and more the domain of her young Billy, though she did not want to think much about this. At around eight or nine, by which time she had finished the meager meal she might have made for herself, he would knock at the door and she would admit him, already closing her eyes in anticipation of the dousing of the lights, and for an hour or so give herself over to him, his kisses and attention, as though the tables were turned for once, and she was the subject and he was the artist.

It was all so different from the way it had been with Helen, at least as different as Chicago, with its high rises and its lakeshore, was from Texas, this place of barranca, cactus, scrub and stony plain. The smells were different, the taste was different, the velocity of motion, the sounds, all different, though she understood, when she took a fleeting second to consider it, that this last had as much to do with their lack of experience as with anything else. Billy was almost childlike—his body told that story even before he spoke or moved—and he loved her as a child loved, with an innocence, and a greed born of that innocence which she could sometimes scarcely endure. With Helen, who was certainly not innocent, she had wanted to give everything and found that she had no time even to find what she had, let alone bestow it on another. With Billy it was—another of these opposites!—just the other way. She found herself trying to protect the inner parts of herself, not the physical, for he was too untutored to try and reach there, but the invisible presence of her, the part of her that hovered and watched, that could never wholly go over to the other side without thinking it a certain kind of blindness—the worst thing to happen—worse even than death.

And as Billy became more and more the man, and his kisses and hands and then his whole body begged for more and more of her, he became more the child, and Ava found herself wondering if she would ever survive this hunger of his that matched nothing within herself. She didn't know how to be a mother, because she had never had one to emulate. Though there was the model of Dora, giving, loving, but here she was, in this boy's arms, thinking of Dora; and Helen, yes, she came to mind, of course, of course, and Harriet's face, fleeting, dark, and then he was thrusting at her, into her, and she felt herself flood with shame and fear and exultation—all together now—and there was her grandmother's face before her, of all things! a feather, dog's body, tall woman, Melissa Tree! And something went *tearing* through her, but in a pleasurable way, and she felt like a glove turned inside out. Her days began to crumble inward onto themselves; she found her hands trembling and her voice quavering when she stood before the class, and she grew thin with worry about conceiving, something which had not occurred to her in all its horror until they were a full half month into their liaison, and she found that she was waiting with great expectancy for the onset of her menses. It came, and she nearly collapsed with relief, refusing to see Billy for a full week thereafter.

He moaned and complained, exactly as he must have when he was about five or six years old, and something—a toy wagon he had wanted for Christmas perhaps? or a horseback ride to town—had not come his way. But that was nothing like his behavior when she told him that she was going to Chicago to spend Christmas with her brother. This news produced the kind of explosion in Billy that must have turned his mother into a willing slave who would endure even the worst torments from her husband in order to please her desirous little boy.

"You can't!" he said in a high-pitched voice that betrayed his sudden reversion to childhood. "I want you to stay here with me!" His eyes did a frightening little zigzag dance in his head.

Fortunately Ava found within herself the instinctive response for self-preservation. She remained calm. "He's my brother," she said, "and you're only . . . a friend."

"I need you more than he does," Billy said. And then something came into his eyes that he must have drawn from some deep well of childhood recollection. "You're staying," he said in a voice a full register lower than it had been a moment before. "And that's the way it is."

But it wasn't.

On a dark morning while a northwester blew in and turned everything to cold whirling dust, she boarded the train, leaving Billy to find out on his own that she had gone.

The train ride gave her more than enough leisure to review in her mind just how much time had gone by since she had last seen Robert. But she was still shocked when she saw him at Union Station. He had grown a mustache, and he had a little tire of flesh around his middle. He also had with him a woman about Ava's age with a shy, pinch-lipped smile.

"Ava, this is Margaret, who is going to be my wife."

Ava felt the words as almost a physical blow to her chest. She felt suddenly embarrassed, ashamed, angry, betrayed, disconsolate, amused, scornful, forlorn, and happy. That, too! Happy! Oh, happy, happy! She was glad she had been fooling around and wasting her hours with young Billy, for where was her love for her brother to go now that he had given his to another?

Thus began the most dreadful day of her life that she could remember, worse even than the gray, painful time of her father's demise—for she *knew* what was going on here, she knew, she knew, and nothing makes pain more intense than knowledge. Nothing! Oh, for the sweet ignorance of her life here before, when she had been mad for Helen and had drawn with such ease! when her fairy godmother had presided over a winter with such gaiety that the worst illness seemed to last but a moment—or so she remembered it—and the worst villains, men intent upon standing in the way of her progress, seemed like comic, mustachioed figures from a melodrama!

The day went by, the longest day of her life, until Robert's fiancée took the train to Michigan, where she taught in an elementary school in a town just over the border from neighboring Indiana. Robert's company rented for him an apartment near the lakeshore. After dinner she asked that she be allowed to go to bed immediately since she was not feeling well. Robert looked as though he were about to ask her something regarding the meal, but the question never passed his lips.

Ava slept like a stone dropped into the lake. The next morning she left her brother still asleep in the other room and went out in search of her fairy godmother's building. She found it easily, but the doorman informed her that Mrs. Finchey had returned to England.

England? She came from Wyoming. So why England? And what if I were from Texas? Would I retire to France? Though I might, she told herself. I might. Or Poland!

A fruitless hour-long taxi ride through the back of the yards brought nothing but misery.

"Hello?" Mister Banks said at the other end of the telephone line.

But what could she ask? Did he recall that Polish girl, the model? And did he know her current address?

And then there was Peter, the father of her new child. Or not so new. What would happen when he came to the door? Time had passed, Ava told herself. Time had passed.

"There's a war on, I'm afraid," Robert said at dinner that night. Ava listened with a growing calmness to her brother talk about these matters with respect, for he paid attention to what was happening in the world around them. All she cared about was her work, and, recently, her pleasure. "The army needs fuel and our company supplies it," he went on. "My job is to find it and pump it out of the ground."

And his little Margaret would help him pump it! Oh, my, Ava felt her heart give a little leap.

"What's that odd look on your face, Sis?" Robert asked.

"I'm worried about your heart," she said.

Robert pursed his lips, seemed about to make a further pronouncement on the war, then thought better of it. "It's been years since I've had any trouble. The doctors tell me to live a normal life. Within reason."

"Does . . . *she* know?"

Her brother looked at her, a strange flash of inquisitiveness and slight annoyance traveling across his face. "Yes, she does."

Ava felt that pain again in her own chest, and touched hands to her bosom, hoping to press in more breath. "Will it be a quiet wedding?" Ava spoke in a voice scarcely more than a whisper.

"Ava, I don't know. Margaret has no family to speak of; it could . . . "

"Make it a quiet affair," she said. "Write me a letter about it."

"Ava," Robert said, reaching for her hand. "Ava, Ava . . . "

But she drew back from the table, glancing over her shoulder at what she took to be a familiar presence entering the restaurant. But it was no one. "I need to work," she said.

"I know you do. And you do fine work, Sis. Fine work."

"No," she said. "I need to work now. Always."

Snow followed her train south for half a day and then turned to rain. The next morning she awoke to bright sun, glowing prairie land. *Tex-as, Tex-as, Tex-as,* the clacking train wheels announced to her. And she was back in her real life with a problem as big as the horizon.

"Hey, Ava!" her problem called to her through the door the day after she returned. "Open up!"

"Hello, Billy," she said as she let him in. "How did you know that I was here?"

"We know everything in Canyon," he said, shuffling past her and throwing himself down on the little sofa. "I was real lonely for you, you know." He looked up at her with great big cow's eyes — and it repulsed her and she turned away, looking instead out at the flat land beyond the window.

"Did you . . . do that work I asked you to do?" she asked. There had been some assignments he'd had to finish in order to complete the semester's work, at which he'd been awfully laggard since the two of them had begun their liaison.

"You know, Ava," he said, reaching down and pulling off his boots, "all I did was drink with my pals." Those eyes — not cow's eyes but sheep's!

"That's not the best way to use your time," she said.

"Use my time?" He swung an arm through the air as though he might fling himself all the way to where she stood. "I just was missing you so much I didn't want to do anything else."

"Well . . . we all have to get back to our work now," she said.

"What does that mean?"

"Just what I said, Billy. I have work, you have work. We have to get back to it."

"I didn't tell you to take a week out and go up to Chicago," he said. "You could have stayed here in Canyon and done your drawings, paintings, whatever you're doing."

"My watercolors," she said. They were watercolors of the evening star, one after another after another, but she didn't want to say anything more about them to Billy. It didn't seem as though anything of that belonged to anything about him.

"I don't know about me and art," Billy said.

"What don't you know?"

"Oh, I been thinking. I know I'm pretty good at it, but being here over Christmas made me think about how good it is, and I don't know if I could go anywhere else and try to do something as an artist."

"You're a talented boy, Billy. It would be a waste if you didn't."

"Well, I was talking to my daddy . . . "

"Yes?" Something about that remark made Ava's heart give a little leap.

"He says he doesn't know why I couldn't just stay here and do both things. Work and draw."

"Of course you could," Ava said.

"I could settle down right here where my home is. I don't need to roam all around the country. My people are here."

"You're a lucky boy."

"Man. Lucky man," he said. "I'm a man. You know that."

"I was just being . . . affectionate, Billy."

"Well, I like that," he said, turning slightly on the sofa as though he were about to rise. "I like that a lot." He suddenly lurched to his feet and came to her. "A lot."

"I'm awfully tired from my trip, Billy," Ava said, pulling free of his arms.

"But I missed you," he said in his little boy's voice, coming close again. There was no getting out of a number of his hard kisses. "When are you going to draw me?" he said. "The way you look at me, I can tell that you want to draw me."

"Did I say that?" Ava took a deep breath and settled back in a chair. "All right. Get undressed." Billy followed obediently, and after an hour or so, Ava had had enough of looking at him. It was amazing to her that the same body that she had found so attractive now made her nearly nauseated. Pleading illness, she asked him to get dressed and leave. He took his time, now and then reaching for her and giving her sullen looks when she stepped back from him. After he left, she drew water and heated it on the stove and made herself a bath, which she sat in until the water was cold. Then she went to work, staying up most of the night with another version of the evening star. She had to go to the grocery the next day, and the trip made her quite irritable even though it was only a short walk. The man in the apron behind the counter, several customers, too, stared at her, and she worried that she must look a fright from lack of sleep. Well, then, the devil with them! she told herself and went about her business. She knew she was a strange one anyway by their lights, a woman living alone, an artist, a teacher at the college.

Still, the looks they gave her! Particularly one woman standing at the counter, who was staring and staring. And then Ava recognized her, the mother of her student, who had brought her the cake. "Hello," Ava said, wishing that she could remember her name.

The woman lowered her eyes.

I must not have given her daughter the praise she wanted, Ava thought to herself. At the moment she couldn't even remember the girl's face, let alone her name or her work. But it would be good to say something pleasant. Ava, in spite of herself, didn't want to be known as someone without the capacity for pleasantries. But when she was about to speak to the woman, she had already turned away, gathered up her purchases and left the store.

She had made few friends at the college. A single woman living alone was considered something of a menace. Ava was never invited to any of the social events she knew other members of the faculty conducted: the dinners, the card games (not that she would have enjoyed cards). But there must have been something about the way she carried herself, because fellow teachers who never said a word to her beyond a greeting stopped her in the hall to inquire if she had had a good holiday—and had she been ill?

After another week of this, when she had overslept—something she had never done before in her life—and missed a class, she began to think of herself as ill.

Her illness was Billy. "I still don't feel well," she said to him through the door on the night when she came to this conclusion. There was a cold wind blowing, nearly all the way down from Nebraska was the way it felt to her when she had come home that afternoon from the college. She built a fire and was staring into the flames when his knock sounded.

"I'll help you," he said. "I'll take care of you, Ava."

"I feel awful," she said, opening the door a crack. "I just want to be alone." Her heart pounded. She felt as though she were an animal trapped at the end of a long chase. But through the opening in the door she could see his eyes, and he appeared to be the one who was wild. "You let me in, Ava," he said.

"Go home, Billy. I'll see you tomorrow. I'll feel better tomorrow."

He moved back from the door and she closed it. A moment later he knocked again and they spoke once more. Then he was quiet. A few minutes later he knocked again and called to her.

"Billy, go home."

"Aw, Ava," came his voice from just on the other side of the door.

"Go."

No answer. She sat in a chair that she had made her favorite since moving into this little house when she arrived in town. She read a while, then dozed. She awoke to a tapping at the door and Billy's high-pitched whining. "A-va!"

She didn't respond.

He moaned and tapped a while, then stopped. She could hear the footsteps as he walked away from the house, and then, again, louder, as he came up to the shaded window to knock.

"Go away!" she said in as loud a voice as she could muster.

Silence. She sat back and closed her eyes. When she opened them again, it was dawn.

All that day she braced herself each time she heard someone come to the door of her classroom. But Billy did not appear. As she walked home that afternoon, she found herself looking back over her shoulder at nearly every step. But no Billy. A letter had come from New York with An American Place as the return address. She quickly opened it and found herself holding a check for several hundred dollars.

I've sold all your old drawings, I'm out of hurricanes. Send me more hurricanes! old Stigmar wrote. *Though I don't suppose that you've seen many in Texas.* She could hear that almost sneering New York voice saying *Texas* in that special way she had noticed in her fleeting visit with him at his gallery.

Well, she decided, I'll send him dog's body, I'll send him fossil feathers, I'll send him arrowheads, I'll send him the entire barranca! She tried to clear her head of all this business with Billy, thinking perhaps that she might get down to work right now and put together a sheaf of drawings for Stigmar along with some of the watercolors she had been working on. But then came a knock at the door.

I know what I'm doing with my work, she wrote to Harriet the next day. *It's my life that's in a shambles.* She then proceeded to tell her friend what had happened and asked for her advice. Before she had a reply from Charleston, Ava came up with a plan of her own. Billy visited her almost every night. The few exceptions were evenings when he could not escape the company of his mother and father. Her thought—and it was nearly mad, she knew—was to invite the family over with him in the hope that it might defuse this crazy passion that he had developed for her. One night as he was dressing—and she lay in her bed beneath the coverlet like some old wife of many years—she made the suggestion.

"Why, Ava," he said, his face lighting up with the biggest smile she'd ever seen, "that's a mighty good idea!"

So she knew she had made a mistake, but she didn't know how, until the actual event itself.

Billy's father was a shopkeeper who, from everything his son had said about him, didn't care one whit for drawing and painting. He tolerated it merely because Billy kept up his other schoolwork. His mother, a good, church-going woman, who was never seen in the store except when she was dressed up as though she were a rancher's wife in to shop for the month, was more sympathetic to her son's artistic side, but she wasn't about to disagree with her husband when he suggested that his son would have to do something more practical with his life after college than waste his days away with charcoal and paper.

"But if they get to meet you and you talk to them, Ava," Billy said, "they'll understand a whole lot better what it's like." He came back to the bed and sat down next to her, touching her on the face.

It was a cold touch—his hands were always cold—and it wasn't unusual that it made her shiver. Gooseflesh rippled up and down her arms. She sighed, and wondered to herself what had happened to her that she had let herself come to such a pass. It was like nothing she had ever known before, though, true, she had not known anyone in any way such as this, except for her few fleeting moments with Helen. She dreaded the boy's presence, and at the same time she yearned for it. Even as she lay here plotting the end of it, she wanted him to crawl back beneath the blankets and rough her again. "Roughing" was what she called it to herself, though neither of them had put a name to it out loud.

"So you'll invite them?" she asked.

"I sure will." And he leaned over and kissed her on the mouth, the kind of kiss she both despised and longed for on the nights of his visits. He was a rude and rough creature with a talent for drawing, and just as innocent as she was when it came to what happened here in this bed. Ava could have had no more idea about what he was planning for the visit with his parents than she at first had had about what was going to take place between them. So for a week or so she lived a life more calm than at anytime since her arrival here. Her classes went well. And Billy actually gave her a few nights' rest, staying at home with his mother and father almost as if he had to prepare them for the evening together they had planned.

And then came this evening in late winter when the wind blowing down the plains made her think that the season and its bitterness might stay hovering over her forever. But the light had called to her, and she had taken this walk, hoping to use what little time she had left before the arrival of her guests to figure something out about her life. But there was nothing, except the vision of the fading day, and darker, older memories that deepened further the passion of her particular distress. At the edge of the barranca Ava tried to gather the strength to throw herself down into it as though she were a dead dog. And then she thought of the fossils there—feather, arrowhead, knife point, bone—and of her drawings. Even as the darkness fell suddenly upon the plain like a hammer, she felt something lifting inside herself, and she turned and found her way home.

Voices outside alerted her to the arrival of Billy's parents. She ran into the bedroom and took one last look at herself in the mirror. Her face seemed to be tinted as red as her hair! No hurricanes in Texas? Oh, Mister Stigmar, how wrong you turned out to be!

Her guests appeared, Billy's mother dressed as though for church, and his father for a businessman's convention. Billy himself wore a fresh shirt—and a fresh grin. Ava's heart sank. Whatever plan she had had in mind slipped from her grasp. She went into a panic, serving little crackers and tea with trembling hands, while the two stolid Texans stared about the room at her drawings. "I like that feather there," Billy's father said. "Is that a—just what kind of animal is that in the other one, the one with the bones?"

Ava fought off the impulse to offer silence as an explanation, telling them about the finds in the barranca and watching their faces as she talked, realizing that a woman out in the barranca drawing with charcoal was as foreign to them as a female physician.

"Isn't it dangerous out there?" asked Billy's mother.

"It sure is," her husband put in before Ava could reply.

"I been out there with Ava a lot of times," Billy said. "Watching out for her."

Both parents turned to stare at him, and Ava was pleased to see that they understood his position here tonight, which was the schoolboy who should remain silent in the presence of his family and his teacher unless they gave him permission to speak. "Billy has been making excellent progress," Ava took the opportunity to say.

"I've seen," his father said. "He drew those bones like yours."

"And the feather," said his mother.

"Not as good as yours," his father said.

"*Almost* as good," said his mother.

"Folks," Billy said.

"What is it, son?" His father gave him a look of such disdain that for a moment Ava began to feel sorry for the boy.

"I have something to say."

"We're talking, boy," his father said.

"I want to say something," Billy said.

"What is it, darling?" his mother said.

His father looked at Ava now, as if to inform her that there would be a slight pause while his idiot son said his piece. "Speak up then."

"Mother and Father," he said, then paused and swallowed, making a click in the back of his throat that Ava could hear all the way across the room. He was a good-looking boy, she was thinking; she should sketch him again before it was over—though she was sure it would be over from this evening on. Of course it would be scandalous if they were found out. A hundred Mrs. Halmes lived here, and that could be the end of her, the end of her employment at the college. Though if they only knew the truth, she was saying to herself. If they only knew.

At which point Billy stood up. "Mother," he said. "Father. Ava and I are in love."

The end of the semester came all too slowly, but it did finally arrive. Ava had packed several times over, sending most of her things on ahead to Nebraska—she was fortunate enough to have a home to return to, if one that she had not lived in for a while—and, on a whim, packing off a number of the barranca drawings and shipping those to Stigmar in New York. Without the prospect of employment for next year, anything that he might get her for her drawings would be welcome. And the hurricane series had sold for over a hundred dollars apiece, so perhaps these might do as well. Who could say?

Everything had come undone since that night when Billy's parents had stormed out of her little house and headed back to town. Within a day the dean of the college had called her in and told her that her contract would be terminated as of the end of the semester.

Terminated! The word chilled her heart. She walked home as though to her own funeral and went inside the house and stayed there for several days without eating or bathing or sleeping. They had killed her—Billy's parents, Billy himself—had killed her dead!

All for the sake of . . . what?

She lay on her bed, fully clothed, quietly sobbing, even after she believed she had no tears left inside her.

For the sake of company in this lonely desert! on this barren plain!

She opened her eyes and found herself looking directly up at one of her evening stars. Seeing it there on the wall, she could feel the wind on her face when she drew it, she could taste air the flavor of dust and saguaro, she could hear behind the sound of her charcoal moving on the paper, below the faint awareness of her own breathing, the music of wild dogs yipping in the distance, she could see the fading cadence of the light.

DOOR

Baby's asleep . . .

Reading and writing my way through Ava's life has left me little time for my own, though it makes me think a lot about it.

Her friendship with Harriet Cardozo – I have no one in my life like that, no one at all. Friends from school have faded away. And Socorro, who works here for Ava, is private and keeps to herself – and my Spanish is not very good, though I'm picking up a few new words every day.

My only friend is Michael – and he spends most of his time with Ava: working, walking. Those hurricane sketches – she tells me that the museums have most of them, but that she has seen one or two over the years. Michael looked for them but couldn't find any.

But now: "This is weird," he says as he comes in the door holding a photograph. "Look."

A pyramid, a camel and driver before it. His father's work? Ava mentioned something about a trip to Egypt he had taken before she moved to New York.

I want to talk about all this, whatever it is, but he waves it at me for a moment, and then ducks back out the door. I see him hurrying across the patio to the barn . . . Socorro comes in from town.

My Spanish – and her English – is very childlike. "Take a walk?" I say to her.

She cocks her head at me, then nods vigorously.

"Is the niño?" she says as we leave the house.

"Is the niño what, Socorro?"

"Niño," she says, with a broad smile on her face.

I shrug, almost give up speech. But then I try. "Do you have children? Niños?"

She nods again. "Cinco," she says, holding up all the fingers on one hand.

"Five."

"Sí. Fife."

"And you took care of your mother, too," I say. "Ava said that you brought your mother to town to live with you."

She shakes her head.

"Madre," I say.

"My mother dead," she says.

We're standing outside the house in a steady wind blowing along the arroyo. Sand whirls around our ankles. Winter gets so cold here, stinging the body and the spirit.

"*Ava* is like our mother," I say, surprising myself. I don't know where it has come from, but it arrives.

"Ava, la madre?" Socorro laughs.

"You don't think so? Ava, no madre?"

The brown-faced woman holds out her arms to me. "Madre, hermana, niña . . . todo . . . "

My baby's asleep, my husband's in the barn helping a near-blind woman make pottery, and I am sitting here with a stack of notebooks and loose pages in front of me on the old pine desk, surrounded by animal bones, rocks, feathers, photographs of sky-scrapers and clouds, paintings of canyons and rock faces, or should I say rocks' face, rock face?—and I am trying to find the words to put some order in the work on the table and the walls, in the barn, and in the museums and houses around the country.

My English sometimes seems to me not much more mature than my Spanish. My words cannot bring the work to anyone's heart. That must come from the seeing of it. I can only point a finger in that direction. Look at that over there, I can say. See how it gathers in the light and shapes itself to a form almost musical. An old music. Antique rhythm. Beat of myth, Stanley might say.

See!

I can't see for you, but I can try to order the feelings that grow out of a viewing of the work, the body of the work, the work that has emerged from the body of this woman's life.

Now a life in a cricket body. My cricket heroine. She has shrunk and shriveled, to the point where I wonder sometimes how it can be the same person who has done the work I see and lived the life I try to picture.

Yet she is one and the same. And once her life flowed out like light, filling all the spaces around her with its brilliance and its heat, and like water, with its all-encompassing fluid.

HOME

Ava

Every cloudless morning feels like a holiday. I awaken and blink and wash and dress, hurry downstairs as if to a birthday party or the moving pictures. Dora greets me from the stove. Despite her terribly infirm legs she manages each day to cook my eggs. In the morning light her cloud-white hair glows like a halo or a crown. "Out again today?" she asks.

"Out again," I say.

"It's a good thing I taught you to draw, dear," she says. "What else would you do with your days otherwise?" She hobbles over and hands me my plate.

"I haven't the slightest idea," I say, attacking my eggs. "May I have the salt, Mother?" Odd how I can call her that now that I'm grown, but her white hair and twisted body elicit all my deepest feelings for her. I love this woman, I love her truly. I just wish that I didn't feel like such a prisoner in this old house.

"I imagined you might have to find something else to do now that the cold weather has set in."

"It's not the cold that bothers me, Mother," I say. "It's the clouds. They kill the best light."

"You could draw them," she says.

"And the snow?"

"Not a bad idea, Ava. You know what I'm saying."

"I know what you're saying. I just don't . . . Oh . . . " I pull my chair around so that I can reach up and embrace her. "Sit," I say.

But I can't stay. Within moments I'm up from the table and out the door, pack in hand. As long as the weather holds, I'll be all right here, I tell myself. As long as the weather holds . . .

DOOR

Of all the material that I've found about Ava's early life, these pages are to me the most depressing.

"Don't use that word," Michael says. "Say 'painful' or 'tortured' or something else. But *depressing*? That's not a word in my vocabulary. It suggests an immature view of real pain."

"Sorry," I say to him. "Excuse me." I can't help but leave the room and go off to cry in another corner of the house.

"Look," he says when he catches up with me, "I didn't mean to get you so upset."

"If I want to say a word, I can say it. If I want to say Ava's life at that time was *depressing*, I can say it. If I want to.. ."

He takes me by the arms and holds me by my back to his chest. "So what was so *depressing* about it?"

"She went back to Nebraska and lived with her stepmother for nearly three years and didn't do much work at all during that time. I think she had something like a nervous breakdown."

Michael makes a low purring sound. "I doubt it. Ava just doesn't seem like the nervous-breakdown type."

"You don't know everything about her," I say. "In fact, you know a lot less than I do. You should read what I've been reading."

He presses himself hard against me, and I know he is smiling, the bastard, even though I can't turn around to see. "I don't have to read to know about her. I do things with her. I'm helping her do her work."

"Yeah, you're the doer in the family, aren't you?" The anger surprises me; it soars up quickly in my voice. "You're the working artist. And I'm just the one who gave birth to your child and who keeps . . . "

143

"We have a housekeeper, for Christ's sake!"

"You could use a more kindly tone with me, you know. Besides, Socorro isn't a nanny."

"She could watch him now and then. It wouldn't be a crime."

"Robby is not her responsibility."

I break away from him and return to my little study where I spend the next few hours—Michael apparently, just as I figured, goes back out to the barn, having given up on soothing me—leafing through the notebook pages that tell of Ava's deepening unhappiness in the house where she grew up.

When the weather turned dark, she grew darker, feeling a little better the next spring and summer, but fearing the worst for the coming winter. Now and then a note from Stigmar. And then dark again. Time. Three years in a few pages of her journal. It's as if she were trying to disappear, writing less and less about working less and less, with an occasional comment about Dora's failing health. And then on top of all this other misery, an influenza epidemic carried Dora away, and Ava was left in the house, alone.

Her brother arrives for the funeral. He's left Margaret, now his wife, behind in Chicago, fearing, he says in a letter, that her presence may upset an already-agitated Ava. They bury Dora in the same little prairie graveyard where their parents lie buried. A light snow falls. Robert reaches for his sister's hand, but she brushes him aside. There's something happening to her that she finds both fascinating and terrifying: the realization that she is now a complete orphan. One snowflake, two, three, four, five—she concentrates on the shapes of the snowflakes; she'll count millions rather than pay attention to the ceremony going on before her.

Robert helps her go through Dora's papers. "Will you stay on here?" he asks.

She nods, not knowing what else to do.

"What about this?" he says, holding up a letter from Stigmar that he has found lying on the dining room table. He couldn't help but glance at the contents.

"I don't have anything new to send him," she says.

Robert returns to Chicago. Ava sits alone in the dark front room of the house in town. It is late January—oh, what a deep, dark endlessness of desperate emptiness on the prairie! Ava has not

144

changed her clothes since her brother departed. She dozes off upright in her chair. She awakens and presses her fingers to her lidded eyes, and pinpoints of light dance before her, the only brightness she has seen for hours. Her breathing slows. Using her feet to guide her, she turns the chair. Then turns it again. And again. For hours she goes around in this circle in the dark room while outside a wind howls, then dies.

Near morning. She must have slept again. She starts upright, opens her eyes to see a pale patch of dawn illuminating the outline of the window. She shuts her eyes again. She is nearly thirty years old, without family except for her brother, without husband or child, without a way of earning money. But for life, she would be dead. She could be dead. Who would miss her?

She turns in the chair again. Her stomach rumbles, most unlady-like. She turns in the chair again.

Outside the wind picks up, despite the dawn. It moans, sinks to a whisper, then moans—and delivers a word to her, and the word that it brings is . . . hats!

Hats!

That's it, that's it, that's it, she tells herself. That is my destiny. I will go to New York and draw hats!

MANHATTAN

Ava

May 1, 1919
New York, New York

Dear Robert,

Yes, I know, this is one of my most infrequent letters and you are
probably quite surprised to receive it. Usually I keep my thoughts in my
notebook, but this time I could not help but respond to your last letter. I
am happy that you have come back to this country, that the Mexico project
has been successful — and pleased that it has not affected your heart! Which
was something I feared. And I am happy to hear that Margaret has made
a good home for you. It is so important, to feel at home, a sensation that
I talk about sometimes with friends, with some of The Boys here, as I call
them, the group of painters and sculptors who have used Stig's gallery as
a gathering place and who never had the idea that they might respect a
woman's work enough to take it for granted that she could be one of
them.

But things happened before that. They began to fall into place from
the moment that I arrived here from Nebraska. Oh, the way life is, all
full of irregular edges, and time all jagged, sometimes smooth, occasion-
ally moving with the velocity of a train!

I'd been here only once before with my friend Harriet for a brief
visit. From the moment I stepped off the train, I felt as though I were
caught up in the middle of a human storm, all these people moving and
milling about and shouting and rushing here and there! You know there
is all that talk always in Chicago about what a bustling city it is, but
compared to New York it sleeps, it sleepwalks.

I gave the taxi driver Stigmar's address—where else could I go? I knew nowhere else!—and the cab bumped and swerved around the pedestrians and the driver honked his horn and the engine roared. I had one small bag with me and another that I had shipped from home. But how, in any case, do you pack a destiny?

Consider my timing. I had not written ahead. Just as I was coming up the stairs of An American Place, the white-haired man with the pince-nez and the white beard was coming down. "I know you!" he said and stopped just a few steps above me. "Come to lunch!"

I shouldered my bag and went along. Lunch led to dinner, and dinner opened into the New York night of starry spires and siren calls, pistol shots and yowling cats, a night you cannot know anywhere else in our land. From that time on Stig and I became as one person, a chimerical many-sided creature both young and old, smooth skinned and hirsute, innocent and wise, gentile and Jew, female and male, western and eastern, New World and Old—all the opposites we could make, we made, and yet we joined together to make sparks fly in the Manhattan firmament.

Stig wouldn't hear of me taking a position as a sketch artist. "No more," he said. "No more of that. It's time that you put aside these worldly things and give us what you can do the best."

He offered me studio space and a separate bed to lie on. Odd—how I, who have never lived with anyone before except you and Dora, and Mrs. Finchey in Chicago, could so easily settle into this new regime. But I love it! We can work together through the day. Now and then Stig sticks his head around the partition, and it thrills me to see the sly little smile bloom on his weathered lips.

"Here," he said one day, and I turned and looked directly into the lens of his camera set on a tripod just inside the room. I'd watched him work, but he had never turned his eye on me before. "You're a sneak," I said.

"Smile for the camera," he said. I could see in him the young man who had once set up shop in his father's department store. So cute! old now and so cute! No wonder his first wife, a merchant's daughter, found him so appealing.

In this space new work is beginning to come to me. I stare out my window at towers of steel and concrete, glass and air—ah, yes, the air around the buildings seems as much a part of them as they are part of the air—and now and then I notice that my wrists are turning, and I am moving a charcoal stick and then a brush, with oils and color, while all the while from his side of the room, my dear old Stig hums such ditties as Daisy, Daisy, give me your answer true . . . I don't sing back—it is not my way—but he knows, he knows that I am there.

And at the end of a day's work, we go out or friends come in, people such as Anderson, a writer, and a painter named Hartley, and other bohemians who frequent this part of town, some of them men of genius, some of them sad facsimiles of the true ones, but persevering nevertheless. These are The Boys, as I've named them, and the name has stuck so well that now they refer to themselves in the same way.

"Well, The Boys are coming over tonight," Stig says to me.

And a shout up the stairwell: "Hey, us Boys are here!"

"Hello, Boys," I say to whomever comes in the door. Smooth-shaven faces, bewhiskered cheeks, eyes glowing from a good day's work or yearning for sleep that hasn't come for days, or sparkling from whiskey or cocaine, smelling of beer and oils and garlic and hair tonic and cologne and must and work—these Boys, they must be Boys.

Some of them flirt wildly with me. Anderson, or "Jobby" as we call him, is the worst of these, or the best. He had his eye on me from the moment I walked into the studio, and he has watched me like a fox ever since. All that flab in his jaws! You'd never know that he writes such plainly beautiful sentences when he wants to. I like him, you understand; I love his work, but the thought of kissing that face, all soft appearing like a child's behind, just gives me the shivers! Doesn't a man know what effect he has on the girls?

Stig notices. He becomes very jealous, or at least plays at it. "Did I see that stag wink at you?" he said one night after Anderson came over for dinner.

"I believe that he had one of my paintings stuck in his eye, Stig," I said.

We were washing dishes together at the small sink in his darkroom—for a man who grew up being waited on by a grand old mother and a number of servants, he does pitch in!

"One of the towers?" he asked.

"A sharp tower," I said, splashing suds around my wrists.

"I love the towers you're painting," he said, turning to squint at me. "I love the buildings; I love your painting."

It was then I heard myself say for the first time in my life to someone other than family—pathetic, I know, but true: "I love you, Albert Stigmar."

And he said the same back to me. He says it quite often.

He is over fifty, but his behavior is more than youthful, sometimes utterly childlike. We'll be standing on the street, waiting for a taxi, and he'll swing around and take me in his arms as fathers sometimes do little girls.

Or we'll be carousing with The Boys over a hand of poker, and he'll suddenly slap down his cards, push back his chair, and stand and announce his love for me.

"Whoo-eee! Whoopeee! Whoopeee!" The Boys will cry.

One night at the movies, while Chaplin did his duck walk across the screen, he grabbed me. "Help!" I said. "Usher!"

"Usher in my love," said Stig to the young man who came running.

Or: walking along Fifth Avenue, past the old buildings where he spent his childhood, in his topcoat and with his cane dangling at his side, he suddenly swung about and grabbed me, stopping pedestrian traffic and even causing a few autos to honk their horns, and shouted, "I love this woman, damn it all!" at the top of his lungs. "Do you know who she is! She's a great artist—and she is the woman I love!"

I thought I had presence; I thought I didn't care. People turned to stare, and I could feel my embarrassment rising up from my toes on the pavement to the top of my head.

And then we were at home, doing the dishes again after an evening with The Boys and their girlfriends, and he looked over at me and made his eyes gleam. "You love me?"

"Yes," I said in a whisper.

Quickly he dashed about the room like a demon, drying his hands on his shirt as he reached here, there, switching on bright lights, snatching up a camera, settling, focusing, snapping the picture. There I was! Here I am in this copy I am enclosing with this letter. A woman in love! Only you have seen this, Robert. Stig immediately wanted to mount it on the wall of the gallery.

"I'm ready, are you?" Stig spoke to me in this odd way the very next morning when he came into the room where I slept.

149

"Ready? Yes, I'm ready," I said. "As always, I'm ready for work."

"Yes, that," he said. "Of course. I'm with you there, my pigeon."

"Pigeon?" I said.

"My dove," he said.

"Your dove?" I said.

"Mon petite choufleur," he said.

"Your what?" I said.

"Listen," he said. "I'm ready."

I got the shivers, I understood; it came all trembling upon me, it was like a fever, it was a big wind out of the northwest corner of Nebraska; I was lying down, but it picked me up and knocked me down flat, pressed me to the bed, to the floor, to the ground, through the ground. Oh, brother, everything has changed for me!

"Hear you're getting married," Anderson said to me one night at a party soon thereafter.

I felt my hands twitch at my sides, as though I had just been shocked. "Yes," I nodded. "And you're invited."

"Figured it," he said, his mouth turning down as he spoke. "Suppose that means it's . . . "

"It's what, Jobby?" I asked.

"Oh, you know," he said, shuffling back from me, staring around the room.

"Stig wants you as best man, I believe."

"He asked me," he said.

"The best," I said.

"The best," he said. "Yes."

"Yes," I said.

"Oh," he made a little moan. "I've never even . . . kissed you."

"No, you haven't," I said. "And that's the way it's going to remain."

"I'm going to die without ever having kissed you," he said, making that hound dog look with his jowly jaws and big midwestern eyes of guile.

"I think that you can count on that, Jobby."

I was talking at the party later that evening to Ramona, the red-haired opera singer who lives with Harry, one of The Boys. He's a painter who always seems to be quite unhappy, except that he lives with this red-haired Amazon with an Amazonian voice and chest. "That Jobby," she said to me. "He's always staring at my balcony."

150

"You—oh, yes," I said.

"And he asked me to go away with him to South America."

"Did he? When?"

"He wants me to go tomorrow."

"I didn't know he had plans."

"Well, not with me, he doesn't, sister. Do you know what he said? He said, 'I'm going to die without ever having kissed you, and that thought will hasten my death.' "

"And what did you say?"

"I told him, 'I'm going to tell Harry and he'll punch your lights out.' "

She took in a deep breath, and her chest moved in massive response. "So, hey," she said. "I hear you two children are going to tie the knot."

"Yes," I said. "Yes."

"So when is it?"

"I'm not . . . sure," I said. I touched my throat. I could feel the very knot tightening around it.

"Well, I sure like Stig, you know," said the redhead.

"I do, too," I said.

She made a little giggle. "Well, that's nice. He's a little old—no offense, I mean—but he's a spry gent, he is, spry."

"Very spry," I said.

"My Harry loves his photographs. He says it's the hardest thing, to make photographs into art."

"I think he's a genius," I said.

"My Harry says that about you, you know." She leaned close and that very chest flowed against my shoulder as she spoke in girlish intimacy. "He gets real jealous, you know."

"Why should he?" I said. "You never flirt. If it's Jobby, well, everybody knows that . . . "

"No, no, no, no," she said, pressing even closer against me and breathing sweet candy breath mixed with whiskey as she spoke. "He gets real jealous of you, I mean."

She shifted her stance, pulling back from me, and now standing with one hand on her hip. She had a little tummy, and, Robert, all I could think was I'd love to paint it. You know how I am.

151

It was a sunny day, it was a rainy day, a cloudy day, a day so clear that you could see every building on the other side of the river; it was a cheerful day, a day for mourning, a dark day, a day filled with glorious light, a day for singing, a day for keening, a day for looking, a day that made you want to shut your eyes . . .

The first thing I noticed about it that made it different from all others that Stig and I had lived together was that I awoke to hear him speaking into the telephone. "Yes, Mother," he was saying. And, "No, Mother." And, "Just as soon as we can, Mother."

"You never speak to anyone before breakfast," I said. "Except me," I added when he gently replaced the receiver on the hook.

"Today's a holiday, my dove," he said, stretching to touch my cheek with his rough finger.

"What did your mother say?" I asked.

"She's going to meet us at the restaurant."

"Not at the ceremony?"

Stig shook his head, and I had never seen him appear more puzzled than at that moment, as though he actually had become a little boy again in the wake of the conversation with his mother, and was confused to find himself trapped inside such an old body. "No, no. Father will meet us outside with the car, though he's not coming in, either. Strange, very strange. They've never practiced any religion, but here we're going to have a ceremony that's neutral, just our vows and a few poems and such, and you'd think we'd turned to idol worship." He made an odd sound with his teeth. "Alas, she's become quite ancient." He held up a hand before his face. "Consider me, for example. I'm no spring chicken, and she is the bitch that whelped me." He laughed a good hard haw! "If a bitch can give birth to a chicken."

"Now, now," I said, feeling suddenly on the defensive for the woman he referred to, even though she was his mother. "I'm an orphan now, so I do appreciate a mother who stays around a while."

"Even Emeralda Stigmar?"

I had only met her once, and it had not been pleasant. She had been a beautiful woman whom age had treated unkindly, and she was not pleased. "Even your mother."

"That's a bully thing to say. If I were not about to marry you, I would ask you to marry me after that remark." With a smile on his usually dour visage, he came over and sat next to me on the bed. "Allow me to bring you some breakfast."

"And how would you know how to do that?" I asked.

"I've observed some very efficient women over the years. Maids and such."

"Not that your mother ever cooked," I said.

"She does know how but pretends not to," Stig said. "I recall a meal or two that she made, when the cook had the night off for a wedding or a funeral."

"Perhaps it was your father who cooked," I said.

Stig laughed so hard it shook the bed. "Not bloody likely, that. He's a true nineteenth-century man." He patted the bed. "Come hither, first, young maiden."

I shook my head. "I'm going to get up and work a bit," I said.

I could hear the breath he took in. "On your wedding day?"

"It's my wedding day," I said. "And I can work on it if I care to."

"Ava, Ava, darling," he said, trying to take me in his arms. "You needn't be so nervous. We're both adults, though I have certainly been here longer than you."

"Stig," I said, pulling away from him. "Don't joke about this. I have something in mind. I want to work."

"And so you will," he said. "For a little while."

"Don't sound as though you're giving me permission, please."

"Never me, that," he said. "Never me."

And so I got up and washed and dressed and went into the studio. I scratched at things, and tore things up. It was a sorry performance. I was in a foul mood when it was time to go to the ceremony, and my state of mind was not altered by the rather crude noises made by some of The Boys when they saw me come down the stairs to the car.

"Never seen you so lovely," Harry said. "Oh, Ava, you've won on all counts." He came forward as though to kiss me, until his red-haired Ramona stepped between us. "Harry," she said, "save that for the wedding." With a quick show of teeth, she led him toward the avenue.

Oh, Ramona, keep a good eye on your sweetie!

We went downtown and a baldheaded little judge performed a civil ceremony. And when I left the building on Stig's arm, though he was there to support me, I felt nevertheless that someone had just cut off both my legs.

Your loving sister,

Ava

DOOR

"I *was* a bit stunned by the swiftness of it all," Ava says to me in that voice of hers, so quiet now that you must lean forward and concentrate so that you catch it. She raises a cup to her thin, dry lips—such a steady hand, I say to myself—and squints at me in the fading light of afternoon. Michael works on firing some pots out in the barn—the new kiln takes up a great deal of his time these days. "The way it happened . . . so unexpectedly . . ."

Robby, playing on the rug between us, makes a squeaky noise, and I look down to see him chewing on some foreign object. I swoop down on him and extract a piece of bone—a flat shard too large for him to try and swallow, thank God—from his tiny lips. His little hand moves with the deftness of a bee darting from flower to flower, but he can't snatch the bone back from me.

There are some things I want to say to Ava, things that I could never ask anyone else, I believe, things that I certainly could never say to anyone like my own mother.

Will it ever happen to me? I want to ask. What do you think, Ava? Does Michael say anything to you about it while you're working? And why, why should I care about it? Why should it haunt me in those peculiar empty moments when I don't have your life on my mind, or Robby's welfare, or the contemplation of some new piece that you and Michael have produced? If he doesn't want it, I don't, and yet . . .

LENS

Albert Stigmar

"Look!" my father said to me, giving me a poke on the shoulder that day in midautumn when he had taken me by the hand and led me around the lake for a little country stroll. It was the smell of his cigar mingling with the odor of the dying leaves that I remember so sharply, and the sound of his teeth clacking together in exasperation when I didn't respond.

"Up there, boy!" He stuck his cigar between his teeth and took my head in his hands, as though it were a block of wood to be adjusted, and tilted my vision upward. I saw only the usual flood of blue and white, all blurred and liquid like the yoke of a broken egg.

"Those geese, damn it!" he said, giving me another hard poke on the arm. "They're flying south!" I began to cry. I was just a little tyke—and I hadn't known until then that I couldn't see at a distance worth a damn.

It was one of our last visits of the season to the country house. In the city the next week, my mother had me fitted with a pair of spectacles, and I haven't been without a pair since. In fact, as I write down these notes for you, my dear new friend, I am wearing my new reading specs. The eyes, the heart, the knees! They all begin to wear just ever so slightly when you reach the ripe old age of fifty as I have just done . . .

Yet I can still see—as clearly as if I were still standing at the edge of the lake—the trees on the opposite shore the first time I stared out at them wearing my new spectacles. It was the next spring, late spring, and I ran to the water's edge early on the first morning after our arrival—it was like a visit to a foreign country, seeing the places where I had been visiting my first six years of life as if with new eyes!

And above us the clouds sailed past, eastward in procession toward the Green Mountains. My father patted me on the head and chanted, "You see, you see . . . " He wasn't looking at the lakeside treescape; he was looking inward, saying to himself, You see how you have helped your boy!

He had helped himself enormously, too, making a fortune in uniforms during the Civil War and using this to found a chain of fine department stores in Manhattan and upstate. I knew nothing of that. To my young mind, the house, the lake, the trees, the sky and clouds—now that I could see them sharply in all their stately, fluid flight—all this seemed to be part of one thing; not anything sought after and gained by my successful father, but part of All: Nature, One Thing, Life, the World. I knew that there were others who had no money or very little, for they worked for us as servants, yet I thought of them as part of us, as limbs belong to the boles of great trees. I could not see that they had lives of their own. How could I, when even my parents seemed mere appendages of my own desires and visions?

Summer, clouds . . . I can see all those old past summers etched against the sky above our lake each time I arrive there, each time I look up and across the tree line. Until those trees die and fall, it will always be only one summer, one time for me. When you come for a visit, as you must, you'll understand. You'll meet my parents here in the city: my father somewhat frail now, though refusing to retire from the business, my mother solid and as unchanging as the landscape; I can't remember that she ever was less than broad and imposing. She'll think that you're as thin as a stick, though as I remember you, you are decidedly just the perfect kind of figure . . . if I may be so bold as to say so. And your drawings! Well, and aren't they just the thing these days, the way they've been selling?

But I set out to tell you these things about myself, musing as I am upon old times at the lakeside, seeing my spectacles here on the table for a moment as I wipe my brow, light another cigar. Cigar smoke . . . this calls me back to the lake again . . . the bittersweet taste of the carefully molded Cuban leaf—I could not have been more than six years old, but the sight of that flame sparking up and smoke billowing all around me just as I tasted the essence of that chiaroscuro creation—bright Caribbean sun and the dark Cuban soil combining to give this special essence to the taste. It was my father's cigar, and I smoked it in the half-light of a closet on the upper floor of our lake house one quiet summer afternoon, the fumes so thick that I could almost swim in them. My breath quickened, my blood pulsed; I stood up, dizzy with the wasteful splendor of my action, and stumbled against the closet door. To my great surprise, it fell open and I tumbled into the room, where Trish, the thick-armed maid, was just coming in to clean.

"Master Albert!" she let out a cry, thinking that I had been struck by some fit—my limbs were all agley and my eyes so wild with the shock of my fall. "Are you all right, sonny?"

She grabbed me up where I lay in a heap on the bedroom floor, and it was then that she caught a whiff of me. "What *are* you doing?" Her eyes flashed notice that she understood perfectly.

Before I could speak, she rushed past me into the closet, where my fallen cigar had ignited a small fire made of discarded hose and old scarves and gloves. "God Almighty!" she exclaimed as she beat out the smoldering mess with the heel of an old shoe. Sparks flew up— and as I watched over her shoulder, I felt an excitement I had never known before. The fire, the way her body moved so fiercely as she put out the little blaze.

Another half-dozen years were to go by before I felt such sensations again: it was summer, and it was Trish's younger sister, Maureen, who was the body responsible this time—her body and mine. In that same room I arranged to meet her while my parents, with Trish in tow for service, had gone off to Saratoga for the races. I had a cigar in one hand—it was possible, I had discovered over the past six summers, to smoke several a month without my father noticing anything out of the ordinary about his supply—and a glass of whiskey in the other.

"Oh, the taste is so bitter, sir," Maureen said after our first kiss. The way she had done it—I had things to ponder as well. With one hand she had disarmed me of my stogie, with another the glass, and with her teeth she had lifted my spectacles from off my face and like a trained bird deposited them on the night table, and then leaned her face back to mine and stuck her tongue in my mouth. It wasn't until I noticed that I was holding my hands out to either side of me like a man about to be crucified that I immediately wrapped

158

them around her and began to pull at her blouse and apron. It was a new and even stranger taste than tobacco leaf that next flooded through my mouth.

"Oh, and you're just a baby," Maureen said, slapping my hands away.

"I'm not," I said, reaching now for the whiskey which, because we were wrestling so, spilled across my shirt front and splashed on hers as well.

"Oh, and now we're going to have to do some laundry," said Maureen, an odd new note coming into her voice.

I was shaking my head and saying that we had better things to do when she began to strip my shirt from me . . .

The cigars, the whiskey, and what we called "doing the laundry" became part of my summers until I went away to Harvard—and Maureen, that same autumn, married a farmhand from the western part of the county and never returned to the lake again.

And as clearly as I remember my first cigar and my first kiss, I recall, perhaps even more fondly, my first camera. It was a small, boxlike affair with a simple shutter and lens and I saw it in the window of a shop in Berlin that summer after I graduated from Harvard and purchased it, and that changed everything. Not that I was very good using it at first; much like my encounter with the cigar and the housemaid, the thrill was more in having it in my hands than using it effectively. At first I didn't know about the need for powder and light, and I knew nothing about the chemistry of making photographs. But I carried that camera with me—minus the stilts upon which it needed to stand; I didn't know enough to buy those until I returned to New York—all over Europe that summer and autumn. Though it was also not until I returned to New York that I sought help in learning how to use it, and discovered that there was not a great deal of help to be gained. Ah, Ava, the view is always fine at the front of the parade, isn't it? But then one must *know* the way in order to lead it! Or pretend to, at least!

So I became a pioneer in chemistry for the camera, and within a few years my father, pleased that I was showing some interest, however tangential, in the family emporium, set me up with a studio in the store itself. And it was in this way that I met many a

159

pretty young woman whose mother had decided that she wished to have her daughter immortalized by this new medium of photography, and the way, a few years later, that I met Miriam, who would become my wife.

She was the daughter of a clothing manufacturer whom my father had known ever since the days of the uniforms, and both families deemed this a suitable match long before either Miriam or I had gotten around to considering that we might want to do this ourselves. She was a pale, frail thing with fearful eyes that sometimes, when she was overcome by the humors, turned beady and mouselike, zigzagging back and forth in a way that I eventually grew to loathe, in spite of myself. What she had was her father's money and her devotion for me. So there was quite a lot of time in which she did nothing but practice her behavior—imagine if people did not have vocations and thus had to stay about the house and do nothing but stare at one another. Well, of course, most people live that way, a situation that accounts for a great deal of buried desire and suppressed mayhem, if not outright murder and, of course, adultery. But Miriam—we stayed together many more years than we should have, though I have to say that I owe my meeting with you to her unquenchable lust for new clothing.

"Paris is the only place," she said to me one night over dinner.

"For what, my dear?" I asked, pausing with a spoonful of her lackluster soup just before my lips.

She gave me a petulant look and I went on with my souping.

But it was clothes, clearly, that she meant, and so off we went to the City of Light, to cover what radiance she possessed with heaps of new cloth.

"You can take pictures," she said while we strolled the deck of the steamship that churned us toward the Continent.

"Please don't condescend to me, my darling," I said.

She shook her head uncomprehendingly. No, she couldn't condescend; she didn't even know the meaning of the word, poor thing.

Eventually seabirds called to me off the coast of France. She went off to her couturiers and I took my photographs, and visited some galleries and the museums.

It was while standing before a Poussin in the Louvre that I happened to fall into conversation with an American chap, a dapper, dark-bearded fellow just under my height from San Francisco, who was a part-time resident of Paris. His sister was a collector of sorts, he told me, and said that if I wished to see the paintings of the future, as well as those of the past, I ought to stop in at her salon some afternoon for tea. This woman, a nearly bald, doughy-faced heap of a female with eyes that shone like stars, had paintings on her walls that nearly made me dance with fever! She and I became good acquaintances—it is difficult to imagine that she might have friends, though Jobby tells me that he was in good with her the first time they met. She became my art conscience. Until I saw your drawings, no work had excited me more than what she showed me that afternoon!

Only a few years later, after a trip to Egypt to photograph the pyramids, I was looking around for a space in which to hang those kinds of paintings here in New York. And Miriam and I decided that we would do well to pursue our divergent interests separately. Fortunately there were no children. Though she had her clothes and I had my photographs and my equipment. And a new lens through which to view the world, my own lens, and the phantasmagorical prism of those new paintings on the walls of my own new little gallery, An American Place, where we first met and that I now call home.

DOOR

"My father's voice! Holy shit!" Michael lets out a sigh—I've never heard such a mixture of exclamation and introspection in his voice before.

"His father's, too," I point out to him. "That's your grandfather he mentions."

"I know, I know," he says, puckering up his lips in confusion. "Jeesum crow! I don't know what . . . " He whirls around in the middle of the floor. "Where'd you . . . ?"

"It was stuck away among her papers," I tell him.

"All these years . . . " His voice sounds that same odd way again, a sigh mixed with exultation. "The Civil War, man! Wow!"

"Wow!" I say in imitation, reaching out to touch his face. I suppose I'm resigned to his usual reaction.

"Hey," he says, and pushes my hand away. "I got to think about this." He shakes his head in consternation. "Give me that? I want to read it again."

"Don't lose it," I warn him.

"Lose it? Hey, Ame! Lose it? I've found it, baby! Hey, I wonder if Cissy knows about this?"

"She probably knows a lot," I say, "if she'd ever tell us . . . "

"Why don't you ask?" he says.

"I will sometime," I reply. "I will."

"Is there more?" he asks, taking the pages from me.

"I don't know," I say. "I don't know what comes next."

"They got married," he says.

"They did."

"And lived happily ever after . . . until she left him to come out here."

162

"She's been here a long while," I say. "But I don't know all of the details yet of what exactly happened."

"But they lived together for a long time . . . "

"Yes."

"So you see there's hope for us, too."

"Don't tease me, Michael. I can respect your principles, but don't *tease* me about it."

"Am I teasing you?" he asks, glancing down at the pages. There's a film, almost, over his eyes. He's off in another mood, dreaming.

I hear something. At first I take it to be the moaning of the wind. "Michael?"

"Huh?" He looks over at me in his way.

"The baby's awake. Do you mind . . . ?"

"My son?" he asks. "You think I'd mind going to look in on my own son?" And then he looks at me in a stranger way still. Oh, it's all fucked up: our thing, his past, the lies we've told to my parents about our life together. The only thing that seems straight and true to me these days is Ava's story. Even the woman herself is almost like a ghost to me, a ghost who lives with us, who works in the barn.

YEARS

Ava

"Hold it right there, my dear," Stig said to me one morning as I stepped out of the bath. There came the flash of his powder – and now six months have gone by, and I'm recalling this incident in the bath, or just after, here in this notebook. What happened to the photograph? He's never shown it to me. Has he developed it? I mean to ask.

An entire day goes by in a brush stroke.

A year can go by and find me working so well that I have not read a newspaper and, if it weren't for the shouting on the street below, would not know that the city has a life that begins before dark.

A year goes by.

Two years.

A truly happy woman working well may not keep a very good journal. And I have been working with a vengeance, as they say. I put in between eight to ten, sometimes twelve hours a day, every day, for months at a time in my studio in the apartment above the gallery. Towers seem to have become my favorite subject. If I have a "subject."

Towers! Towers of light! Spires reaching into the purple impossible sky of New York!

Towers like ocean liners racing vertically toward the port of sky!

Massive needles of light, plinths of light, spears of light shooting toward heaven!

Where, oh where, is that?

Right here in old New York, Stig would say.

He does say.

He said at dinner the other night, "The dance was in Paris a good long while. Paris was where you had to be if you wanted to dance. If you wanted to hear, no, if you wanted to *make* the right music, and follow the right steps, and find the right partner, but I truly believe that that is over now, and that if you want to dance, you get up on the floor right here, right now, where we live, where we work."

" 'I truly believe,' " Anderson says. "When Stigmar says that, he means he's making a good guess and he knows it."

Anderson — he dogs Stig's heels. (He also makes love to my friend Harriet, in spite of his married condition. And she sits quietly through dinners such as these, as if drugged by her own lack of caution.)

"He could be right," I say, and continue to pick at my food with my fork. I've learned to cook this last year. I don't *love* to cook, though, and this affects the way I eat my own food.

"Oh, we don't dance anyway," Stig says. "We work and we eat . . ."

" . . . and we love," puts in Anderson.

"Jobby," Stig says, "that is absolutely correct. I should have mentioned that." He glances my way, a sly smile on his lips.

"You can't make me blush," I say.

"I've tried," he says, setting down his fork and raising his hands in mock desperation.

"Real artists don't blush," I say.

"She's quoting me," says Stig.

"Because they are without shame, or must be, or else their work would never show the truth behind the mask."

"You've got her well trained," Anderson says.

I tap my knife on my plate.

"Quite the contrary," says Stig. "It's just the other way around."

"It's true," I say. "He used to sleep in the morning . . ."

"One of the perils of growing up a rich boy in the city," Stig puts in.

" . . . but he knows that if he wants to see me, he has to be awake before late afternoon."

"Oh, now, Ava, it's not *that* bad. She's exaggerating, Jobby."

"Not much," I say. "I wake up early and get to work early, and for a while it used to be that just when I was thinking about closing up shop for the day, my *husband* . . . I love that word! . . . was thinking about wandering into his darkroom and playing with chemicals for the rest of the evening."

"Perils of a two-artist family," Anderson says. "I've tried never to do that. Haven't always succeeded." His eyes buzz around the room and land momentarily on Harriet.

"No, you haven't," she says.

Many, many meals go by like this, with one or two friends, or with mobs of painters and actors and actresses and dancers, and now and then only Stig and me, gobbling our food so that we can get back to work, or eating soup at midnight at the diner around the corner where they once graciously accepted a drawing of mine that I made on the back of the menu in lieu of cash—we'd just forgotten our pocketbooks. We have no problems with money in the least, not in the least. My new father-in-law's department store keeps on growing and growing. This is a prosperous time, and even in New York where trolleys and the elevated and taxis will take you anywhere you want to go, we know more and more people who are buying automobiles—the people who are buying our work are buying automobiles, I should say. Our closest friends travel light.

Such as my dear Harriet, who has given up music and teaching and everything down in Charleston to live here in the city and try her new love: poetry. And some of it is not bad. And she's getting better, having published one poem in *Poetry* and another in *The Dial*. I only wish she hadn't developed such a terrible affection for Anderson, a longing that can only get her feelings horribly crushed. Never fall in love, I say, with a man whose eyes roam about the room and land on a woman's breasts like a fly.

But as for love, oh, if it were only as redeeming as work!

This man I married, he, all of it, is oh, so interesting. Above all, it is interesting!

Now there was never a great wildfire between us, nothing to light up the prairie that you could see from hundreds of miles away. It was, instead, a firm yet gentle . . . affection. And respect. He made me feel as though from the start he understood who I was and what I was doing – and what I wanted to do from then on.

As for his age, which none of my friends remarked on but which I know was, still is, perhaps, on their minds, I pay it little attention. His hair was already turning white, his beard and mustache, too, when I first met him. And he moved a little stiffly even then, holding himself erect as though he were royalty about to give an audience to some of his subjects – this might have put off some women, but not me. I find it rather engaging, the way in which he holds back just ever so slightly, except when I use on him the ways I have learned that bring him forth. Which, I suppose, I shouldn't say here. But I will anyway.

For instance, on nights when we stay in and have no guests, so we do not have a lot to get us talking, I will pick up a book and read to him.

"Do you think I'm a child to be read to?" he said the first time I tried this. The book was Richard Henry Dana's *Two Years Before the Mast* (a great personal adventure, and all true, and for a prairie girl like me filled with the perils of unaccustomed great oceans).

"No, I'm the child who's proud of reading," I said.

"In that case, continue," he said.

And so it has been on those nights at home for a few years now.

The child in the white-haired man comes out in the bath. "The backbrush, please," was how I first discovered it, one of the first of many new things I learned about Stig and his habits.

I handed him the brush, but he pushed it back to me. "Can you do it, please, Ava?" he asked.

And so I learned to bathe him, as though he were just out of infancy. I wasn't surprised. No one who had met his mother would have been surprised.

I wish sometimes that I used a camera.

Emeralda Eisemann, my mother-in-law, was named after a gem by her father, a German-Jewish shop owner who, within a few years of his arrival in New York from Hamburg, had turned a small group of linen stores into a large chain of department stores. His only

167

rival was named Stigmar, whose marriage to his daughter joined
the two empires in much the same way that the marriage of two
medieval European houses might have created a territory larger than
each of their two respective nations. When I first mentioned these
facts to Robert in a letter, he replied that it was probably the case
that one of our grandfathers had arranged to buy material for the
uniforms he brokered from some of the same larger jobbers whom
the Eisemann-Stigmar stores employed. "Large country," he said,
"but very few of us here on the plateau are looking out across it."
He was in the West at the time, scouting for some variety of mineral
or another, and mentioned how much he enjoyed climbing these
tablelands. Oh, flat west Texas, I don't miss *you*! Only the tiny part
of my soul I left behind!

But Emeralda. "Rather than 'Mother,' I would prefer that you
call me by my name," she said to me the first time that we met after
my marriage. I was relieved since, believe me, dear notebook, I had
no intention whatsoever of ever calling her "Mother." She is no
Dora to me, the only mother I've ever known. This big-boned
German woman who wears clothes the way a sofa wears uphol-
stery is not my mother. She didn't so much pamper Stig as never
recognize that he grew beyond his infancy. This was easy when he
went to college—Cambridge was just a train ride away to the north—
and so she could imagine that though he was gone for weeks, sometimes months at a time, he might be out on an errand or a stroll
across town to the zoo. When he left for Europe after college, she
treated that, too, or so he told me, as though he were going away
for a weekend with family friends. When he returned she did show
him a certain respect for his new-found maturity. It would be difficult to treat a man with a handlebar mustache like a child, though
now and then, as he was courting Miriam, his first wife, she did
give it a try.

"Alby likes his breakfast this way," she would instruct the new
bride. Or, "Did you send Alby's cigars over to the darkroom? He
should be running out of cigars by now." She kept track of her
baby's cigars!

For a long while he tolerated this in her, shrugged it off like
rainwater while he was out taking pictures. Around the time we
met he found a way of turning her impulses elsewhere. Not on me.

But on herself. He learned how to do this quite by accident. It was a turn, in fact. For the first time in his life as a photographer, he turned his camera on her. And it had a curiously satisfying effect.

It was at the lake house upstate, in Cossayuna, the family's habitual residence from late spring through early autumn, a place that when I first saw it convinced me that I had married the perfect man, because he had given me the perfect places to work – the city in winter and this large house by the water in the warmer seasons. It had been Emeralda's wedding gift from her father – Stig had been born here and found his first words here, and it was here more than anyplace that she treated him as though he had never grown past the age of five. A dozen rooms, a large porch, the lakefront, a garden, a girl who cooked and cleaned. The only thing it lacked was one of those pretentious names that easterners who have money that goes back only one or two generations sometimes adopt for their large country houses. But the Stigmars had never suffered from pretension. So while Emeralda kept herself quite reserved and never deigned to acknowledge that her son was over fifty and might be able to make judgments about his own life by now, beneath the layers of expensive clothes and jewels, and her face that seemed to have hardened like the earth after a dry spell, there lived a girlish heart. I saw this one morning as we stood out by the lake and she was going on about something or other to Stig, and he turned and playfully pointed his camera at her and without any preparation at all clicked the shutter. (Or perhaps he had been preparing, studying the light, gauging her position, I don't know.)

And as they say around New York, she melted, she absolutely melted. "Oh, Alby, I'm not dressed for this; you give me no warning; I . . ."

"The shore, Mother," he said, "look at the far shore." He rested the big camera on his chest and snapped off another picture.

"I thought he would never want to take a picture of his mother," said Emeralda later back at the house. "Everyone but me, I always thought."

"And you were wrong," I said.

She looked at me as if she had suddenly remembered who I was – the bohemian usurper who had taken the place of the perfectly respectable daughter-in-law she had chosen personally for her son (or had convinced her husband that he had chosen, I should say). She smiled anyway.

Every spring as we open the Cossayuna house, Stig takes her photograph, and somehow with that ritual she gives up her hold on her little boy and allows him to assume the role of the middle-aged man that he was when I met him.

Ah, the power of art!

I suppose it would have been easier if he had had children of his own, but he had none with Miriam, and the two of us have decided that we will not even try to have any ourselves.

"They are soft underfoot," Stig loves to say. "Why, I might step on one in the dark and crush it. And then there's the problem of what to do about them if they live!"

I don't know that I find his joking as amusing as he does, but I'm certainly in agreement about the issue of issue. I cannot imagine giving up the time from my work in order to tend children.

It is Harriet who brings the subject to mind again. It is a late spring afternoon in a time when I have taken to working up on the roof of our building when the sun is good. On the "tar desert" is what I've come to call it, looking out across the landscape of tall buildings from a slightly better, and now to me more interesting, angle than from my studio windows. No frame, thus. Only the wavering lines of heat rising from the roof, the curious visual sensation of watching the light bend between my eyes and the towers that stretch out across from my view like vertical slabs of native stone. No use to try and paint the stars from here—at twilight the city turns to a million pinpricks of light, ten thousand streaks of moving stars, stars on earth. But this—these rising sheathes of man-made rock and glass! I stand and work all morning and on into the afternoon.

And it is on one of these afternoons that the door to the stairs bursts open and Harriet comes upon me. "Ava, I need your help," she says.

I turn back to my canvas, with a few clucks of my tongue. "I couldn't write a sonnet if my life depended on it, darling," I say.

"I am not talking about writing a sonnet, or any kind of writing," she says. "I need moral support."

"Well," I say, "I will support you as best I can." I turn to look at her. She is dressed as if for a tea party at some dull apartment, and she doesn't look happy. "Ava, I do need you to help me."

"He's done it again, has he? Oh, sweetheart, I'm full of paint, otherwise I'd hug you. Is it Jobby?"

"Yes," she says, "and this time he's got me pregnant."

"You make me feel as though I'm your real mother," I say, reaching for my turpentine rags so that I can clean off and take her in my arms.

"Oh, Ava, I could never speak to my mother this frankly."

"Then what's a mother for?" I say, hurrying my cleanup.

In an hour or so we are walking up the steps of the brownstone in the Village where Margaret Sanger has established, in the face of great public outcry, her clinic for women who wish to make a choice in such situations.

I knew the way since I had come here just before my marriage. Stig might joke about children—and I think that the force in his jocularity is double-edged, to tell the truth—but unless we were not to sleep together, someone had to take practical measures about this matter. It was left to me.

And even with my protection in place, I sometimes shudder in the middle of our meetings in the dark, because I know that if there is a slip, it will be up to me to take care of that as well. I don't accept this as the way it has to be, yet I recognize that this is the way The Boys are and I take measures.

"Ava, please tell me, quickly," Harriet says to me in the waiting room. "This doesn't hurt, does it?"

"What doesn't hurt?"

"What they're going to do to me."

I shake my head and pull her head to my chest. "Darling, I've never had it done, so I can't say for sure. But if there's pain, it will only last a little while."

I can feel her settle quietly against me. She is thinking . . .

I have done my own share of thinking on this matter, to be sure. Haven't I been a schoolteacher? Every schoolteacher, no matter how high the grade she teaches, thinks about children and what they would mean in her own life. I understand that all of the time that I labored in those fields taught *me* something about my life: I do not want children. Children would tear apart my workday and thus tear apart my work.

But I can't say to Harriet, "Be ruthless." That would sound utterly heartless. My heart beats for my creations, my work: the work I have done, the work I may do. But I can only speak for myself. Art is my progeny, my child. I love it, I long for it, I nurture it, it is mine and yet not mine. And if it is any good, it will not need to be taught but will teach instead.

Having said this, I wonder if it sounds too harsh. Do I sound like Lady Macbeth? I don't mean to. I have merely made my choice about my life and my future.

The male artist does not even have to think about this as a choice. Oh, he may make noises about choosing between his family and his work, but this is not the kind of visceral choice that a woman must make. The work! I choose the work! The world is full of women choosing the life. I choose the work!

[there is a hiatus here in the notes, mostly blank pages with some sketches and designs scattered about, mainly wings, windows, a flower here and there, a skull]

early mornings at Cossayuna
    the lake giving up its breath to the new sun
    loon calls, flutter of wings
    I'm alone, all eyes and heart

City and country – years pass, and while I know that the world goes on, and not much of it in good shape, this is the rhythm we live by – city and country, country and city . . .

Stig returns from a doctor's appointment looking very unhappy. "He says that I'm drinking too much. Am I drinking too much?"

We burst into laughter together. "I drink twice as much as you do. Whatever does he have in mind?"

Stig squints at me over his spectacles, perched there on the end of his nose. I study the gray hairs, like tiny wires protruding from his nostrils. "I've been having some trouble," he says.

"I hadn't noticed," I say, laying my ear to the gray pelt that covers his chest.

"I'm old enough to be your older brother, of course," Stig says with a certain stiffness in his voice, "but I'm also nearly old enough to be your . . . "

I place my palm lightly across his mouth. "Don't say it, please."

He gently removes my hand. "It's true. Perhaps if you have heart trouble from early childhood on, you become resigned to it. But not if it comes now."

"Now?"

"Toward the end."

I shove him away from me. "Don't get me angry, Albert Stigmar! Don't get me angry!"

My father-in-law, at eighty, decides that he wants to give up his business. "It's time," he says. "It's high time."

I hope to be working past eighty myself.

And now I look back and see that it's been six months without an entry. The work has come on instead!

Wise old man, my father-in-law. The stock market has sunk like a stone in Cossayuna Lake, but he has been well out of it for almost a year. He has gone up to the lake to sit on the porch in a rocking chair and contemplate the end of autumn.

Seems like a fit subject to me. I go up to spend the weekend there and find that I'm drawing leaves and branches, just as though I were back at the Art Institute.

"Daughter," says the old patriarch, looking down at my sketchbook. "You have a good hand."

"Thank you, Papa," I say, closing my book and going over to put my arms around his grizzled old neck.

Robert and his wife come to town and I discuss his heart with him. "Just age," he says. "Just age. Why shouldn't souls get tired after a long time on earth? Rocks do."

"Rocks," says Margaret. "Rocks are all you talk about, Robby." (Rocks to her! I don't like her, have never liked her.)

173

"Don't call me that, please," Robert says. "It makes me sound like a child."

"You're my baby," says Margaret. Clearly she's been drinking, the only one, oddly enough, at our table who has.

"I'm not your baby; I'm not anyone's baby," my brother says.

"Rocks," I say.

"What?" says Margaret.

"Do rocks have souls, do you think?" I ask my question and drink deeply of the wine myself.

"Do souls have rocks?" asks Robert with a smile.

"I sometimes think that rocks and trees have souls," I say, "and that air is the breath of trees."

"What do you mean by that?" says Margaret.

I can hardly suppress a groan. Robert sails tomorrow, and Margaret will be staying with us overnight before she takes the train back to Chicago. I look over at Stig, who seems perfectly happy to have her at our table, and I decide that I'll go up to Cossayuna first thing in the morning.

"But now that I think of it," Robert says, "perhaps rocks *do* have souls, or the earth does. And oil is its blood."

"Interesting," I say.

"That's what I've been trying to do," Stig puts in. "Trying to photograph the earth's soul. I see it now and then in the clouds."

I drink more wine, unable to get through the dinner any other way.

"How can souls have blood?" asks Margaret, holding up her glass.

"Look," I say. "We're very lucky souls ourselves. Very lucky. Look around us. The sky's falling on our country and we're surviving."

"The sky is falling?" asks Margaret, taking a sip.

"Sis," says Robert, "that's a good point. I'm not sure what it has to do with what we were talking about, but a good point nonetheless."

"It has nothing to do with it," I say, "and everything. Like the best things — nothing and everything."

"My wife's not just a painter but a philosopher, too," says Stig.

174

Now I'm beginning to think that *everyone* else at the table has been drinking much more than I have.

"I mean what I say about how fortunate we are," I tell Robert after dinner. "So many people out of work. So much misery all around us."

"I'm doing what I can," Robert says. "I'm going after oil. It's oil that's going to take us out of this mess."

"You're a great heart to be able to think that," I say. "I'm just doing my work – and I don't know what it has to do with anything."

Since my father-in-law has retired, he seems to be growing younger, and Stig has aged very quickly. They appear to be more and more like brothers, rather than father and son.

. . . . [pages torn out]

Something's happened to my reading. I used to read poetry and novels exclusively, never the newspapers. Now I scan the headlines every day in the *Herald Tribune* and the *Times*. What's come over me? It's what's coming over the world that's so upsetting.

But all I can do is what I do: I do my work. Short of prayer, what else is there? And I was never one for prayer much.

What's blocking pedestrian traffic on the avenue? The line going into the gallery for our show overflows the curb. One night I wait until it slackens a bit and then follow it in and up the stairs, trying to see my work as others see it. It's dark up here, but gradually one's eyes adjust and as they do, emerging all around on the walls is a living forest – leaves and branches, thickets and stands of maple and oak and elm painted in such a combination of painstaking detail and rush of subtle light that it gives the impression of seeing these trees just as the dawn comes up on the first morning of spring – or is it the First Day of Creation?

Thank God I gave up towers for trees!

And then you look up at the ceiling – which has become the firmament itself with photographs of clouds like cushions on a divan piled up above, clouds like spiderwebs, clouds in rows like buttercups, clouds very like a camel, a woman, a whale . . .

Did I say woman?

175

In the center of the ceiling floats a large photograph of a woman emerging from her bath — of clouds — the moment that Stig captured me years ago . . .

And as I see it I clutch my breasts, feeling naked to the eyes of those around me.

And then I laugh at myself, at the power of his art.

And I go through the gallery in search of him, this man, my husband, of whom I say to myself, father husband second brother friend, and when I spy him, I take him by the hand and plant a kiss on his white beard.

DOOR

The time that swept across my mind while Ava talked me through that period of her life came on like a wave, like a forceful wind, leaving me a bit flattened in its aftermath. So much, so quickly! But the one thing I can't show in words—the drawings and the paintings that she worked on during that stretch of years—that's the most important of all. She dug in during that decade and started to become herself, the artist that we know and love, and here words become irrelevant. Except without them we cannot know the woman. And without her there would be no work.

Time passing. Absence of speech. A feeling that has no form except in the painting after painting—the drama of the emotional life, a chronicle of the action that made the canvases—here words fail me, and I need almost to think in images in order to make you see, Michael. Michael! At least he will be an audience of one for this project. And yet, paradoxically, living with these papers—these notes, letters, notebooks, clippings, jottings, photographs, essays, reviews, sketchbooks, paintings, catalogs, newspapers, magazines, bus tickets, boat tickets, plane tickets, telephone bills, poems, dreambooks, stories, rumors, myths—all this has made me feel so distant from him. Socorro and I talk more than he and I do.

One night when I couldn't sleep—my head was so filled with all the work that I'd been doing—I wandered through the house trying to find a comfortable place to perch. At dawn Socorro arrived and found me asleep in the big chair in the living room. She brought me some coffee and told me that she had seen an owl and a blue jay flying together just at first light, and that this was a sign she had never seen before and she was pondering its meaning. When her mother had died, she explained, there was an owl that came to her and spoke in the woman's voice.

Her story reminded me so much of the old days at school when Stanley would tell those kind of tales and then explain the significance. I miss him. I miss school. This adult life—how have I come to it? Michael snoring in the other room. I can hardly bear it.

But Robby, oh, Robby, I do love!

Owl and the blue jay. Ava the owl? Michael the blue jay? I can't tell Socorro my interpretation of the sight.

I'm worried that after several long sessions of talk I'm suddenly avoiding her—Ava. Though she does spend a great deal of time with Michael, mostly out in the barn, I feel as though I should try to get closer to her. Here I am, a witness to the most intimate moments of her life, and there she is, shuffling about on my husband's arm, within my reach, too, but never present anymore for me to get to know *now*.

Though since Michael has read almost none of the papers, he knows Ava mainly through things she has said to him, what his mother recounted to us, and what I let him see.

"Ava," I say at dinner one of those times, rarer than ever, when she has decided to come and sit with us. (She doesn't ever seem to eat anything herself.)

"Socorro's a good cook, isn't she?" she says.

"Yes, she is," I say. "Ava?"

"Yes?"

"Honey," Michael puts in.

"Just a moment, Michael. Ava, would you like to take a walk with me after supper?"

"We're going back out to the barn," Michael says. "Ava's only got a little good work time left in the evening—"

"I want to read," Ava says.

"We could do that, Ava," Michael says. "I'll read to you."

"I want *her*," Ava says.

"I'll be happy to," I say.

"I usually do it while you're putting Robby to sleep," Michael says.

"You can work," I say. "I'll read to Ava."

I notice that Socorro has been watching us, the three of us, while Robby plays about our feet. "Socorro?"

"Si, Señora?"

"Will you help put Robby to bed tonight?"

"Si, Señora," she says.

"Well, Michael, that frees you to work," I say.

"I guess it does," he says.

"What would you like to hear?" I ask Ava after we have left the table. Michael has disappeared, out to the barn, I figure. I can hear Socorro and Robby making noises to each other from the far side of the house.

"The same," Ava says from her soft chair before the fire.

"I don't know what that is."

"Cather," she says.

"Uhum," I say. "We never read her at college. But I'd love to do it now. Which book?" I ask. "I'll find it for you."

"*Death Comes for the Archbishop*," she says.

"I don't know it," I say.

"A good one," she says.

"Where is it?" I ask.

"On the top shelf," Ava says. "Worn copy. I've read it over several times."

"What's it about?" I ask.

"New Mexico, New Mexico and . . . " She pauses, takes a breath, poised on the brink of a new thought.

"You love it here, don't you?" I say.

"I love . . . *everything*," Ava says.

179

IN THE FIELD

Robert

Ever since that Sunday morning by the river all those forty-plus
years ago, it has always been water that has haunted me, and I suppose in a way this fear might account for the way in which I have
tried by means of my profession to sometimes bury myself in the
earth. Water may wash away earth if the gods want to flood us, I
know, but short of that, you can heap up a pretty good-sized dam
against the rising flood or tide and live fairly safely behind it for a
while. So all these years earth has been the best of life for me, earth
and the fruits thereof, the bubbling black viscous liquid that I have
helped to pump from her bowels. Some scientists like myself go for
earthquakes; I have gone for oil and gas, and that has made the
difference. Earthquake men tend to stay in one place, now and
then going out into the field to check the cracked surface of the
planet. Oil men like myself move around a lot, go deep, and that
has suited me just fine.

Not so Margaret, the dear girl I courted while at college and
married before going to graduate school. Margaret, the poor wretch,
spent some years practically living on prescription elixirs – the cause
of which, she claimed one morning while she was shrieking at me
as I was trying to pack, was my profession: "Your job is what's killing me!"

But even as I looked up from my suitcase, I could have told her
that one of the reasons I left so often was to get away from her.
Though I didn't say it, I tried to put it in my look.

"Say something!" she called out, stumbling over to the bed and
whacking me on the arm with her open hand.

I stood my ground, stoically, the only way I knew how to respond
to her since this variety of behavior had begun.

"You leave me all the time!" she said, hitting me again on the arm. I caught her by the wrist and turned her away from the bed. "Let go!" she said, her voice rising into another scream.

To show you how much I had become inured to this kind of insanity, I took it all as merely another good-bye; it was buffered by all my vivid memories of the first violence I had known – those moments at the river so long ago with Mother and Father – memories buried under strata upon strata of mad nights with Margaret.

No wonder that it was around this time that I began to try and find answers for some of the questions I had outside of my science – where was I going? where had I been? – by reading books in which one is supposed to find some truth. I began with the Bible, a book that I had not really read while a child, but rather had had read *to* me by our grandmam. In its pages I found conflicting news. The Old Testament says the world is powered by a dark and angry God; the New Testament says he is a God of Love. Well, which one? Both? or neither? Later I read the mystics. Then I read the Hindus. They make the world too much of a flowing, and my work helps me understand that things are a bit more complicated than that. All theories came undone when I got to Shakespeare, and his genial greatness made me look back to the Greeks and find the heritage of all that I had read before. I understood that beginning with the Bible had been a false start, a narrow, if powerful, distortion of the marvelous reality and faith of the pagans. I understood that I was a pagan, that all scientists by nature of their work are new pagans, and that such a notion does not exclude a sense of the divine, merely the narrow Christian sense.

But in this quest for philosophical truth that I undertook while out in the field and on nights at home while Margaret lay snoring in our bed – outside our little house blazed stars and whirled storms through season after wondrous season, and within my chest cavity my heart beat on, unsteadily but nevertheless doing its job, quite against all medical predictions – I wanted to find a way to yoke the scientific view of the natural world and the old notions of the godhead. Then I discovered Freud, whom a few of my sister's friends in New York had already been talking about after a lecture tour the great doctor had made in our country just a few years before. What

ιe Oedipal conflict seemed to me, in its own way, a the-
ιan geology.

hings moved along. I read and I read, and read some
ι to this the loud sleep noises of Margaret for a realistic
picture oι the scene on many a night, or me sometimes in my field
clothes still smelling of oil and grease and sun-baked clay and spicy
food while in the field, alone, all alone in my bed, pondering the
news that there were many things in our philosophy that could not
be explained by Freud's paradigm.

Thus I began thinking a great deal about my sister, and how it
was the artist who was anomalous; it was the artist who, once sprung
free from the service of the church, soared higher than the limits
imposed by the Judeo-Christian God—broke free of such clouds
and looked back down upon the world and saw it as a beautiful
subject for expression. And if there were a deity, it was not a god
who spoke in words, but one who emitted light. God was light, and
love was clarity. And seeing with the human eye was the truest
form of worship.

It was on a dark night in winter in a company house in Odessa,
Texas, when I came to this conclusion. I remember it well because
in my foolish rush to test my theory out on someone, I hurried into
the bedroom where Margaret lay sleeping and touched her on the
shoulder. She made a small noise out of sleep but would not open
her eyes. I went back out to the living room and began to compose
a letter to Ava.

"If you're looking at an artist," I wrote, continuing my theorizing
on these matters, "you can't just look at the person herself. You have to
see the field you find her in. And in the case of a life, that field lies both
in time and space. Emotions may be nothing but the weather of place.
And the lines of force link that field with the rest of the rock and pressure
in that region, and in the larger world. You may stand calmly upon seemingly solid ground and paint a rock face that has been in place for a
million years, but painter and object both have a certain motion. And
emotion. Yes, even rocks have feelings, if you look at them in a certain
light: the vibrations that created them, the speed at which they're moving
toward or away from one another. Am I making any sense, Sis? Am I at
least amusing you? Oh, rocks again, you say. He's at his rocks again. I
know, I know. But bear with me . . ."

182

At which point Margaret peered bleary eyed into the room. "What are you doing?"

"Just writing a letter, dear. I tried to wake you up. I wanted . . . oh, never mind. But here you are! Come and sit." I got up and went to the sofa, motioning for her to sit alongside me. Coming out of sleep this way she sometimes had the look of the schoolteacher I had married, and I still had a big soft spot in my heart for that girl. "What are you writing?" she asked.

"Just a letter to Ava," I said.

"That damned sister of yours," she said. "You're always thinking of her. Never of me." She fixed her eye on the old buffalo-calf skull that I keep on my desk. "This dumb thing," she said, reaching for it.

"Please, dear," I said, blocking her arm.

"Don't you 'dear' me, you bastard," she said. "I wish it were her skull here on this table."

"Please don't speak like that," I said. "You're . . . "

"Going to break your hard heart?" A wicked smile such as I had never seen before crossed her face, and it made icicles in my chest despite the relatively mild Texas winter night.

"Write your stupid letter," she said, and turned and went back into the bedroom. A few moments later when I went after her, she was already snoring again.

Then came a spring when oil was crowned as king and I was its courtier, and the train carried me southward into Mexico, its lower kingdom. In the dark tomblike cabinet of the Pullman car I slept a relaxed and dreamless sleep better than any I had had in a year, lolled into slumber by the steady rocking of the train.

Tampico, if a bit drier and dustier than Texas, offered great promise. Spring stretched into summer. No one in the company wanted to be down here in this season that could make you feel as though your bones themselves were melting from the heat. I stayed, and that was when I met a woman named Maria Elena Marcado, called Malu, a secretary in the company office. She was a smart girl about twenty-five who had never gone to college but had learned English on her own. She had family in the states but it was never clear to me where. I asked Maria Elena to come for a drink with me

183

one evening after work. She knew a bar, a place where some English and Germans and a few Americans drank. Cool beer made us sweat all the more. That was what we did each evening, from that point on: drank and sweat. Through the front door of the bar I could see some of our men on their way to the brothels down at the low end of the street. Mine was a more elevated variety of debauchery, with a name better than whoring. Adultery. I could hear the word in Mrs. Halme's voice, over all these years.

Other voices soon drowned hers. The voice of Maria Elena crying out in pleasure: such a sound I had never heard before, having been married to the mute Margaret who turned all of her feelings inward, and then drank. And I heard a man's voice raised in laughter, and I looked toward the sound, and discovered it was my own. And then there was the loud, though unspoken, sound of the sentences in my letters north. The work on the company project had become more complicated than I had anticipated, and I was going to have to stay another few months. And a few more.

Take me with you. She never said that with her voice. But it was there in her eyes each night that Malu and I spent together from that point on. The way she touched me, the way she clung to me at night while we slept, the way she spoke to me upon awakening— all of this should have convinced me to take her with me. But I was a man with a head thicker than the rocks he sometimes drilled through, and when the time came to go, I left her behind. My heart pounded, but my tongue stayed tied.

Margaret's tongue loosened upon my return to Texas, aided by a quantity of whiskey. "You despise me, don't you?" she said as I walked in the door. But before I could deny it, she let me know that the reverse was certainly true. "I want to know what you were doing down there. Tell me all about what you were doing."

"I was working," I said. "You know that." And I began to explain in technical terms the nature of our project.

"Oh, yes, some work!" she said, cutting me off.

She went on for some time in that odd slurred voice, as though tongue had cut loose from sense. She sounded as though she would pass out in each next moment and yet was indefatigable. Now and then she would duck into the bathroom, and I finally went in after

184

her. "Get away from me," she said, holding the bottle behind her
back.

I grabbed for it, and in our struggle it fell into the tub and
smashed to pieces. A hot, sour smell rose from the tub.

"Monster!" my wife shouted at me, down on her knees as if in
prayer. And in one of those moments of prescience she added, "Don't
think I don't know about her!"

She didn't. But I couldn't hide the truth any longer. So, fool
that I was, I told her about Malu, and then came weeks of ferocious
argument, and then I moved out, went up to Chicago and worked
in the main office a while, and finally there were lawyers.

I had in mind that I would return to Tampico, find Malu, and
make her mine. But that was not to come about. The company had
other things in mind for me, namely a sojourn to the mesa country
of New Mexico, where they had bought some cheap land. My task
was to evaluate its potential for exploration. So it was the company
that changed everything for me. And, at least indirectly, changed
everything for Ava.

DOOR

Amy's lesson for the decade: that children grow more rapidly than I had ever imagined, and the old decline just as swiftly. A year! And Ava seems to have begun to shrivel up into herself. As I write this, I can see her through the open black door. She is walking very slowly—or should I say v-e-r-y s-l-o-w-l-y?—toward the house. She doesn't see me watching her, and she's showing the pain. Her very bones seem to have knitted together, and she's becoming a sort of living fossil. Horrible of me to put it that way, but that is how she appears against the blue-white sky—as though engraved upon it by the pressure of time and wind.

Suddenly a small, fast-moving shadow comes up behind her and I stand up with a start. "Robby!" I'm fearing rattlesnakes, God knows, eagles, too! I'm two steps toward the door when Michael rushes up and scoops him up from behind.

"You mustn't . . . " I start to say to Michael as they come in the door.

"I was right behind him," he cuts me off. "He was watching us throw pots."

I glance over at Ava, poised in the doorway, not in, not out. She seems to be looking at something, though I know her vision has deteriorated to the point where, months ago, she gave up trying to paint again and has devoted herself to the making of pots with a vengeance. "Ava?"

She shakes her head. I don't know whether she's looking or listening. How nice to have the time for such contemplation! I have been keeping up with Robby and keeping up with the Boldin papers and have done nothing for myself or my own work in over a year now.

186

Michael and our son wander past to the front of the house. "Yes?"

Socorro comes to the table. I don't know where she's been, out hanging the wash or at the well, somewhere. "That's all right, Socorro," I say. "I'm talking to Ava."

"I'll make the meal, Senora," she says, giving me a look. I recognize it as one that speaks of a yearning to return to a quieter time, when it was just she and Ava alone in this house. She once mentioned to me something about her mother. Maybe it was the three of them.

"Ava," I say, picking up my pages and going to the door.

"Cheerful girl you are," Ava says.

"I'm not sure what you mean," I say.

"Care to walk?"

"Sure. Where shall we go?"

"To the mesa," she says.

"Do we have time?"

"Eternity," Ava says.

"Oh, now, Ava, don't be silly."

"I feel so useless," she says, leaning against me with no more weight than a dress on a hanger. "These eyes of mine! If they weren't screwed in so tight, I'd tear them out!"

"No, no, Ava," I say, patting her on the shoulder. It's like she's a feather and at my touch floats gently down. I catch her.

"I tripped," she says. "Life tripped me."

"I'm not so sure about that," I say. "You've had a good life, once you got started living it."

"Oh?" she says, something sly in her cracked old voice. "You've been following me?"

"I've been reading," I say.

"Good girl," Ava says.

"I'm not a girl, really, anymore," I say. "I'm going to be twenty-four."

"And what does that make me? If you're a woman, then what am I?"

She's got me struggling, never having been challenged this way by her before. "I don't know," I say. "I don't know what you mean."

"Am I the mother?" she asks. "Am I the grandmother?"

187

"You could be," I say.

"Or I could be this," she says, pointing at the ground.

"What's that?"

"Dust. Or this." She holds up a fist and then slowly unfolds her fingers.

"What?"

"Wind."

NEW SKY

Harriet

I always felt a little provincial coming up to New York, no matter
how much time we spent there, no matter how comfortable our
surroundings while we stayed. But after Benjamin and I separated
and I continued to come to the city, I gradually came to understand that what I brought with me from Charleston served me well
up here: that sense of morals and its relation to geography, the
matter of tide and the passage of time. Love and water: that's a subject poets might well take up. I know that lately I have been trying
to write about it without much success. But then I've never been
much of an artist, certainly not much with my music, but only an
admirer of the artistic, and so my poems will probably come to
nothing.

However I do know something from observing Ava over the
years, something about the artist's life that has been valuable to me
in my own. Most people—ordinary people, I want to call them—
usually discover that they love one person, or perhaps two people,
in their lives, and they make their plans for home and hearth,
the future, accordingly. But the artist—he, or in this case, *she*—
discovers gradually over the days of her life that she may be
capable of loving almost everyone she meets for the lines in his face
or the light in his eye, the tilt of her head; just about everyone has
some redeeming quality or three for the artist's eye. A thrill here, a
heart lighting up there, and the next thing you know, the artist
may discover that because she loves everybody, she can love nobody
truly deeply, not with a powerful passion that stays constant, like a
flame at a monument, or the constant light of a star to steer by.

Nobody! Only her work, and not ever her work that's past, but
only the present work and the work to come.

189

ʋhat Ava and I were talking about that afternoon in
ɪ while sitting on a bench in Gramercy Park, only a few
ards from the building where I was living in the apart-
. Benjamin had left to me before he returned, his tail
ᴜᴇᴄ. ʜis legs, to Charleston some years before.

On a park bench on a slowly darkening afternoon, with the
interspersed towers to the west of us jutting up to stripe the pink-
paling sky over New Jersey, she broke off our small talk—which is
what we usually made of our visits on these late afternoons, when
Ava had finished in her studio and wanted to take some exercise in
the form of a walk over to the park to meet me—and she told me
in a firm, quiet voice (she had never raised her voice in all the years
I'd known her) of her current dilemma.

She was trembling a little, as if there were a breeze cold beyond
the season. "My brother wrote to me. He's found some land in New
Mexico, and he's invited me to come out next summer and spend
some time with him. And I may do it. We're the only two left now,"
she said, "Robert and I, the only survivors of a family that felt like
it was shrinking fast even when it was at its greatest
number. So it tempts me, but it has also plunged me into turmoil,
Harriet, of a kind that I thought existed only in romance novels!
Stig won't go—I know he won't. He just won't. He says he's
traveled long enough and far enough, and he wants to stay in one
place. Harriet, I pleaded with him . . . "

It was difficult for me to imagine Ava pleading with anyone,
but I gave it a try.

" . . . but he was adamant. He said that the trip he took to
Egypt was the last long trip that he would take. I told him that New
Mexico was hardly as far as Egypt, and he said, 'Do you want to
wager on that?' Harriet, I worship him, but he is slowly killing that
glory, and I think he's trying to kill himself as well. He's done some
marvelous things with his camera, and I know that he could open
up even more, but when I tell him so, he folds his arms across his
chest and gives me such a look—the I-am-the-master-and-you-are-
the-apprentice look; oh, I hate that!—I am nearly forty years old,
and no one needs to look at me like that anymore! The *fool*! I told
him that I just wanted to go out for a month, that Robert had
made arrangements for me to have a place on the property—and

190

I'm not sure what that means out *there*—whether it's a house or a shack or extra rooms or whatever, it really doesn't matter to me—but there's a woman he met when he was on a rock hunt—not a romance, I know my brother well enough to say that. The end of his marriage has left him a bit stunned. But this woman . . . she has a house in the middle of a village called Taos, north of Santa Fe. Now you can't see the look in your eyes; you can't see it, but I see it, and it's a lovely look . . . "

"Thank you, dear."

" . . . no, listen, the way your eyes are opening wide, and wider, the more I describe the trip, the place, the possibilities, and do you know what happens to Stig's eyes? They glaze over, they nearly close, those wonderful eyes of his that have allowed all of us to see clouds and sky as no one has ever seen them before; the eyes that looked upon New York in winter and gave us such remarkable photographs: the snow in the streets, the parks, the automobiles. Oh, Harriet, I am so furious with him I could pluck out those eyes when he does that to me!"

She rose from the bench as though she were about to sing an aria. "Come with me on the trip. I promise you it will be like nothing else you've done before."

"Ava . . . " I stood alongside her, as if we were about to commence a duet.

"Come up to the lake when my brother visits next and listen to him talk about the West. If he describes it the way he has in his letters, you'll be convinced."

"Have you shown Stig these letters?"

"I've read them to him." Her eyes flared wide, almost as if she were already looking out upon one of those western scenes she wanted to travel to see. "And it's made no difference. He's dead to adventure, Harriet. And it pains me, pains me for him, and pains me for me. He's such . . . such an . . . *easterner!*"

I laughed at her, at her anger with his timidity at travel. If I hadn't known her as well as I did, I might have thought she was attacking him because he was a Jew.

"He won't leave that damned lake," she said in rising anger, "and I've begun to use it up. I need something new, someplace my eyes haven't tired of. I never want my eyes to grow tired! Oh!" She gave a little shudder, pulled back her hand, and looked around as if she had just come out of sleep or a trance to find herself in this park beneath these trees. "I want to walk," she said. "Come walk with me?"

I walked with her, Ava setting quite a vigorous pace, tiring me after a while in the way that usually only a man can tire me. It was twilight when Ava and I finally parted. All the light from Manhattan seemed to be slipping westward toward New Jersey, as though the red sky there had magnetic powers, drawing toward it first any light brighter than itself, and then, building in color, anything less bright, with a kind of celestial tidal power. Yes, and I thought what if all this sky were water, and the waters became sky, and with this notion of all earth and heaven turned upside down churning in my mind, I hailed a taxi and rode uptown, leaving Ava standing where she wanted me to leave her: on the ferry slip at the Battery, just another woman in the crowd.

The first time I met Robert Boldin his visit caught me in an odd state of mind. He turned out to be quite different from what I had imagined, not at all the way I had pictured the head geologist for a large oil company. He was taller than Ava—that wasn't unexpected, since you can usually assume that brothers will be taller than sisters—and his hair was completely white, though there was a lot of it, more than, say, Stig's, which is also quite white but comes to a widow's peak that makes his forehead stand out. Robert stood tall and slender, but not desiccated, certainly not the picture of a man with a bad heart. His face, though leathery from years under the sun, reminded me so much of Ava's that I wondered if they might be twins. When I said so at dinner, he gave me an odd stare.

"We could not be more different and still have emerged from the same womb," Robert Boldin said, finally flashing me a smile for my wonderment. "I'm an artist and she's a scientist."

Everyone at the table broke into laughter.

"Seriously," he went on, "we've never had much in common except our family sorrows. But if you look at us today . . . "

"And they are looking right now," Ava said in that dour way she can put on when she wants to, so that you would never imagine, if you didn't know her well, that she had a sunny side at all, ever.

"Then, Sis, they can all see . . . "—*all* was Stig and me—"the resemblance that comes from life. We are two battlers from the plains, and we have fought our way to a large, flat, sunny place on a rock face. Or we're climbers, then—whatever the metaphor. One thing I'm not is a poet but . . . "

"Harriet has been writing poetry," Ava said. "She used to be a pianist but she's given that up for verse."

"I'm not a poet," I made a protest, "only a writer of verses. And poor ones at that."

"Not so poor at all," my friend said, making me blush. By the end of the evening she had me forgetting my initial embarrassment—I don't know how she did it, but she has a way, she does—and reciting my "Island" poem, not just once but twice.

"Bravo," said Robert, standing and applauding when I was done. I had to leave the table and hide in the bathroom. Seeing my face in the mirror, I wondered why that man had kept on staring. My cheeks were so lined and red—lined from age, of course, is what I mean to describe, and the blush from having retained some of my girlhood through all these long years. But even as I studied the fixed lines time had etched in the corners of my eyes and mouth, I marveled at the fluidity of my emotions. I had given up Charleston, Benjamin, and music, and taken up the writing of poetry and an affair with Sherwood Anderson. "I'll be your poetry coach," he had said. He had tutored me in other matters as well. But just when I thought my work was progressing nicely, his wife had tightened the reins on their marriage. "Run with me," he had said, "and I'll leave her." I shook my head. When it was a game it had been fun, but suddenly it had ceased to be a game. Fickle, fickle, fickle, I scolded myself in the glass. But then why shouldn't we be fickle, when life itself is the opposite of constant. That much I had learned from watching the ocean meet island, wind stir wave.

Fickle? I didn't yet know the meaning of the word. If I had known what lay ahead for me, I might have fled back home and buried my head in the sand.

"Harriet?" I started at the sound of Ava's voice.

"I'm awful, I know. But I just couldn't bear to stay in the room another second."

"My brother won't bite you," she said. "Come back and join us." She reached for my hand. "When he was married, he was as faithful as a rock, and then one day it all came undone."

"What are you saying?"

"She was perfectly dull," she went on. "A schoolteacher. He went on his expeditions and she stayed at home. I never liked her."

"Could you like anyone who captured Robert's affections?"

A cloud hovered over her face, then passed. "Perhaps," she said inscrutably, "if she had the right sort of affections."

When we returned to the dining table, her brother was discoursing on the glories of that place—and I was sunk in a sort of paralyzing ecstasy. Oh, love and sex electric! A moment before and I had been perfectly in control, and now I was like someone bitten by a snake! Everything felt as though it were changing. His voice! I paid close attention to his voice, and I liked the little smile he made when he caught me staring at him.

"It isn't the best place for a man with a heart like mine," Robert was saying, "because of the altitude, but it gives me a thrill to work there—walking that desert! Oh, Sis, it made me think of you and your wonderful eye, and how much you'd want to see there!"

"She'll see it alone," Stig said, his voice unusually rusty, as though he hadn't used it in days. "I wouldn't cross the Mississippi for any amount of cash. I wouldn't cross the damned Harlem River if I didn't have to get up here to Cossayuna. My traveling days are over. As for yours, Ava, why the hell do you want to go west again? You spent that awful time in Texas—awful it was, to hear you tell about it. Stay here in the woods that you know, with me and my clouds, and our lake."

I saw flare in Ava's eyes the only mean spirit in all the years of our friendship, but it subsided quickly. "I must go west, for part of the summer at least."

"You're a free woman," Stig said. "Go for all of the summer. Go and . . ."

"Stig," she said, and it was as if he had been the only one in fearful agitation, the way she calmed him with her voice so soon after she had allowed her own ferocious response to show.

194

"Do what you want," he said, getting up from his place and going over to the window. Something about his movements spoke of his age in a way that I hadn't ever noticed before. He might have been weeping as he turned his back on us to walk away, his shoulders heaved so, but I don't think that it was any out-of-the-ordinary amount of emotion that was making him tremble, just the way his (I suddenly realized) old body moved at an angle as he took himself across the room.

"I will, I will do it," Ava said. "You know that. It's not good for you to fret about it."

"Of course," he said in a small voice, his back still turned to those of us remaining at the table.

"Stig," Robert spoke up, and I admired him for it. "You don't know what you'll be missing by not taking the trip."

The white-bearded man at the window turned to face us: me, Ava, his brother-in-law. "Oh, I know, but I'm too old to adjust to new light . . . "

"What kind of a thing is that to say?" Robert asked.

"Oh, Stig," Ava said, her voice now packed suddenly with the sound of charity and forgiveness. "I want to stay with you, and I want to go west for a time. Why can't I do both?"

He turned to his wife and inclined his head a little, as though listening to some sound other than her voice. "Our kind of people, we want to do everything all at once. Well, my dear, you must try it. Go west for the summer, and Harriet will go with you. Won't you, Harriet?"

I flinched, feeling as though he had caught me staring too intently at his brother-in-law. "Yes, yes, I will."

"Bravo!" said Robert, reaching for my hand. His touch felt as hot to me as a poker.

"Oh! Oh! Look at the clouds! Look! Look! Poor Stig!" Ava said as we climbed down from the train in Albuquerque. I was tasting the oddly flavored air while Ava hopped about in a little dance among the baggage. "Stig!" she hollered. "You poor fool! You damned fool!"

Dark-eyed, dark-skinned men in dusty clothing hefted our suitcases.

"There!" Ava said, pointing toward a cloud of dust rising in the wake of a large black automobile roaring toward us.

"Here *you* are!" said the big-boned, red-faced woman in the large yellow sun hat as she stepped down from the passenger's seat. It was someone named Mabel Dodge, who had written to Ava saying that she would pick us up at the station after Robert Boldin had told her that we were coming. I knew this about her: that she was a pioneer woman in many ways and had come west to give herself room in which to live her life larger than she could comfortably in New York. Among her famous loves had been Jack Reed, who had died in Russia of typhus about a dozen-or-so years ago, and recently, or so we'd heard in New York, David Lawrence, the British writer. He had brought his German wife with him to this part of the country, and she might not have enjoyed the spectacle of Mabel working her charms on the man. As I watched Mabel direct the handlers with our luggage, I noticed that she had very large charms, or could put them on if she so desired.

A man leaned out of the car window, and I could see that Mabel Dodge was currently employing her charms to good advantage. "This is my husband, Tony," she said to us.

Tony, his face as dark as old clay, moved his mouth in a smile, though his eyes did not waver. He was the living picture of an Indian chief in his prime.

"Hello, Tony," Ava said from where we stood on the pavement. Silence.

"Hello, Tony," I said. Silence.

"Darling?" Mabel spoke as if to a child or an animal she had trained.

"Welcome to my land," the man spoke at last. His eyes were large, beautiful black pools of emptiness. I watched him watch us, and when I wasn't watching him, I was watching Ava watch him. It was as though she had just turned her eyes on a large tree the likes of which she had never seen before, or a waterfall at the edge of a forest. Or—or—I couldn't find the words to describe it, the way she stared at him. This was new to her—the air, the glow, the men, the sound of Tony's odd, uninflected voice on our ears—and new, very new to me. The only thing I found familiar was the way that watching her excited me.

We drove north out of Albuquerque and saw something of "Tony's land": the desert that fell straight away on either side of the narrow highway, the mountains—the Jemez, Mabel named them—to the west, the Sangre de Cristo range growing more and more visible to the north . . . and the great thunderclouds already gathering over both stretches of peaks. Tony's land included the sky. The sky seemed almost half the land, so close down did it bear upon us, and so broadly did it spread out above us. In the East if you see that much sky, as when, say, you're floating on your back just off our Isle of Palms, you don't truly look upon it; the sun makes it so bright that you have to blink and blink and quickly turn away. And when there is no sun, you see clouds only, or only parts of sky. Here you could stare at the sky all morning and not be blinded—the light, the sun was so distinctive.

We bumped along the bad road past Santa Fe at far too great a speed for the car—and for us, the passengers—but Mabel was in a hurry to get us settled before dinner, and the bad roads be damned. "Hurry, Tony," she said to her companion behind the wheel, "hurry it up—watch out for that rock!—here's the curve—hurry it up!" Tony remained silent, concentrating on the road that led northward into a vast blank space of sky.

Ava had grown up beneath such skies as these, though nothing, as she later assured me, as pure and empty all the time as this New Mexico space. But she at least knew something of what to expect. For myself I kept noticing how in this great dusty valley between the mountains and the horizon, you could put all of my home state, and still have room left over for much of the ocean besides.

Ava seemed steady, quiet, as though she were imitating Tony the driver in his silent Indianness—but I couldn't help myself for pointing out, in counterpoint to Mabel's instructions to Tony, that rock formation, those mountains, that stretch of valley!

Here! We arrived! And then there was Robert waiting for us in the doorway—Robert, whose presence I had allowed myself to play hide-and-seek with during our long train trip.

He looks at me and I look at him, I look away, and then look back to see him just looking away, and then I stare, and he comes back to looking at me. My head is spinning—all this space around us—this man here with us, when we repair to the patio to drink wine and stare at the land falling away on all sides.

"Why, it's as though . . . " I started to say.

"As though what?" Robert stared down at me with his pigeon-wing gray eyes.

"As though . . . I'm trying to find the words, Robert . . . as though the ocean off Charleston had evaporated and all that was left was the bottom of the sea. That's what it looks like to me out here."

"And *we're* the sea creatures," Mabel Dodge stepped up behind me. "Though the water's been gone so long, we're all dried out, not so wet and wriggling as you might imagine."

"We're the what?" Ava came over and touched a finger to my bare arm.

"Sea creatures," Mabel said.

"Sea?" Ava looked puzzled.

"This was all once a great sea, a great ocean," her brother said. "Here where we stand."

"Even the peaks were underwater for a time," Mabel said. "That's what I like. An entire world underwater."

"And we've risen from beneath?" Ava asked. "We've come back from a world all drowned?"

"I like that idea," I said. "I feel that way sometimes."

"Do you really?"

Something crumpled inside me, as though she'd taken one of her small drawings on paper and crushed it in her fist—and then tossed it in the trash basket. I couldn't explain it to myself, but my knees nearly went.

"Here," Robert said, taking me under the arm. "You look as though you can hardly hold up that glass. Too much traveling in one day; that can get to you. Too much train, too much car. I know. In my work I do too much of it myself."

"Yes, you do look a little tired," Ava said, staring at his hand on my arm.

"It's the altitude," he said. "I pay a price for coming here."

Ava touched his cheek in a fashion almost maternal. "Robert, I forgot about your heart. I shouldn't have, but I did."

By this time evening had descended, like some huge muslin curtain that had dropped quickly from above and caught us all with glasses in hand, still thinking about the light. A net of odors fell upon us as well, a mixture of dry wood that had soaked up sun all day, all season, and something like the memory of moisture, the last vestiges of recollection in the senses of the old sea that might have boiled here a million years ago.

"A hundred million years, give or take a million," was how Robert put it. "Some people think when I talk like this that it's godless, but geology makes you realize greater glory, if you consider it, the way it enlarges any notions of creation you might have. It makes you think big, so it makes God bigger."

"Have you been worrying about these things?" Ava said to him.

"When your heart worries you, you think about such matters," he said.

She touched his cheek again. "Are you having more trouble?"

"No more, no less than usual," he said.

Mabel and her husband floated up to us, moving quite lightly for two heavy creatures. She was a big woman, but Tony in his bulk made her seem, if not diminished, at least normal sized. Her curiosity was not. "What are you discussing?" she asked.

"We're talking about geology and mortality," Robert said. "Such matters as that."

"Look up and you'll feel better," Mabel said. "The stars are coming out. You can't worry about mortality under a sky like this, not out here."

All of us turned our attention to where millions of gallons of light seemed to have spilled across the vast landscape of the sky at sunset. Silence weighed on us for an uncountable series of minutes; silence buoyed us up closer to these brilliant, unclouded heavens, where all the turbulent water in the old oceanbed below seemed to have found a luminescent second home.

Robert did not stay more than a few days with us before heading off on company business. "To the Jemez Mountains," he told us.

"He's always on the trail of some powerful fuel or other," Ava said as we waved our last good-byes and he drove away from the hacienda, south through town toward the main highway south. "I've always thought him as solid as the rocks he chases," she added. "Despite the trouble he's had with his heart."

"Yes, he seems so."

She had noticed something in my manner, and she wasn't about to let it go. "He *is* a good man," she said.

"Did I say that he wasn't?"

Ava shook her head. "No," she said, giving me a sly look.

I excused myself, turning quietly back to the house. With Mabel ensconced there, it was not a place to talk about anything one cared about. She was one of those people, artists without an art, who made it her business to be in charge of everything that came her way, on the excuse that she had a need to make a design of it all.

I got to think of him a lot that night after bedtime when I stole from my room and went out onto the patio and stood beneath a great cascade of stars—stars stars stars stars stars—a balcony of stars—more stars—wondering what was to become of me. For something had come over me, or left—it was difficult to describe the sensation of these past few weeks; meeting Robert and deciding to come: the two things compounded in my mind; and after we moved the next day to the small house high up the mountain where we would stay for the rest of our time here—admittedly, thanks to Mabel—Ava painting and me working on my poems, I thought a great deal about my new condition. My premature change of life is what I'm referring to. There is not a lot of talk about this situation, though, unlike childbirth, which will always remain a mystery both to me and my friend Ava, it is something that all women will eventually know, no matter how they choose to live or how the world chooses for them. Remain alive and it will come to you—or should I say, it will steal from you the old feeling of knowing always since young girlhood who and what you are about.

Some mornings I followed Ava's progress with my eyes from the house to the point where she disappeared behind the tall rocks to the east of us where she would spend the day at work, and before going in to sit at the little table with my paper in front of me, I wondered if everything I had done before was a prelude to what I

had recently become—an aspiring poet and a woman in meno-
pause—or if the life I had now entered was the coda to all my other
days. The vast plain before us had been a seabed so many millions
of years before, and I had been a girl in Charleston, a not-ungifted
pianist with suitors at my door, and, I thought: Look at me now.

"This must be what a lobster feels like when he's being boiled
for dinner," I said over our meal one night soon after.

"Don't demean yourself," Ava said. "Take courage. It's part of
your life."

"Courage?" I took out one of the cigarettes I had borrowed from
Mabel Dodge before we left for the mountain and smoked on
through dinner, the first time I had ever done that.

"Does smoking help?" Ava asked.

"Don't you know anything about this?" I asked her.

Ava shrugged and offered me more salad made of the greens
which Mabel's mozo—a sort of handyman, janitor, and houseman—
had plucked from the little garden he tended behind the main house.
It had cheered us at first to see the inviting patch of green against
the dry, clay-brown earth, a touch of the East against this blank
western ground. I suppose that by this time I took for granted that
someone out here would work to grow such familiar things, despite
the hardship of a land where water was as precious as mother's milk
in a nursery.

"I don't know, actually," she said, and shook her head. "I haven't
gone through it yet, and if anything, I'm afraid my girlhood's coming back, now that we're west of the Rockies."

A thunderstorm lighted up the western sky after dinner. Ava
and I stood out on the flat roof of our little house, careful not to
damage any of the tiles, and watched the sharp white-yellow flashes
of light, bright explosions that showed up the edges of clouds that
might have been hundreds of miles long and eight, ten miles high,
up to where they faded in the afterlight back into the night, where
the stars used to be before the storm.

"What must it be like out there right now?" Ava asked.

"Out where?"

"Out in those mountains, under that storm. Great bolts of lightning so close, striking trees nearby? Can you smell the burning of

the gases in the air? Hear the hiss of the clouds as they evaporate in the heat?"

"It would be quite frightening," I said. "Caught in that rain that must come with it."

"It would be like suddenly finding yourself underwater," she said.

"I don't know," I said.

"I'd love to find out," she said. "When I think how the colors might be, the storm from the inside, I wouldn't mind trying to find out."

I slept rather fitfully that night, with the storm rumbling hour upon hour. Once I sat up in what seemed like a dream, sudden utter stillness in the midst of the thundering, and imagined I saw Ava standing at the foot of my bed. Next I awoke to light—that was a dream, I know—and the next time back into the storm, with the night air around me in my room like water stirred by a stick, and sticking to me, too, as though it were more like makeup or paint than something we breathed. Taking myself to the window, I looked out upon the last traces of the storm, faint flashes of light where the road led out across the old oceanbed, spurts of light bursting faintly across the tops of mesas, those little mountains worn down as if by the gods pressing weights against them for eternity. If I had walked out into the surf off Sullivan's Island, might I have seen, if I descended far enough, scenes somewhat like this?

The next time I awoke it was fully light, nearly seven o'clock, and I took my breakfast alone, Ava having already gone off to work out-of-doors. My body felt extremely heavy to me, and I walked through the first few minutes after breakfast as though dragging weights. A bath seemed in order, but I didn't yet know how to light the little charcoal heater that would prepare the water to my liking. I sat in the new sun for an hour or so, notebook on my lap. But nothing came. When I retreated inside, it took me a while to adjust my eyes to the interior shade. My mind, it appeared, couldn't adjust at all. For no reason I began to tremble and then I sat in tears for even longer than it took my eyes to become accustomed to the absence of direct sun. I tore myself from my chair and dashed outside again, getting as far as the edge of the patio, where I saw a lizard sunning itself on the tiles. It skittered away at my approach, and against all reason I once again burst into tears.

Lizard
Scale down my heart to your size
So I may take in sun through every pore.
Wise you are to sleep and bake
Your soul instead of opening it like a door.

I was in and out of this sun the next few days: the shade felt like still, cool water, the raw light like pure heat, water like liquid stone. My baths amazed me. I shivered, and then laughed, laughed and called out so loud that the mozo came running. "Pardon!" he said when he appeared at the door, averting his eyes and backing away. And well he should have averted his gaze, for what man could look upon a dried-out, freckle-chested stick of a woman as old as I—forty plus!—her dark hair all askew from rubbing her knuckles across her skull, saying to herself, "Where has it all gone? Where has it all gone?"—without turning to stone?

Stone
Air water fire stone
Elements of my life alone.
Stone fire water air
Birthmarks of an old despair.

I admitted that much to myself over the next few days. What had I come to in this time on earth? No husband or lover (now), no children (ever), a few friends only (and each of them caught up in her or his own problems and projects, if not despair), no family (all dead or dispersed). Bathing and sitting in the shade, sleeping during the hottest part of the dry, dry days, standing out under the stars on the patio at night, this woman was slowly finding her way toward her new condition.

Old Song
Once a green place, where springs
Flowed sweet, this valley sings
Of a life long gone.
Willows thrived here, meadow things;
Now mesas haunt us, all alone.

Old volcanoes, dry riverbeds,

The rocks show what I will become.
Deserted ledges, tattered banners,
Knocking of a cast-off drum.

"What is going on with you?" Ava asked at dinner.

"Ah, you've noticed. Could it have been that the pistol I was pointing at my head caught the reflection of the early morning sun and you turned to look?"

"I *didn't* notice that, no," Ava said with a twirl of her wrist. "But I *have* noticed you. I'd like you to sit for me. I want to break my rule about no more people in my work, and I want you to sit for me."

"Why?" I found it exceedingly odd, my Ava ignoring her iron rules like this. Years ago, she had once explained to me, she had vowed that she would never paint portraits, never again.

"I can't say, really. Call it a whim. I'd just like to do it . . . if you'll agree."

"Ava, we came out here so that you could paint the land, the air and the sky, the clouds. I can sit for you anytime, anywhere."

"Are you saying no?"

I shook my head.

"As you like. I'd at least like to sketch you," she said.

"And capture my last days as a desirous woman?" I asked.

Ava gave a shake of her head, as though trying to toss off a bothersome insect. But none flew in this thin air. "Why did you say that?"

As sudden as any flash flood in the mountains all around us, tears filled my eyes, blurring the soft lights of the candles at our table.

"You dear," Ava said, coming around to my side of the little pine table. "You poor thing. You poor thing." I shivered at the touch of cool fingers on my skin.

I might have agreed to anything right then and there: to sit for her, or whatever else . . . and I did agree, but without words, because a knock came at the door at that moment, and Ava stepped away to call out to the party (or parties, as it turned out) on the other side, and in came Mabel and Tony, bearing several large, covered picnic baskets.

204

"We've eaten, thank you," Ava said with a smile. I could tell that she was slightly annoyed at the intrusion, but this was, after all, our hostess and host, and so she accepted it in her usual quiet fashion.

"But you haven't eaten tomorrow," Mabel said. "And here is food for tomorrow." Her eyes moved from Ava to me and back again, and then she nodded for her husband, the big, dark Tony, to set the baskets on the table near the door.

"And what's tomorrow?" Ava could scarcely control the annoyance in her voice.

"Tomorrow is a good time to walk up into the mountains," Mabel said. "The weather will be wonderful . . . "

"The weather seems always wonderful," Ava said.

"At this time of year," Mabel said, "except for an occasional storm in the mountains. Well, we won't sit down, thank you, we just wanted to drop off these baskets."

Ava stared at the table where these gifts rested. "If we did decide to walk tomorrow, it would be difficult to carry these heavy things," she said.

"Oh, one of the boys from the house will carry them for you," Mabel said.

"A bearer? No, no," Ava said. "If we were to go, and we hadn't thought of going, to tell you the truth . . . "

"We're working well," I put in.

"Yes," said Ava. She looked at me and I looked at her. And we laughed. Together.

"It was only an idea," Mabel said. "There's homemade jam in the basket, and hard-boiled eggs."

"And where do you suggest we walk?" Ava asked.

"Oh, no, Ava," I said. "You're working . . . "

"It might help you," my friend said.

"Help her?" Mabel asked.

"Harriet's looking for a subject for a new poem. Rocks might be good. Ever since my brother taught me about rocks, I've always found comfort in them."

I couldn't help but laugh again.

"Rocks?" Mabel seemed puzzled, but we didn't mind. She and her Tony stood there silently, as though they themselves might have been carved out of the dusty stone of the region.

"We have many here," Tony finally broke the pause.

"Most of them in my head," Mabel said. "I didn't want to disturb you. I just thought that you might like a suggestion or two about what places to see. It's been days now . . ."

"We came to work," Ava said. "I don't mean to be rude, but that's what we came to do."

"And it *is* going well?" Mabel asked. Her large-boned body shifted beneath her large muslin dress.

"Very well," said Ava.

"We'd love to see some of it . . . when you're ready to show it."

"When it dries," Ava said.

"Oh, of course," said Mabel. She turned to Tony and gave him a knowing nod of her head. "When it dries. We'll have an art festival. Harriet will read her poems and you will show your canvases. We'll lack only musicians and dancers."

"We'll try to find them," Ava said.

"Oh, we could find them," Mabel said. "Easily. But . . ."—and here her lower lip curled up and you could catch for a fleeting moment the way she might have looked as a spoiled child some fifty or sixty years earlier—". . . you aren't making fun of all this, are you? It means a great deal to me that you're here."

"Oh, no, no, no," Ava said. "We're *having* lots of fun, not making fun. Of you? Dear Mabel, is that what you thought?"

"She is like a leech of the mind," Ava said after they had gone. "I don't see how anyone stays here very long. She has no vocation herself and so lives off the vocations of others." She got caught up in a little shiver, and turned back to me, though with her eyes still on the door through which Mabel and Tony had recently departed. "I know it is her very own house . . ."

"Just what I was thinking!"

" . . . but it is my very own soul that she'd like to catch and put in a cage! Or tack up on her wall!"

"No," I said. "No, no, no, no, no . . ." And I burst into tears again.

"There, there," I heard Ava say as I stood with my back to her, my hands pressed over my eyes.

That night she came to my bedside and spent some long minutes calming me down. I was so upset, though why I couldn't say. I felt as though some cold spirit hovered just outside the range of my fingertips if I stretched out my arms, just above my bed in the dark.

"There, there," Ava tried to soothe me, patting me on the shoulder, on the back.

"It's all so bleak," I heard myself say, thinking back on the years and years. "It means nothing," I said in a wail, "no-thing. You know, I remember the day my first flow came. I took it calmly, until my mother said something about the coming months. Every month! I remember crying out. Once was a trial that I could stand – but every month afterward for the rest of my life? And now I see that I should not have complained so much, since it *won't* be for the rest of my life."

"So you are slightly more optimistic now?"

"No, it's all still dark before me. It still means nothing."

"What, my love? What is it? What means nothing?" Ava's voice lingered at my ear, so close that it was both breath and sound in one.

"Everything that I have done and haven't done in my life," I told her.

"I know that can't be true, since we did so many things together," Ava said. "And we're here now. And we'll do things tomorrow." Her hand lighted gently on the back of my head.

"We may," I said. "But all the things we might have done, what about them?" I turned in my agony on the bed and faced her in the dimness of the room. The slightest tinge of blue had seeped into the night beyond the window. No moon, or if there was a moon, then only a sliver somewhere out of sight beyond the frame. There was a slight taste of tar in the air, or some kind of burning wood I had not smelled before. A dog barked somewhere far away.

"Push over," Ava said, and I made room for her alongside me. "You've set me to thinking about my own first blood. And of my twin sister . . . " There was a catch in her voice, and I waited expectantly; for what, I couldn't have said. ". . . who died as I was being born . . . and whose spirit lived with me a while. Until my own blood came. After that I scarcely heard a whisper from her, and then it was, I was sure, only a memory of the many conversations we had had all through my childhood. Since I never knew my mother, this ghost girl was a kind of friend to me no one else could become. I thought then, and I'm convinced now as I tell you about it, that my first blood was *hers*."

"Oh, Ava," I said, "what a life it is, what a world to live in!"

"It's nothing," she said in a whisper. "Just an old memory. The crazy things we carry from childhood. Up here, in this rare atmosphere, it all seems to stand out more purely: recollections, old shapes . . . "

She began to tremble in my arms, and for a moment I thought that she might be crying. But when I touched a finger to her eyes, they were dry. "Let's sleep," she said, turning slightly against me.

"We will," I said.

Our breathing settled, and I listened to the sounds of the particular night around us, a night so dark that it might have been a palpable presence carved of ebony, or a wall of coal black stone. From where we lay, you couldn't see any stars.

I awoke into sunlight as thick as dew, as warm as the faintest oil. Ava was gone to work, leaving me to stare at the covered baskets on the table.

"What if we take that walk Mabel suggested?" I asked over a late lunch of goat cheese and tea.

"It's more a hike than a walk, I'm sure," Ava said. "She takes and says things very lightly, that woman does. If she says walk, it might be miles. If she says sleep, it might be death."

"You don't want to do it," I said.

Ava tilted her head at me in a childlike gesture, rare for her. "You do, I can tell. So we will."

"Thank you," I said.

It took another day to get this plan going and by that time, whatever food Mabel had put into the basket for us had turned stale. We packed our own, and with a few directions from the mozo started off toward the hills to the northwest. I soon slowed us down to admire the plants: the devil's claw, the spiny cholla, and patches of blooming morning glories, and the diminutive verbena—the mozo

had walked me this far before we started out, telling me the names —
the poppylike Arizona caltrop, the wand of the desert spoon, tall
and spindly in the light wind, the desert marigolds brilliant alongside the path toward the hills.

"You've been busy," Ava said, admiring each plant as I pointed
it out to her, as the mozo had done for me.

"No more, no less than you, though in my own way," I said.

"I've painted some of these plants without knowing what to call
them."

"To name them doesn't mean that I see them as well as you," I
said.

Slipping a hand around my waist as we walked, she gave me
the sweet assurance of her companionship. It was a perfectly clear,
warm, sunny morning, a beautiful time for walking, but as the sun
grew stronger, it made us want to dally, too, and we stopped
frequently, now one of us, now the other, calling attention to the
great bowl of the old oceanbed to the west, or to rocks heaped here
and there as though flung down by some childlike deity in a tan-
trum. The farmhouse and outbuildings below appeared to belong
to that same child, so small they had become, though when we
looked up and ahead we could see an occasional hawk, to whom
we must have appeared as much in miniature as the buildings did
to us. The idea of climbing hadn't occurred to me until I saw the
beginning of the cleft of rock we were to hike into and up for the
next hour or so.

"Do you see?" Ava asked, pointing to the enfolded, water-carved
indentations in the rock face.

"I see," I said, shaking my head at the way in which nature
seemed to have mirrored — in such vast proportions — the lower parts
of the female body.

"I will see these things, and you will put them into words."

A mile or so further we left the rutted path and began to climb
up, and into, a small, converging, enfolding hollow, much larger
than the cleft had seemed from a distance: a vibrant, shady place
where small birds nested and moisture flowed down canyon walls
to form a wet creekbed. This moist bed marked the place where
water and rock face met, the softest, most-receptive region, the locus,
evolution, and promise of this clefting that we had both seen so

clearly as we approached. And as we walked single file up and into the small cut, we slowed to move our hands across these familiar ridges of the canyon's mouth, wondering to ourselves, or at least I was wondering, how something so accidental as these walls could seem so absolutely made for us to notice. This appeared to be no ordinary trail, and the excitement we felt belonged as much to the landscape as to ourselves.

"Do you think Mabel planned it this way?" I asked.

"Which?"

"This. This path."

"She's not that smart," Ava said. "Though even she might have noticed these things."

"This place certainly makes me think about *my* body," I said. "And without any Tony or his kind to make me think it, either."

She stopped to lean against the rock and I stopped with her, looking up beyond the ascending canyon wall to the rim, where dwarf cedars and piñon pine pointed at odd angles into the bluest sky I had ever seen.

Had I walked from the beach at Sullivan's Island out into the water and proceeded until the ocean covered me, and then looked up from one of the undersea hillsides that slant down toward the bottom of the Atlantic shelf, I could not have felt more remote from my old life than I did now. The wind splashed through the tree branches above us, as though it had turned into a marvelous liquid, something palpable that we might touch with our outstretched fingers before it ran off along the canyon walls and turned into the moisture at our backs and feet.

"Listen," Ava said. "It's as though the world's breathing. With these walls around me, the sky up there, I feel as though . . . " She was staring straight up the rock wall, with its striated markings giving it the appearance of old clay that some child had scratched upon with a stick or knife.

"What?"

"I . . . saw . . . " Her warm breath bathed my face.

"Yes?"

She glanced up, and then jerked her head down again, as though someone might have slapped her on the skull. This trembling began, the kind that we hear comes with electric shock.

"Ava, what is it?"

"Ho!" Her body leaped in my arms.

"Ava?"

"Hee!"

"What? What is it?"

"Hi! Hee!"

"Ava!" I clutched at her as I might a squirming child or a large cat that tried to evade my grasp, and then she seemed to settle herself slightly, and it became more like embracing a wounded bird, its wings fluttering but carrying it nowhere.

"I'm all right now," she said, taking a deep breath, but she was not all right until long minutes after, when her spasms ceased at last and we sat, our backs to the rock face, on a sunny ledge, our legs stretched out in front of us.

"We're quite a pair, aren't we?" I said. "You taking care of me the other night in my distress, and now . . . "

"I'm not in distress," Ava said in a voice quiet but determined. "I know it looked painful, but I was not in pain." Her eye was on the slice of sky above us, where the sun washed through, bathing our bodies in heat and light.

"Oh," she said, getting to her feet. "I want to look." Without a glance back at me, she was suddenly heading up the path, the bag with her drawing materials bouncing against her back as she bounded along. I followed her, leaving the food behind except for the sack that I held in my hands. In a moment she had reached the top of the tablelike mesa, and I arrived soon after.

"Now I see nothing," Ava said, surveying the vast space all around us, a view with more sky than earth. The sky was so vast it seemed to lead our eyes into regions closer to the moon, just rising to the east, than to the puny habitations we had left behind and below.

"What was it that you saw before?" I asked, watching her, then staring out all around us. I could not have been more amazed at this view than if I had gone to sleep on earth and awakened on another planet.

When she didn't answer my question I asked another. "Did you know all this was here?"

"This?"

211

"This . . . this space . . . this air . . . this light . . . "

She was silent a moment, though I saw her lips move, and I could hear the wind pouring over the pines just below us at the canyon's lip, like water spilling off a table onto paper, or leaves. That wind was cool, and if it hadn't been for the sun on our faces and chests, we would have been shivering at noon, or whatever early hour it was—time? all time faded into something we had left behind: with the farmhouse, with the traveling, with New York and the lake, Anderson, Stig, the conversation Ava and I had had in Gramercy Park—all that became part of a strangely distant past, not just distant in days and miles, but as if it belonged to another life, another plane; as though we had been in those moments another species, as foreign to the way we felt now as, say, these hawks circling above us were different from the lizards we might see clinging to the canyon walls.

"What I felt was something else," Ava said after a while. "All this and more. I don't know that I can tell you . . . "

"Please try." I sighed deeply, my breath sounding faint and hoarse, like the wind at a distance.

"While we were climbing."

"Yes?"

"In that odd way up through the rock . . . " She took a deep breath now, and I could see in this special light all the new lines at her eyes and the corners of her mouth.

"Tell me."

"I thought I heard something. But it might have been the wind."

"What did you think you heard?"

Ava shook her head. "Let's sit and eat now. Did you save some of the food?"

I held up the sack I had lugged this entire way. "We've got apples and chocolate," I said.

"I've got water in my pack," she said. "Along with my materials. I always bring water when I go outside."

"Outside," I said, giving in to a little laugh.

Ava gave me one of her appraising looks, the kind I sometimes saw her apply to objects as she made a mental cartoon of them, preparatory to putting them in her sketchbook. Well, I don't actually know if that's what she was doing when she looked like that, but I always imagined she was. I could have been a hawk or a rock or a spiky plant the way she looked at me.

"I thought I heard someone calling to me."

"Someone?"

"A voice. Like . . . " She broke off, and with a quick toss of her head tried to turn her attention to the plants around her.

"Who was it?" I asked, trying to get her to look at me again.

She said something in a whisper.

"Who?"

"My sister," she said.

"What?"

"My sister Eve," she said in a voice as dry as the dust and stone around us. "I heard a blue jay and when I looked up, I saw her face."

By the time we returned to the house, we were both so exhausted that it was an ordeal just to nibble at the meal we found prepared for us on the table—stew, tortillas wrapped in a cloth, a warm bottle of beer standing at each table setting—let alone talk about what had happened up in the canyon.

"Tell me about her," I said when, after our early supper, I had gotten into my nightgown and washed in the bowl before the small mirror and climbed into bed.

"I don't know much," she said. "I don't know much at all."

But she talked a while, telling me family stories, which got me to thinking about Robert again. Oh, those nights under this new sky! what things showed forth! But if it could bring me a poem or two, then I would say it was welcome, this odd part of my life, our life, together.

Ava must have fallen asleep alongside me again, because when I awoke in darkness, her weight had pressed against my shoulder and made it numb. Dogs howled outside the house, and my bladder ached. Slipping out from under the weight of my friend, I walked out onto the patio and opened the door to the dark ocean of the desert night, taking a few steps out onto the grainy plain, raising my nightgown, and squatting.

Oooh, the wild dogs, coyotes, whatever, called out around me.

Hooo, I said silently back to them.

Hip,hip,hoo-woogh! they called to the high white stars.

In the silence that followed, a great roar of nothingness rushed in around my ears. A terrifying chill came over me, and I saw myself suddenly alone under the huge milky canopy of the universe, nothing between me and the emptiness but the thin nightgown that brushed against my bare knees.

Hoo-hee — hoo — hee-wheee! the coyotes called after me as I hurried back to the temporary safety of the house and my dear friend Ava, asleep and dreaming of who-knew-what more-urgent matters than these.

DOOR

The mysteries of family — I will never fathom them. Robby and I fly east to Alexandria to see my parents and then to visit his Grandma Cissy, while Michael stays at Blue Mesa to care for Ava.

"Socorro can handle it," I say to him.

But he won't agree. "She needs me," he says.

"Your own mother might like to see you, too," I reply.

"Aw, she'll take one look at Robby and she'll forget I'm even there. Look, you go and give me a full report."

That was one of the things I hoped to get — his mother's story, that is — though I couldn't really tell him. He'd accuse me of being a soul stealer or something like that, or at least devious and disrespectful. How conservative he's become since Robby was born. I know that it's probably good for the baby, but I'm not sure that I like it.

I should be thinking about the mysteries of family, I tell myself as the airplane banks to the northeast. "See the clouds, darling," I hear myself say to Robby. "See the beautiful clouds." And when he finally sleeps, I try to doze myself, and the mysteries of family become lost to me.

I wander off, I dream. Of a perfect moment with Ava, in which she leads me out onto the mesa and shows me the space around us glowing with a light more pure than anything I've ever seen . . .

And I turn to smile at her, filled as I am with a feeling that seems similar to the illumination, as though I were glowing from my soul outward. She returns the smile, pointing a finger to her forehead where, within her skull, a manifold rose appears to be growing through the bone and flesh . . .

We visit Alexandria first, though I certainly haven't admitted to myself just how fearful I am about seeing my parents.

"Have you misplaced your wedding band?" Mommy says to me during our first few moments together. She may be slightly tipsy, as usual, but she notices these important details.

"My fingers swell when I fly," I say.

"Her fingers swell when she flies," she says to Daddy, her voice the changing barometer of all our conflicts from my childhood on through college.

"That happens," says my father, taking Robby from my arms and holding him up for inspection, as if he might, if he looked carefully enough, find a flaw that would make it possible to return my son to the store.

"Let me," says Mommy, wrestling Robby from his hold and whirling him around the room. "Careful," I say, instantly sorry that I've spoken.

"Oh," she says, "I carried you and your brothers long enough; I can carry this little package."

Daddy invites me to lunch the next day, just the two of us. But I'm wary of leaving Robby alone with Mommy and so I insist that she come along.

A day and a half into the visit, Mommy finally inquires about Michael. I'm ready for her then, having slipped on my finger the wedding band that I've bought for myself downtown after our funny little lunch, at which Robby entertained them both to the point of near ecstasy. "Love you," he said.

"Love you," Mommy said.

"*Don't* love you," he said.

And then she pretended to cry.

"Love you," he said.

Daddy took photographs of this exhibition.

"Love you," Robby said.

I never stopped in Albany for more than a traffic light until I met Michael. Now it seems like a safe harbor after Alexandria.

216

"Oh, look at this, will you? Look at this!" Cissy scoops Robby from the floor and disappears with him into the kitchen. It's only after she puts him down for a nap that she allows me to bring up the subject of Ava, and it's an hour or so before she seems to feel even a little comfortable about talking.

But she talks. . . .

UPSTATE

Cissy

Men just have no idea of the amazing lives we women live, not unless we tell them. And even then they may still never comprehend. They are always daring themselves to bravery or hardship— you see it in hunting season up this way each year—and I think this is so because their lives are really so simple and easy, at least in comparison. Finding work so you can feed those hungry mouths at the table, even work with your hands, is not such a tragedy, as my mother used to say, not compared to giving birth to those children in the first place, and then raising them up. They should have to be the ones to open their legs, and then where would we be? Humans would die out within a generation, for no man would want to carry a child to term. He likes his adventure discontinuous, the man does. With a lot of rest between. And servant girls to wait on him. Girls like me, who've had circumstances such as her parents dying on her, and she had to take work with a rich family with a grand summer house on Lake Cossayuna, which, in case you haven't yet figured it out, is where I come into the story of this glorious artist's life, and into yours as well.

After the fire at the farm that killed my parents and my little brother Mike, I was taken in by my mother's Aunt Lydia, but she wasn't long for this world, either. "Aunt Lydia," I remember myself saying to my darling aunt one snowy afternoon when we were sitting around the fire with the quilt that was our winter project, "when I see the mean fathers that stay alive and mine being dead, it makes me hate the world, this cruel awful place!"

And I began to shed tears upon the quilt. It was a farm design, with animals and corn and trees and houses, all in little squares, and two little farmers, the farmer and his wife, and the sun in one

218

corner and the moon in the other. It was a pretty picture indeed of Washington County that we were finishing up, although the reality of life on the farm, at least as I knew it, and what showed on the quilt were as different one from the other as life is from dreams. I remember mostly the cold and the dark and the work, and nothing to resemble the pretty design beneath our fingertips except, perhaps, now and then in a tender moment with my mother and father, and they were both gone in the fire.

It was just after my Aunt Lydia's passing that the doctor who attended her made his suggestion. "I know of something you might do, Cissy," he said, throwing an arm around me for comfort's sake. But I was feeling so solitary already while waiting for the grief to come that I pulled away. "There's a family from New York City," he went on, "that keeps a summer house on the lake . . ."

And so it was that I found myself walking one afternoon soon after my Lydia's funeral up the old road toward Cossayuna Lake, thinking more about the needs I would have in the weeks ahead than the great future lying before me.

The Stigmar house, a dozen rooms and more, was built right out to the edge of the lake, where fireflies danced over the little lawn at night, and you could hear birds call over the water at sunrise and sunset so you didn't need to set no clock for waking, or know what time it was when you went to bed. Larks and bobolinks, bobwhites and hoot owls, now and then an egret, and sometimes flights of ducks and geese whirred across the water, and I could see them from the little window in the third-floor room my mistress, Mrs. Emeralda Stigmar, gave me as my own, where I set up a neat little dresser with my comb and brush and a bracelet or two, a few things I had inherited from Aunt Lydia, may she rest in peace, and with my quilts piled high atop the narrow but comfortable bed, I made myself a home that I would keep for a good while.

The previous maid, whose room I was taking over, had out of the blue gone off and eloped, according to the doctor, who had heard about it from his summer patient, the lady of the house and the wife of a department store owner—or he heard about the vacancy, in any case. If anybody was gossiping, it wasn't Mrs. Stigmar but probably Jesse, the old houseman, who lived out in back of the house in a small cabin where the tools were kept. It was recent the maid had run. And I was the lucky duck to get her job.

"They're good people to work for, though they's Jews, you know," Jesse said while partaking of one of my meals in the big white kitchen I was pleased to make my own.

"So what's that supposed to mean?"

"They crucified our Lord," Jesse said. "Though these particular Jews, they seem all right to me. Mister Stigmar is a real nice gent. He don't come up much, working as he does in his big store down in New York. And the missus. Big woman. But never cross. It don't go with me, a big woman with a bad temper. But she's always looking out for me. 'Jesse, did you get your meal? Jesse, can you use a pair of trousers?' Always like that, like I was a little boy and not about her age—which is, hum, maybe say, getting up there in her seventies. 'Jesse this, Jesse that.' She's got a boy. But he's all growed. That be Mister Albert. He's a picture taker. Don't work at anything else. His wife certainly don't work, neither. She paints pictures in the little house out near the water. Used to be a playhouse, I think, though nobody ever said to me what it was. That's a fine couple; they don't give me no guff. 'Cept it seems strange a man don't work; now when the woman don't work, I can figure that, but it's for the man I wonder about.

"But you don't have to worry. You'll be keeping busy: cooking the meals, cleaning, fixing the beds, ironing, sewing. Though Missus Emeralda—and what kind of a crazy name that is, I never could figure—she will not work you to your death, if that is what you're fearing, and the master of the house you'll hardly ever see, because he's always down in the big city. Mainly in the hot days you'll see Mister Albert and Missus Ava, and if the whole world was as easy to please as these two, Jesus never would have had to come into the world. Even if they is Jews."

"Jesse, I don't want to talk religion," I said, serving this good man his apple pie, which I had learned to bake from my dear old ma, Mama so long gone now, "and I don't have to listen about it, either. They could be Jews, and they could be Catholic. They seem to treat you real nice, and I hope they'll do the same to me."

"They might," he said. "You're real cute."

220

"Get out of my kitchen," I said, giving his chair a playful little shove.

He took the rest of his pie in one gulp, and chewed it while he said, "Just don't be ungrateful, like the one before you, and run off with some tractor salesman."

"Is that what she did?"

"You getting ideas?"

"Jesse, you better have some respect when you speak to me."

"Who said I don't? Why, I knowed your Aunt Lydia since she was a little girl. Now we buried her, and you got to make your way. I respect that a mite."

"Would you like another piece of pie?"

"You don't make it bad for a town girl."

No, I didn't, and there were a lot of other things I did pretty well, considering that I hadn't had much experience at doing them: all those house chores and the cooking, which I remembered from working with my mama, plus the little things, like learning how to serve the missus to her own special desires. The doctor came over once or twice—did I ever say what his name was? It was Heevey, Doctor Heevey—to attend to some ailment or other of Missus Stigmar, and he tried to make out to be my master somewhat, asking me this and that about how I was doing, what and thus. He asked me to feed him a meal. I couldn't begrudge him that. But afterward he asked me if he could see my room, so that he could be sure it was a healthy place for me to live. I stared at him. Just stared. Not saying a word. Until finally he rubbed his knuckles across that bald skull of his and turned and left the house. For a minute or two in this quiet of the country night, I could hear him whistling some doodle tune or other as he walked toward his car.

Such are the things you discover in our town: that the kindly doctor may have helped you through the funeral for reasons other than the genuine goodness of his heart. But then I had a great deal more to learn about life, and not all of it was bad.

My room. It was far too sacred to me to show to this man. It became my own little family house in the upper part of this larger building. My room, my room, my room, with its narrow bed piled high with quilts and pillows embroidered by my own hand and my Aunt Lydia's, making both a field and farm and a town, as well as the four seasons, all in eight large squares upon the puffy surface. Farm animals—Lydia loved to do these, saying once to me that it made her feel for an hour or two that she was back home out in the country, and that if I let myself go, I could allow the same feeling to come over me from time to time—and on the other side, forest animals, deer and raccoon and fox, and each of these animals had its little space, with weather to go with it: falling leaves and snow and sprouting plants and the hot sun of summer, all done in the appropriate pastel threads.

Lydia was right. There were minutes before sleep when I could lie there and put my mind to dwelling on the design, in the field and forest, or in the little town with its three shopfronts and its motorcar and its horse and wagon, and here and there a tiny person in a dress or suit, and I played games within these places that I never could have imagined playing when I was a child out on the farm, though why I can't say for sure. Maybe it was the freedom I was feeling in this house, no matter how hard I worked. Maybe it was the food. I don't know. But my mind was working in such ways as this before I fell asleep, and when sleep came, the feeling followed me in dreams.

It was the beginning of summer when Master Albert and his painter wife turned the entire lakeside upside down. Many, many friends of theirs came up every weekend from New York City, and it seemed that when I wasn't tending to a party in the house, there was tea on the veranda or a cookout at lakeside or a picnic on the meadow alongside the hilly road to town. Singers came up and crooned and yodeled along the lake, sometimes to the accompaniment of guitars and mandolins. Dancers, girls who flitted through the trees with long gauzy scarves floating behind them like spiderwebs torn by the wind, moved to the beat of the music. And poets, the likes of which I had never seen before this time—I had never even known they existed outside of the rhymes we had had to read aloud at school—poets came up in platoons! Here they chanted, there they called out their verses in singsong voices or in bass—how do you call them?—profundos over the windy surface of the lake. And the musicians, well, I mentioned the guitars, but horn players sometimes came, and now and then a pianist, though no one liked staying inside much even on the cool nights when the best of

Washington County weather hovered over us and helped us forget the heat of the day.

"It's like a carnival, don't you think?" old Jesse said to me over his dinner plate after one of these weekends, trying to make me think that he disapproved somewhat of these goings on. But by the light in his eye, I knew that whatever it said to him in his Bible about parties and enjoying yourself in music and song, he could interpret his scriptures to make a little room in his life for wine and dancing, for he liked to take a nip of it himself now and then; and to see him staring off in the distance at some of the young female guests, some of which would undress down to their fancy underwear and wade into the lake, I understood that Jesse would tolerate the activities of his younger master.

Though I didn't know that I could, at first. I was no innocent, but remember where I had grown up, on a farm out in the county, and so when girls wore makeup on their faces and danced about in the woods one afternoon, I didn't know whether to cover my eyes or stare. Missus Stigmar, Ava, gave me no clues. She sat on the veranda and read or talked with the guests, or now and then took a walk along the lakeside as though nothing out of the ordinary were going on.

Maybe it was nothing out of the ordinary to all of them. That's what I told myself. The girl who had worked here before me had run off, but I wasn't running. I had nowhere to run to and no one to run with. And so I tried to get into the spirit of things, tried to enjoy working on the costume party they held at midsummer, with Master Albert as a Greek god and his wife Ava as his girlfriend— they explained it to me the night before, with straight faces.

"Zeus, the head of the Greek pantheon," Master Albert said to me, and I'm saying to myself, pantheon? what's that? and Greece? over in Europe, ain't it? "He takes a human lover . . . " What other kind are there? I'm asking myself, trying not to look too uncomfortable, but sorry that I had asked about what sort of costume he was going to wear.

"And that's me, Cissy," said Missus Ava, all wrapped up in gauze and string, but not covered so much that you couldn't see almost all of her chest, including the little half-moon of her left breast. "And what will you be?" she asked me.

"Me? Be?"

"Won't you wear a costume?"

She always had that odd way of looking at you, which I could never find a way of describing until years later when Michael had to go to the hospital, and they used the X ray on him to find the break in his arm, that time when he was a boy and fell out of a tree. That's what she had, Ava, what I'd call X-ray vision. She looked at you and you felt as though she were seeing all over you, inside as well as out. With those eyes that changed color. And now was she ever giving me the look-de-doo with those eyes! I wanted to run and hide from her stare, but it was so strong it gave me the idea that no matter where I went, behind a door or under a rock or even at the bottom of the lake, there was no place that she couldn't find me. Talk about gods! or goddesses! whatever they called them! See how much I learned working in this household in my early days? And that ain't nothing yet.

"I doubt if Mother ever suggested to her that it was part of her job to wear a costume," Mister Albert said, smiling warmly at me.

My face turned red, and I looked away, staring at one of the scenes on the wallpaper of the dining room where we were talking, a summer scene with flowers and hills a lot like what you could see by stepping outside the door, except for the lake. "Do you want me to wear one, sir?" I asked, keeping my eyes off him.

"It might be fun, Cissy," said the master.

"I wouldn't know what," I said.

Master Albert cocked his head at me sort of like a large bird contemplating a small one and said, "A shepherdess?"

I made a sound in my throat when I was wanting to reply, but it was his wife to whom he was really speaking.

"Do you think so?" she said.

"I do."

"It might work," she said.

"And then again . . . "

"A . . . shepherdess," I replied. "That sounds all right."

And so a shepherdess I was, wearing a hoopskirt that Ava found for me in the attic. Now on these occasions not all of the guests stayed at the house. We had only five bedrooms in this cottage, which was a bigger house than any I had ever imagined living in, to

224

be sure, and so Master Albert had had to make reservations for some of the arrivals at the Adelphi Hotel in Saratoga and bring them over by automobile. Oh, it was quite a jolly sight seeing them chug up to the lakeside in the old car, masked bandits and pirates and their merry wives all in flowery silk and flimsy, but pastel, cottons, the likes of which I had never before laid eyes on.

But then for a girl who had left school early, I was learning a lot of things that I had never dreamed of. And some of the things I did dream about were becoming part of my waking midsummer night's day.

"What is that that you're wearing?" the old Missus Stigmar said to me as I brought her tea out on the veranda.

I explained with some embarrassment that I was playing a shepherdess for the party, and that Master Albert had . . .

"Oh, he loves a good time, my boy does," she interrupted me. "But you mustn't let him make you do things that you don't like yourself."

Oh, and did that bring the blood rushing to my face, for with the skirt allowing the wind to brush along my stockinged legs, and the thought of the others all in strange costumes mingling around me as I served, there were some things that I had begun to imagine. The kind and straightforward way that Master Albert spoke to me had stirred up some of these and turned them, if not into what you would call hope or hopes, at least into little daydreams that sometimes flitted through my mind like the warm breezes that stirred now and then off the lake on an afternoon in July such as this, breezes that stroked my legs and touched my fancy as well.

None of this became so clear to me as it did on that day of the midsummer's party, when both Master Albert and his wife Ava took charge of the house and its occupants, and made such a party that I have never forgotten it. And I wasn't invited; I was only working there. Imagine how the real guests enjoyed it. The music. A flutist and guitar. Even I knew, and I knew nothing about music, how odd that combination was. "A voice ahead of our time," was how I heard Master Albert put it when announcing the musicians.

And poetry. Read by a man named Anderson, one of their friends from New York. I tried to catch some of it as I served the early picnic supper at lakeside. What I caught didn't sound like

225

poetry to me, but ugly instead, more like words from the news-paper, not the way poetry is supposed to be. Pretty, I mean, and flowery, if you like.

"Jobby Anderson is our best," Albert said in a little introduc-tion he gave. "Since the end of the war no one has been writing better stories. Our Jobby." He began to clap and the others fol-lowed along, clapping, too.

"No, no, no," Anderson said, moving his big doughy face in a smile. "There are some better ones and I have to tell you. There's a boy, a veteran, out in Chicago. And a fellow down in Mississippi, or New Orleans, still, he might be. They're better than I am. That's why I'm going to read you poems today. Those two can't write poetry, and neither can I. So we're all equal at this." Whatever else he said, he was right about his poetry.

A sort of play came next, a play without words with actors in strange costumes: a man with the head of a donkey and another with the head of a lion. A girl—I supposed it was a girl—played a fairy who darted back and forth among the trees, bewitching these odd creatures and making them do mighty funny things: walking backward, walking on their knees, even trying to fly like a bird. There was some farting, which embarrassed me something awful, though I had to turn away for fear of laughing.

And for those who wanted something more exciting, the mas-ter was conducting people, the ladies at least, down the hill on a bicycle built for two that he had brought up from the city for the occasion. "*Daisy, Daisy*," he sang as he wheeled the funny contrap-tion away from the house with a pretty actress—the fairy from the play, as it turned out—and onto the dirt road down the hill. The full sun had slid down behind the hills by then, and the western sky had flared up suddenly with pinks and dark blues and yellows, as though someone had spilled Ava's watercolors from her shed all about the horizon, when Master Albert came up to me and asked if I wanted to go for a little ride.

"Me, sir?"

"You. And stop calling me 'sir' and start calling me 'Stig,' which is what all my friends call me."

"Sir, I am not your friend."

"How dare you say that, Cissy! I'm hurt."

At which point the Missus Ava came along, a wineglass in hand. "Cissy, is he troubling you? If he is, we'll just throw him in the lake."

"Oh, no, Missus," I said.

"*Ava*," she said.

"Oh, Lord," I said with a loud sigh, and just clenched my teeth and from then on called them by their names.

And I rode the bicycle, too, after a while, when it was almost dark, and after I cautioned Stig not to try the hill again. But he would not take no for an answer and bade me hoist myself up on the seat behind him, hoopskirt and all, so that I could hardly touch my feet to the pedals without great difficulty. But he did most of the work, sending us off with a great whoop and a kick— for a man of his age, so much older than Ava, not to mention me, he had such wonderful strength and power and, what's the other words I'm looking for? such a love for the things he was doing, whatever they happened to be. All of these things are invisible qualities if you look at the photographs he took of himself, pictures that make him out to be rather sourlike and without much happiness—but then off we went on the bicycle, rolling swiftly down the road.

The guests who saw us go let out some shouts of their own. Someone tooted a horn—and I hadn't even known that anyone had brought one—and there came a general cheer as we passed the veranda where the elder Stigmars sat, and they nodded as we rolled by, as though it were a normal occupation, this party, and Stig and I their children of a pleasant summer eve's outing. Oh, I didn't know who was crazier then, them or us!

"Steer with me," Stig said in his good firm voice as we rounded the first turn and began our descent of the hill in earnest. It was dark below, a pool of darkness, while the light still colored the sky above the trees, and as we picked up speed, it turned cold on us, too, and my legs grew goose bumps, and I could feel the air rushing up my blouse as though the wind had fingers and wanted to tear it away. This was fast, this was speed, this was the ride I wanted to take away from town, though it was happening on the downhill road toward the village itself. The speed, though! I didn't care about the rest.

"Mister Stig!" I cried out to him, scaring myself by how brazen my voice sounded on the wind.

"Don't be afraid!" he said over his shoulder.

"I'm not!" I said. And that should have made me more afraid than anything else.

Oh, and then he turned too quickly into the last curve, and we went spilling off the bicycle into the weeds. There was a snapping sound or two, and if it hadn't been for the absence of pain, I would have thought it was some of my bones. But it was the stays in my hoopskirt, cracking like bones as I went head over heels down the slope.

"Cissy?" Stig's voice sounded a little cracked, too. "Are you all right?"

I picked myself up and went toward him. "Yes."

"I've lost my spectacles," he said, sounding all forlorn.

I took his hand and led him back onto the road where the machine lay in a heap, as though it had fallen from the fading pastel sky. "You stand here, sir, and I'll look for them."

"*Stig*," he said.

"What, sir? Oh, yes, *Stig*, you stand here and I'll look." I went on my hands and knees, fumbling through the underbrush, and found his eyeglasses dangling loosely from a small weed tree, and when I turned and stood up, he was standing right there in front of me. "Your spectacles," I said.

"Thank you," he said, placing them on his face and then without even a thank you, pulling me to him and giving me a dry-lipped kiss on the mouth.

"Sir!" I said, drawing back from him as though I'd just touched the hot part of a stove.

"Thank you for the company," he said again, a smile spreading across his face.

It seemed a long walk up the hill with the bicycle, and he was talking all the while. "I don't know what you think of us, me and Ava and our friends, but we are just trying to have a good time, you know, when the rest of life isn't so swell, is it? and you could find a lot of dull misery to dwell in if you let yourself go in that direction."

"I . . . I suppose, sir," I said.

My knee was beginning to throb from the fall, and here he was going on about something or other, and I wasn't sure why. These were people, I decided, for whom it wasn't enough to show that they felt a certain way, but they had to give you two or three reasons for it as well. But as far as I was concerned, a kiss was a kiss, and that was good enough. And so when Stig—for that was how I began to think of him, at last—set down the bicycle right there in the middle of the road and suddenly took me in his arms again and kissed me on the mouth, I wasn't thinking anything more about it except that this time, now that I was better prepared for it, it felt good, and I looked up into the purple-black sky above the trees and saw the first star.

I could see many more by the time we had reached the top of the hill, but the house was lighted up, too, and Ava came running from the veranda when she saw us come out of the shadows. "Oh, Stig!" she said, and there was something in her voice that made you know right away that there was trouble.

It was the kiss, I was sure, and I was already packing my little suitcase in my mind, ready to head toward town, jobless and without family or friends.

But Ava rushed past me and took my master in her arms, and I have never seen her so tender as that. "She's gone," she said. "Your mother."

"Gone?" he said, perhaps thinking for a moment that she meant that Missus Stigmar had returned to the city.

Ava immediately ended his confusion. "Just a few minutes ago, on the veranda. I went to say something to her, and she was gone."

I had never seen a grown man cry before. Men just didn't do that up in these parts. But that night I went in to bring the master his tea, and there was Stig, sitting next to his father, both of them in tears. I wanted to reach out to the younger one, tell him that I had been through this grief and knew that it would not last forever. But here at the beginning it was too ferocious, and so I could not come very close to him at all. Things remained draped in funeral black for a while: no weekend guests, no parties. Although his father did come up now and then, most of the time he stayed in New York City and began to waste away himself. Within a few months he,

229

too, was gone, and Stig and the missus became the masters of the house. The next summer Stig went about doing what he usually did, making his photographs of water and clouds and sky and leaves and rocks. And Ava did her work, making paintings of rocks and leaves and sky and clouds and water. They had, you see, a great deal in common, though none of it seemed much like work to me, not work such as I did: scrubbing the floors and dusting and doing the wash, and the cooking, of course, always the cooking.

Jesse was the one who first pointed out to me that there might be more to what they did than just a pretty waste of time. "Oh, I seen him in his darkroom," he said. "He showed me how he mixes the chemistry and it's like what the doctor does, it looks like to me. He takes this blank paper and like magic he puts the picture of the lake on it. I watched him, I told you, and it's like putting in the corn. You got to know what you're doing, and you got to do it at the right time, or else it don't come in good at all." He picked a piece of straw from his trousers and began to chew on it idly while he continued to speak. "He took my picture," he said.

"No!"

"Eh-yup, he did. I got it in my room. He ask you yet?"

"Oh, he's asked me, but it's just a lot of . . . oh, I just didn't want him to do it."

"I kind of like the ideer of it," Jesse said. "No one going to remember what old Jesse looked like until they take a peek at that pitcher."

"I'll remember you, Jesse," I said, heaping more potatoes on his plate. I enjoyed serving him. It made me feel at home, and almost with a family again, or with a father, at least, or grandfather.

"And when you go? Who's to remember, without that pitcher?"

"You have a point," I said. "You have a point."

I had seen Stig at work myself, not in the darkroom, but before that stage, when he aimed his camera at the things around him: at the lake and rocks and clouds and sky. That all seemed so strange to me, to want to make a picture of something that you could see all the time anyway. It wasn't until an afternoon one summer when he was down at the waterside with Ava and that Anderson friend of theirs and Anderson's wife, both of them looking sort of pasty and white from living in the city all winter, with Ava and Stig looking fit already from their first few weeks of the season under the sun, that I began to understand something of what he was doing.

"Don't look at me," he told them. "Now Ava, you stand with Jobby. And there—yes, that's it—but look toward the house, not at me, and now . . . "

He pulled that trigger or whatever he called it on his camera, and then had them move again into another way of standing. After a few minutes he turned and caught me standing there staring. "Come and join us," he said.

I shook my head.

"As you like, Cissy." He went back to his business, but after a while he let his friends go and came up to me. "Are you afraid?"

"It seems just a nuisance," I told him, rubbing my hands on my apron.

"Come along, Cissy," Stig said and took me by the arm, leading me into the house and down to the cellar where he kept that darkroom of his. Just another excuse to kiss me, I told myself, though it had been a year or two since he and I had stood there on the road under the umbrella of trees and growing dark, and since that time he had not done more than now and then slip his arm around my waist.

So, like those heroines in the romance novels that people read so many of these days (though I can't say that I've turned the pages of more than one or two without getting bored to tears, but it was enough for me to see what they were about), I descended into the cellar with the master of the house. "It smells funny in here," I said, feeling in the dark for his arm.

"Stand still. I have to do this . . . " He moved away and I heard a faint rustling, and saw a small red glow up near the ceiling, where he had installed a special curtain that filtered out the light from outside but wasn't so much that it would ruin the film he was working with.

"I didn't know it was this complicated," I said as he mixed and washed his chemicals and papers and film.

"Pose for me and people will remember you," he said. "But not until I develop the film."

"Why do you want me to pose?"

"I like the way you look."

231

"Oh, go on, now, Stig. You'll have to think of a better one than that."

"Don't take it personally," he said. "It's *you*. It's the way you appear, which isn't really *you*. I want to arrange you, like flowers, Cissy. I want to put you into a *composition*."

"Into a schoolbook?"

"Never mind. Listen. When I'm through here, I want to do a portrait with you and your bicycle."

That word called me back to our little ride together and, you guessed it, it made me blush to recall that kiss, no matter how much I tried to make it trivial in my mind. "Oh, all right, Stig," I said, "you can pose me. I'll be happy to help out."

"Then let's go up," he said, and he finished washing some of his paper and then hung it up to dry on a little clothesline he had made for himself—and I had to laugh because he seemed so much like a young boy playing at these things of his—and we went up and met all the folks at the lakeside who were there for the week-end: that Anderson, and some artists with pointy black beards and several girls my own age, who had lifted their skirts and were wading up to their bare thighs in the water. And this time along with the painters and the writers, there was a neat-haired man, dressed so nicely that he might have wandered over from one of the fancy parties at Saratoga, who, as it turned out, was Ava's older brother, a scientist or some kind of doctor, I heard someone say. He had a fine laugh and I enjoyed hearing it all the time I was serving dinner.

These people having such a good time made me feel left out, and yet a part of a family at the same time, and I listened and enjoyed them even as I moved back and forth from the kitchen to the dining room, doing what it was I had to do in order to earn my keep in the world.

"That's a smart brother she has," Jesse said from his place at the kitchen table. He was spooning up the summer soup I'd made for the party, though he was still dressed—flannel shirt, heavy wool trousers—for winter, last winter, and for the winter we knew would follow this summer pretty soon. "He was out there with me this morning looking at some rocks, telling me things about the land here I didn't know, and I've lived here all my life." Jesse sloshed another spoonful of soup into his mouth and wiped his lips on his sleeve.

"Don't know much more about her brother, except he's a rock doctor of some kind, like I said, and he's been telling her, he told me, about places out in Mexico or New Mexico or some part way out West, and he said that one day she ought to go out there to take a look. Something about the light she needs to see, though I think we got plenty of good light right here in Washington County, if you ask me. I never had no trouble with it, myself."

I heard about it next from Ava herself, without even asking, in the middle of the next week as I was bringing a little lunch out to the shed where she did her work—when she wasn't painting out-of-doors, that is, out in the woods or near the lake.

"Come in, Cissy," she said as I came to the door. "Come in and take a look."

"Oh, I don't know, Ava," I said. "I'm not much of a judge of art, that's for sure."

"Come in, come in," she said, taking the lunch tray from me and then standing back so that I could enter the shed. "It's not *art*; in any case, it's not separate from nature; it's part of nature, as we all are; even though we think, we're still animals, thinking animals, and these paintings are made up out of nature. If we say that the dams built by beavers are part of nature, and anthills, too, then why not paintings?"

I must have shown her by the look on my face how confused this talk made me, because she stopped it at once and took me by the arm and led me to the canvases lined up on the bench at the far wall. "All these leaves," she said. "Do you like them?"

I could only tell her how beautiful she made them seem.

"But I'm using up these woods," she said. "I'm looking for . . . something else. Up here things have grown too thick in summer: thick air, thick light. I feel as though I have to peel away layers before I get to the thing itself. I want something more pure. Like a laboratory. Though I know that's not what I want, either. Stig has his darkroom. Do you know what I want? I want a *light* room! Yes, and I'm going to find it one day, I know. Does all this sound ridiculous? It doesn't have much to do with cleaning and cooking and feeding us and putting up and taking down the drapes, I know that.

233

But it's part of life, part of nature . . . " She stopped suddenly and put her hands on her lips, flashing those eyes at me, those X-ray eyes! "I'm going to keep quiet. I'm going to eat this sandwich you've made for me. What kind is it?"

"Turkey, Ava, left over from dinner."

"How lovely. So. I'm going to eat this and never say another thing to you about this. My ravings. Sorry."

"It's interesting to me," I told her, bringing the tray over from where she had set it on the bench to her main worktable.

"You're a good listener, Cissy," she said.

"I do like the paintings," I said.

"Thank you. You didn't have to say that."

"But it's true. I mean it."

"Thank you."

"I only wish I had some of your ability."

"I'd give you some of it if I could. Cissy, I could teach you to *draw*. Would you like that?"

"Oh, I'd like to try, Ava."

"Good. Well, why don't we set aside some time beginning tomorrow afternoon?"

"I have to go to town with Jesse then, Ava."

"The day after?"

"That would be all right." The big question lay on the top of my mind, but I couldn't find a way to ask it.

Then someone knocked. "Ladies," Stig said as he entered. "Anyone for a walk?"

"I've got to work," Ava said. "Take Cissy."

Stig's eyes never left Ava. "Are you sure you won't come?"

"Work," she said.

"I thought that you had used up all the local light."

"It's going for me. I didn't say it was all gone. I said that I want to renew it. That's why I want to go west. Just for a month. I'll come back for the rest of the summer."

"Oh, I guess then Cissy will come for a walk. Won't you, Cissy?"

"I've got work, too," I said.

"You work for me. Come for a walk."

I never thought I'd see Ava get annoyed. "Oh, go with him, Cissy," she said. "But don't forget about the day after tomorrow."

234

"What's the day after tomorrow?" Stig asked, touching a finger to that snowy white beard of his.

"I'm going to teach Cissy how to draw," Ava said. There was something in her voice that I could notice but couldn't describe to myself.

"That's fine," he said. "Then she can amuse herself in those long winter months when we're away and not here to entertain her."

"Is that why we're here?" Ava seemed to be quite amused herself by Stig's remark.

"Sometimes I think that's why we're here," he said. "To amuse others. And sometimes I think that we're here to amuse only ourselves."

"Go for your walk and ponder it," Ava said. "Go with him, Cissy. He will enjoy the company. And I have some of this light left still to use." She came toward me as though I were company rather than the help and leaned to me and gave me a kiss on the cheek. "Tomorrow."

"The day after," I said.

"That's right. The day after."

And so Stig and I took the first of many walks around the lake. The sky that afternoon was as blue as teacups and touched with tiny wisps of cloud that might have been painted on with a fine brush. It gave me the chance to remark on something I thought would interest him. It gave him the chance to tell me how acute he thought my eyes were.

"Have you ever thought of becoming an artist yourself?" he asked. "Perhaps after Ava gives you a few drawing lessons, you'll just have to give up working for us and completely join the family." He slipped an arm around my waist as he said this, and gave me a sly wink, then withdrew from me and kept on walking. It was hot— I could feel the heat in me—still the country girl, whatever else it was I thought I saw in life, living with these strange people as I did.

Then came my lesson with Ava two afternoons later, which would change my view of things somewhat. The small shed where Ava kept her materials and sometimes worked had a number of windows, which she kept closed against the mosquitoes. When I arrived for my lesson, she was wearing scarcely anything: a white cotton blouse and a skirt that was stained with oils and grease and no shoes at all. Her usually flowing hair she had tied up on her head under a scarf, and she had a brush stuck in the left side of this bun. "Ready?"

"I suppose. How do we begin?"

"By beginning," she said. "Now, here, take this pad, and we'll go out to the lake."

Thus began what was for me a very strange afternoon.

"You have been a great help to us both," Ava said.

"I do my best, Ava."

"Stig enjoys his time with you."

"He is a very nice man."

"It's been difficult for him sometimes with both his parents gone. He looks his age, doesn't he? But he doesn't feel it or act it. He needs all the help that we can give him."

"I try," I said, remembering one of our walks and the way it had seemed so natural for him to talk with me, as though we had almost grown up together, father and daughter. Yes, it came to me then: that was it.

"The world's in such a mess. I can't bear to read the newspapers much anymore. If we're lucky enough to be able to escape out of the city and come here for the summer, I believe that we should concentrate on it. That's what I want to try to do, Cissy. To focus on my life the way that I focus on my work. And I try with Stigmar. I do try. But now I'm losing ground again and I can't help it. I have the chance to go west . . . "

"Yes, so I hear," I said.

"And I desperately want to do it, to see what's there. I may *need* to go there sooner or later. I have the feeling, I've told you, that I have truly used up this place. I know it must sound strange to hear me talk this way because you've lived here your whole life . . . "

"I'm trying to understand, Ava."

"Good. But even I can't fathom it sometimes, this restlessness that goes along with the great stillness I need for work. Sometimes I think that I'm a mad person and should be locked up."

"Oh, *no*," I said, and shook my head.

"But here you are; you're bound to this place, and I'm babbling to you about leaving for reasons that must seem so silly."

"I like it here, it's the only place I know," I said, "but I'm not a farmer. My parents were farmers but not me. So I'm not bound, as you call it. I could leave."

"Where would you go? Do you think about leaving sometimes? Do you dream about it?"

"Oh, Ava, I don't know that you could say I dream about it. But I think about it sometimes, yes."

We both turned at the sound of a fish breaking the surface of the lake.

"In the winter sometimes, it gets so cold, and I feel like a prisoner in my house in town. I think about it then; about a warmer place, I don't know where. I've never been anywhere. So I don't call it anything. It's just . . . a place in my mind."

That was when she put her hands on my shoulders and held me still, as if she wanted to pose me for one of her paintings, though I know she didn't ever paint people, just the things in the world. She kissed me, and her mouth had a funny taste: oils, a touch of dirt, and a bitter tang that reminded me of lake water, and a sweetness, too. I said to myself, that's probably how my own mouth tastes to somebody else.

When Ava went west, I didn't know whether I felt worse or glad that she was gone and I was alone in the house with Stig. "I do miss her, though," I heard myself say on one of the very first nights that I was serving him his dinner.

"Of course we do," he said. "It's not so bad, Cissy. She needs to be out there for a while. You wouldn't catch *me* in such a place. Cossayuna was good enough for the Mohawks and the Iroquois and it's good enough for me. Look at it this way. We'll miss her, but when she comes back, it will be better than ever. That's what I tell myself."

After the meal he told me that he had something to show me, and he went to his studio while I was cleaning up and came back with a bunch of large photographs. "We had a bang-up winter," he said. "Both of us got a lot of work done, and we had a good time. Look at these."

He showed me a series of pictures of Ava, naked to the waist, in various poses in their New York studio: first as a dancer, then a

237

ı, and wearing a top hat and carrying a cane, and then with
erfly wings made of gauze. Even with her breasts showing—and
y were beautiful, full and firm—it was still her eyes that caught
most of your attention. That at least was what I told myself until I
went to bed that night and dreamed of naked Ava leading me along
in some kind of dance or parade, and there were Jesse and Stig—
waving flags, they were—and it all seemed quite bizarre to me, who
was still a country girl despite everything.

A week or so passed, with me keeping the house and sleeping
in my little room upstairs in the back over the kitchen, and Stigmar
working long hours in his studio and then going out with his camera to hunt clouds. And then there came her first letter, which sat
on the dining room table at Stig's plate waiting for him, and it
made me feel as though it were alive, I was so nerve wracked waiting to hear what was in it. And what could I imagine it would say
after all? Nothing about me, certainly. But when Stig came to the
table and saw it and opened it, what he read to me soothed my
heart.

"Listen to this, Cissy," he said. He touched a finger to his beard,
and then to his spectacles, and began to read: " 'It is five in the
morning. I have been awake for nearly an hour watching the moon
grow pale and the dawn begin. I walked around in the wet grass
beyond this house belonging to Mabel Dodge. One bright, bright
star, so bright that it seemed like a tear in its own eye . . . ' " Something stuck in his throat, and he coughed sharply before he read
on. " 'The flowers here are so lovely. I walk to the mesa so that I can
see the mountain line, so clear-cut where the sun will appear . . . I
don't know whether you know how important these days are for
me or not. And I am not sure that I am really certain about it
myself. But I feel it is so. They seem to be like the loud ring of a
hammer striking something hard. Ah, the surface doings of the
days are only important insofar as they do something for an under-
current that seems to be running strong in me. As I can't tell where
it's going, all I can say is that I am enjoying the way, and the many
things it brings to me . . . ' "

The hot point of Stig's eye where it focused on the letter seemed
to soften all of a sudden, and I saw that it turned all watery.

" 'You know,' " he went on, and for a moment I thought that he was speaking in his own words instead of continuing to read Ava's, " 'I never feel at home in the East the way I do out here, finally feeling in the right place with the right light. I become more myself, and I like it. One perfect day of light replenishes each morning with another . . . ' "

He set down the letter and stared at a point in the air above his head. It was a little above *my* head, but I listened for a while longer to this talk about light and visions, until he looked over at me and said, "Tell me, Cissy. Have I made a mistake in not going out there with her?"

What did I know? What could I say? I gave a little shrug and excused myself and went about my chores. I kept my distance for the next few weeks, and, I suppose inspired by Ava's beautiful words from the West, I tried to look at the light before me with a different eye. On one of those afternoons in late summer, I was staring off toward the lake when I heard an automobile engine, and here came Ava in a taxi from the village, just off the train from New Mexico. "Howdy! Hey, hello!" she called.

A new way of speaking. I could hear it in her voice and, although she looked the same, if a bit more brown than when she had departed, her eyes! she looked at me now in a different way, a woman who had seen another sort of world than the one we lived in.

Stig came to me the next summer in the dim night in my room. "Can you . . . ?"

I heard his voice through the coverlet of my sleep. "Oh, Stig. Go away!"

I felt the bed sag as he sat down alongside me. "Come walk with me."

His breath smelled of cigars and whiskey, odors which, believe it or not, I didn't find unpleasant. It was just *him*, the sign of Stigmar in the dark room. "Do you like the night?" he asked.

"Do I like the night?"

"Yes, very important to know. Frankly, I detest it. This dark. Covers us all. And I can't work. I need the dark to develop, but I can't *use* it, damn it! It's all a waste. Half of the day, half of our lives, all of it under cover. And then there's death! Ah, goddamn death!

239

Though everything goes dark. Can't do any serious work when you're dead, either. Can you come with me, Cissy?"

He stretched himself out alongside me, and I edged away from him toward the wall. This moment was the one I had both loathed and desired since Ava had apparently begun making part of her life away. But he soon began to snore, and I carefully slid out from beneath the covers where he had me nearly pinned, and spent the rest of the night on the sofa in the downstairs study.

The next morning I pretended as though nothing had happened, which was best, I thought, when you are working for someone for your living. And thus our summer went, without any more of these strange visitations, until Ava returned from New Mexico, on what seemed her regular purpose now over the months. And a few days after her arrival came some crates from New Mexico. The three of us huffed and puffed our way with them out to the studio, and as she opened these packages, she talked about the desert air and the light—light, always the light—and some Indians she had met at the house of a friend, and about the Indian dances she had seen. "I wanted to strip off my clothes and join the dance," she said. "But it was only men! Oh, the lucky men! But I felt it in my blood, those drums they played, I felt them!"

Stig puffed on his cigar and continued with the unpacking. "It sounds quite wild," he said. "Which is precisely why I've been quite pleased to stay right here."

Ava looked over from where she was unwrapping the first canvas they had freed from the crate. The sun had scored creases at the corners of her eyes and at her mouth, too, when she smiled. Her hair seemed to have kept its usual red stain, not lightened very much by the sun.

"You might as well be in Europe as here, Stig," she said. "This placid atmosphere, those clouds you love, they've floated over here, the last detritus of the big thunderheads we see out West. Why don't you come out next summer and look at the originals?"

"I like the placidness of this place," he said, picking a few threads of cigar from his mouth. "Art must be wild, but artists don't need wildness. If it were wild all around me, I couldn't work. I'd be too distracted."

240

"Here, Cissy, help me," she said, lifting a canvas from the crate and, with me alongside her, setting it up against the wall of the shed. "It's not the way you imagine it, Stig. What you say is just talk; it's not the real stuff about the place. You can't know the real part of it until you see it."

"I don't need to see everything in the world," he said. "I take my pictures of a few clouds, a few trees. All clouds and all trees grow out of them. Should I hunt around the world and take ten million photographs of all the clouds and all the trees? Tomorrow, every day, and ten years from now there will just be more. It would be like photographing the waves."

"Of course," she said, and I could hear her trying to keep things calm. "Cissy?" She bade me take up a knife from a nearby table and cut the cord around this frame.

"What's this one?" Stig asked as we pulled away the paper.

"Oh, just some wild thing," Ava said.

Oh, was she ever right! The paper fell away and I stepped back to stare at this enormous desert rose, its color so bright that it made me blink, its shape and lines so suggestive that they made me look away out of embarrassment.

"Ava," was all Stig said. Over and over. "Ava, Ava, Ava, Ava . . . " He reached out for her. She reached out for me. He noticed me out of the corner of his eye. I'm sure I turned the color of the rose.

It was the next summer that it happened, the main thing that you've come to find out—the time when Ava began what became a regular habit of staying away for three to four months, leaving me to care for Stig and help keep the lake house running. And care for him I did, in more ways than one.

"Keep him walking," Ava said to me just before she left for the train west. I assured her I would, though it troubled me to hear her speak of him in that odd way, as though he were her child or her aging parent. In any case, I had come to love our strolls around the lake in the late part of the evening, when now and then a little breeze off the water would give you the thrill of thinking that this was the best time of year, when you could have the feeling of the best of all our seasons at once: the cold edge of winter and the warm touch of summer nights. Oh, well, and I'm not so good at describing all these things I was feeling then, but it was something like that: a closeness that Stig and I came to feel together, not that, mind you, of housekeeper and master, either, and certainly not that of daughter and father, though I have to admit that every once in a while during that time when he was talking to me about the world, about the Europe he had once traveled in, or a famous trip to Egypt he took once when he made his pictures of the pyramids, or about growing up as a boy in the city down there in New York, or even, bless him, when he would say something about Miriam, his first wife, and the trials she put him through, or when he would take a deep breath and sit up like a boy just full of himself for the first time and talk about Ava and how he thought her work was getting so wonderful—which it was, it was, for all of the people writing about her in the newspapers when she had a show were saying that, too—it got so that I couldn't help but notice how I was weaving my days around this man, not so much as his employee but as his devoted . . . friend, you might say.

He even got me to reading, something I had never done much of before in my life; poetry, too, like the poems of the great Irishman W. B. Yeats, and those of Wordsworth—worth a lot of words, by my lights, that one!—and sometimes he would read stories to me, getting me so scared once telling me "The Legend of Sleepy Hollow" that at the end of it, I leaped up from my chair and hugged his neck, saying to him, "Stig, for heaven's sake, a girl likes a good scare now and then, but this is a bit much!" And now that I think back on it, it frightens me to think of how little I understood what was happening to me.

Now and then, maybe twice a month, a letter would arrive from Ava full of wonderful descriptions of the local flowers and such out there, and descriptions, too—I have to confess I thought this—of just how happy she was out there and how fine her work was going, which, considering that she had left her husband behind to go out there, seemed to me sometimes a bit much to put into words, words that he was reading, in any case. Sure, for in those days, I have to say it, you could look at Ava and notice that she had a bit of a love affair with herself and her own work, which, for somebody like me, who never had a talent for anything except living her life in a simple way and trying just to make a living of it, caring and fending for herself so that she never would become a burden to anyone else, was quite something to behold.

And upon us, it seemed to me, Ava put her blessings, pleased, in her own way, that Stig was not suffering in her absence. No, he was actually living a part of his life that he had not enjoyed ever before, if you know what I mean; a new phase of it, as they say, when just at that part of his life when most people would think he would be ready to give it all up and take to his chair with a blanket across his lap, now and then glancing up at the walls to see the best work he had done in his lifetime that was nearly all behind him, he found a lot of things he wanted yet to do. It was then that he asked me to pose for him, and he did those portraits with the face all blurred—a kindness to me, of course—but it was the bodies—the body, my body, that he showed many times over—that got him such good notices, and that I've kept copies of all these years up in my attic here: a little gift from him to keep me warm in old age was how he put it, since he said that he was knowing directly just how cool it could become at the upper end of the register of years—his words. And because he gave me the house, or the money to buy it, in any case, I've never had to even think of selling those photographs. One day you and yours might want to, I suppose.

But it was on those nights, those summer nights at the lake, lying there in his arms, the air outside settling down over us, on the house and the woods and the lake, with now and then only a bird call, or a dog barking way off in the distance to break the silence, I would touch a hand to his soft white beard—it always surprised me with its softness—and he would turn in his sleep and make sweet little sounds just like a baby, and I would think to myself, who could have imagined? who could ever have said? And I thought of my long-lost family—father, mother, my baby brother Michael—and it was then that I got the idea that Stig could give me something else besides the photographs and the money for a house to keep me warm in my old age.

DOOR

"'Night, Mommy."

"Good night, darling," I say, tucking the light red wool blanket with the turtle design in around him and then leaning down to kiss him on the cheek.

"Dream, Mommy," he says.

"Dream sweet," I say, the little ritual we've made these recent months, me and my little walker and talker.

I close the door to his room, once Socorro's room. Thinking about Robby and his future: sweet little boy, he doesn't have to ever even touch a paintbrush; I would like him to enjoy art, to love paintings, but everyone doesn't have to be an artist. My life until now would have been a lot easier if I hadn't had to think that I had to be great: a great sculptor, painter, writer, whatever. I want my son to be ordinary if that is what he is: just ordinary and happy; that in itself is a kind of great thing.

I've got to find Ava for my evening reading. She seems to tire so easily of late, and she seems to eat nothing but a tortilla or two now and then. We're getting close to the end of a new book, slowly but surely: Dante's *Purgatorio* in a little blue-covered bilingual edition, from which I read Ava one canto a night.

Socorro has been wonderful about pitching in and taking care of Robby during the day while I spend more and more time with this work. She seems naturally to exercise her ability to love this child, which my family has merely *strained* to do. Michael, meanwhile, stays out of my sight. He's off in the barn, or in the little office, always on the telephone. Ava thinks this and Ava thinks that, I hear him saying now and then. What's best for Ava, he sometimes adds, and, The way Ava puts it.

"I want to go out" is the way she puts it to me while I'm in the middle of a paragraph.

"It's late," I say. "And dark and a little chilly, too."

"Dark doesn't bother me," she says, trying to pull herself up out of the chair.

I rush to aid her, setting down the book along the way. She's so light, I find, as I help her to her feet, as light as a child.

"Let's go," she says. Something in her eye—I can't read it, but I see it.

It's around nine o'clock, but we bundle up in sweaters and head out the door. I can feel the heat at my back, the cool wind on my face. "Which way?" I ask, taking her by the arm.

"To the mesa," she says.

"Oh, Ava," I say, "it's too long a walk, and it's dark . . . "

"I told you about the dark," she says.

It's not completely dark. The way the western sky holds the light even, it seems, when it's long hours after sunset, that's how it is up there now. Faint pale glow. If you were confused, you could think you might even be looking east, and the glow was the dawn rather than the end of the day. Here and there a long-tailed cloud catches the last light, glowing like some piece of tinder in a fire flaming into nothing.

"Let's just go part of the way," I say. "Robby's alone in the house."

"We'll try," Ava says, pulling free of my hand. Now she's shuffling slowly alongside me, touching my shoulder now and then with hers. We go a few yards without speaking, and I can hear the wind and the yipping of wild dogs far off in the distance. But mostly I can hear the silence, the kind of absence of sound that takes on a presence of its own. Nothing is ever completely silent back East. Where we walk now, nothing seems ever to fully come into sound.

"It's my secret, child," Ava says.

"What is, Ava?" I say, staring, staring, staring at the top of the sky where so many stars have suddenly appeared that it might be that the few dark spaces are the celestial bodies and all the brilliant rest of it is bright and wonderful emptiness, nothingness with a presence all its own.

"What you're looking at," she says.

"Ava, how do you know what I'm looking at?"

"Because you're not talking," she says, touching my shoulder with hers. "There are no clouds. And you're looking up at the sky."

"I am," I say. "It's . . . it's . . . "

"No words," she says. "There are no words for some things. That's why all my life I did what I did."

THE EAST
Harriet

Some letters Robert wrote to her:

. . . I had a letter from a lawyer in Chicago which suggested to me that some things remain constant back home. Margaret was asking for more money, and my first response was, Why, gee, does she think that just because I help pump the stuff from the ground that I can just siphon off a little for myself whenever I feel like it? My next response was to spend a long evening at the saloon that the company runs for our exclusive self-destruction in our air-conditioned compound in the middle of this dry country—dry in that it's mostly desert, and dry in that these Moslems don't allow alcohol. Here we have booze and Chaplin movies. I drank much too much and stumbled about like Charlie himself, railing against women and marriage and deserts and oil, against rocks and sand and dunes, against dust.

"What the hell is this life?" I heard myself demanding as some of my men helped me to my room. "Just what the hell is this?" But I know what life is—it is thinking of you; it is my sister and her good work; it is this business I'm in, pumping oil against the disaster of those Nazis who are trying to take it and all the good things away . . .

The next few days at the drilling site, I sweated and stared at the sky, at the walnut-skinned nomad children, at the women in their veils, and at the camels and the trees that grew dusty and tall along the wellspring, at the grizzled salt-and-pepper beards of men in thick, pearl white djellabahs, and I said to myself, Why, they know what they are doing. Do we know what we are doing? And then I remembered you and Ava, and I said to myself, Yes, we know, we know, we're each doing what we must do.

September 1, 1939: a sad day for the world. I drank myself into a stupor, bad example for the men. I did it anyway. And the next day I wrote a letter to the president of the company telling him that I was going to volunteer. "Your heart's in the right place, Robert," his reply came by courier, "but keep the oil flowing. It's the blood in our veins. Our business is business . . . "

A letter from you, at long last! I took it with me to the edge of our compound, where the oasis ends and the desert stretches west for days, and there I read your good description of your latest visit with Ava out in Taos, but you say nothing about poetry. Please send me some of your latest. I hope you're still writing them. I'm still writing my poem—or living my life, I should say, working nine- and ten-hour days under this incredible sun in a landscape remarkable for its merciless heat, wind, and, at night, the cold, the stars.

    All this sand, wind and sand—sand hills of my childhood, the beach where our great mother Melissa walked on the water, these children digging in the sand—I don't so much see a pattern in all this but feel a strong affinity for locations such as where I now sit, scribbling to you—as if the entire world were connected in a way that I sense but can't yet explain . . .

    Rocks, I said to myself, oh, rocks! I was out for a walk under the cold night stars; my heart beat rapidly, but I could still hear the spring trickling up along its course through the oasis strand, and I conjured up a much older Arabia, an Arabia of rivers and forests, old Arabia whose waters flowed with the first rush of power from the Biblical flood, which every good geologist knows is not a story made up out of whole cloth, for we have seen the traces, traceries, markings here and there where we dig and drill, and these reveal to us that the world has not been the same since . . . as if we didn't know that the forests died and sank into the earth, and under pressure like that of a fist from the stars, after millions of years became underground lakes of oil; as if we didn't know that this Nebraska might one day become a new Arabia: all the trees swept away and the sand hills taking everything, and the slender rivers sinking into the ground, and the small rocks ground to sand, and the winds sweeping it all away. Out of this we could recapture nothing except for what those of us who can read the earth might interpret, or what artists like my sister would make, paintings that go directly onto the rocks and sand and give the feel of what the old life on the planet was like.

The war heated up in Europe, and Robert's company pulled him and his men out of the Arabian desert, and when he stopped in New York on his way to Chicago, I was touched. I needed his visit more than I would have liked to admit at the time. I had stopped writing poems; I didn't know anymore what I wanted to do with my life. Ava and I seemed to be, if not drifting apart, at least seeing each other less and less as she took up what seemed like nearly year-round residence in New Mexico. And Stig and I were seeing a lot of each other.

One day at the gallery he turned to me and said, "I need you." I closed one eye and stared him up and down.

"Oh, for God's sake, woman," he said to me in a voice of almost complete exasperation, "I'm talking about *art*. About this *place*." His eyes flashed more impatience than I had ever seen in them before, even in the days when Ava had first talked to him about traveling west. "I'm tired of business. Not *this* business, but the business of running it. I've known you a long time now, watched you over the years. I'd like you to come in with me and help me take care of things. I started this place on a lark. All I ever really wanted to do was take pictures. If you handle the business, I can go back to that." His dark expression turned to a smile, and raising his right hand, he tugged at his white beard.

"Did Ava put you up to this?" I asked.

He leaned closer to me and said, "I haven't said a word to her about this."

I don't know why it was that I wanted to do this on my own, just between me and Stig. Well, perhaps I do know. My dear friend's work was still selling now and then out of the gallery. And when the war was over, there would be more money around for art – and more artists. I could enjoy her success, and I would enjoy it. I just didn't want her to think that I was trying to take advantage of it.

"I'll do it," I said, and gave Stig a big hug, breathing in the cigar smell and the familiar cologne that he sprinkled on his beard, and thinking to myself, it's a start, a new start. Music, poetry, now this. Business. Very well. I'll do it.

I just didn't know that when Robert returned, we would make a start between ourselves as well.

He arrived by ship from Arabia by way of England, scheduled to visit for a few days before leaving for Chicago and his home office. *A few days* was what his wire said. It was early spring, and Stig had gone upstate to see if it was warm enough to work, leaving me behind to tend the gallery. Which was the first place Robert headed when he disembarked.

He arrived. My heart leaped. We drank coffee, went out to dinner, and then returned to the apartment above the gallery where he was to spend the night. The rest is history. Two people like us falling in love—most spectators might think of it as rather ludicrous. Age doesn't put you off at our age, though. In fact, it draws you along. Here is someone to whom you don't have to explain very much because he understands a great deal of what you have lived through. He has lived it, too.

Did it seem a touch incestuous? Now and then in the light of that first morning when we awoke together, I noticed some resemblance in his face to his sister. And some similarities, as well, in our own bodies: my soft and flattened breasts, his own puffy chest speckled with liver spots and long white hairs. But when we pressed our chests together, we made a number greater than our two parts, and suddenly it came to me, the feeling that I had longed for ever since I was a little girl.

All through the war we remained lovers, visiting back and forth between Chicago and New York. The news from Europe grew more awful by the month, the rumors flying about what was happening to the Jews and the gypsies, to communists and priests. Many a night I went to bed in tears, and on the nights that Robert was there to comfort me, I thanked a God I had never prayed to since I was a child. It was like that the day I heard of Jobby's bizarre death in Panama; it was like that the day the war ended, and the doors to the death camps opened to reveal horrors beyond our imagining.

My bad dreams went on for a while. It made me physically sick when I read the stories about the survivors of the camps, and so after a while I had to ignore them. Another spring—and Robert arrived for one of our occasional rendezvous at the lake house, which was actually only a few miles from the train line between the two great cities where we lived.

Sometimes Ava was there, too; sometimes she wasn't, depending upon the season. For more and more of her year, she lived out in New Mexico on the property that Mabel Dodge had offered us that first summer and later sold to her. If I hadn't been long aware of how much it meant to her work that she stay out there, I would have thought that she was avoiding the sight of me and Robert. I don't know what Stig thought about it. He passed most of his time in his darkroom or out-of-doors himself. When we talked, we talked about business, which was flourishing.

"These new painters we're seeing," Stig said to me one afternoon as we were setting up a new show that included Ava and a few of the old gang. "Who can tell what they're doing? It's a different time and a different style. Not necessarily better."

"Thank you!" Ava called out from her work space on the other side of the room.

"I wasn't saying anything about your work."

Ava came toward us from the window. "He wasn't saying anything about my work, except by omission."

"I was *not*, Ava," Stig said, standing up and waving a hand at her as though he were her old schoolmaster — or her angry father.

"Never mind," Ava said with a vigorous shake of her head. "If I measured my success by my sales, I never would have gotten started in the first place."

"Well," Stig said, still on his feet, "I did buy the first drawings you made."

"They weren't the first," Ava said. "I've been drawing since I was a child."

"I'd love to see those," I broke in.

Ava gave me an odd look. "I'll bet you would."

"What do you mean by that tone?" I asked.

"Ladies," said Stigmar.

"Who's that?" Ava said, reaching for my hand. "Ladies? Are there any of those creatures around here, Harriet?"

I gave her hand a squeeze. "I haven't seen any."

[pages missing]

Another year or so went by, another year in which, now that I was running the gallery by myself, I listened as new male painters began to be talked about and written about in the way that made me see just how much had changed. Abstraction was becoming everything, and artists such as Ava, for whom the world still held an attraction in its actual shapes and configurations, were less and less interesting to the people who believed that they took art seriously. I certainly got caught up in that fever myself for a couple of years, though I always kept the door open for Ava's work, and now and then I found a buyer for some of the cactus flower paintings and the other desert flora canvases that she was bringing east each year now from her New Mexico sojourns. These days I saw more of her work than I did of her.

I just cannot imagine how things would have been without Robert. Would I have thrown myself on Ava's mercy and moved out to New Mexico with her? Or would I have suffered the miserable life of the unattached women in New York City: a grand success with our gallery in public, and in private a suffering, lonely soul prone to covering over her unhappiness with a variety of diversions and perversions?

He saved me from that, bringing a great deal of joy into my life. He was kind, understanding, smart, and successful, and for a man who was supposed to have a weak heart, he certainly exerted himself in making love to me. On some visits he made me so sore that I was relieved when the week was over and I could return to my celibate life. Yet there were times when, alone in New York, I would awaken in the middle of the night and miss him so powerfully that I felt as though I would die before the night was over if I couldn't have him by my side.

"Oh, my dear," he'd say, in that old-fashioned way of his, when I'd call in a frenzy of despair and wake him in his Chicago bed, "seems as though I should pay you an emergency visit, does it? Or do you want to come here?"

Once or twice we did it that way, on the spur of the moment, but Robert's work had changed in the years since the war ended. He was no longer in the field but a vice-president in charge of exploration, and it was difficult for him to turn his plans around and come east — and by the early fifties, the gallery had become so

252

successful it seemed as though I were tied to my place of work as well. Even though I didn't particularly *like* the style, my eye for the best of the abstractionists was good, and I picked them earlier on than many of my competitors. A few of the young, smart critics began to write about these painters and their style, and the whole thing got out of hand.

"I'm making good money for them, and for myself," I said to Robert one dark winter night after I had ridden the train for what seemed like days in order to spend a few hours at his side. "But I think of Ava, you know? Out there in that house in the desert, working away, working away; I don't know what's going to happen to her."

"Happen?" said Robert, rolling over and looking up at the ceiling. He was smoking a cigarette, a bad habit for a man in his condition, but then he had reached a point in his life, or so he told me, when he would rather have pleasure than be prudent.

"I sell one or two of her little canvases every year," I said. "The rest, and there are a lot of them, I keep in storage. But I don't know that I'll ever have the opportunity to unpack them."

"Has she gone out of style?"

I couldn't help but laugh. "Out of style?" I grabbed for his cigarette, but he kept it beyond my reach. "It's as if she's working on another planet."

I lighted up a cigarette of my own and watched the smoke make tenuous patterns as it rose up toward the ceiling of Robert's bedroom. "I worry about her," I said. "What would happen if we closed the gallery? I don't know that she'd ever find anyone else to represent her."

"If you closed the gallery?"

"One day it might happen."

Robert turned to me, and I could feel his curiosity flow in my direction, a palpable thing, much like his desire.

"You're getting close to retirement, Robert, yes?" I said.

He sat up in bed, and I could feel his interest fill the room, like our smoke. "So I am." He turned his face to me, the face I'd come to love so much: those gaunt cheeks, the sparkling blue eyes, all of it beneath that wonderful sheaf of white, white hair. "Though I have a few things that I want to do before that."

"Such as?"

"Oh, just technical stuff. Science stuff. But I'm pretty close, yes."

"Well . . . "

"Well?"

I tamped out my cigarette and laid a hand on his chest. "I have a plan."

He listened carefully, nodding now and then, and I could picture him as he would be, or had been over the years, out in the field, as some technician reported to him about the readings of the drill or the quality of the findings, or as he had been in recent years, presiding over meetings where they devised their strategies for implementing exploration in Saudi Arabia or taking over a group of uranium mines in the Southwest. Among other things, I reminded him about the retrospective that I had been wanting to produce of Ava's work. "It's high time," I said. "It will take at least a year, if not two, to get it all together, and I think by that time the public will have had its fill of abstract impressionism, or at least enough of a taste of it that they'll want to see something different."

"That's my sis," Robert said. "Something different." He was staring up at the shelf on the wall where, in the new light that had begun to wash in through the bedroom window, I could see books and books and rocks—and the small polished white skull of a calf or cow.

"So we'll do this retrospective," I said. "And by that time you'll be ready to retire."

"Maybe," he said. "Maybe."

"And we'll take a trip together."

"I see," he said, reaching down and stubbing out his cigarette in an ashtray at the side of the bed.

"Do you?" I asked.

"I think so."

"But what?" There was something else in his voice.

"Well," I said, "I thought I would pay her a visit."

"With me?"

"If . . . you'd go with me."

254

"I don't know, Harriet," he said. "I'm . . . up to my ears in work at the moment."

"I'll go see Ava by myself," I said. "It might be easier."

"Easier to ask her about the show?" He took a deep breath, the kind of breath you hear cigarette smokers take, but in a heart patient like Robert, you hear it even louder. "Or to tell her that we're getting married?"

I let out a screech! Just like those little girls at the Taverner School where Ava and I used to teach oh-so-many-long years ago in Charleston. "That wasn't part of my plan," I said, planting a large wet kiss on his smoky mouth. "It wasn't part of my plan; I swear it wasn't."

"It is about time," he said. "A man should make a second marriage before he retires, I think."

It was a bit later before I managed to speak about the rest of it to him. In fact, from the way he relaxed and started to light up another cigarette—I batted it out of his hand—after we made love, I knew that he thought he had heard all of it. "There's something else," I said.

"Yes, I know. I'll stop. I promise. And I'll put in for retirement just as soon as you get back from visiting Ava."

"Promise?"

"Darling, I just proposed to you. What's ending a little habit like smoking compared to getting married again? Remember what it was like?"

"Oh, I do, I do."

"You do? Then I thee wed."

"Robert," I said, feeling myself fairly melt into him. Oh, it was so spectacular, our plan, it took me a while before I could recover my senses enough to talk to him about the rest of my idea.

"And you want us to do what?" he asked. He was already climbing out of bed when my words stopped him.

"It's what I said. I've been thinking about this for a while now— since the end of the war. I want us to go to live in Israel."

He gave his head a little shake, as though some invisible hand had just punched him in the face. "Israel? You mean Palestine?"

255

"Robert, it's a country of its own now, and I'd like to take a trip there, if that makes sense. And if we like it, after you retire we could go there to live."

He lay back on the bed and curled up next to me. "I didn't mean to play dumb. Darling, I've been to that part of the world. I've worked there. It's all sun and sand, darling. It's hot—not pleasantly warm, but hot. And . . . "

"You haven't been to Israel," I said.

"I've been to places quite near . . . "

"It's not all desert," I said. "They're reforesting; they're planting thousands of trees, tens of thousands . . . "

"You haven't been there, either. How do you know about it?"

"I've been reading. I've been talking to people."

"To people who've been there, lived there?" There was something in his voice that I had never heard before, the way he must have sounded when he was at meetings: at his company, in the field.

"Yes."

"There's a war on there, you know, a continual state of war."

"I thought that we would . . . just visit and look around. I know that it may sound crazy to you . . . "

"Oh, not that crazy. Not as crazy as some of the things I've heard in my life. But you've never said a word to me. I just assumed that when I retired we would move somewhere in the Southwest, probably New Mexico."

"With Ava, of course."

"At least near her."

"It *is* very beautiful out there . . . "

I wished that I could have better explained my plan, but whenever I started to, it came out sounding all wrong, with words about wanting to be among my own kind, which sounded silly even to me, considering where I was and who I was saying them to. But I vowed that I would try to make my case to Robert just as soon as I returned from seeing Ava, and the night before I left, I gave him some pamphlets and newspaper articles that I had been saving, saying that if he read those, he and I could talk better about the subject when I got back.

And I said to myself, *promised* myself, that I would have a good visit with his sister, too; that I would convince her that the time was ripe for the retrospective, and that I would talk to her about me and Robert—and that above all I would try to love the desert place where she had chosen to live for the rest of her life. It seemed to me good practice for living, or trying out a life, anyhow, in the desert land now so much on my own mind.

DOOR

We've had a real scare. Michael came running up to the house shouting so loudly that I thought: oh, my God, Robby's been bitten by a
scorpion, until I remembered that he had gone to town with Socorro
in the old car, and then I thought: oh, my God, Ava, there's been
an accident.

And I ran to the door just as Michael came in wildly waving
his hands. "She's bleeding!" he said.

And I thought, what, what? and I shouted back at him, and
then ran with him to the studio where we found Ava standing at
the door, blood streaming down her face from what turned out to
be a major nosebleed. She smiled through her fingers, stanching
the flow, or trying to, with clean rags from the studio, though where
she had found them I don't know.

We took her to town, all the while making her sit back and
hold the cloths to her face, though the doctor in town told us we
might have made her gag on her own blood. He checked Ava's
blood pressure and said that, given her age, it was slightly below
normal. We left feeling better, for all the trouble.

On the street we met Socorro and Robby. They were mighty
surprised.

That night Michael and I looked at each other and I said, "One
day . . . "

He shook his head vigorously. "No, no," he said, "too much to
do."

I had meant Ava, but I think he took it to mean himself, or the
both of them together.

258

BLUE MESA

Ava

Of late I have spent much time alone with clouds. And I have discovered that when I am out under the sky and notice these configurations that only he could truly capture with his camera, I think of Stig, and all the desert land around me, and the sky itself seems to contract in an instant into an ice-cold pain no smaller, I say, than my fist – all of it exquisitely there, compressed and pressing into my stomach. But I can shrug off the pain.

And then I sigh, and I wish with that sigh that he were walking with me along the trail northwest to the top of the mesa, so that we might take home with us the sight of those clouds on his photographic plates.

He and I certainly had no quarrel about light.

The way he looked at me that morning, you'd think he had forgotten whose eyes were looking back at him. I saw the terrifying flash of recognition that he had given up on his own work, or worse, that he believed that he didn't have to change anything in it anymore. It would be clouds, a trail of clouds, mares' tails, wisps of cirrus, all the way to the end. I saw – and this terrified me – just how close to finishing he had come.

"You can't pack it in, Stig," I told him that night. "Please come this one time with us. You've seen some of the work I've done because I went out there. Think of what *you* could do. It's everything you've always wanted to put into your work, the space out there: the American space we've always talked about."

"It's here," he said, thumping his chest.

"What's there? Do you have pains again?" I leaned toward him, over a tablecloth loaded with empty dishes and a half-filled bottle of blood red wine.

259

"No, no, no, no pains." His voice made him seem weary, as though something in his spirit had suddenly sat down in the middle of a long walk. "The space you're talking about. I have it here. American heart." And again he thumped his chest. And then he tapped his skull. "And American brain."

His hair had long ago turned completely white, but there had always been that sparkling quality in his look that had kept me wondering how at his age he kept on going every day, but now it was as though someone had left a room, and then recalled something and stepped back inside to pull the string on the bulb. Darkness.

"The clouds," I said to him before we went to sleep, "do you know what you could do with those clouds out there!"

"I might think about it," he said, and then shut his eyes.

"So you might?"

"I might," he said without opening his eyes.

In the middle of the night I awakened to ferocious thunderclaps: the kind of upstate storm that you read about as a child, the resounding carooms and boomings that make up the bowling alley of the gods. "Stig," I said, "the windows."

I touched his sleeping body on the shoulder and got up to shut the windows. "I can't see a thing out there!" I called to him over the noise of the storm. But I was wrong, for just then I saw something large, either a deer streaked with rain, or who knows what? a stray dog or whatever, an animal—I thought it was an animal, a huge beast—caught at the edge of the lake in the jagged glare of a vast, unfolding accordion of light. "Stig!" I wanted him to come and see it. But the light faded just as quickly as it had flashed upon us, and the deer or dog or whatever animal it was disappeared, was swallowed by the night as certainly as if it had sunk into the lake. I wanted to wait until the next flash, to be sure about what I had seen.

But Stig called to me from the bed and I turned away from the window. "Camera!"

"I wish you had it, too," I said. "But how could you photograph the dark?"

No answer from the bed.

260

"No one could have solved this problem with the light, or the dark, to be specific, not even you."

No answer.

"Stig?" I reached over to touch his forehead. In the lull between thunderclaps I could hear the sharp intermittent rasps of troubled breathing—my own chest's noises—but no sound, not even a breath, came from Stigmar's dry pursed lips. I leaned down to kiss him. It was like touching my lips to a stone. A moan erupted from my throat, and I flung myself down on the bed alongside him. I grabbed him by the shoulder and shook him; the lightning flashed, and I could see that his head remained at an unnatural angle when I roughly moved him on the bed. "No no no no no no no," I moaned again, feeling suddenly the greatest terror I had ever felt in my life. An astringent, almost winelike odor stung my nostrils and I could feel the wetness beneath me. At first I thought that in my fear I had suddenly wet myself, but then I realized, as I rolled away toward the edge of the bed, that it was Stig's bladder which had emptied—and everything faded away for me then, including the noise of the storm. I found myself back in my own childhood bed, sometimes soaked in urine, as if no time had elapsed between then and now, as though I had lived it all in the single ever-widening span of a huge elongated moment, my life not so much a story moving forward through time, as it was a spreading stain, soaking into the unprepared linen of a canvas.

"Dora!" I heard myself call into the storm, which was fading now, and so I could hear the sound of the door opening.

"Ava!" It was Cissy, come to see if we had closed our windows. One last major flash of lightning turned the room for an instant into something near to day. In that light I saw her look of surprise; I saw the large growing dome of her belly, the way her nightgown seemed to flow away from it toward the windows, toward the departing storm.

"Great God in heaven!" she cried out. Rushing to the bed, and without more than a glance at the body of Stigmar, and no complaint about the winy damp in which we lay, she flung herself down alongside me and took me in her arms.

So we lay there a while, ever mindful of how much time was passing – the light told us, the growing light – and how much time had never elapsed.

We held the funeral upstate. Harriet arrived from New York, with Robert. He happened to have been in the city on company business, he said, and took the train up with Harriet.

I told them of my desires for Stig's body, and they seemed a bit staggered themselves. "The airfield is in Albany," I explained. "I have found this out."

"Did he state in his will that he wanted it this way?" My brother appeared to be quite concerned for me, despite his apparent attention to Stig's desires.

"Don't worry. This is what he would have wanted."

"No Jewish burial?" Harriet asked.

"We won't do it this way for you," I said to her, and then I tried to soften my voice. I frightened even myself by all the anger I had put in it. "Not that I'm wishing this for you, Harriet. Please, understand."

She put her arm around my waist and said, "He loved clouds. It makes great sense to me."

"Thank you," I said. "I know what I'm doing is right. Robert, don't you think so?"

My brother had his eyes on the ground and raised them to address me. "I'll go with you."

"You two can come to the airfield, but I want to go up alone. Just the pilot and me."

And so they accompanied me to the airfield and watched as I climbed in behind the pilot of this small one-engine airplane that made a racket when it started up, like a freight train in a tunnel. Under any other circumstances I would have been terrified, but somehow the presence of Stig's ashes in the small urn I carried gave me strength.

I so enjoyed the surging, the lifting of the aircraft as we climbed. My heart swelled as we banked to the north. The pilot had made me wear goggles and a helmet. As we roared along about a thousand or two feet above the ground, I slipped up my goggles so that I could see the various colors of the clouds and the squares of farm and splashes of forest beneath us, and then the blue mirror of our little lake, without any screen.

"Here!" I motioned with my gloved hand, pointing down over the edge of the cockpit. As he had instructed me before takeoff, I turned toward the rear, took the stopper from the vase and let the ashes stream out behind us into the current of the wind.

"You'll run the gallery now, won't you?" I said to Harriet over the cold dinner that Cissy, with some effort, had prepared for us. I had told her to take the night off, to try and sleep, and I knew that she had taken a bottle from the liquor cabinet before going to her room. Good, I thought, well and good. At the table I couldn't help but keep going back and forth between Robert and Harriet, Harriet and Robert, until I had to stop, or else my curiosity would have been all too apparent. Lord, how even in my grief there were these other questions on my mind, about my brother and my friend – but what could I know without them telling me? and about my work, oh, I was thinking about Blue Mesa and the sky at twilight, the strands of pure color tortured by the wind into threads of luminescence beyond my capacity to say how they looked in words.

And I thought very little of Stig, because of the odd sense I had that he was sitting next to me, and then after I climbed into bed, lying next to me, almost as though he would be there if I were to turn around and speak to him. To preserve that feeling, which I knew was a little joke I was playing on myself so that I wouldn't have to remember that he was gone, I kept from turning in the direction that I had decided was his. All night I lay there, without moving my head in that direction.

I sold the house. I wanted Cissy to come west with me but she refused, saying that she could never live anywhere but in Washington County. Stig had left some money for her in his will, and with it she bought herself a little house in Albany and waited for her child to be born. I sold the house that had once belonged to Mabel Dodge and bought this ranch house. I liked the solitary location, this old adobe house with a beautiful wooden door and the barn behind it. I thought that solitude was what I needed – until I hired

Socorro, whose name literally means help or sustenance, a few months after my arrival.

Long ago I had sworn never to use human figures in my canvases. Socorro made me think I might break my rule. She had the kind of skin that changed in delicate tones under different light *always for the better,* and the relationship of her eyes to the light, the lithe lines of her hands, fascinated me. I finally asked her to pose.

She looked at me for a long time—showing me nothing but the darks of her eyes—and said nothing but began to undress.

"Socorro, let's walk instead," I said, and she slipped back into her skirt and blouse, and I set aside the paints, and we went outside and walked toward the top of the canyon. "You almost made me break my vow," I said.

"I do not understand," she said.

I tried to explain.

"I still do not understand," she said, holding her head high as she walked.

"People, *gente,*" I said, "human beings are part of nature. But not the most interesting part for me. I like to paint these canyon walls, these cliffs, a star, now and then a sunset. The human figure . . . "

"Sí, Señora?"

"Please, Socorro," I said, "call me Ava."

"Como la primera mujer?"

"Sí. I am named after the first woman. But I am not the first woman, and I am not the last."

There was a breeze blowing up the canyon, the cirrus clouds drawn out to nearly ropelike strands above us. The sun had risen full, a sulfurous ring with ragged edges blurred into the egg-white sky around it. My breath came in short bursts, and I could feel a billowy sort of looseness in my knees. A blue jay burst out of nowhere and screeched at us, then flew off.

"What would happen if we just kept on walking?" I asked my friend.

She shook her head, as if to say she didn't know . . . or she couldn't say . . . or it didn't matter.

Time passed, and more time. Some nights, while I lay awake staring out the window at the brilliant splash of stars in the southwestern sky, she came into the room and stretched out alongside me.

I heard myself ask on one of these occasions, while I was still wobbly in my head from a few shots of tequila that I had thrown down while star gazing on the patio just before trying to sleep, "Are you my desert flower?"

"Flores," she said in an odd voice, as though it were not her own but instead that of some vendor, or namer of things who was going through a list of nouns pertaining to the world. "Flores, agua, aguilar, caballo . . . "

There is a kind of romantic statement—you know what I mean, you hear it in books, you see it on canvas—the design of which is to make you think some deep emotion holds sway, as in "He took her in his arms and they clung together all night"—some such nonsense. A swirl of sky, ocean, flowers, that variety of things, and in the case of Socorro and me, there was some element of romance, though, of course, it was a bit narcissistic on my part, wanting to see myself in this younger woman. And on her part she saw, well, what she said was, "La madre."

She told me that. I enjoyed hearing it. That was the week that I finally did break my vow, and I set about making the first of the Socorro figures, a watershed time for me since I had not done a figure for many decades. I was quite nervous when I first started. I didn't know until I picked up the charcoal for the sketch whether or not my wrist would remember how to draw. But it knew. It worked. It drew. This was the kind of work that was completed even before I began it, a certain treasure of feeling already there. The Socorros were alive before I set a line on paper, the kind of thing you hear about but always as someone else's experience. There were mornings when I believed in the old magic of taking the subject's soul and putting it on paper.

This figure, whose skull with the rose contained within it so that the woman seems to be holding up both the cow's skull and her own head—here, see how she shows herself so sweetly below the waist and makes it seem, or so I wanted it to seem, that her upper torso has been transformed into something other than anything we might have imagined for woman. Some may say that I am becoming European, putting this late surrealist touch in work so otherwise the opposite. But then I would reply that all of my work until now has shown a certain fantastic quality: faces of the earth larger than real, bigger than life, beginning with what the eye sees and then transformed by the eye. For in a way all that I see is already within me, even as I move through the world with my eyes open.

I had begun to slow down a little—and it took about two or three years for me to do most of the pictures in the series. I had painted all but the last pictures, the woman with the cow-skull head containing the rose, and another, the woman with the snake head, one of my favorites—I can't say why—when Harriet arrived from the East. It was an odd situation, but I found that I had very little to say to her. At first I told myself that the problem was that since she had taken over the gallery, she had gotten very bossy.

"You're back to *figures*? I thought that you had vowed never ever to paint figures again?" Her strident voice upset me. It was as if she had finally, after all these years, become a New Yorker, but there was something else, too, on my mind. "Well, then, Harriet, I've broken my vow. Don't you like them?"

"Darling," she said, "nobody does landscape the way you do, but figures? How can we sell figures at a time like this?"

"Like this?" I walked her over to the far wall of the studio and turned the last drawings toward us.

"No," she said, after scrutinizing my most recent Socorro for a few quiet moments, "not like that. I admit it, no one has done anything like that. Oh, no, no, you've done it here, Ava. You've really done it here."

"These may be the last," I said.

"What does that mean?"

"The last figures for a while, anyway. My eyes have not been good," I explained.

"They've been good enough to get you this far."

"They tire easily. I don't have the concentration that I used to have, and it takes a lot more out of me to produce."

Harriet had been staring at the drawings all this while. "So you don't have any more of these?"

"You want to put them in a show, don't you?"

"Don't you?"

266

I shook my head. "I don't know what I want to do with them. I want them to sit a while."

"Who is the woman?" Harriet asked.

"Socorro," I told her.

"Socorro?"

"She helps me."

"She works for you?"

I nodded. "But she's away for the week. You can't meet her."

Harriet took a step back from the canvas and then turned to stare at me. She recognized the change that had come over me, and I saw that now she, too, was jealous. "I already have."

Harriet brought the subject up again at dinner. "Tell me about her."

"Oh, there's not much to tell. To see her is almost everything. You saw her as she really is. In the flesh she's like everything else: only the possibility of becoming something other than what she is."

"Oh, come on, Ava, please don't give me that song and dance."

"What a funny way to put it."

"Don't be coy, please. We are both getting too old for that."

"Don't be jealous," I said, going to her and taking her in my arms.

In the next moment her fate arrived. In the form of my suggestion about a hike the next day. "I'd love to," she said. "Remember our first hike together? The first time I came out?"

I remembered, of course, all too well, and I spent a mostly restless night, the voice of my long-departed sister in my ear, but around that hour when I had been given to getting up out of bed and going to the window to try and count stars, I heard Harriet in the main room, a certain heaviness in her breathing.

"Yes?" I could hear my voice, sounding a bit anxious it seemed to me, and for no good reason I could know at the time.

"I can't sleep."

"Oh, you come here," I said, and took her hand and led her to my bed where I tried gently, as in the old days, to soothe her into sleep. In a few minutes her breathing turned even and deep while I lay there still awake, wishing for what I did not know: some peace outside the body that could still be called *alive*, something such as this.

* * *

The next morning the sky had the appearance of a deep concave bowl that had been gouged out of the light and worked so carefully with a smoothing tool that no mark showed on its interior surface. A single star remained in the west, a reminder that in some parts of the world night still covered all. I studied that star, and thought that if there was a possibility of new work, it would not be stars again, though something about that tiny winking emblem trans-fixed my attention, and would have continued to longer, if my friend had not been making morning sounds at my back.

What if I traveled in the direction of that star? The thought occurred to me that if such were my wish, I had better plan on it soon. Plan a trip. Travel to California, see the Pacific. Fly to India— see Asian mountains—I wanted that. And then come home to my canyon cliffs, my red desert plateau.

Blue jays called to each other. A hawk hovered over the trail to the west, far too early for lunch. He'd be looking for lizards, or some pale owl chick too small to know which way to turn at the sound of those terrible wings. It would be over before the poor dear knew.

We'll take our hike, I decided. We'll walk a lot, talk a little, and perhaps something salvationary will come to mind.

It turned out to be late morning before we started out. After a breakfast of cornbread and chocolate and coffee, Harriet wanted to see the rest of the recent work. "Besides the figures of Socorro," she said. "I've got a good idea about those. And I know that they are going to sell like crazy."

"I don't want to sell them."

"Please, Ava, don't be crazy. They'll go quickly."

"Let's not discuss it now. I'll show you other things."

"Clouds," she said with her mouth all pinched up when I showed her what stood against the wall in the barn. "You're picking up where Stig left off, aren't you?"

"He made me look at them. And the last few years I couldn't help but try to do some of his work. Now that he's gone."

"Yes," she said, "he taught me to look at them, too. Look at those thunderheads, gathering there over the mountains."

We started our walk a short time later in that direction. The destination of our hike was Blue Mesa—not a mesa, really, but a little ridge resting a few miles on the other side of the canyon, where some dry streambeds converged to create a small peninsula of rock somewhat higher than the desert floor. I painted there sometimes, working with cactus and rock wall, the distant mountains, all starkly outlined.

After a while Harriet stopped to stare out across the space between the ridge and the mountains which had filled up with large tablelike clouds. "Beautiful," she said.

"And dangerous sometimes," I told her as we set down our baskets and made up our picnic spread. "We have huge sudden thunderstorms out here, nothing like your hurricanes back home."

"Remember . . . ?"

"Oh, I do," I said, spreading before us the large blanket made by Socorro's mother many years before, that my helper had brought into the household for just such occasions as this. It contained the figure of the rose within the cow skull that I had taken for my own in those last canvases. When I had first seen it and inquired of Socorro about its origins, she had said she did not know whether it was an old insignia that the woman had sewn into the center of the cloth, or something she had found or seen or made up out of her own dream visions. Stars in the faded blue of evening sky, bleached skulls from the dusty ground, patterns on cloth sewn by an old woman out of her Navajo eye: it was all the same to me. I've always taken my inspiration where I've found it.

"The wind is coming up stronger now," Harriet said.

"Yes," I said, setting out bread and cheese, and the goatskins with the wine and water. "Though it may storm here or it may not. See those clouds, . . . "—the sun had slipped down behind them, leaving the giant valley below us to fill up with dark, as though it were a bowl and dark were liquid—" . . . they can just as easily blow north of us as move directly here."

"I'd prefer not to get wet," Harriet said as though she could hear my thinking.

"Me, too," I said. "Though this is the West, and sometimes you can't hold to old habits."

I studied her face. Light was quickly disappearing even up here on our little table, and though I had not taken a single sip of wine,

269

I felt that I could see Harriet fading into the dark: her skin eroding and then the bones and then the very imprint of her presence. I shuddered involuntarily, and then took a drink from the wineskin.

"Thunder," she said, and I could hear it rumbling in the distance, as though some huge animal were clearing its throat. "Shouldn't we go back?"

Along the line of the horizon, the clouds had turned pitch black, with little spokes of lightning leaping out from above them, and above the lightning were clouds as thick as I had ever seen out here. "It's moving away from us," I said.

"I hope so."

"See up there?" I motioned for her to look directly above us, where blue sky still remained, as promising as when it had first appeared at sunrise. Harriet nodded. "Yes, clearing."

"We have enough space out here so that there's room for storm and for stillness both," I said.

"The wind's still blowing," she said.

"And it's raining hard far off there; you can see it now," I told her, motioning her to look where dark fists of rain seemed to beat against the far northern valley with an angry kind of pulsing. "If I were working, I wouldn't stop."

While we ate, the storm appeared to shift even further northward. We could still hear the thundering and see the lightning that flashed in vast sheets against the dark wet northern sky, even as the brilliant western horizon grew brighter and brighter with the rejuvenated afternoon sun. Such a mixture of frenzy and calm, all in the sight of a single person's vision!

Some jays skirted up out of nowhere, screeching at each other as if in the middle of some long debate, and then flashed down behind the rocks to our right where an old dry creekbed led down toward a plain of boulders stretching toward the east.

"Let's talk about your work," Harriet said. "Will you?"

"What do you have in mind?"

"I have a plan," she said. "But first I have to . . . " She stood up and looked around, as if she were in the house of Mrs. Trenholm back in Charleston on that afternoon that had begun blowing in the storm that had changed my life.

"You're still Southern and modest, aren't you?" I nodded toward the rocks. "Over there. But don't wander off."

Something odd fluttered across Harriet's face. "There aren't snakes, are there?"

"Just be careful where you squat."

"Ava!" she said in mock distress that turned into a moment of laughter for both of us.

And then she walked off and disappeared behind the rocks, leaving me to think about the proposal that she would bring up again when she returned, about a show that she wanted to put up, the show that I supposed I was ready for now that Stig was gone, one in which I could feel that the work would stand or fall by itself, and I was thinking, then good; we'll do it, whatever you want, Harriet, and if you want my brother, too, for you have already had him, or he you, then good for that, too; I can make my peace with the world just as I have faced up to my work, never understanding much of it but feeling the power of the driven spirit as naturally as those fierce dark clouds I see now herded before the strong high winds of the upper world, so high and far now that they might be raining this very moment into the distant fork of the North Platte where I first found my brother his buffalo skull, where our mother first tried to drown the both of us, driven as she was by her own twisted art, the art of death, the death of art. I was thinking this, and I called out to Harriet, *"Don't go down into the arroyo, darling!"* but I'd told her not to stray, thinking about the story of our great family mother, the tall bark painter, Melissa Tree, who had rescued us, the future, when she helped her children to walk upon the waves.

Slowly Harriet descended the path, and I don't know whether it was some antiquated notion of eastern shyness that sent her, or if she had been startled from her first stopping place above on the rocks by the sound of a blue jay hopping away in its own surprise, or if she thought she might have strayed too close to what she took to be the lair of a rattler. But she started down toward the canyon floor, not a long way down, but far enough, oh, yes, far enough. Stones rolled out from under her feet, and she could hear them come to rest an instant later. Not a long way down, only a few feet really, no, not a long way.

She heard the wind draw down the pass; she heard the wind shaking the mesquite branches; she heard a bird whistle in the sunlight, or might it have been a lizard? What did she know? Could lizards whistle in the mesquite trees?

It had been only a very few minutes since she left me up there on the mesa. Perhaps she glanced back up in my direction and saw the first star over the canyon rim, and I wonder if she smiled to herself as she found the bottom, halted, undid her clothing and squatted, thinking: we have missed the storm, we have missed the storm. She was happy in her voiding.

All fell quiet. In the sudden silence surely she could hear the gushing of her own urination.

And then came a new sound, not wind but rather like the wind, not the galloping of horses but something like what she imagined their sound might be—I am imagining all this, of course, but then I knew her, I knew her! And I have had plenty of time since then to imagine this, to imagine much, to imagine a great, great lot of things!

I heard the sound at a slightly different pitch, because I was higher above it. And I knew! It came from so far away, but it had been building; there was no way that I could have known that it was coming, and yet I had warned her; I had warned her, but alas! not sternly enough.

"Harriet!" I called out, and I was up and running to the edge. A dog howled, hooted! a bird screeched! a child screamed! or it might have been that bird again, yes! And the flood waters that poured around the bend on the canyon floor rushed ahead with the power of a train engine, high and as deep as forever.

DOOR

Michael flies east, to see some people about a plan he has for a Boldin retrospective–Harriet Cardozo's last dream. There is plenty to do here, and during the day a number of workmen arrive, at Michael's behest, to do some work on the barn studio. And yet I am quite alone. When I walk out by myself toward the mesa, I feel more comfortable than I do in this house.

Ava complains that she feels suddenly too tired to walk with me. My guess is that she misses Michael. "Has he called?" she asks me at nearly every turn. She can't see my face very clearly, but she can hear me breathe. "I want to know about that show," she says, as if to put me off the trail. "Should I do that show?" she asks.

"Of course," I say. "How could you not?"

"Easily," she says, "easily."

One afternoon while she's napping, I put Robby in the car seat in the van and drive all the way to Santa Fe to the bookstore. Reading takes my mind off all this sometimes, though of course the work I'm doing at the moment is more writing than reading. I buy some things to read to Ava: *The Professor's House*, a Cather I think she might perhaps not know, since there isn't a copy on her shelf; *Wuthering Heights*, figuring that she might have read it, but long ago (I haven't seen a copy of that, either); and for myself a Doris Lessing novel and a Joan Didion novel, and essays by someone named Annie Dillard that look good when I flip through them – and I wonder to myself, how am I ever going to do this project on Ava? How can I ever make her *known* to people who have only seen her work but never met her? Words? When she herself chose a path around words. Though I love painting, finally I am a writer, or think I am, or perhaps I should say, I want to be, or maybe I am at

273

least during the time that I am putting all this down on the page. So how can I convey a sense of the *paintings* in my *language*? I won't even try, is what I have decided. Where Ava writes about such things in her notes, that can stand on its own: her struggle to say in words what she wants to do, to describe what she sees she has done.

My job, I think, is to do what I can to make some sense out of the life, so that it can shine forth on the page: in her words, in the words of those who loved her, lived with her, and in the case of some, also lived *by* her. Because she was, of course, some kind of emblem for a lot of people—more and more women, and even some men.

(All this was going through my head—I'm trying to record now the way it was at that moment in the bookstore—while I was completing my purchases.)

Her work is an emblem—I'll put it on a flag and march beneath that banner—a charge to life!

And her life? Because she is who she is, because she is the woman she is, because she is a woman, I believe that her life has some power to show us things, too—more so than the life of some artists, male artists?

But then what is male and what is female when it comes to the work? I don't know, I don't know that I can ever know.

And the art? and the life?

Excuse me, I have to make my purchases.

VERMONT

Michael

You grow up the way I did, it's always your mother's voice that you hear in your head. Which is, like, all right if you're a girl, but not if you're a guy like me.

It started back when I was around twelve years old. I always knew I was a little different, not having a real father and all, so I used to go out of my way to show the other guys that I was tougher than they were, and smarter, too. It affected my brain, I think, what with getting punched a lot for one thing, and also from busting my head to get better grades than the rest of them. For a normal kid I suppose one or the other would have been enough. But not for me.

My mother—you know a little about what she's like—she didn't know what to do with me when I would come home all bashed up and bloody, except wash my face for me and sit down and collapse into a heap and start to cry. "Michael," she'd say, "please help me, not hinder me. Every day I got to earn the money to raise you; don't make it such a chore."

So I would go into these cycles where I would study like crazy and bring home these report cards that nearly made her swoon. And then I'd be out fighting again on the way home from school, and she'd be moaning again.

In eighth grade I took a shop course and that changed things a lot. I loved working with metal—it was just tin, but then it was prophetic; however you want to call it. Anyway, I couldn't get enough of metalwork—and so halfway through school, I found a job after school working at a sheet-metal place out near the railroad yards. I'd see my mother looking at me over dinner sometimes, and I could see her thoughts as clearly as though they were posted on her

275

forehead: here's my boy, and it looks as though he's got a future at the sheet-metal place forever. It wasn't like she was a snob. She was caught between who she knew my father was, and who she thought she was.

As far as who I thought I was, I was the bastard son of a fancy photographer from Cossayuna and New York City. You want to make something of it?

"Ma," I asked Cissy one day, "where's those drawings that I did when I was a kid, the ones you said you were keeping?"

"Whatever do you want those for?" she said, speaking from the stove where she was fixing supper. It was just before that time when I came over to Vermont looking for Paul Feely, an artist I had read about in the newspaper.

"I want to look at them," I said.

"Well, I don't know where I put them," she said. I didn't know at the time that she was lying. I never would have believed that she was capable of telling a lie, not my own dear mother. Boy, was I in for a surprise!

I had finished high school and had served a couple of years in the army—most of that time on godforsaken bases from Texas to North Carolina—and I had come back to Albany to see my mother and found myself working again for the same sheet-metal shop. There was a girl there, an assistant bookkeeper, and she and I got engaged, and I knew that look in my mother's eye when I brought that poor thing home with me for supper one night to the little house on Washington Avenue where I had lived all my life, within walking distance of the bakery where my mother worked—she gave me that same look.

"Mom, I'd like you to meet Teresa."

And she gave me the eye—so this is who you are?

It wasn't Teresa's fault. She was a nice girl, Polish—and even though nobody in Albany liked you to marry outside your tribe in those days, it wasn't that. It was another thing.

But something happened between us—I don't mean some incident, but more like something that was there all the time and getting stronger. It was like I lived on another wavelength. When we went out with our friends and I got drunk, everything was okay.

276

But then when I'd sober up the next day and Teresa would be on the telephone talking to me about what we were going to do that night, something would just come over me. Like it was a veil between me and the girl. Between me and that life.

If my mother had known it then, she maybe would have said, Ah, and it's *him* at work in you. But I don't know.

This went on for a while, a couple of years. I was making pretty good money at my job and saving some of it, and giving my mother some, too. But I always kept out a little for what I told myself was special dough. You know, and it's like there is a plan or something at work in us sometimes, because how could I have known what I was saving for, except that when the time came, the money came in pretty handy?

And that time came after the day when I drove over the line to Vermont and went up to the college. Your college. As you know, I hadn't been to college at all myself, and Bennington was just another place in the fancy part of Vermont, was all I knew, if I thought of it at all, but I had been feeling that itch—waking up one morning, thinking as I lay there smoking my first cigarette of the day about building something out of metal, as though that were just what I thought of *every* day when I woke up: shapes and the way the light struck the angles. Maybe some guys suddenly get the thought that they want to walk across Australia or climb a mountain or build a new kind of bicycle. What came to me that morning was what I said.

And it was that story in the *Knickerbocker News* about one of your art teachers up there that made me think I ought to drive up and talk to him. What did I know? Teachers were people you just went into their rooms and talked with. College wasn't high school? News to me. So I called in sick at work and drove over to Vermont. And it's just like our old Stanley said: it was all part of an old story, all that Stanley called mythic passages, right? Crossing the river.

It was a sharp, bright, etched-against-the-sky kind of autumn afternoon. The leaves had turned into that raw brilliance just before I took each curve to see them—that's the way it appeared to me— and would fall just as I put each stand of trees behind me. The air smelled of the smoke of burning leaves. What a time! what a day! I could swear it was magical, because I know that if I had stayed in Albany and gone to work, I couldn't have looked up at the sky from the yard where I would have been standing and felt the same sense of possibility. Crossed another river, the Hoosac, and rolled into town. It took me a few minutes to find out that the college was in *North* Bennington, and then all of a sudden there I was, parking in front of the little bar on the main street in this village, thinking I would have a beer before I went up to ask around for the artist I wanted to meet.

Because deep in my heart I knew this *was* different from everything else I'd ever tried, different from high school after all, and certainly different from the army. A beer was in order to cool my soul. So was another. And after another I sat there just sort of paralyzed wondering if I was ever going to get up the courage to do my errand. Guys came and went in this place: mill workers from some furniture plants along the river was what I learned from listening to them talk in those funny, cramped Vermont accents of theirs. I bought one of them a brew and found out there was a metal-working plant down there, too, and I was thinking about going over to ask about a job when a couple of girls came into the bar and reminded me, by their age and their looks, that there was a college in this burg, and that I was a man with a mission.

It was nearly suppertime when I got up to leave the bar and nearly dark outside, too, one of those full-sky pastel sunsets just coming to an end in the western sky—well, where else but the west!—over the Hudson Valley. I was thinking, leaning back a little against the high I was feeling from all those beers, the sun was setting on my mother away out on Washington Avenue, and further west, all the way to the end of the country—it would be coming on dark there soon, too, and then I was thinking back at myself, Well, hey, Michael, like, here you are in this dinky little hamlet in Vermont, and you've blown it; it's too late now for the reason you've come, and what are you doing but following the path of the sun where it's fading out west? Hey, what is going on?

The air grew chilly all of a sudden, and I was sort of teetering there on the sidewalk in front of the bar, asking myself, should I go and try to find this guy? or should I just say the hell with it and drive back on home? Home—not much of a home, with me so bored with seeing Teresa, and feeling at that moment like where I'd stood for a lot of years now was like having my back against the wall. All I had was this dream of mine, out in the open now that I had said it to myself in my head standing there in front of the little Vermont bar: I wanted to make things out of metal, call it whatever you would.

So I turned around to walk back into the bar and use the telephone to try and find this artist guy at the college anyway, even if it was too late, and nearly collided with this barrel of a bearded man in a three-piece suit, clearly as out of place here as I was going to be, I thought, up at the college. "You one of the teachers here?" I heard myself ask him.

"What's it to you, man?" he said back at me like he was some sharpie out on the street in front of the racetrack at Saratoga.

I shook my head, thrown a little off balance by the way he was talking. But then I had had more than a few beers and wasn't caring about my manners—and figured out in a hurry that he was not exactly sober himself. "I'm looking for somebody," I told him.

He leaned up against the front of the bar and asked me who it was. And—you guessed it, this was Stanley—of all people to run into, your favorite professor—but then it wasn't such a coincidence, looking back on it, to meet the town's thirstiest camel at the only oasis for miles around.

So we went back inside and had a few more drinks, and he asked me a lot of questions about my life and what I was really going to do with it. At first I was real suspicious. Nobody was ever that curious about me before this, not even my own mother. But as you know, he's such a funny man—that great big laugh, the way his whole body shakes when he tells a story he thinks is funny—and he had me convinced before too long that he was just being friendly because he wanted to be. That doesn't happen much, as you know, outside the world of the college.

A few more minutes went by, the bar was filling up with a different crowd now: more girls—students—than mill workers, the changing of the shift. A lot of girls came over to our booth to say hello to Stanley. Some of them he scowled at, some he bought a beer for. And for a special few he raised his voice in song:

Hit the road, Jack!
And don't you come back
No more, no more, no more, no more!

This odd duck, he thought the blues was a special kind of poetry that a lot more people—white people, rich girls, the kind he taught— ought to listen to. "It's all a road story, when you come down to it," he said, his voice elevated in that special intonation that I eventually came to recognize as his teaching voice—and his preaching voice as well, since he was a kind of preacher, too. "On the road—we're all on the road." He raised his hand and stuck out his thumb. Some of the girls giggled and jumped back from the table. Who the hell do these rich bitches think they are? I was saying to myself, looking at their good teeth and their nicely cut hair, when all of a sudden I saw this face in the row behind the others standing there, and I was seeing you for the first time, and our eyes met, and that was all, and then you went off somewhere, and I was staying there with Stanley, and there was more beer, and he was getting up to call Feely, and the next thing I knew, we were leaving the place for destinations unknown.

Because I never knew my father, it may account for why I've always been attracted like nails to a magnet—with that same kind of admiration that soldiers have for great officers—to men like Stanley, so full of himself and so ready to dispense advice and wisdom about the world, however much he had. So I followed along, and within minutes, he had led me to Feely's studio. It didn't take much longer for the man to hire me to clean up the place in exchange for a little space that I could use to work in.

"I want you to read these," Stanley said to me later that evening in his living room after his wife, a huge woman, had fallen down on the floor as though someone had hit her with a slaughterhouse hammer and begun to snore like a freight engine. He stepped around her body and handed me a copy of what I quickly discovered was one of his favorite books of all time, Lord Raglan's *The Hero*, and invited me to come and talk with him about it when I'd read it. "You need to start reading, Michael," he said. "It can't hurt your sculpture and in fact can only help."

280

I shrugged and threw back another drink.

The big woman stirred now and then, like some huge sea animal washed up on a beach. Stanley caught me staring at her. "She's haunted," he said. "She writes about the house across the street as if *it* were haunted. But the real ghosts are in her own mind. She's got a haunted *head*." He raised his own glass again and stared at the tanish liquid before swallowing it all. "Can you imagine how difficult it must be, to be a woman and have to deal with the likes of us? No wonder her head is haunted!" He roared out a laugh, and I couldn't help but laugh with him. What did I know about anything back then?

But I did get to work, serving, as you know, as Feely's assistant, and working part-time for maintenance during the day and trying my own stuff at night: painting a little, learning from another teacher how to throw pots, but mainly discovering that what I really felt happiest with was working with metal. The college was a place then where so many of the best guys passed through – all those guys who worked with steel – and it inspired me to meet them and drink with them, even though they were famous and I was the one who was sweeping out the work space and finding time, mostly at night, to work with my torch over in one corner of the space. But everyone was so great to me: Stanley, Paul, not to mention you girls. Well, hey, I'm really only kidding about that. It was, what? one or two of the painting students I went out with before I met you?

Or you met me, is really how we should put it, right? There I was, wearing my goggles, bent over a piece of steel, my torch flaring, and I must have been working for five or ten minutes before I turned off the torch, pulled up my goggles, and took a deep breath and saw you standing there against that tree looking over at me. What month was it? Early March, I guess, and it was one of those freak Vermont days when you get a false reprieve from winter. I was wearing a couple of layers of shirts and a mackinaw and a heavy work apron. You had just come out of the painting studio, and were covered with streaks of various shades of oils, your hair stuck with little bits of paint, too.

"Don't we know each other?" you asked.

What did I know? I thought that was a straight question. Yeah, go ahead and laugh at the memory of it! "No, I don't think so," I said, feeling the heft of the torch in my hand. Jeesum, if I had turned it on both of us, it couldn't have burned us hotter than how we got those first few times.

And the next autumn when I told Cissy about you the first time, you know what she said? Guess. "Amy *Cross?*" Her hands flew into the air in distress. "She'll be a cross for *you* to bear."

"Ma," I said, "she wants to be an artist, just like me. She understands what I'm doing without me even saying a word."

"Oh, oh, sweet Jesus," she said, her hands doing a little dance before her in the air, "it's coming out; it's all coming out!"

"What are you talking about, Ma?" I said to her, reaching for her wrists.

"Don't try to sweet-talk me, Michael," she said, stepping back from me. "You know there's little you can do that's wrong to me."

"So what's to complain?"

"What? what? Oh, nothing and everything! My whole life – oh, Michael, you're turning out to be your father's child!"

And then I brought you home to meet her. "We'll take a walk, why don't we?" she said after she served us a supper of stew, and some of the season's last corn on the side.

"Great idea," I said. "We'd love to. We walk all the time over in Vermont, Mother. Especially now, when the leaves are starting to turn; it's . . . "

"Michael, my love," said my mother. "I meant just me and my new friend Amy, here. You are going to stay home and do the dishes."

We all laughed, the three of us together.

So off you went walking, down Washington Avenue toward the park, with all its grand trees now turned and past their final glory, while I stayed and washed and wiped.

Don't you mess this up now, I said in my mind to Mother. If you mess this up, I'll take a . . . a stick to you, thinking of what she used to threaten me with when I was a child. Though she never did strike me; not once. "You are my love child," she used to say. "And it goes against nature to do anything to a love child but give it more and more love."

You two came back, chattering together. And you were smiling and she was touching your arm. "Now let me see out in the kitchen if this boy has done his job," Mother said in a playful voice I hadn't heard her use since I was a child.

"I want to show you some things," I said to you, remember? and I excused myself a moment and then came back into the kitchen where I found my mother drying the dishes I had already dried. "Ma . . . "

"Oh, I'm just touching them up," she said.

"No, I want to know where you put those old drawings of mine. I want to show them to Amy."

She gave me the sweetest smile and said, with a shake of her head, "I told you, I can't find them."

"Did you look?"

She nodded.

"Ma . . . "

"Your girl's waiting for you," she said. Then she lowered her voice. "I like her, Michael. She's got a good heart and she's smart as a whip."

Driving back to Vermont, I felt as though we had her blessings upon us. But the climate of things changed a little when I called her the next day. "What do you think, Michael?" she asked over the telephone. "Do you know how much money you'll have to earn in order to keep Amy in the style to which she's accustomed?"

"Ma, where'd you learn to talk like that?" I said, thinking I could make a joke out of it.

"You know what I mean, Michael. As nice as she is, she's still one of those rich college girls you make fun of when you tell me about that school."

"She is and she isn't, Ma. Think about me, what they could say about me: just another mick from darkest Albany."

"Your father was a Jew."

"You know what I mean. So I'm *half* Irish. I work with my hands."

"My house was clean when you brought her here."

"You know what I'm saying."

"Do I, Michael?"

283

I swallowed the spit in my mouth and I said, "I'm in love with her, Ma."

She made a little outcry, sort of like an *oh!*, as though someone had kicked her in the shins at the other end of the line.

"Ma?"

"I loved your father, too," she said in a whispery little voice, the way she had spoken to me when I was very small but a tone I had not heard in a long, long time. "And he's very proud of you, I know, from wherever he's watching."

"Aw, Ma."

"Because you are an artist. That's what he was, you know."

"I know."

"And I know that if he had lived, he would have recognized you."

"Please, Mom."

"No, no, I want to say it. He would have. He was a decent man. He was just old, getting old. And his marriage . . . "

"You've told me a few things before, Mother. I know, I understand . . . "

"But you don't understand what it was like to live . . . beneath him," she said. "He didn't treat me that way, but that was what it was; that was the way people saw it. I don't want you to have to live like that, Michael."

"Mother, for Jesus' sake . . . "

"Michael. Please."

"Sorry, sorry, but listen, this is a different time . . . "

"Oh, is it?"

"Yes, it is, and first of all I don't work for Amy's family."

"No, no, you're not a servant, are you? Just the son of a servant girl."

"Mother!"

"Don't yell at me, Michael, please."

"Sorry. Sorry, sorry, sorry. I didn't mean to raise my voice."

"It wasn't easy my working at such an early age, and it wasn't easy admitting to myself what it was I was getting myself in for, and it wasn't easy carrying you, my boy, with your father dead; and then raising you, wasn't that a picnic!"

"Yes, Mother. You've told me some of those things; I remember you telling me."

"Raising you."

"Yes?" I could hear her doing something on the other end of the line, and then I could hear her blowing her nose. I breathed a little easier myself, having said what I had said.

"Michael?"

"Yes, Ma?"

"She's a nice girl."

"Hey, and Ma, . . . " I said, trying to lift this conversation a little out of the valley of tears, " . . . did you find those drawings of mine yet?"

"Is that all you can think of at a time like this?" she asked, and blew her nose again.

When we drove down to Rappahannock, your parents took things a little easier. I remember your father looking at you kind of wistfully, almost with envy in his eyes, asking you about your courses. And then your mother took me into the kitchen to help her with the dishes while you and your old man stayed at the table, talking. I remember thinking to myself, What is this? Isn't the father supposed to be the one to take me aside and ask all the pertinent questions? But no, first it was your mother.

"What are you working on?" she asked, as though she were just one of our friends up at school.

I told her a few things about my sculpture and about some of the pots, too.

"Will you be able to make a living out of that?" your mother said, showing me how to stack the dishes in the dishwasher.

I was thinking, this whole house is turned upside down, as I rinsed the last of the dinner plates and handed them to her. "I really don't know," I said. "But I would like to be able to make some kind of living, don't worry about that."

"Oh, I wasn't worrying about anything of the sort," your mother said, showing me a profile quite like yours.

"Ma-om!" That's when you came into the room, calling out to her like you were about twelve years old and she had just embarrassed you in public.

Your father and I finally had a little talk, too, down by the river where we walked after meeting each other in the kitchen early the next morning. There was a heavy mist, almost fog, over the water, and it was chilly, though you could tell that spring was well on the way—there was just some kind of hope about it you could feel in the air in spite of the cold.

He asked me about work, too, and I talked a little about what I was doing. He nodded, but I could see in his eyes that he considered that making art was an appropriate activity for his daughter and his daughter alone. Grown men didn't do such things; they went out into the world and made buildings. And you had told me how successful he had been at that.

I was rubbing my hands together, watching the water churn up the light as the sun pushed against the slowly thinning curtain of mist. And he started asking me about my father.

I played it down. Back then I didn't really know that much about him, not anywhere near as much as I know now, thanks to you. "A photographer," I said. "He was a photographer from New York."

I don't know; all in all, I thought at the time that they were taking our romance too seriously—I had no idea back then that we would still be together a year later, your last year before you were to graduate, when we were both getting ready for the show that Feely had arranged for a couple of us on campus.

"Amazing!" That's what Feely said about your painting.

"I like the way that she keeps the action in the center of the field," said the slightly dumpy, slightly balding art critic from New York who came up to advise Feely from time to time. He took you to lunch—I don't have to remind you, but it sure sticks in my craw—and put it to you quite boldly. Or baldly, I should say. You sleep with him: guaranteed show in New York. A group show, mind you, but a show.

I guess that's when we both started thinking about other things. You started taking a writing course along with your art. And we both started thinking about getting out of there.

"Hit the road!" Stanley rubbed his hands together and looked at us both when I mentioned it. "That's the greatest story ever told.

A guy – a chick – set out on the highway! Or else they ride into town. And look for a nice room at the inn."

That's when I should have figured it, when you looked at me just then and blushed. But I thought it was just you and your usual shyness, the way I liked you so. I know you're smart, but at the same time you're so damned cute and innocent! Hey, but don't walk away! You asked me to tell you about this, and that's what I'm doing. Because, remember, you got really put off by that proposition, and you . . . look, if you're not going to listen . . . hey, look, so remember?

We wanted to get out of there, but we just didn't know where to go. Canada, I thought, maybe.

"Are you crazy?" you said. "I'd freeze to death up there."

"Then south? Atlanta's a big city. Maybe they have an art scene there?"

"Whatever I had in mind," you said, "I don't think it included going south."

"So . . . west?"

You looked at me – it was just an idea – but I remember the way you looked at me the first time it came up.

"I could write to my Aunt Ava," I said. "She's living out there."

"You've never even met her," you said with that steely skepticism of yours.

No, but I had mentioned her a few times, I guess, to you; only in the vaguest way though, because thinking about it – about her and Stig and Ma – gave me a headache, the three of them all tangled up together back then, the little that I knew about it. Ever since I had known about who my father was, I always kind of told myself that they had gotten a divorce and she had gone west before he and Cissy got together. Some story that was!

"Is she still alive?" had been Feely's response when I had first mentioned Ava to him. "I haven't seen any new work of hers for years. I honestly thought she was dead. She must be eighty or ninety years old."

I had shaken my head and dropped the subject, the whole thing still making me a little ashamed. I didn't know how old she was – I didn't know anything back then except you and my work.

So I said to you when I brought it up, "Well, maybe I could get Ma to write to her for us. Maybe we could head out there and pay her a visit. At least it would get us started." I saw that look come into your eye just then, so I wanted to reassure you. "And once we get out there, we could think about . . . you know . . . "

"It's not such a horrible thing," you said. "A lot of people do it." Your face turned a little red. "Get married, I mean."

"Maybe they do," I said. "I know you don't like telling stories to your folks. It's just that I'm not ready for it yet."

"What am I supposed to tell them?"

"You're taking a writing course, right? So make something up."

It was your turn then to change the subject. Which was all right with me. "I got another letter today," you said.

The art critic from New York had been writing to you every week, suggestive letters, and though you did not reply anymore, he still kept sending them.

"Look," I said, "I'm going to call him up. Or better, I'm just going to go down there and shove his teeth down his throat."

You laughed, I remember that, and you told me how cute you thought *I* was—getting a little of your own back, uh-huh!

But your interest in painting fell off long before you finished the pieces for your senior show. You'd started that writing course with a friend of Stanley's, the novelist from Brooklyn who had made a new life for himself and recently come to teach at Bennington by way of Oregon—strange route! I was there that afternoon in the lounge of the barn, a place I always thought was a funny location for classrooms—so many animals had been born, coupled, shit, and died there.

He touched a finger to his nose, leaned forward a little and said, "I don't usually say this, but I'll say this to you, Amy—not just because you seem like a nice girl—and in your presence, too, I'll say this, Michael, and not just because you seem like a nice boy. Amy, from the first story you showed me, I can detect a hint of a possibility."

"A hint of a possibility?" You showed your white teeth in a nearly perfect smile.

"A hint," the man said. Coming from Malamud, we knew what that meant. It was almost the same as the Pulitzer Prize.

"So now you're a writer, huh?" I said to you that night.

You shrugged and went back to your typewriter. "Words, shapes, sounds, steel: it's all a matter of giving them form and color," you said.

"That's all?" I said.

"That's enough," you said.

Not long after that—I think about this a lot—we drove over to Albany to see Cissy, remember? And we were talking, and I brought up the subject of those old drawings of mine again, and she looked me right in the eye and said, "Look, Michael, darling, I have to confess to you—I can't keep it in any longer—I sent those drawings of yours to your Aunt Ava."

"You what?"

"You heard me, darling."

Amy, you looked at me, and I looked at you, and that's when you said, "Well, why don't we just drive out there and have a look at them?"

DOOR

"Hi," I say to Michael as he slides into bed alongside me. His weight tilts me toward him, and I hold onto his shoulder, inhaling the must of clay and acid that has become his aura since he began working with Ava in the barn on their pots.

"Hi," says Michael.

"Nice to see you."

"Amy," he says, "I got to get me a suit."

"A suit?"

"Yeah, if I'm going back East again, I've got to have a suit."

"Are you planning to go again soon?"

"It could happen at any time."

"Well, tell me about it."

He shakes his head. "It's unlucky to talk about it. But it could happen . . . "

"Goddamn you, Michael," I say, "tell me what's going on."

"Well . . . remember what's-his-name, the critic?"

"Not *him*—you haven't been writing to . . . "

"I've been talking to him."

"On the telephone?"

"Well, yeah, on the telephone. How else would I talk to him if I'm out here and he's in New York?"

"Please don't be sarcastic."

"Okay, okay. But I've been talking to him about . . . "

I can't take it, and I burst out, "You're such a hypocrite."

He pulls away from me and sits up. "I beg your pardon?"

"You heard me. I didn't mean to make it sound so ferocious . . . but I'm not taking it back."

"Just because I talked to him?"

"You know what you think of him."

He turns around and faces me in the dark; I can feel him against me, feel him breathing. "Well, it could be that I've changed my mind. Actually, he had some interesting things to say about Ava's work and I was won . . . "

"Jesus! That is so . . . low, Michael. After you got so pissed at him because he wanted to . . . "

"To put you in a show."

"In exchange for a one-night stand."

Michael swings both his arms back behind him as though he's about to fall backward and is trying to catch his balance, and takes a deep breath as he swings his arms forward again. "Well, that's modern life for you, ain't it? He's mellowed since then, and I've mellowed . . . "

"Honestly, Michael," I say, with a good shake or two of my head. "Will you be trying to fix him up with Ava next?"

Smat! He slaps me across the face, and I go slamming back against the wall — it is a terrible thump!

"I'm sorry, sorry, sorry," he says really quick, over and over, as I get up and run into the bathroom and lock the door. The tears, the fear, the humiliation, the disappointment, all feel much worse than the pain. "Amy," he says through the door, "look, I'm sorry."

My hands are shaking as I reach for the faucets, the shower nozzle, as I flush the toilet over and over, hoping that the sound of all that running water will drown him out.

"Amy," he shouts through the door, "let me in!"

"Quiet," I say, "or you'll wake Robby."

"Open up!"

"You'll wake Ava, Michael!"

Silence on the other side. I turn off the water and listen. "At least you've still got *some* shame," I say, rubbing my face, the back of my head. I'm a mess, my book is a mess, my life is a mess, my marriage, or whatever you want to call it — not a marriage, no, no, not that; that might encumber us, weigh us down, destroy our art!

"Amy, open up," he says.

"Go to hell, Michael."

291

"Amy, I am so sorry; please believe me, I am just so sorry. Hey, please, open the door a little and take a peek. I'm down on my knees, Amy; I'm begging your forgiveness."

"You goddamned roughneck; you thug!"

"Amy, please."

"Are you down on your knees, really?"

"I am, Amy, I am."

"Well, while you're down there, fuck yourself."

ABOVE THE CLOUDS

Ava

Work—work cures all.

I have been interviewed relatively few times, having kept so much to myself for decades out here in the desert, so I remember quite well what it was I said to that girl who telephoned once from New York for *Vogue* magazine. The call came at that time just after Harriet's death when I could not work at all. I was paralyzed, the only time that's ever happened to me.

The girl kept on asking questions about the erotic content of my natural surfaces and such things as that, and I told her she was being silly—that I was merely painting leaves and rocks and bones—and she got quite upset; and I recall standing there looking out at the mesa with the telephone receiver in my hand, the girl's voice like static, thinking that everything would be all right again if I could just go back to work.

But my eyes had been bothering me lately, something that I had really begun to notice even before Harriet's death.

That night I had wept all the way down the mesa, stumbled into the house, and called for Socorro. She in turn went for Carlito, the mozo who helps with repairs around here. I sat on the sofa and could not stop weeping. When Stig died, as you know, it was not like that at all, perhaps because he and I were so much a part of each other that if I had let any of that grief take over, it would have killed me. But with Harriet, it was more like losing a limb, and so I felt that pain acutely.

And everything went black for a while, and I suffered intense pain in my eyes. This didn't stop me, however, from going out in the morning with the sheriff's patrol to look for Harriet. This didn't stop me from watching them lift her poor, pathetic, waterlogged body from the arroyo. By noon I had Socorro going into town to find me a curandera, an Indian doctor, who could mix me something that might cure the terrible black headache that was afflicting me. I had been trying to reach Robert in Chicago but there was no answer.

The telephone rang and it was Mr. Montoya, the funeral director from town, asking what instructions I had for the body. "Instructions?" I said as much to myself as him. "I . . . don't know. Please let me call you back."

"Very good, Miss Boldin," he said and hung up, leaving me to ponder the possibility of commanding a funeral with this pain in my eyes and a black headache holding my head in its fist. I pondered — what? what? and it was only when Robert finally called back that I figured it out.

"My God," he said when I told him what had happened. "I'll be on the next plane."

"Your special tea, Señora," said Socorro, coming out of the kitchen with the curandera's brew. By the time I had made a few telephone calls, my headache was clearing up, but my eyes still throbbed and teared, and I had to do a lot of my talking while daubing at them with a cool, wet cloth that Socorro dutifully kept continually soaked.

It was a long day after that, and though I said to myself, work, work cures all, I couldn't bring myself to go out to the barn until the next morning when I prepared a new canvas. Robert arrived around noon, having flown most of the night and changed planes twice. He asked me what had happened and I told him. After a while he inquired after the arrangements, and I told him about those.

"I've buried only one Jew before this," I said, "but that was Stig, and if you recall, Harriet didn't like the idea that I was having him cremated. And so we're not going to do that to her. I've found out that there's a Jewish cemetery in Las Vegas, just the other side of Santa Fe, the cemetery of the congregation of Montefiore, and there's a rabbi in Santa Fe who will officiate, and we'll do all that this afternoon."

"If they have a cemetery for Jews in Las Vegas, why don't they have a rabbi?" Robert asked.

"How should I know? I'm only telling you what I found out by talking to the funeral director and then to the rabbi. He's just come up from Albuquerque himself. Robert, please don't ask me any more because I don't know any more."

"I suppose it means that the Jews in that Montefiore congregation have all died out," he said.

"Please," I said to him with some urgency.

"It means," he went on, "that the only Jews left in Las Vegas, New Mexico, are dead Jews and the few living Jews who keep up the cemetery. And soon they'll be gone."

"Why are you doing this?" I asked.

"Because I'm drunk," he said. "And because it's very hard for me to breathe up here when I'm drunk."

Oh, my brother!

And so we drove to Santa Fe and met the rabbi—Jonathan Cohen was his name, a slim dark-haired man about thirty-five or so, I expect he was—he was wearing a dark suit, and he was wearing sunglasses, which I didn't like, but he took them off when we got to the cemetery in Las Vegas where we were met by Mr. Montoya and his helpers—and the casket. Two Indian men were just completing the grave.

"Now can you tell me something about the deceased?" the rabbi asked me and Robert. Much to my surprise, Robert told him that both her parents were dead and gave him their names. He told him a few other things, and the rabbi made a few notes on a small pad. My eyes began to pulse and burn again, and it was all I could do to stand there during the ceremony, though it wasn't a long one. I listened only with half my mind to the prayers in a foreign language. They sounded so oddly familiar in their singsong way to me, and I wondered if the two Indians didn't understand them, since to my ears it could have been something chanted around the Taos pueblo. Nothing about this reminded me of anything about Stig or Harriet, however, and it was the thought of Stig that did me in, because I had the thought just then that I should have had this ceremony done for him instead of cremating him, and this brought back my grief for him on top of my grief for Harriet, and I became a terrible mess, and Robert had to help me back to the car.

"Is all we do from now on bury people?" I asked.

"Well, there's just the two of us left," Robert said. "So it's not so bad." He took out a handkerchief and began wiping his face. "If I keep on visiting you here, I may go before you though."

"Very funny, brother," I said. And when I thought a moment, recalling what I had just told him, and the way I had spoken it, my grief returned fullfold. Robert gave me his handkerchief, and I blew my nose and saw through the car window that the rabbi and the funeral workers were standing at the grave site, silently, it seemed, having finished their work. A beautiful blanket of blue sky lay behind them, and remembering Harriet alive and tall on our way only yesterday to just such vistas as these, I sank again into the darkness of my misery and grief.

"I don't know what I want," I heard Robert say a little while later, as we drove back west toward Santa Fe and the road to the ranch.

"What do you mean?" I said to him, blowing my nose and feeling as though my brains were going to come sliding down between my aching eyes.

"I'd like to lie back there next to Harriet, but that means I won't be able to lie next to you."

"I have no immediate plans myself," I said.

"Ah," said my brother, "your old self returns."

"Shush you," I said, "you'll scare this rabbi into thinking that we gentiles don't grieve for very long."

The rabbi had put his dark glasses back on, even though the sun was descending rapidly in the west and the mesas around us, leading all the way to the southern horizon and the mountains to the north, were beginning to sink back into the shadows of themselves: sculptures superimposed on sculptures.

"I'm not scared of that," he said, turning where he sat alongside my brother who was driving, and reaching out a hand as if to try and touch me on the arm. "I'm afraid of just the opposite: that you won't recover quickly enough. You have your work. You must go back to it as soon as you can. That is what life is all about."

"How do you know what I do?" I asked, wondering if he could hear in my voice the strange sensations I was feeling.

"Miss Boldin," he said, "I know who you are."

"They told you about me in town, didn't they?" I said to him.

"Yes," said the rabbi, "but I knew about you already."

Robert stayed a week, and we were up late night after night, drinking and talking: about old times, friends, even politics, a subject that has never seemed to me to be anything worth bothering about.

"I can't convert when I'm this close to retirement," he said. "It would be unseemly and treason against all our past. So I suppose, Sis, that I won't be allowed to be buried in that Montefiore cemetery. That leaves me next to you."

I gave him a big hug and a kiss, that brother of mine, at the thought of the two of us lying side by side, which was not the craziest idea I've ever heard, if you know what I mean. I don't know how we got so rowdy when our dear lost love was still so fresh in her grave—or do I know after all? Do I know that she was with us, helping us to laugh, her spirit hovering in the air?

Things settled down to somewhat like the normal life of the old days before visitors. I looked around the barn and found a small canvas—lizard and rose—and sent it to that rabbi down in Santa Fe—and I thought of buying myself a pair of those dark glasses for use when I wasn't actually working with paint. They seemed to help my eyes a little, as the teas that Socorro now made on a regular basis helped my headaches.

Time seemed to move very swiftly after Harriet's death, as when in an hourglass the sand on the top is clearly a smaller amount than the sand on the bottom, and you begin to notice how much sand you have left rather than how much you have used since you first tipped the glass and the sand began to flow. This was the image in my mind. Robert—despite the problems he made for his heart by staying at this altitude—paid me regular visits during the next year or so. He had another way of putting this, this idea about time: and he did it in the language of his profession.

"Time may be like the plates that make up the continents," he said. "Consider time as *place* . . . we might think about it geographically rather than temporally, linearly, so that the past and you and I and our presents and our futures are all in plates; and now and then when the pressure builds, the plates, each of them moving in its own direction, buck and scrape together. Think of it . . . we may have many years of quiescence . . . and some years become earthquakes, changing the landscape of our lives."

We looked at each other, knowing quite well if we adhered to his theory which years would be which.

And then one day there was a knock at the door to the barn, and I had a most unexpected visitor: a lanky young man in a blue suit wearing dark glasses. "I know you, don't I?" I said to him.

And I did, because it was the rabbi from Santa Fe, Jonathan Cohen. "It's been a year since your friend's death," he said, "and I thought I would come by to see how you were doing."

"Oh," I said, "that's very kind of you." And I invited him to come into the house with me and have tea.

"That was very kind of you to send me that painting," he said. "I treasure it, I really do. And my wife thinks it's the most beautiful piece of art we have in the house."

"I'm pleased," I said. And we talked like that, small talk, and after a while he left – and I thought it was very nice for him to have come out, considering that he knew none of us, and especially since the only one of us who had been Jewish was lying in the ground over in the cemetery in Las Vegas. I don't mean to sound cruel or cold, because that is simply where she was, and I knew that very well not only from having buried her there, but because more often than I would like to admit my thoughts went in that direction: to the grave site, to pictures of the jays and owls swooping over the cemetery there in Las Vegas against that turquoise sky, the same as covers us right here at the ranch.

Now I don't want you to think that I'm rambling, because I don't think that I am, and don't think that I'm dwelling only on the mundane and accidental here, either, just because I'm bringing up the issue of tea with the rabbi, because something came of that. When Robert visited me next and we began to talk about Harriet in a way that we hadn't before, having moved somewhat further away from grief, the subject came up of her plan for them to visit Israel, and I said, "I'll find out about that," and the next thing you know, I was asking Jonathan Cohen for some pamphlets, and then Robert spoke to a travel agent in Chicago.

As it was, another year or so went by before we actually took our trip—or Harriet's trip, as we both thought of it—because I had changed galleries after her death, and the new gallery wanted me to do a show—I might have become obscure to a lot of people, but I was never completely without a following and for that I am grateful—and so I wanted to put in another half year of work for that event. So we timed our trip to coincide with the show, which was a moderate success, thanks mainly to collectors who wanted to have some flowers on their walls, I suppose, since it turned out that I had done mainly flowers during the time leading up to the show, and then we flew on to the Holy Land.

But even before we got there, I was in a kind of mesmeric state because of flying, since I had only been in an airplane once before, that time when I went up with the pilot in that little plane to scatter Stig's ashes over the lake. So what I saw from my window—the clouds, banks of clouds, cliffs of clouds, walkways of clouds paving the way from one sphere of heaven to another—these sights thrilled me in ways I had not known, and I was drunk on the view and on the feelings and memories—Stig, mostly Stig!—that came from this vision.

After we landed in Israel, Harriet's ancestral homeland, which, I suppose, is the way she had come to think of it, I had the odd feeling that she was trailing us about from the moment we stepped off the airplane, an eerie sensation that translated itself, once we drove south, into a kind of soothing familiarity. I certainly felt at home because the land was so much like here, my desert, but also because Harriet was buried in land much like this, I felt some sort of inexplicable connection. "I think we did the right thing, coming here," I said to my brother.

And he agreed. "You know I've spent plenty of time in this part of the world, but never having actually set foot on this particular section of it, I can tell you that it seems special here: all those thousands of years of wandering tribes seem to have left some kind of trace of themselves. The Saudi desert seems empty, vacant, lonely by comparison."

"I think it's because of our mission," I said. We did have a mission, one that my friend the rabbi had suggested. "You'll go there," he had said. "And you'll plant a tree for her."

299

"Plant a tree? Sounds awfully pagan to me, Rabbi."

"Pagan, Jewish, Christian: it's all the same finally, if you have the spirit," he said. "Plant a tree in the desert. It will stand in for her and make a little fresh air, and hold the soil a little, too."

So we had arranged to go to a particular commune—or kibbutz, as they call them—and pick up a young fir sapling that we could carry to the edge of a new forest and plant in her name. A fair-skinned young boy from the kibbutz in white shirt and tan shorts walked along with us, and I kept seeing the rabbi's boyhood in this child, who was quite helpful and helped us dig the hole and didn't even take a penny in recompense. I picked up a handful of the sandy soil and scattered it to the wind—it was just dirt, sand, but it felt cool and reassuring to my touch.

We returned to Tel Aviv in only a few hours—the country is that small. All of it could fit in the old sea bottom that I can see from the mesa back home was what I was thinking, and also, looking at the Mediterranean as we approached the city in our vehicle, I realized Israel was smaller than the state of South Carolina, and I was remembering Harriet, and finally having a good cry, recalling my days in her native city by the sea. Neither of us could ever have imagined then the direction that life would take us in, or that we would know each other for so long—because we couldn't imagine the *so long* of it—and we couldn't ever have believed anyone who might have told us, though who could predict such things? That I would have buried her and then flown all this distance to plant a tree in her name in this country fighting back the Orient desert?

I listened intently then to the sounds of my own weeping, and through the rest of the day and into the evening, my brother stayed even closer to me than usual, giving me comfort as best he knew how.

The night was filled with the sounds of automobiles and here and there a child's cry, dance music, the braying of a mule; the odors were of sesame and olive oil and the salt sea from the beaches only a few hundred yards or so from our windows. Everyone in the dining room looked familiar, though of course there was no one I knew. "It's like an oddly oblique mirror image of New York here," I said.

"So not really foreign?" my brother asked.

300

"On the contrary," I said. "All the more foreign for seeming so oddly familiar."

"So you like it?" Robert said, raising a bit of meat on his fork.

"I do," I said. "I do like it here, and I could work here except for the light. It's a strange light, almost on the verge of being plentiful, but not quite."

"You and your light, Ava." He stopped speaking and seemed to glance away at a corner of the room. I followed his glance, but saw nothing that looked unusual.

"Someone you know?" I asked. "From the oil company?"

Robert shook his head. "No, no, it's just . . . " He patted his breast. "Just time for my medicine."

Up in the room I watched him wash down his pills with a glass of mineral water, and it was just something in the way he held his head—I can't explain it, but it reminded me of him as a young boy, when I had come up from the riverbed and handed him that buffalo-calf skull, and he had looked at me with eyes so wide, amazed that his little sister could have been so resourceful. "We've come a long way from the river," I said to him, just letting it slip out.

"What river?" he asked.

But I was tired from our trek and tree planting, and so I just said, "Nothing, nothing," and got ready for bed. We were sharing the room—twin beds; it just seemed like the natural thing to do on our trip—and while he was in the bathroom, I climbed under the covers and let my thoughts go: thinking about Harriet, the years we had spent in Charleston, and everything after; how much I missed her—I missed just knowing that I could see her if I wanted to see her—and then wondering about how Socorro was doing; thinking about the house and the barn and the light on the mesa at sunrise, the light on the west cliff at dusk; and I heard Robert coughing and I called out to ask if he was all right, and he came out and said, "I'm fine, I'm fine, Sis. You know, I sometimes think that the rest of me is going to die *around* my famous sick old ticker before it gives out—and wouldn't that be a joke?"

"Here," I said, patting the bed next to me.

He smiled and came over and lay down next to me, and that was how we fell asleep that night: two old pals together in the desert dark.

301

You know, there is the myth of Tithonus, the lover of Aurora, the goddess of the dawn, who was given immortality by his mistress, except that was all he was given: the ambiguous gift of eternal life; and as he grew in years beyond the normal human span, he began to shrink in size until some eons later he was no larger than a cricket, so that the goddess kept him in a little cage of reeds at her bedside, and his early chirping startled her awake, and thus she brought light every day to the world. I've felt a bit like that in the years since Harriet's death – the shrinking part, at least – for as I've grown older, I can see that I am becoming smaller and my hide is becoming thicker, and my eyes have become quite weak to the point of near blindness, as you know, as you know. But I have canvases to show for it – this little retrospective of my life:

The cloud paintings that came out of my flight to Israel and back, and how I longed to be able to look up from that project and say, Ho, Stig, come and see what I've done with clouds! Look! the clouds are like stepping stones from your eye to infinity, the very air (I hope it works this way) transformed into a plane uplifted toward your eye as if by a wind from the other side, so that you can see that, in a way, our very planet is walled around by space and cloud and air and light.

Next came my new lizards – dozens of them – lizards and flowers, for I recalled the painting I had given to Jonathan Cohen, which was one of a kind, and it pleased my eye to imagine a row of these, at least a dozen, with every kind of spiny-thorned and armored creature engaged in posing with the various flowers of the desert floor – beasts and beauties, if you'd like to think of them that way.

And here, take a glance at these – while we're looking at them together – which grew naturally out of that time as well: the gravestones, desert gravestones, each one different from the other, but all, of course, a version of one another, as we are all versions of one another; dark stone and light, up against the canyon wall or, as with this one, bedecked by a wreath of thorns and bone.

And then, the seasons of this place, the series that I began in summer, so that quite ironically, I suppose I have to say, the cycle goes from light through fading heat to cold and winter, with here and there some snow, which I have hardly ever painted, an aversion, I suppose, that I developed while living in Chicago, though we, of course, had snow in Nebraska when I was a child . . . a child! I've come some distance from that long time ago, now haven't I? but as I was saying about these: here, look, you see: from summer through autumn and the dark folds of winter and on to spring again. I call this ironic–not that I intended it that way–since I myself am moving through my final season, and am not about to begin another; but don't look so upset, for I'm sure that I have a few more actual seasons to go. I meant it in the general way: that if you look at our lives against nature, you can see that we move from spring to summer to autumn to winter–and that we have no second spring to look forward to, unless we accept the stories that we hear in church as children, which I never did; for some reason they just never took.

All these canvases! It's not that I'm such a quick painter, either; it's just that I have lived so damned long, and for the longest time now lived alone with no distractions and all the time in the day to work; and so here they are: these products of all of those days from all these years between, these images of time concentrated, as we might say that trees are concentrated sunlight, and when we burn them, they give off the light of the sun that has been stored within them, however long.

I have been here so long now that Socorro, a girl when I first employed her, has grown old; so long that my mozo, the handy-man, has taken sick and died and been replaced by his son; and now you have been here long enough to see your child crawl and then walk upright on two legs, and now he is talking. He'll be reading soon enough, too. And when you're old, perhaps he'll visit you now and then and comfort you, as you have me, with stories out of books.

I don't mind all this change around me because, the hell with it, I have lived so long in the desert that even the small transformations of color and arrangement–the kind wrought by wind and water and the combination of wind and water and light–have come to please my eye. I have enjoyed many of the changes.

The way my dear Harriet has changed for me in memory, the way my brother changed over the years, and I am ready now to enjoy the change that I myself will undergo–sea changed, except that the sea has long ago receded here, and we're left with the old oceanbed that resembles nothing less than the surface of the moon. Old land, old woman, dry as dust, though I am still working; yes, I am still going out each day to face the light, though one day, I know that, too, will fade.

What if I had said all this to the girl who wanted an interview? That life was nothing but these encounters with the light. That all of what she cared about would fade, so quickly fade away, and one day the sun itself would go out and the light would fade, bereft even of eyes to observe it. Time would run down to nothing, with all the riverbeds dry, the waters having flowed away?

Yet I am still working as best I can, using my hands now for eyes. Oh, I sometimes say to the night—if the dark were to interview me—I say, grow dark as you like, dark as you can, and still the work will come! Still the work will come!

DOOR

Clear night, a million, million stars splashed all about the sky. I come in from a short walk, hoping to work again, when I see Ava sitting up in my chair. "Ava, you're still awake?"

"Michael," she says, clearing her throat. "Michael says that we shouldn't."

"Shouldn't what?" I'm staring down at her. She's so small, even more so it seems to me than when we first arrived. But there's a . . . I want to say sweetness, but that's not the word. Just say, a certain aura about her: something very strong and yet positive, nothing at all frightening.

"Walk," she says in that tiny rasp of a voice. "No more walks. He thinks I get too tired."

"Is Michael your doctor now?"

"What?"

I lean closer to her. "We've all been worrying about you since your nosebleed. But the doctor couldn't find anything wrong. And you feel all right, don't you?"

"My age," she says.

"Sorry?"

"I feel my age."

"Oh, Ava," I say, laying a hand on her shoulder. I can feel her breathing, the way she moves against my palm.

"Perhaps we'll walk again," she says. "But for now . . . "

"For now?" I ask.

"For now, I would like you to help me to bed."

"You do need your sleep," I say.

"No, no, no," she says, giving her head a shake, and sloughing off my hand. "I don't sleep. I lie there. Thinking."

"Thinking? Ava, tell me what you're thinking."

"Oh," she says, and I can hear a kind of sadness rising up in her words. "Oh, if I could tell you. And I would tell you."

And as I help her into bed, I'm thinking: if I could only throw away these notes; if I could only read her mind!

On a sunny morning in October, we pack Ava into the pickup and drive south. Time for her regular physical. She spends a night in the hospital.

We pick her up the next morning and find a strange look on her face. "I don't like places like that, Amy," she says to me, taking me by the arm. "They stick needles in me and tell me I'm doing well." She gives a little cough. "I've always done as well as can be expected."

"Doctor says," Michael begins to explain, "that you can keep on working with me, and that you can take a little walk once a day."

"But you want me to save my strength for work, don't you?" she says.

"I want you to have your walks with Amy, too," he says.

"What do *you* want?" I ask, seeing her eyes leap out to me in a smile.

"What do I want? What do I want?" She says something in a whisper, glancing over at Michael.

Ava whispers again as Michael leaves us at the entrance to the hospital to get the truck. I lean closer to her, a natural inclination, having lived with her all this time now. I look more closely at the wrinkled contours of her face—the surface of her skin resembles some roughly approximate map of the plain of stone and dust we live upon. "Ava, what do you want to do?" I ask again.

She replies: "Same as always. Everything."

NORTH SOUTH EAST WEST

Ava

Here, these letters, some to do with my dear, lost Robert, some others you may recognize.

Dear Robert,

I have sent you a painting for your room, to set beside the blessed buffalo skull that you claim you still possess after all this time. The painting shows the mesa that I have been working on for the last few years. It takes me about two hours to drive there in good weather, and I have been doing it daily with only the most minor interruptions: a few big snowstorms in the winter, once or twice a flat tire. If I sit there long enough, someone comes along to help—last time it was an Indian boy in his rattletrap pickup. Another time it was an eastern couple on a tour that had taken them off the beaten track. As a reward, I told them about the mesa. Oh, they just couldn't believe that they had found this old woman sitting by the side of her car reading Emily Dickinson while lizards stared at her from their vantage points along the rutted road.

Each morning the drive; the work all day; then the drive back.

Setting up in the still, early light is almost like setting up underwater, under water as clear and thin as air. One morning last week it rained, odd for the season—long needlelike streaks of water that seemed more light than liquid—and it washed my canvas, and the gouache streaked as though from beneath and within, as though the color were seeping up through the surface, rather than raining down upon it from my brushes. Some few cloudy days the light never comes up full, and I work beneath a shroud of pearl gray netting.

A scorpion crawled on my shoe once. In ten years it never happened again.

Other dawns have burst upon me as though light were the fireworks of the gods, and I was the celebrant of my own fiesta. Nothing comes between my eye and the surface of the sky, the cliff, the desert floor; my wrist and hand behave as though they belong to another being who has reached through me and slipped its hand into my appendage and picked up the brush.

I heard a rattler, only once. Once a thunderstorm passed overhead, and the scent of the water made me weep for what seemed like hours.

I return home in the dark, feeling as though I have made a long tour of some Asian archipelago.

The drive, the work, the drive.

Only the clouds, if they are present, the sky, always present, seem different each time that I arrive at my mesa.

And then I awoke the other morning with a searing pain in my eyes, as though all these years of sight had been limited to a certain number. I cried out for Socorro. And she came running to me, friend and helper that she has been over all these years. And she bathed my eyes, and out again I went that morning, if a bit later than usual, on my drive to the mesa again. I had gone only a mile or two down the road when the lights began to flicker, and a shutter closed over my left eye almost as though I were one of Stig's old cameras, and some god or photographer had clicked the shutter in my head.

I sat in the car a long while, until the mozo came up the road from an errand in town, and found me there, and helped me to return home.

Oh, brother, you in your hospital bed, me in my foggy vision, and who will there be now to help us if we do not help ourselves? If I could only find a way to work a little longer, if I could only find a little more time and light, then afterward I would gladly walk into the desert never more to return, giving up my already rather dried and desiccated body to the small animals and beetles, and my bones to the dust.

Love,

Your Sis

I had a letter arrive sometime after I wrote this one—not from my brother, but from another family member, of sorts. You'll know the signature.

Dear Ava,

I hope that you are alive and well as you read this. I know that sounds silly. It's hard for me to write. After all these years, I worry that you won't remember me. But I hope you will. I am still living in Albany in the house that I bought just after you moved to New Mexico; in the house where I have brought up my son, Michael; in the house where you so kindly sent those checks when I needed them just after he was born. It has been a long time, though, and so I wasn't sure that you would remember.

I once saw your name in the newspaper, when you had a show of your paintings in New York City. I don't know why I had to tell you that. It was so silly of me. I guess because you have lived out West for so long I think that you don't know the East.

I haven't been up to the lake in a long time, either, myself. I took Michael there once, when a friend had a car and we took a drive one Sunday afternoon. The old house hasn't changed much, except that the owners have built a dock on the lake, and there were cars in a new garage, and there's a house now on the other side of the lake. And a main road only a mile away now, through the woods.

But I don't know why I should be going on like this to you. I just wanted to say hello and ask how you were. I would like to send you some drawings by my son. He shows signs of being an artist himself, and I want you to see some of what he has done. He is only fifteen and having some trouble in school, but I try to let him understand that it was a special sort of love that brought him into the world. Sometimes he gets so angry, and curses his school and sometimes even his life. I am hoping that you might look at his drawings and maybe write something to me about them? If that is not too much trouble.

Sincerely yours,

Cissy Gillen

Michael's drawings — there was something there, though I tortured myself by looking and looking in the hope that I might discover signs of his father, when all I found were the marks of a talent that might become something if everything else fell into place — if he could

survive and thrive and live a life, despite his gifts. That, after all, is
the most difficult enterprise.

I sent Cissy back a pleasant, equivocal note—and received, in
return, another letter and another.

Dear Ava,

*It was so kind of you to write back and send me those kind words
about Michael's drawings. I hope that if you ever come out this way, we
can get together. It would be like a dream of the old times, to see you
again. Now and then I wonder what it would be like for all of us to meet
somewhere, something like a family. My boy has always lacked that, the
family gathering. He has grown up a loner, with only his mother and his
special talent. I worry about him, he has so much of his father in him he
has yet to discover. . . .*

Then arrived the last letter from my brother, the final words from
the keeper of the buffalo skull I found for him so many long years
ago, in childhood—another place in time, where the rivers still run
in season and every object stands out in perfect illumination—every
stone, tree, leaf, cloud, moon, stars near and distant, the fall of
wave, strand of hair, pupil of the eye. . . .

Dear Sis,

*Here I am after all these years still in Chicago, lying almost abso-
lutely still in Chicago, to make a joke; the only parts of me working are
my poor heart, my eyes, and my fingers moving this pen, making this
letter.*

*The way things fall off, the strength fades so rapidly. Why only a few
years ago, I was making long pages of notes about life: your life, my own;
and now there's only this scribble where once I strode the hills and delved
deeply in them for the energy to fuel the world to come, from the world
that perished long ago. Now everything has shifted with so many of us
gone, and yet we go on, however feebly. My heart pumps; it goes on.*

*And I think upon my theory—so much time in which to do it—I
think of time, and time as location, each moment a little location of time,
each occasion a plot of time, and all of these spaces folding in upon one*

310

*another, moving inch by inch in space; and I am thinking that if, as these
boys have now hypothesized, because of this creep of the plates beneath
the surface, oceans will change their shape, and seas arise where deserts
now lie burning, and great seabeds become high deserts, and cities—cities
such as Los Angeles, say—will one day—if we wait long enough, if time
waits, if light waits, for we will be long gone—Los Angeles will live next
door to San Francisco, and who knows where Chicago will travel? north
to Canada? south toward New Orleans? I have to read the charts of all
this potential progress; I must do more homework; I have some time to do
it lying here, Sis, staring at my prize skull on the table, and if this is as
true about time as it is about space, then one day the past will inch along
to where it will scrape against the present, and the future will fold back
into the past, and what once was all over will become possible again, and
all our yesterdays will become tomorrows, and the present in which we
find ourselves growing old, and in our solitude so separate, as we have
always felt from time to time—if I can use that phrase while I am speaking of such patterns as I sketch for you here—and the present will be able
to be everywhere: back and forward, north south east west, up and down,
inside outside, behind and before, below and above. Then alive and dead
will mean nothing, and nothing and everything will be one together, and
the male and the female, and the young and the old, and the beautiful
and the ugly will all be one with the past and the present and the future,
and dark will be light. And the knowledge I have, such as it is, of what I
know and knew, and your talent and your insight—all of that will be
together, and I will love you, and you will love me, and we will live apart
together and together apart, and all we know and knew, and all those we
cared for, will come back to us whole because they never left. . . .*

Over the years there had been a little gallery in Chicago that had
been handling my work. Now and then the owner would look in
on Robert in the rest home. It was she who called to tell me about
him, and to help me with the arrangements.

"It's expensive to fly a . . . coffin," she said.

"Not just the coffin," I told her. "I want the body, too." I could
hear her on the other side of the telephone line, a little shaken by
my joke. But at my age you can say anything and do anything,
anything you care to. Even joke in the face of this blankness. Joke
in the absence of your brother who has always been there.

311

"I'll fly with him," the woman said.

"That is very kind of you," I told her.

It was the son of Mr. Montoya who now ran the funeral business in town, and he met the flight in Albuquerque and drove the
casket up here so that we could all gather in his little parlor—oh, all
this talk of coffins, caskets, the grave site in the little churchyard
where the priest, for a good price, said a Mass in Latin and Spanish, a ceremony that meant nothing to me except that I wanted
something for Robert, and in this part of the world that something
has to do with the old ritual of the Mass. If I could have hired a
medicine man to say words, I would have done so. But I was too old
to tramp about the pueblo.

As we were burying him, I had the thought—I wondered if that
nice young rabbi was still in town. I wondered if I should have
called him. I wondered if he had heard the news of my grief. . . .

Blue jays squ-squ-squawked behind the near gravestone, frol-
icking in a light so pure it might have been honey poured down on
us that morning from the jar of heaven.

Work hasn't been much since that time, my eyes have gone so bad.

But I could read Michael's letter; I certainly could read that.

Every morning after that—it was a good few months, too,
wasn't it?—I went out to the barn and did something I had never
done before: I fooled myself into thinking I was doing something
worthwhile.

But what I was really doing was waiting. For you.

312

DOOR

I'm standing in the shower, feeling the warm water stream down, over and between my breasts and over my belly, trying to imagine myself part of the great flow of things—and funny how I have to do this *apart* from Michael and even from Robby—and who should burst into the shower but . . . Michael!

"Hey," I say. "Come on in!"

"Listen," he says. "I just talked to Washington, and we're going back there for a meeting tomorrow, all expenses paid!"

"Wait a minute," I say, and pull back the curtain. He watches me while I grab a towel and as I dry myself off, he explains to me that the National Gallery wants to confer about a retrospective of Ava's work.

"I can't go tomorrow," I say. "I have to take Robby into town for some . . . "

"No, no, you stay here. I've already booked the flight for me and Ava. She is really excited. She hasn't flown a lot, but she loves it!

"Michael, why can't we all go? Just give me another day to . . . "

"Look," he says. "It's business. They're not going to pay for your fare. But I'm going to fix it so that you'll write the catalog," he says, blinking like a schoolboy caught red-handed by the principal.

"If they approve of me," I say. "Whoever *they* are."

"It's going to be part of the deal," he says.

"I'm so glad I'm part of the deal, Michael," I say.

"So then . . . " It takes him a moment before he actually hears what's in my voice.

They leave early in the morning. Robby and I wave from the window as Michael helps the fragile Ava into the van, and Socorro waits dutifully alongside to hand up the baggage.

"I can't believe he's taking her," I hear myself say aloud.

"Ma," says Robby.

"Yes, dear?" I ask.

"Mama," he says again. "Where Daddy going?" I hug him to my chest.

The day goes much faster than I have feared. Pretty soon it's lunchtime for this little boy, and then it's his nap time. I put him down, ask Socorro to listen for him, and head out toward the mesa. The day is unusual, with clouds here and there, hinting, I suppose, at the winter weather to come, though the air remains still quite warm. Not much wind. Visibility excellent—as they're probably saying at this very moment, I think to myself, on that airplane heading east. Clear, clear weather. The cliff face I'm walking toward seems, in fact, so close that I have the illusion that I can reach out and press the flat of my palm against it.

I climb a while, climb and climb, until I can look to the west and see that same ancient seabed that Ava herself has observed so often, a reminder of how even the most solid things in this world do change, if sometimes only over the longest time. Michael has changed, I tell myself, though with that thought comes the assurance that he could just as rapidly become again the old self I knew back in Vermont.

He means well, he means well, I say to myself, and walk, and walk. Until I come to the edge of a drop of about fifty feet, a deep cleft in the mesa that runs along the northern side, where the entire rock formation seems to point toward the far mountain range like a ship under steam on the ocean.

It is so dry down there now where waters once flowed.

I no sooner walk in the door on my return from my excursion when the telephone begins to ring.

"Oh, Señora," says Socorro, stepping out of the bedroom.

"What is it?" I say to her as I pick up the receiver.

"*Amy?*" says Michael from the other end of the line.

314

"Michael? Where are you? Have you . . . ?"

"I'm still in Albuquerque," he says. *"Jeesum crow, where the hell have you been? Socorro didn't know where the hell you were! I've been trying for half an hour . . . "*

"Well, excuse me," I say, "but I was out for a walk. What's going on?"

"Ava," he says. *"At the airport. She fell down. She . . . "*

"Oh, Michael, is she . . . ?"

"She's in the hospital. Come down as quick as you can."

I leave Robby with Socorro and borrow her old Chevy. It's bright, brilliant sunlight the first part of the trip, but just south of Santa Fe suddenly large storm clouds gather, almost as though some huge fist had gathered up clouds and squeezed them until they bruised a purplish black. I'm speeding along in the car, the car is vibrating, my heart is beating wildly—it's as though I've just swallowed Dexamil, the way we used to so that we could stay up all night working, talking, singing, dancing, loving—and suddenly I have the sensation that the car, with me in it, is like a missile shot along this highway; we're hurtling so fast-forward and downward-southward toward the city, as though the continent itself had tilted and North America were higher than South, and I were tumbling in the southerly direction. Oh jeesum, I am saying to myself, oh jeesum, what is happening to me? I must be going crazy because I haven't taken drugs since we came out here, and I haven't taken a drink, and I am having these strange sensations in my stomach, oh, my ovaries and my chest. And that is when I realize that it is a new baby that I am registering; oh my God, that strange and wonderful change that comes with a new baby inside again—only this time I am actually aware of it the instant it's deciding to stay around. How can that be? I don't know but I can feel it clinging to me deep within and that is when the rain comes down suddenly without a warning, except for that glimpse of the huge, dark cloud so far south when I first saw it, and now it is emptying itself like a shelf full of hard water, like tons of ten-penny nails, onto the hood and roof; and the wipers work but do no good, and I am frightened and elated and shouting and singing, and the car is sliding and rolling forward and skipping

315

and hopping, and then it feels as though we are flying, and then the rain passes as suddenly as it began, and I am heading straight down the highway again into the bright sunlight of a cloudless day above Albuquerque alive and in that moment, in that passing instant, it doesn't matter why.

THE ROSE AND THE SKULL

Ava

Amy, lean closer to me so that I don't have to raise my voice. Don't be afraid; I have fallen before and I know that though it may take some effort, I can rise again. It was in a time just before you and Michael arrived. I was making one more version of that painting of the rose in the skull, and I awoke to find Socorro laving my forehead. Where did you find me? I asked her. On the mesa, Señora, she said. You must not go there again. How many times have I been? I asked her. She shook her head. Too many times. Not enough, I said. Oh, yes, she said. Sí, sí, many times. But not too many? She shook her head again, and I was left without knowing exactly what had taken place. I stayed in bed for the day, staring out the window at the translucent sky. The moon rose in the afternoon, and I was still lying there, brooding, disturbed. I slept and then opened my eyes onto the dark window full of stars. New stars, I want to call them, as though they had just burst forth from some fresh and quickly hatched brood of celestial eggs. They called to me in a low voice, a low chorus of voices, and soon I slept, I slept. Next morning I awoke and *knew* it was time. I climbed out of bed, feeling my bones knock together. I dressed and boiled water, drank a cup of tea. How many, how many mornings had I done this? A lifetime of mornings! A mesa of teacups! A mountain range of mornings! Mama was gone; Eve had been born only as a ghost and then she had flitted away, borne away in the blood of my womanhood, and then Dora had died, and my Helen – ay, ay! – she, too, had disappeared. Stig was long dead, Harriet washed away in the flood, and Robert now, too; and yet here I was, sipping my tea, ready again for work. I was ready. But I have to say that no matter how steady you are, no matter how fierce is your devotion to work, a certain sorrow creeps

317

in, a tinge of sadness, in many ways natural, like the coating of
pollen on your hand when you brush against a flower in certain
seasons. Nevertheless, I pushed ahead and never ceased for years
and years until my eyes began. Or ended. But here is what I dreamed.
Up on the mesa the light blinded me. In my barn there were too
many shadows. I said to the mozo that morning, Take off the doors.
I prepared a canvas while he worked. Pretty soon he had removed
both doors. Let the lizards wander in. That's what I thought. Let
the desert enter in. And desert light. I'll try to make something out
of my failing sight. Fusion of shadow and light. What was I thinking? Just that, just that. I moved about; here I was, wandering about
the barn, preparing a canvas, near blind. I was standing sideways to
the wall where I had nailed up the linen, sneaking a look from the
corner of my disintegrating eyes. Socorro called to me, What are
you doing? Working, I said. How silly I must have appeared to her,
looking sideways at the wall. I was in that state, the work trance, I
call it: when you are in the world, but in a different time – perhaps
sideways might be the way to put it, sideways in time; and even as I
stood there, feeling myself fill up with the promise of work to come,
the way an athlete prepares for a leap or jump or mile-long run, I
never felt so empty, not knowing what I would do – the charcoal in
one hand, brush in the other – with the not-knowing in my head,
and only the leap-feeling in my heart, my heart coiled like a snake
about to strike. I let out an old-fashioned cry. Spun around, hands
in the air. My eyes began to burn: wanting an image so, desiring it,
the image! The feeling of the image! you know, you know, and I
swiped across my face, felt my spectacles go flying away! Calling
Robert! Robert! Turn-ing my-self a-bout! Hours went by, as though
I were a rock in a fast-moving stream. My eyes so bad, I could see
what normal eyes could not, the very passage of the air, the winking on and off of time in light. All the objects in my life flashed
past, as though I were the one drowning, drowning in this mixture
of light and time: stone, feather, rock face, skull bone, rose, rose,
and with that picture in mind, my hands began to move as if with a
life of their own, striking here, flying out there. I do not even remember touching a brush to canvas, though the tip of the brush must
have moved like a thousand stinging bees protecting the queen from
danger: here, there, there, here, here! Who knows how much time

went by? Look at my life. Where has that gone? One moment a girl on the prairie, now a woman in a city, now a trembling old hand holding a brush, a pair of failing eyes peering up close at the canvas, slowly tracing the lines of the flower. That was when I discovered it: the rose, the rose unlike the others, the rose from within. It took me weeks to finish it, and in many ways, it will never be done. But even as I made out the first curves and early angles of its presence in the rough drawing, I had that feeling, the feeling that comes with something strange and new, the voice in the head saying paint it over, and you ask why, and the voice tells you, You have never seen anything like this before, so therefore . . . Paint it over? you interrupt, Paint it over? Go on, says the voice, because it is unlike anything, and therefore must be destroyed. And I understood, of a sudden, an old story, the commandment against graven images, and I saw, even with my weakened glance, I saw within why we are punished, those of us who work this way: because we stand against the commandment, and are punished by the law that says: Those who would give their lives to painting the gods would take away their sense of time, and then blind them to the light. Oh, this wandering talk, the wavering words of an old woman painting a rose. But that blossom! See it for yourself. It was as if while working that day, I had planted a rosy bush within the skull of the steer and stood still long enough to watch it grow. The rose, like a single eye within the steer's head, seemed almost to watch me watching it, even as I worked on its creation. A certain kind of inward-tending pressure began to blow between us, from the center of the flower to my own eye, a link like a fishing line, though whether the flower was the fish, or I the bait, I cannot say. Yet it tugged at me, and I knew that I was drawing it into existence: petal by petal, layer by layer, line into line into line. It drew me, making me, yes, but pulling me at the same time; that kind of draw, draw and draw, creating this lift in me even as I was touching up its own curves and surface self, the picture of action complete and pure in a realistic flower. This was what I wanted! All the grit of the real, all the heart of life beyond the visible! Because. Because in my waning vision, I could see something beyond all the actual, beyond the hard winking of flame points worrying into expiration the last glimmer of normal sight. I could feel the edge points of vision that lie on the

319

surface of all things. I could see from the viewpoint of hard matter; I could see for a fleeting moment how I looked outward from the cave of my own skull; I could see the stuff of the world looking at me, not back at me, but at-to-into me, and I knew that if I could ride this beam of light back into the source and turn it around on me, then I could have a way of seeing like no other I had ever known. I walked away from it then, giving it time to set in the light. So I went to town with Socorro, the first time in a year. It was another world, all the cars and people, yet I saw that I could continue for a while and that I could go on working. I was not entirely alone. Socorro was with me. That gave me strength. Even in my earliest childhood I always had someone with me, to comfort me. Oh, Amy, I have to tell you this, though it is the part that no one ever admits to anyone else. But I trust you with the secret, with the news, and you must keep it to yourself, because it carries with it too much of my deep soul, the part that you must never give up if you are to live and survive, but I have to say that before all of this, before they came into my life, before Robert and my father, before my old house-keeper Halme, and Chicago and the lessons, and dear, sweet, Black Madonna virgin-mother pungent-smelling Helen of the stockyards, before that passion, before paint became everything to me, before Harriet and hurricanes, before Stig and clouds, before Texas and New York and Charleston and a boy named Billy, before Jobby and parties and drinking and smoking and towers and trains and stones and lakes and clouds and more clouds, before Mabel and dust and sunsets like the beginning of the world and the end all in one, before bones and blossoms, before great rushing waterstorms and lightning slashing the face of the night, before all this long slide into my own private darkness—and now this new fall I have taken, even just as I was about to rise once again into the air on the modern wings of airplane power, just as I was about to see the clouds once more from above—back before all this in the smallest glimmer of the earliest light of the first time, I arrived in the world, pushed forward by the strong hands of my water-walking Melissa, who in a dream came to me only the last hour before I awakened here in this bed and you arrived, and she said that it was she who told me to begin walking, and to take the hand of my little sister Eve, whose tiny fist seemed like a bud never to blossom, but when I clasped it in my own small hand, felt moist enough to bloom at least in my mind. And whether these are mere stories I had, or whether these visions be true, makes no difference to the generations that come after the next generation, for to them the hard bone of skull or the vision in the air, each has a truth all of its own devising. People are always asking what my paintings mean. Perhaps the new one means something about my loneliness and my new resolve to continue despite it. Who knows? Must it mean something? I mean about light and the shape of that skull, the flower in the brainpan, opposite perhaps of the snake in the garden. Say it is all an epitaph. Say, why not, that I have done it all for my little sister who never was. That's as good a reason as any, isn't it? To declare that I was driven by a ghost on the wind? I was thinking of such matters, feeling my way toward something of an idea that I might admit was true for me, as I stood before the new work the next morning. That is, I think, where you found me when you first arrived, Amy, you and my family-to-be: out in the barn, leaning on a long thick stick, contemplating that image I had seen in the cave of my skull and put in my own way on the canvas; thinking about light, thinking to myself, it is my first work. All work is first work. And this was not bad for a beginner, though I knew I still had a long way to go. But no hats; at least I have not had to draw hats.

DOOR

As quiet a funeral as we can make it here at the old churchyard. A few mourners come from town: friends of Socorro's, a man who once worked as mozo at the house with his son, a priest from the clinic over in Espanola, a slender man in dark suit and dark glasses, whom I recognize from Ava's own description as the rabbi from Santa Fe – and I'm wondering even in my grieving how he has heard – and a reporter up from Albuquerque – how did *she* hear of this? – who remains blessedly without questions throughout the brief Mass.

"It doesn't matter that she wasn't Catholic," Michael says, loosely holding a large paper sack he's carried with him from the car. "It doesn't matter that she wasn't anything. This is my gift to her. She'd understand. She . . . this . . . needed a frame . . . "

I don't understand, but I go along with it, tending mostly to Robby who is weeping and confused. The dank adobe odor of the place is mixed with the smell of incense, perfumes, soap and flowers, rank males who have trod here under the hot sun, women who have bathed and splashed on a little store-bought scent. Socorro weeps quietly into her lace shawl, having buried her own mother here years before.

The priest says his words in Latin and Spanish.

A wind stirs up suddenly, as though someone had just opened a door onto the mesa in late afternoon.

And then it's over, as simple as that, and I make ready to leave the little graveyard, when Michael reaches into the sack and takes out the calf skull, a few pieces of charcoal stick, and one of Ava's long special brushes and tosses them into the open grave.

322

"You were hiding that from me, weren't you? But it was the right thing to do," I say to Michael as we walk out to the dusty road. We're alone, together, Socorro having taken our Robby by the hand and led him out before us.

Michael turns to me. There's something about the way he looks. He moves his lips without sound, then clears his throat, and reaches for my hand. "Amy," he says, "marry me," and then bursts into tears.

I'm crying, too, and we're holding onto each other—do I tell him about the new baby? I say to myself—Tell him *now*! comes a woman's voice in my ear—urgently, as though it's freezing cold at midnight instead of blazing hot and noon. *Tell him now!*

A CHORUS ON THE WIND

Eve

Tell me about color. Tell me all the colors you have seen within your eye and without. Tell me about blue, blue without cease, and red—tell me of the nature of red: its fiery menstrual challenge, its lingering embers; tell me about the ocean depths of green, tell me green; and pearl, off-white pearl, cream of petal; green-blue stem; and gray stone, gray, gray stone; ochre rock, tortilla earth, desert orange, slap of yellow wildflower in the eye, the come-hither look of violet, lush of purple, vermilion's odd assertion; tell me the turquoise passage of winds shaping the pliable cloth of clouds.

Louise Boldin

Tell me about the white of absence,
    the black of presence
    these shades . . .
    tell me, tell me, tell me how water bleeds the colors across the
space of vision, how tense the oil; tell me of the sheen of cobalt blue
at rest, of the flash of first crimson, the garden of insight watered
by the fluids of exterior shapes.

Melissa Tree

And line, too, speak of lines, the way a stretch of black moves across your eye and takes on the curvature of the earth; tell me of rock and rising hillside, mesa of mesquite and distance, earth and dirt, the texture of stone underfoot; of air in the lungs, the weight of my breasts and arms upon the water; tell me of the buoyancy of my body in this plane of mine in the flash flood of insights that come unawares upon me; tell me, show me, how oceans spill out from the motion of your wrists, and I will learn how to perfect this story; how to write it in ink made of seashells and paint it on the bark of trees.

Eve

I see by the light that you show me, I see what it is like to walk upon the water and continue on across the plain of years, over the mountains. Sister, mother, daughter, oh, you give me hope, you give me promise that I might try and try, and if I fail, and if I fall back into the territory of darkness, at least I will have had a glimpse of what lies beyond. Show me then if color has a sound and how line creates music, and if the shape of things takes on a shade visible near darkness, oh, Ava, and if light, if light is the old metaphor for infinity, and if color, if color is light given in terms of the world. Succor me with this knowledge; that when I awake from my dream, I may know something other than before I slept.

AFTER AVA

An Afterword

It all began for me with an image – an old woman standing straight and tall, staring off into the sky to the west, a stick or, no, a paintbrush in hand, behind her a red barn (with a black door? no, the black door came later), this woman a figure of fortitude and mystery, an ancient mother, a desert relic.

Who was she?

The novelist wants to know as much as the reader eventually seeks to find. This woman's identity was much more enigmatic to me than you might at first imagine.

I had traveled through the Southwest on a number of occasions, visited friends there, hiked the canyons, climbed a mesa, got drunk on the landscape.

And I found myself involved in another love affair as well. I had read a bit about the life of Georgia O'Keeffe. Her paintings thrilled me with their quintessential Americanness, in much the same way that Aaron Copland's music thrilled me. And the choreography of Martha Graham.

The color, the shapes, the movement, the sound of the best of our country's native values: I wanted to make a novel that resounded, caught the eye, the ear, in all these ways, a novel that could move a reader the way that Copland's music and Graham's choreography and O'Keeffe's paintings moved me.

So I found myself reading and reading and reading about her early life and her marriage to Stieglitz and her life after, but I also read as deeply as I could in the lives of a number of other American women painters from around this same period, with Alice Neel standing out nearly equal with O'Keeffe. The struggle these women had to make to

327

become artists included all of the struggle that men had to endure, with all of the added difficulty that women must face.

And not just American women. The agony of the young German painter Paula Modersohn Becker, who is roughly contemporaneous with O'Keeffe and Neel, is exemplary in this regard, encouraged as she was by her family up to the moment when she said that she wanted to do more than just study art, when they brutally cut her off.

So I had caught more than a whiff of great courage among these female artists, women as bold and brave as any young boys from the country who wanted to prove themselves by running off from home and joining the army or the marines, as tough as any turn-of-the-century city boys putting up their bare fists to defend their home turf.

Ava Boldin – the name I gave to the mysterious old woman – serves as a metaphor for O'Keeffe and all the other women who struggled to perfect their art in our tumultuous century. To me, O'Keeffe is emblematic of all that an artist needs to be in order to triumph. It's part of what I see as the essential Americanness in her – that need for solitude mixed with the desire to make a way in the world.

Of course, I changed some things. O'Keeffe, unlike my native Nebraskan Ava Boldin, was born in Sun Prairie, Wisconsin. And her early family life was quite different from the particulars that I invented for Ava. Where the two biographies begin to truly coincide is with Ava's enrollment in the Art Institute of Chicago. But then O'Keeffe went to Charlottesville to teach in a private school and Ava goes to Charleston. Then they both go to west Texas to teach.

(If you are interested in making some detailed comparisons, you can pick up a copy of the very good biography of O'Keeffe by the story writer and novelist Roxana Robinson.) While my story wasn't determined by her life, it was certainly influenced by it, and certainly inspired by it. I think of it as a variation on her life as a musical variation on a theme takes from an original melody and makes its own way. Or a *rhapsody*, yes! I see the book as a rhapsody on the life of O'Keeffe! a rhapsody on the color of the country, of the rocks and the canyons, a rhapsody on the light that plays across this western space of ours! A wedding of a life and a geography, the union of a way of seeing and a way of feeling about our particular space and time.

But how to make this all work? As I've done with the other novels I've written, I went through a number of drafts, with the editorial guidance of my old friend and (now) former editor James Thomas (a fiction writer in his own right). The title came last. I had used as a working title "The Rose and the Skull," and, in fact, an excerpt from the novel appeared in *Story* magazine under that title in the autumn of 1990 just before the publication of the book. The cover showed a painting of a mesa by the publisher Gibbs Smith, a Sunday painter of some talent. I had always imagined an O'Keeffe work on the cover, possibly even the very same painting that adorns this beautiful paperback edition. But we could not get permission from the O'Keeffe Foundation to reproduce any of her paintings, let alone this one. The painter had died in 1986, and there was a battle going on within the foundation over the ownership of paintings and rights of reproduction.

As for the title, I can't recall now just who put up so much resistance about that title for the novel itself, but whether it was me or James, I found myself with one weekend to go before the publisher had to set catalog copy. That weekend I holed up with a copy of the complete poems of Walt Whitman, convinced that I would find the right phrase for my book somewhere in the luminous body of his work. Before the weekend came to a close, I was drunk on Whitman and "The Rose and the Skull" had become "The Light Possessed."

When the book appeared in the autumn of 1990, the reception was heartening: an enthusiastic review full of praise in the *New York Times Book Review* by novelist Kit Reed; a wonderfully appreciative review by Roxana Robinson herself in the *Washington Post Book World*; and positive reviews from many other places around the country. (The only negative review I recall came from an ex-nun in the Hungry Mind bookstore throwaway publication – may she return to the cloister, forgiven.)

In the readings I gave around the country, I felt as though something was going on between Ava and the audiences for which I was serving only as a medium. (When the original paperback edition appeared from HarperCollins I noticed the same sort of response. People loved Ava, which, I had to remind myself, meant that they loved the novel.) But how was it, some readers and some journalists asked, that I wrote a novel about a woman in which I used the female voice? Was this strange?

Strange? All writing feels strange, and wonderful. Whatever the gender, it's all strange. If you write about something utterly familiar, it wouldn't be interesting to you or the audience. You try to imagine a life, and that makes for discomfort. All writing in that respect is exotic and uncomfortable, and at least as difficult, as Norman Mailer has been wont to say, as learning how to play the piano. But every book has its own difficulties, and a lot of the pleasure in composition comes in learning how to surmount them. Maybe we can amend Mailer's keen insight to say that each time you start out to write a new novel it's like learning how to play a new instrument.

So the metaphor takes us back to music. That poetry is best which is closest to music, Ezra Pound has written, and that music is best which is closest to dance. And I'm doing a little swaying back and forth right here on the page now, pleased that my Ava – and yours, if you like her – is reborn again in a second paperback edition.

Alan Cheuse
January 1998

About the Author

Alan Cheuse is book commentator for NPR's *All Things Considered*. Cheuse is the author of a memoir, *Fall Out of Heaven*; three novels, *The Bohemians*, *The Grandmothers' Club* (reissued by SMU Press in 1994), and *The Light Possessed*; and two story collections, *Candace* and *The Tennessee Waltz* (reissued by SMU Press in 1992). His stories and reviews appear in the *New Yorker*, *Ploughshares*, the *Chicago Tribune*, and other literary venues. He teaches in the writing program at George Mason University in Fairfax, Virginia. He and his wife, Kristin O'Shee, a dancer and choreographer, make their home in Washington, D.C.